MY AUTHOR IS DEAD

My Author is Dead

Michel Bruneau

CePages Press

CePages Press, First Edition, September 2016
2nd Printing, November 2019

Library of Congress Control Number: 2016906629

CePages Press ISBN: 978-0-9824752-8-7

To my Muse—unpredictable, wild, and surely insane.

The problem is not when somebody's watching you.
It is not when nobody's watching you.
It is when nobody's watching over you.

Algebra [Al·ge·bra. Noun. Relationships of abstract entities
for which A-B=0 is true for everybody]

My Very Own Prologue

All I want is to be normal like those kids without mad parents, bruises, and broken bones.

The rapes were horrible, but it was the killings that were unbearable.

It was the best of times, it was the worst of times.

That's how my story might have started if the Author had really existed.

But it doesn't.

Bad Start

I was born in a village of morons where nothing ever happened. So the trial was quite an event.

A very big deal.

An order of magnitude more exciting than the inaugural of the telegraph depot a couple of years ago, when the first message received launched frenetic celebrations—quite a feat for an uninspired "This is a test STOP Please reply END" sent by an anonymous bureaucrat miles away.

The trial generated a lot more excitement, for sure, but it was also a frenzy of a different kind. Like a visceral feeling that the world stood at the edge of a cliff and that all living souls had to be conscripted to prevent Armageddon—although, in reality, that world at the edge of a cliff was only a dumb village in a rut.

The excited patrons, as turbulent as self-enlisted soldiers eager to fight, filled all the available space in the village's meeting hall. Bodies were squeezed in chairs in a continuous mass of overheating flesh, from the front of the stage all the way to the back where five layers of agitated observers stood in what was intended to be one row of standing-room space. Makeshift stands, built overnight and added along the walls, wobbled when all stamped their feet in unison, chanting improvised slogans. The luckiest of the late arrivals blocked the doorways, followed by the rest of the village and curious folks from everywhere else, arrayed as if funnels led to the doors. The mob outside, blind to the proceedings, was impressively silent, trying to hear the commotion inside. Criers were posted on the roof, ready to provide to those outside a verbatim play-by-play of the case, as transmitted to them by a chain of whispering colleagues spread through the rafters.

It was quite a show, and I likely would have enjoyed it too had I not been the defendant.

Now, don't get me wrong.

I never committed any crime.

Except for stealing a dictionary, once *[Dic·tion·ar·y. Noun. Alphabetical list of words whose meanings are dictated by the same invisible rascals who define what constitutes a crime; compendium of definitions in process of being revised by yours truly]*. I admit, this was a reprehensible act and it crossed my mind after the fact that it might get me in trouble someday. But this trial had nothing to do with that dictionary. In fact, most of the people in the room had not opened a dictionary since school—and most hadn't stayed in school for longer than a nap. No, this trial was about serious matters.

This trial was about having taken the wrong side.

In a village of morons, you can't take the wrong side.

I should have known.

It was all foreseeable.

Even though, in my mind, I wasn't guilty and had committed no crime, to those in the room I was guilty as charged, and the trial was a mere formality—but an entertaining one for sure, as it provided a welcome distraction from a life so dull that even roosters slept through sunrise out of boredom. One couldn't have distilled an ounce of doubt about my guilt from the cocktail of hate and anger percolating in the room. Even the presiding, hooded magistrate had a hard time keeping decorum to give a semblance of solemnity, as he would much rather have been in the bleachers cheering with the lynch mob.

"Order. Order in the courthouse," he repeated with little conviction, enjoying the ruckus. That hammering was also the cue for the guards to bring me to the dock where I was to sit silently during the proceedings. All the excitement and disorderly chitchat turned into a focused rage as soon as I entered the room.

On the stage, although overshadowed by the towering judicial bench, I had a perfect view of the audience. I could see all the village's familiar faces contorted with anger, some with foam at the mouth, among a sea of unfamiliar thrill seekers presumably attracted by the smell of blood. I particularly noticed Cassandra's father—whose big nose always reminded me of a can opener—making obscene gestures from the second row, acting as if the single row of flesh in front of him prevented him from jumping on stage to beat me senseless. Even my parents, at the left end of the last row in the stands, had joined the crowd hurling insults, carefully hiding any incriminating love they may have felt toward their son—if any. Grandpa, clearly embarrassed by them and exasperated by the whole circus, sat in silence at the other end of that last row next to Barbooyee who, as always, was likely mumbling the "t't', tap t'tap, tapt', tap tap tap, t'tap tap," that mirrored his incoherent thoughts between long, lazy jaw pauses—although that stuttering disability turned out to be a blessing as it landed him the job of village telegraphist. The Small Visionary was perched in a makeshift box—although barely a couple of feet higher than everybody else—smack in the middle of the last row where he observed the proceedings in absolute delight.

Facing all that intimidating madness, I felt blessed to have a public defender. Imagine if I had been ordered to defend myself like it used to be before our modern times. I'd be lost. How could a fifteen-year-old know all the things one needs to master to appease a hostile crowd and win over a magistrate?

Sure, it would have been better if my public defender owned a comb, some soap, and clothes without holes. And if he hadn't spent the days leading to the trial emptying barrels of rum one glass at a time in an attempt (unsuccessful) to cure the chronic case of hiccups that plagued him since childhood.

Sober, he was a nice person who seemed knowledgeable in the rules of procedure. He had told me that what I had done was "humanauthorian," and his strategy was to plead accordingly. I had no clue what that meant, but given that it took him a while to come up with this defense, and that it was a huge improvement over his initial counsel to plead guilty and beg for a lenient sentence, I didn't argue and remained optimistic.

After much hammering from the magistrate to finally silence the mob, he gave my public defender the floor for his opening statement. While unable to drown his hiccup problem, he had learned—with thirty years of practice—to keep his mouth shut to transform "hics" into "gulps," thus muffling their impact, minimizing embarrassing moments, and making it possible to carefully time short sentences between two hiccups.

"My client is the victim of a judicial farce," he blasted before two gulps.

The crowd immediately responded, booing, hissing, yelling "Burn in obscurity!"

"Order. Order," hammered the magistrate, without much effect.

"What happened is entirely not his fault," insisted my defender, with great conviction, trying to shout above the rumble—even though he and I seemed to be the only ones buying it.

"Order. Order."

Adding to the general commotion, a roaring outburst started outdoors—out-of-phase with the indoor one as a result of the crier's delay in relaying the play-by-play of the proceedings. I felt surrounded by thunder, wondering why lightning hadn't struck me yet. Fists were pounding the air above screaming heads. Threats were unintelligible, drowned by the general shouting, foot-stomping, explosive outrage, and taunts of hysterical patrons *[Pa·tron. Noun. Social or financial psychopath who expects the world on a platter in grateful return for having showed up—or for having bought a beer]*.

The magistrate, amused and enjoying his position at the helm, fueled the freak show by a deliberate "laissez-faire" discipline, banging his gavel as required by protocol, but without muscle. It took him a quarter of an hour to silence the mob before the trial could continue. The jumping shoulders of my public defender testified to an intensified hiccups crisis.

"You may resume your opening statement," calmly instructed the magistrate.

Taking a deep breath, timing his delivery, and clustering his words in small bunches, he resumed: "None of this (gulp) would have happened (gulp) if not for the silliness (gulp) of a silly little (gulp) silly girl—hic."

He missed one, triggering some laughs, as if the slip revealed his incompetence, relieving concerns in the crowd that I might have had a shot at evading justice.

For emphasis, he added: "All that has happened (gulp) is entirely the fault (gulp) of a little harum-scarum (gulp), irresponsible, unscrupulous (gulp), and hair-brained girl named (gulp) Cassandra Dew Hawkyns."

That's when the riot broke loose. Everybody stood up at the same time.

Fortunately for me, the crowd had been packed so tight that, with everybody up and the empty chairs becoming obstacles impeding movement across the floor, the mob got jammed in place.

The generalized pushing and shoving match that this triggered only made things worse, perpetuating the paralysis.

Strangely, from what was first a cacophony of anger and outrage, slowly emerged a rhythm, as if hate had a pulse.

"HERESY! HERESY! HERESY!" chanted the crowd.

Those at the front, crushed against the stage, unable to free themselves to jump on it, swung their extended arms wildly, hoping to grab me in their claws.

"KILL THE HERETICS! KILL THEM BOTH!"

My defender shuddered at the thought that a mob could link his destiny to mine. Given his opening statement though, it wasn't a surprise.

Everyone in the Dominion knew Cassandra Dew Hawkyns by then. Arguably, nobody would have disputed that she was a little twerp—particularly those from the village who had known her for years—but after having been glorified by the Small Visionary for her recent actions, she was untouchable. Not adulated, but off limits, even though—as correctly stated by my defender—she was the harum-scarum, irresponsible, unscrupulous, and hairbrained initiator of this entire mess. Even I could have told my defender that attacking her wasn't a brilliant strategy. Had he warned me that this was his grand plan, I would have told him to slack off on the rum; I would have chosen to defend myself instead.

It's on days like those that I wondered why I had to be born in a village of morons. Was there really no other option?

More pressingly though, why did I land in such a hostile courtroom, awaiting the only sentence that would appease the vicious pack of wolves that was once a peaceful flock of sheep? A flock to which I once belonged.

There's an explanation.

A long one.

Let's start from the very beginning.

No Better Start

Cassandra was a little pest whose perky righteousness could be your worst nightmare. I didn't know it then. We were only seven years old.

What I knew at that age was that Cassandra would cling to you like burdock; once the damn thing was glued to you, getting rid of her was challenging.

Some people cling to others because they have no life of their own, no initiative, no imagination, or simply because their sad puppy face is desperate for a sympathetic person that could serve as a pillow. Cassandra wasn't such a poor sap. Her clinging was instead driven by an unquenchable desire to spy, admonish, and denounce—with a determination most exhausting to her victims, because once she had latched onto a prey, ditching her wasn't simple.

One might think that simply stopping all activities and sitting on a rock while waiting for her to get bored and leave would have done the trick, but that strategy only offered her a tribune to lecture, endlessly repeating word-for-word the millions of rules we were taught in school, while emphasizing the need to obey those rules and the consequences for failing to do so.

One might think that telling her outright to disappear, get lost, or eat shit and die would have hurt her feelings and left her running home crying, but it only served to harden her shell and her resolve in catching deviant behavior—if there is indeed such a thing as a hardened seven-year-old criminal.

One might think that hurling rocks would have kept her at bay, but it only gave her ammunition—and satisfaction—to denounce improper behavior liable to harsh punishment.

No, the best way to get rid of her was simply not to be found by her in the first place.

One day, it occurred to me that a good way to do that might be to sneak into the forest first thing in the morning—escaping the village before the monster left her lair to start annoying people. This was a relatively simple thing to do given that my house was at the edge of the village, so I gave it a try. For extra safety, I traveled deep into the woods, far from the village and from the reach of Cassandra's stalking, until I eventually discovered a hollow, near a stream, that seemed like a safe haven. For a while, day after day, right after sunrise, I would travel to that peaceful hideout with a homemade sandwich, only to return for dinner, and it worked: for the entire week, I didn't see Cassandra. I didn't see my parents during daytime either, for that matter, but they were too busy running the general store to care about how I kept busy during the summer holiday.

So my plan was phenomenally successful—except for the fact that spending entire days alone in the forest was utterly boring, even when I brought along playing cards or puzzles to kill time. Swimming in ponds along the stream while trying to catch crayfish got old too after a while. Yet, I continued to go every day because in my unexplored, uninhabited, undeveloped piece of forest, the company of shy squirrels, ugly toads, dull slugs, and biting flies was a thousand times better than that of shy, ugly and dull kids who were not particularly friendly—and it rid me of the most unfriendly and biting one.

As I arrived at the hollow, on the eighth consecutive day of my self-inflicted exile, convinced more than ever that absolute solitude was better than suffering the nagging personality of Cassandra, a girl sprung up from behind a rock. She had hidden there when branches snapping underfoot announced my approach, fearing the arrival of an adult, and was both surprised and pleased that I turned out to be a non-threatening presence.

Her name was June; we were the same height; and she was the total opposite of Cassandra. She also had lilacs in her hair— hair that, some might say, was of golden flax. I didn't know where she came from, but it definitely was not my village.

Unfortunately, I don't remember all the details of our encounter. I was seven years old, and this whole escapade-into-the-woods story is one of my earliest childhood memories. There are holes in that story that time will never be able to fill, but while many specific details are forever lost, what remains is a certainty that her presence was soothing. She was the first kid my age with whom I was at peace. We met for many consecutive days at the hollow, and I thought of her as my first friend. Even though childhood remains a fuzzy memory at best, some powerful images forever remain etched in one's mind, and I have kept two such images from my chance encounter with June.

The first one is of me giving her my leather necklace. It was a rather ordinary leather rope at the end of which dangled a small apple carved in basswood. Not a big gift—just a trinket—or so it seemed. A gift presumably offered as token of my love—as far as a seven-year-old can be naively in love, of course *[Love. Noun. Mysterious and uncontrollable binding force and affection for a person; known to trigger bouts of insanity and ripping apart daisies; sometimes incurable]*. Since we weren't of an age to carve initials in trees, I gave her a little bit of sculpted wood.

The second image is more vivid. Unforgettable.

It starts with June and I, stark naked in the woods, staring at our differences. Two seven-year-old kids, baffled by the mystery of it all, trying to figure out why they were physiologically mismatched. How it happened, I don't recall. What I do remember though, is feeling like an explorer discovering a new continent.

In those days, even at that age, boys, as a group, knew they were somewhat similar to each other—thanks to pissing contests and other crude sillinesses of youth. Presumably girls also knew they were the same within their group, for reasons a boy wouldn't know. Furthermore, in villages, naked babies are a sort of permanent exhibit, so June and I knew that the flagrant differences confronting us weren't anomalies within our gender. We had been created that way, for reasons unknown; with time, and paying close attention to animal life, we would eventually figure it out, but at seven, the fact that animals and humans behaved similarly in some aspects hadn't been realized yet. That extrapolation would come in due time.

For the time being, in that mesmerizing moment, it was just an unprecedented and privileged opportunity to scrutinize the mysteries of the other sex, free of parental obstruction. Besides, naked June was a lot more intriguing than a naked baby. I particularly remember that we stayed connected in some delightful way for a long moment.

Warm as the sun.

There was no shyness, no shame, no flaw in that shared experience.

I was in love.

It was all innocence.

It felt good.

Until we heard the scream.

A horrific noise—scorching, like lungs trying to escape the body in one blow.

This is how a dream turns into a nightmare.

Cassandra.

It turns out that my prolonged absence from the village had been noticed by creepy Cassandra—obviously—from the very beginning. So, keeping vigil in the wee hours to figure out how I had managed my disappearing act, she had caught one of my earlier escapes, followed me from a distance to the hollow, and spent a day spying on my activities, crouched behind a rock. Fortunately, that day spent hidden like a hunter had happened before I met June, otherwise she would have woven a sordid story about suspicious meetings in the woods with a stranger not from the village—embellishing the lies as needed to get me in trouble. However, as there was nothing irregular to denounce during Cassandra's initial stalking, she found my solitary exile too boring to watch on a continuous basis and postponed her bloodhound game for a while, focusing instead on other preys; there were plenty of other kids to harass after all.

Unfortunately, one morning—that very morning—she decided to return to the hollow to check if I was still a bore to watch or whether I was committing some reprehensible act that deserved punishment. She arrived there at the very moment when I was busy enjoying June's tender handling. Cassandra screamed when she saw us, entangled in a naive exploration that admittedly, in her mind, was a most unorthodox pose. Scared witless, she had found more than she bargained for. She ran back to the village, hysterical all the way.

Fear in her eyes, June grabbed her clothes and ran in the other direction.

I was alone, again. It was the end of a beautiful moment and the start of an ordeal.

Cassandra went straight to her parents. It didn't help that the Hawkyns were a family of Perfectionists: the most persnickety, intransigent, unforgiving bunch of raging fanatics—an attitude which I attributed at the time to a possible constipation problem, not knowing what I know now. By moral duty, they felt compelled to first inform my parents of my scandalous and pernicious behavior, and then to spread the news to the entire village for good measure.

My disgraceful behavior and the shame it brought to our family—thanks to the Hawkyns' proactive preaching—created a hysteric scene at home. I don't remember much of what my father said. In fact, he might have remained mostly silent—maybe even, for once, proud of his son in some ways—but I do remember that he was tasked with dispensing the corporal punishment required for educational purposes with enough vigor to imprint some lasting memories as part of one's life-long learning process *[Ed·u·ca· tion. Noun. Process of filling a blank slate and editing its content to achieve desirable communal ends and rectitude]*. Interestingly though, what I more vividly remember is my hysterical mother's incessant crying and moaning.

She repeated the same lament over and over, emphasizing that I had ruined my life, that I'd never be a protagonist, that I had shamed them because they'd never be respected anymore by the other Authorians. Actually, to be exact, I only remember that she kept repeating "pro-something" and that I didn't understand what it meant then. I can only assume that she said "protagonist." Authorians don't teach the word to kids before their tenth birthday. Before then, for simplicity, they use "good character." In grade school, every hour, they'd make us stand up and recite: "Be of good character to become a good character," which, frankly, was equally cryptic to me back then.

It's funny what we remember from childhood. Being passionate about those things, I'm sure my mother started to drill me to be a good Authorian from the instant I was born, but my first awareness of belonging to that group comes from that day when my mother feared that my actions had disgraced our family in the eyes of the entire community.

The second part of the ordeal was the second serving of corporal punishment I received—adding to the curriculum of my education—when my father discovered I had "lost" my necklace. Thankfully, I had the presence of mind to lie and not tell him that I had given it away, otherwise all the members of my family—

including aunts and uncles I had never met—would have relayed each other to educate me, in a session I might not have survived. That's when I learned that it was not an ordinary leather rope at the end of which dangled a small apple carved in basswood. Rather, it was a family jewel keeping our coat of arms close to my heart. The fact that my family could only afford leather and basswood instead of gold and gems, and pledged allegiance to a fruit where others did so to lions and dragons, didn't make it less precious. The apple was our ancestral symbol of strength and unity, and keeping it close to our heart was our only guarantee of good luck. Admittedly, there might have been some truth to this as it seems that all my bad luck started not long after I lost my basswood apple.

The third part of the ordeal was the medical treatment *[Med·i· cal. Adjective. Relating to the most respectable field of unquestionable and unwavering knowledge]*. I don't recall everything the doctor did, but I remember being confined to bed rest for a week, with a leech on my forehead and one on my heart. Given that leeches can suck only so much blood, they were replaced by fresh ones every six hours. The blood sucking wasn't that painful, but the swelling and itching that followed was horrible and lasted for weeks.

Not as horrible as the return to school, though. Even before the incident, I was an outcast: the weird kid that made everyone uncomfortable. Admittedly, some of it was my fault; I probably was the only kid who thought that a week at home, away from school, with leeches slurping blood straight out, was a golden opportunity to read the dictionary once more, reviewing forgotten parts and brushing up on synonyms, as a distraction from the leech-inflicted pain.

At the same time, I was caught in a vicious circle. Not having any friends, the stolen dictionary became my only friend—I even started to memorize it, at the rate of one letter a month—and the resulting weirdness kept potential friends away. So, words became all that mattered. They flowed in my veins—even those starting with J, Q, X, and Z, because it only took a week to memorize them. As a result, I started to use words that most people didn't understand. In fairness, some words I didn't even understand correctly myself until much later.

It didn't help either that it took me a few years to discover that synonyms were context-sensitive and not all interchangeable, and that blindly abusing a thesaurus wasn't a wise thing to do. Nobody could figure out that when I said "I masticated delightful munchies," "I fancy hieroglyphs and terms," and "now is the most protracted twenty-four hours of the vintage," what I really meant was "I ate good food," "I like letters and words," and "today is the longest day of the year." No wonder everybody thought I was weird.

After I cleared up all that confusion in my mind and started using the appropriate words in their proper context, people still did not understand me because I was trying to drop all the words from my stolen dictionary in sentences longer than what the basic "subject-verb-complement" structure allowed. Even my teachers hated me. "Stop talking in a foreign language," or "Speak English!" is pretty much all they ever said to me. On a good day.

Now, thanks to Cassandra, there were no more good days in sight. The leech treatment had been bad days all the way through. My first day back to school was worse—a truly bad day. The other kids in the village had suffered the grumpy mood of their parents on a daily basis since Cassandra's revelation. These parents were upset that I had shamefully tarnished the village's appeal to the Author, and they had taken out their frustration on their defenseless offspring. Those kids were ready for some serious retribution. So the day I returned to school, I didn't even make it to the middle of the schoolyard before a mob, led by Cassandra's older brother, beat me senseless. Apparently, the pummeling and kicking continued while I was unconscious. My left arm was so badly broken that bones healed in zig-zag lines. As a result, my elbow bends so weirdly that a thumbs-up is impossible, and ten pounds is the most that arm can lift. All that after another month away from school, covered in leeches.

Apparently, some of the kids were scolded for their cruelty—if "Don't do that, it's not nice" can count as a reprimand—but most Perfectionist parents didn't even bother because they were pleased that the village's weird kid got beat up well. Clearly, not all kids had as effective an educator as my father—and certainly not the precious, little Perfectionist darlings who knew that "don't do that" is just an unthreatening and ineffective admonition by a spineless, dull-brained, idiot parent too weak to educate kids properly.

On the positive side, that was supposed to be my last beating for a while. For some reason, being condemned to live the rest of my life with an almost useless arm was deemed to be an adequate penalty for what I had done, and all concluded that further disorder wasn't going to help the village's image at that point—all, except the Perfectionists, always lobbying for more pain and suffering, always complaining that being too lenient was the road to obscurity.

Needless to say that at that point, I vowed to never ever again say a word to Cassandra, nor look at her for that matter, in spite of her never-ending and unrelenting lecturing, taunting, and badgering. For the rest of my childhood, every time she came within striking distance, unable to outrun her, I closed my eyes and sheltered in my head, waiting for the storm to pass, imagining her being dropped in a boiling caldron of cow pies, dissolving into a soup of feces, and being forever erased—as all Perfectionists should be.

If the story had ended there, it wouldn't be so bad. In fact, for a long time, it seemed like it did. I came to think that I had been the victim of the worst thing Cassandra could do to a person, and that the whole incident had taught everybody a lesson.

Was I wrong!

What had happened to me then was nothing compared to what was to come a few years later.

The Sordid Affair

The crisis happened on my fifteenth birthday. Coincidentally.

"Adam. You're a man now, so come with me," my father said.

The words suggested that I might have been able to escape the whole thing if my birthday had been a day later; in hindsight, it would have made no difference. What was clear, though, was that we weren't out to get me a birthday gift. Quite the contrary.

In those days, my father was a member of the village's Review Panel. Given the size of our village, we only had one Small Visionary, and the Rules required him to seek counsel from a Review Panel consisting of no fewer than four Lackeys.

My father served as Second Lackey, which I guess was a prestigious position. At least, that's what he kept telling my skeptical mother, who was convinced that this whole panel gimmick was just an excuse for guys to escape domestic responsibilities, to instead play cards, drink booze, and make dirty jokes—to my mother, all men were ordinary, weak, lying, and untrustworthy, except for the Visionaries, as she believed that truth only lay in the rulings from those consecrated to speak with wisdom and moral authority.

Unfortunately, the Lackey's meeting room had no booze, no playing cards, and the stern faces of those sitting around the table didn't forecast a shower of dirty jokes. My father had warned me on the way that this was an emergency meeting.

"Gentlemen, this is a major crisis," announced the First Lackey, to break the ice.

"It surely is."

"A sordid affair."

"Scandalous."

All four Lackeys nodded, presumably already aware of what had prompted this emergency assembly of the Review Panel.

"It's a major pain."

"Worse than ever."

"Worse than sitting on a protruding vertical root."

"Worse than screwing a sandbag," said the Fourth Lackey.

Maybe there were to be dirty jokes after all, but the frown from the first two Lackeys quickly shut down that avenue.

They remained silent for a moment, evidently taking their counselor's role very seriously.

"Do we know for sure?"

"We know."

"But do we really? It wouldn't be the first time with these Perfectionists, you know."

"The Small Visionary has personally questioned her, and concluded that her testimony will stand."

"But what if she lied?"

"Her testimony will still stand."

"You can't get the cat back into the toothpaste bag," added the Fourth Lackey, again displaying his brilliance.

Silence again. This didn't seem to leave them many options to contemplate, or much room for debate. So much for providing counsel.

"I'm not convinced," timidly offered my father, to test the water.

"Why?" responded the First Lackey.

Taking some time to look at the others, trying to gauge if his disagreement could find some footing, he suggested: "This is the testimony of an Authorian who broke a rule. Shouldn't her transgression render her word suspicious? At least a bit?"

"So what if it did? The Visionary has already made up his mind."

"The Rules require the Visionary to seriously consider our recommendations," countered the vertical root guy, rescuing my father. "We've discussed many times the fact that he has grown to systematically disregard our counsel, but we've never done anything about it. Maybe this is the time to bring him in line?"

"Maybe this is not the time to do so," countered the First Lackey, visibly upset, and waiting for the sandbag-screwing guy to side with him. Unfortunately, for him, the sandbag lover was

Jasper Stone, owner of the village's only funeral home, a man respected enough to end up on the Panel, but whose prosperity had been achieved without the need for any decision making—clients continued to show up, no matter what he did. Even a fifteen-year-old like me knew that it would be futile to wait for him to commit one way or another if there was dissension. I guessed that his usual role was to cast a vote when unanimous decisions were obvious, and abstain from fueling any fire otherwise.

"Actually, if there was ever a time to do so, this may be it," insisted my father.

I wasn't sure if this was brave or foolish. Probably brave, but I had never thought of my father as being brave before.

The First Lackey, much like the Visionary it seemed, didn't like being contradicted. One can safely assume that Woodruff Oak, as owner of the door manufacturing plant, owed his First Lackey appointment to his ability to please those above him, and that confronting the Visionary was the last thing he would ever do. There weren't enough buildings in the village to use all of the doors his plant produced, even if it had been decreed that all building walls were to be three feet thick and entirely built of piled-up doors, so his prosperity depended on his servility *[Ser·vil·i·ty. Noun. Art of keeping political friends happy; plucking lips on the big cheeks where power sits]*.

"That's beyond the point. We've been given a specific task within the scope of this crisis, and it is our duty to fulfill our obligation—but nothing more."

"I'm still not convinced," insisted my father. "This will be a dangerous expedition. Before risking the lives of our sons, our only real obligation is to be absolutely certain about the facts."

"That's why it's good to have your son here," replied the "First Oak," quick to erase the ugly smirk that had started to form on one side of his face.

My father was clearly upset, seemingly understanding at that point how the slick politician had played him—although I had yet to understand what was going on.

"The only reason you asked me to bring my son was to see how our youth would respond when learning of our mission for them—on the basis that his reaction would be representative of the more timid and less daring among them—and we will keep it at that. On the other matters, I think we can make our own decisions here."

"You are correct, and I'm not interested in asking him to decide for us either. But since you questioned the validity of Cassandra's testimony to the Visionary, essentially questioning her character and suggesting that she may have lied, it may be enlightening for us to hear from your son of his... say... 'experience' in this regard."

The political maneuvering behind the scenes might have been thicker than I could follow, but Lackey Woodruff was probably eating from the hand of the Visionary. I was starting to feel like the sandbag mentioned earlier. I obviously was more than an accidental tourist to the Panel.

"Well, I'd like to hear that too," added the other Lackey. It was two against one—and the usual abstention.

"Let's be serious here. He was only seven years old. He doesn't remember," said my father, as if I could have forgotten all the education I got when I was seven.

"So if he doesn't remember, you can't possibly mind if we question him then."

"Even if he remembers a few things here and there, how credible can childhood memories be? Memories from a seven-year-old kid! Not eight, not ten. Seven!"

"We certainly can trust that the Author will put the right words in his mouth."

That always was the killer argument. Invoking the almighty Author for the right words.

The right words.

Now, that's an argument I never understood. Lies happen. In fact, there are lies everywhere. So how can we trust the Author for the right words? This is like admitting that lies can be the right words, that lies can be as legitimate as truths. What is right then? To me, it was one of those mysteries without an answer. Actually, there was an answer, the one we were force-fed in school, the official answer that the Visionaries professed with conviction: The right words are whatever the Author wants. The Author's wisdom cannot be questioned. There's a greater purpose. It may escape us, but in due time it will be revealed.

My father intensely looked at me. The signal was unequivocally clear. He wanted me to answer "I don't remember," no matter the question. All I had to do is repeat that answer, over and over, to make my father proud and (as I now know) nip this whole thing in the bud. Yet, I could see the fear in his eyes: the fear that I would fail him.

"Adam," smoothly said the Oak, with a broad grin intended to reassure, as if that was ever possible with so many missing teeth—it was a mouth forever free from the annoyance of a stuck piece of lettuce between teeth, unless an entire head of lettuce got jammed in there.

"You wouldn't mind answering a few questions now, would you?"

I couldn't answer "I don't remember" to that one.

"Uh-huh," I replied.

"You know who Cassandra is, right?"

Another one I couldn't answer with "I don't remember." That Lackey was slick.

I wanted to reply: "Yes. She's a snake with crooked fangs, a wart-covered monster, a rotten-egg-smelling witch. She's an annoying wheel that always squeaks, oil or no oil. She's a fork scratching a plate. She's garbage that even quicksand refuses to swallow."

I wanted to shout: "I don't want to have anything to do with this living nightmare, this stupid bird of ill omen, this righteous freak, this slanderous fanatic, this vicious twerp that only lives to do harm, this malevolent weasel who would do anything to satisfy her thirst for violence."

I wanted to yell: "Get me rid of her! I don't want to know her!"

I was trying to remember all the synonyms for revulsion, dread, and hate that I had learned from self-study in my stolen dictionary and scream them out to bury Cassandra in them.

But it was impossible to get rid of Cassandra. She was like a fruitcake so horrible that people preferred dying of starvation to touching it.

I knew it.

They knew it.

"I asked if you know who is Cassandra."

"Everybody knows her."

"Indeed. And your father is a good father, isn't he?"

"Of course he is."

"So when he educated you, he did it well, didn't he?"

"He surely did."

"That's good. I thought so. For sure, your father would have never failed in his duties to properly educate you—that would have tarnished his reputation. Only honorable men like your father can serve on this prestigious panel."

My worried father seemed to know where this was leading and I was trying hard to guess where that was.

"Now, I'd like to ask you a few questions about Cassandra's character."

I burned to tell him that all her angelic posturing was nothing but a fake front to her evilness, that she was a corrupt devil rotten to the bone. I sure was ready for his questions.

"So, Adam, tell me. In all the years that you have known her, has she ever said anything about you that you know, with absolute certainty, was not true?"

That took me by surprise. He hadn't asked me if Cassandra was of good character at all (she was not), or whether she had less compassion than a worm (she had), or whether she was a nuisance to society (she definitely was).

I didn't immediately answer. "I don't remember," wouldn't have helped. I had to say something to discredit her.

"Your hesitation is telling."

"No, no. Wait. She's... she's..."

One had to pick his words carefully when describing the little darling of the Visionaries. More education was the last thing I wanted at that juncture.

"Kid, I don't care to know what she is. Everybody knows her. We know her. She's a Perfectionist after all, isn't she?"

"Yes." It was an undeniable fact.

"What I asked you is whether she ever said anything about you that you know, with absolute certainty, was not true. With absolute certainty. Has she?"

Obviously, if I said yes, I would then have to explain in detail what it was that she had said that was untrue. Everybody knew that I had purposely avoided talking or listening to her since my earliest childhood memory—there's only one school in town and no secrets in a small village—so my answer to this question could only refer to the day of my adventure with June, and it would no doubt be extrapolated to serve some dark purpose I ignored.

"Yes there is."

There was no doubt in my mind that, like the vacuous girl she'd always been, she had embellished her story to transform my sweet and loving encounter with June into a horrible deed that deserved no less than a crippled arm.

"There is?"

"Yes."

"That's interesting. Can you tell us when that happened, Adam?"

My father stared at me. His eyes screamed: "Say you don't remember!"

"Uh. I was seven."

"That's not a problem. I trust your father has educated you well, as we discussed."

"He did."

My paternal education had been impeccable.

"So what happened then?"

As if he didn't know what happened then.

"Well, there was the whole incident. Remember?"

"So what were Cassandra's exact words?"

"Exact words?"

It just struck me that while I knew that Cassandra had run to her parents, I didn't know the words she had used to denounce the activities at the hollow. I didn't hear firsthand what Cassandra's parents had told mine either. To be honest, all I remembered was the education.

"The exact words, I wouldn't know, but the facts—"

"You don't know the exact words."

"No, but the fact of the matter is—"

"Adam. It's pretty simple. Yes or no. Has Cassandra ever said anything about you that you know, with the upmost, absolute, unquestionable certainty, was not true?"

Giving Cassandra any credibility was worse than sitting on a porcupine while holding a fifty pound rock. The pain was sure to last.

The other option was to lie and claim that Cassandra had made up the whole story about June. However, the Lackeys would then probe as to why I didn't deny the accusations back then, instead of shaming the entire village by my deception and, worse, embarrassing my father by letting him educate me on false pretenses. Besides, I had been found guilty and had paid my dues, so contesting my sentence and complaining eight years after the fact would have sounded disingenuous. My own credibility didn't stack-up.

"Is it a yes or a no, Adam?"

"No"

"There. That's all we needed to know."

The strained grin vanished.

Like a swaggering rooster, shoulders pulled back and chest thrust out, chin slightly up, he surveyed the room, daring others to dissent. In a sense, my mother was right about the Panel: this was a big poker game.

Addressing the other Lackeys, the First Lackey added with authority: "Are there other concerns that need to be aired about Cassandra's credibility?"

"It remains that this is the testimony of an Authorian who broke a rule," replied my father, without skipping a beat.

"Yes, she broke a rule. And she'll be educated for it. However, it's not a sacred rule."

"It was sacred under the previous Kritikillar."

"Well, it's not now."

"She associated with Kafkaists. It's not a small thing."

I didn't understand why my father was suddenly so scrupulous about the Rules. If anything, he was far from a Perfectionist, even though he never openly criticized the Rules and the Kritikillar—not even within the confines of the family walls.

"Association for commercial purposes is not forbidden," underscored the First Lackey. "Not anymore."

"The fact we can sell doors to Kafkaists doesn't make them less wicked and insidiously dangerous."

"He's right," supported the Third Lackey.

"Insidiously dangerous they are. But remember that we are talking about a Perfectionist here. Perfectionists have the moral rectitude to counter the moral turpitude of the Kafkaists."

For a tense moment, all remained silent.

My father seemed particularly exasperated. I couldn't tell if it was because I had failed to support him by falling into the First Lackey's trap, or because he despised the First Lackey as much as I despised Cassandra.

"So there's nothing else to discuss then," my father said, standing up. I followed.

"We still have the duty to advise the Visionary as to whether we support his proposed course of action."

"As if he didn't already know that nobody here has the balls to stall him," shouted my father. "He's going to start a big mess—a very big mess. All because of a damn, stupid girl who couldn't mind her own business."

"She gave the rite—"

"She could have fornicated with a snake for all I care! It's still going to be a huge mess. It's happened before, thirty years ago, and it was a mess then. Imagine what it will be now, with the new freedoms and liberties."

"There's only one solution to—"

"Just tell your boss what he wants to hear. I'm going home."

I rushed through the door before my father so that he could slam it on his way out—the superior quality of the doors crafted in our village makes them slam louder than any competitor's products, which is apparently a selling point.

I had no idea what the Panel had been talking about in that meeting, but it looked serious.

"I should have drowned you in a barrel the day you were born," is maybe what my father would have told me if our entire father-son relationship had not been built on a solid foundation of silences and unshared emotions.

Important Rules

There are so many rules.

Rules dictating how to put on socks (right before left, and always sitting on a chair), which day one is allowed to sing (only calendar dates divisible by 3), where not to put your fingers (in your nose, among many places), what to drink before six o'clock (only water) and how much (two quarts, minimum, unless the water is darker than your nails), when to get married (eighteen), which side of the bed to sleep on (wife to the right of husband), how many children to bear (tons), how much skin to show in public (depends on age, gender, and location of skin), who can talk to Kafkaists (nobody, except for business purposes), and so on.

Important rules to follow.

Rituals one cannot violate.

For example, one must remain in character. Being found out of character is a serious offense. One small slip, by a single person, could bring obscurity to an entire village. Too many slips and it's the end of the world as we know it. One cannot recover from that.

Basically, there are rules for everything. That's the problem.

To make things worse, there are sacred rules too! That Cassandra could get away with breaking a sacred rule—of all rules—was outrageous.

And most upsetting.

To think that I had the chance to call her a liar, to wipe that smirk off her ugly mug, to tarnish her aura of invincibility, and to prevent the mess that was to follow—and I blew it. If there had ever been an ounce of doubt that maybe the sacred rule had only been broken in her vivid imagination, I had stupidly spilled that ounce down the drain before it could be used. It was now indubitably real *[In·du·bi·ta·bly. Adjective. That which cannot be doubted, chal-*

lenged, or questioned, even though it may be far from evident, or be absolutely untrue].

Yet, it remained that she broke a sacred rule and got away with it.

A sacred rule!

I can't even break a silly one without creating a commotion.

Like how one opens an egg.

It shouldn't matter from which side you open a soft boiled egg. But it actually does, because that's what the Author has apparently dictated.

In one of my first acts of defiance—as a ten-year-old rebel way back then—I had decided to open my egg the wrong way.

On purpose.

So I did.

Disappointingly, the world didn't explode when my spoon crushed the top of the shell. Now, it so happens that when I cracked that first egg of doom, I was alone in the kitchen. Maybe there had to be a witness to the crime for the world to end. So I repeated the experiment the next day, making sure that my mother was in the kitchen at the critical moment, but she didn't notice my transgression.

She didn't even notice!

I repeated my sacrilegious deed every morning, day after day, wondering if she would ever notice. On the seventh morning after the start of my rebellion, my ritual was no different than on the other days, but, somehow, for some reason, from the other end of the table, her blank gaze caught sight of the egg. She looked at it, emotionless, for a minute. Then, the blankness evaporated as she focused more intensely on the egg, puzzled, suspicion kindled by maternal instinct, sensing an anomaly but unable to put her finger on it—until she noticed that small but important detail. That small lapse that shouted anarchy.

She should have laughed at the naive defiance of a silly ten-year-old kid trying to push the boundaries of decorum.

But no.

Instead, she freaked.

Totally freaked.

To the extent that she didn't wait for my father to educate me. She schooled me on the spot, with her own hands, drilling the Author's rules into my brain by using a lower contact point.

"Adam Chad Kilroy! What are you trying to do?" she'd scream in synch with each bit of corporal education. "Are you trying to kill me? Are you trying to stab your mother in the heart? Are you trying to become a Kafkaist?"

Why would I have wanted to be a Kafkaist? First, I'd never met one. Second, it was made pretty clear by all those educating us that Kafkaists were lower than worms and cockroaches in the Authorians' world.

Once calmed down, mostly due to exhaustion, she pulled me against her chest, crushed in a bear hug to remind me that mothers love their kids—that she loved me, in spite of my flaws. She whispered in my ear: "Don't ever do that again. Don't ever tell anybody what you did. Let's keep this in the family."

In the family.

Of course.

What else?

For all practical purposes, my mother was crazy. The Small Visionary had told my father that having kids solidifies couples because it helps parents discover their true nature. Indeed. It turned out to be so true that, after discovering my mother's true nature, he decided to never have another kid. No matter how much pressure the Small Visionary put on my mother to expand the family, my father resisted all her cajoling, pleas, and sneaky attempts to do so. If she was passionate about the Author and the Rules before their wedding, she revealed herself to be totally insane about the whole thing after my birth, and once she realized that I was to become her only offspring, I had to also become perfectly obedient to all rules—the perfect son, in her eyes and, most importantly, in the eyes of others.

I suspect that my mother would have loved to be a Perfectionist. It sometimes seemed as if all women in my village would. Why they so fervently honored all rules was—and is still—beyond my understanding.

But Cassandra was a Perfectionist, and—damn it—she broke a rule and was getting away with it.

To be frank, it shouldn't have surprised me. As far as I can remember, she always got away with everything. As a little girl, she was a monstrous critter poisoning the other kids' lives, who could at the same time play the innocent victim, batting her eyelashes with a sad face to make everybody—particularly Perfectionist mothers—swallow her side of the story. When kids slapped her, usually in an attempt to shut her up and chase her away, she ramped up the drama, with exaggerations that far transcended reality, to ensure that the reactions would always exceed the actions.

From those formative years, perfecting the art of embellishing facts without having to lie, she grew up to become vicious, rotten to the bone, and always scheming, finding satisfaction in spreading injury and suffering.

Sticking like cobweb, she has been a living nightmare to all those who inadvertently came in contact with her. To the point that a few kids at school would have been willing to run straight into quicksand if only they were certain that the hound tracking their footsteps would have followed them all the way there—unfortunately, she was despicable, but not dumb.

I long wondered who would want to marry such a mudslinging, self-righteous, sermonizing witch whose only pleasure in life seemed to be officiating as a rule-police, dutifully denouncing violators with more spite and virulence than even the Visionaries and Kritikillar themselves—maybe with a vengeance, out of frustration that women were not allowed to hold such positions of authority. But I later learned that Small Visionaries, in their presumed infinite wisdom, typically brokered arranged marriages to help the Perfectionists deal with their little demons. These grand matchmaking schemes also served to impress upon the Perfectionist parents the idea that the Author will always reward their daughters for service to the cause—the reward, in this case, being the poor sap ordered to wed the otherwise unmarriageable girl and spawn multiple offspring of Perfectionist allegiances.

The thought of a brood of little Cassandras growing up into a whole pack of intolerant Perfectionists always made me shiver. Not to mention the bloodcurdling vision of a dozen nagging mini-Cassandras, all hung up on details and denouncing the transgressors of stupid rules, but conveniently allowed to break a sacred rule. An army of little Perfectionists, crawling around, spreading their antipathy toward all fun things to do in life and their ingrained hate of Kafkaists.

In fairness, everybody hated Kafkaists—understandably, as this was required by a rule taught at a young age and regularly reinforced, that also prohibited kids from any contact with Kafkaists. Given the grim portrait of the typical Kafkaist painted by our educators, the rule protecting us from such a frightful encounter was understandable. But Perfectionists hated them more and better than all of us. If Kafkaists and Authorians were like cats and dogs, Kafkaists and Perfectionists were like cats and skunks.

Sometimes I wondered if Perfectionists didn't just hate everybody who was not a Perfectionist. They sure didn't miss a chance to act as if they did—even though they always said otherwise, claiming to be servants of the greater good.

Damn it, they even hated magicians!

That animosity alone was sufficient to discourage any kid from trying to learn a few tricks from the traveling magicians that visited the village every now and then. Yet, all—except for the Perfectionists—loved these shows improvised in the middle of the street during which cards, scarves, eggs, birds, rabbits, appeared or disappeared in exchange for some applause and a few coins. Of course, money and jewels tended to disappear more than they appeared, often discovered days after the fact, and as a result these buskers tended to get blamed for more than they deserved. For example, once, a villager claimed that his wife disappeared with the magician, never to be seen again, but that was eventually discovered to be a lie when her remains were found buried in his basement.

Yet, Perfectionists didn't despise magicians because of their skills of larceny. No. They hated them on the belief that making things appear and disappear is creating illusions that are perverting the Author's narrative. Typically, a magician who couldn't run very fast always risked being stoned to death when Perfectionists were numerous enough in the vicinity of their impromptu magic show to rally themselves into a raging mob.

Anyway, I always liked talking to magicians. For sure, I found the exoticism of a traveling life attractive, but more importantly, I was fascinated by the illusions and wanted to learn the truth behind the trickery. In particular, many times, I begged them to teach me how to make Cassandra disappear, but they knew it wouldn't have been wise to teach magic to an Authorian kid. They had enough problems as it was.

This didn't stop me from dreaming that I could, someday, in a grand feat of magic, make all the rules disappear. All the stupid rules about eggs, socks, and noses. All the pure nonsense that had cost me loss of functionality in an arm. Make all the Perfectionists and Visionaries disappear too. All vanishing down in a magician's hat, leaving nothing but a clean slate on which to rebuild a better life.

Kids' dreams.

In the meantime, coming back to the egg incident, as a ten-year-old kid who had survived—at the cost of a limb—the contemptible judgment of Perfectionists a few years earlier, I wasn't about to tell anybody that I had broken the egg rule. I followed my mother's wise advice.

The problem, however, is that I sure wasn't about to stop breaking rules. There were so many. So many so easy to break.

In that sense, it's somewhat ironic that I ended up entangled in a huge mess because someone other than me broke a rule. And I sure didn't expect to be dragged into that mess by my father.

Punishing Reward

"You come with me!" snapped my father.

Last time he had said that, I ended up at the Review Panel and things didn't turn out so well. Now, with the same order, again stripped of any justification or explanation, I feared the worst.

Usually, when he barked, "come with me"—which was already more words than he'd say to me on a good day—it was to push my face in some mess I had created, as a visual explanation for the stern education that followed. But this wasn't about tools I left out to rust in the rain or bees in the basement that came through a window I left open. The same few words now sounded like a much bigger "come see the mess you could have prevented while you had a chance."

Although he didn't tell me where we were going, it sure wasn't another visit to the Lackeys because my mother gave me an egg sandwich—made with motherly love and properly opened eggs—an apple, and a gallon of water. A trunk was also loaded onto the cart behind the horse.

When we arrived at Visionary Square's gatehouse—by rule, the westernmost dwelling of the village—twenty of the strongest young men from the village waited there for him, including some of those who had beaten me up and crushed my arm when I was seven. They were sitting on ten carts filled with weapons and chains. For a moment, I wondered if that intimidating pile of muscles served a deadly purpose to be executed immediately on the square, but thankfully not.

All the meatheads lined up behind our cart, like a group about to leave on an expedition. Clearly, my father wasn't pleased to be there. Best I could guess was that he had been tasked with this duty as some sort of retaliation for having voiced his dissenting opinion at the Review Panel [*Re·tal·i·a·tion. Noun. The act of biting an ear in return for a punch in the face, or doing the same with words and a smile*]. My father wasn't a zealot, but he knew better than to contest orders from the Small Visionary, so he was there, fulfilling his duties.

Our cart led the way. Without a word, the others followed us around the village, heading east. Technically, the convoy should have cut through the village, using Main Street, as this was our prestigious hundred-foot-wide avenue and the shortest route eastward, but on a rainy day, the logical path isn't always what it seems—and it was pouring rain that late afternoon.

Winds had long ago blown away the thin layer of top soil that once covered the village's main street, leaving a clay roadbed that was fully functional on a dry sunny day, that was still passable in the damp of the night, but that became a bottomless mud pit on a rainy day—a problem particularly exacerbated by the fact that Main Street was the lowest point in the village. In other words, our most prestigious avenue had been perfectly laid out on the flats of a hundred-foot-wide mud swamp. That's what you get in a village of morons.

The logical thing would have been to recognize the mistake the first time it happened and move the village far uphill, or at least out of the seasonal mud pit. But no. Instead, in a village of morons, people don't move; they adapt. Piles were driven deep to stabilize the foundations of existing homes or to build new ones, and everybody learned to live with the seasonal Main Street problem, suffer with it for as long as possible, complain, complain, complain, and wait for the day when someone comes up with a brilliant accommodation—which, in my village, happened the day "complaints street" reached about a mile in length.

In a burst of creative genius, our village leaders developed a system of covered wood sidewalks (also on deep piles) elevated above the roadway, that quite conveniently allowed villagers to reach all the little stores and businesses along Main Street while remaining dry, even in torrential rain—as long as it wasn't windy at the same time. While the sidewalks had their critics, mostly lamenting that the unaesthetic appendages had destroyed the architectural character of our town—as if it had any—I, for one, have always been appreciative of the luxuries of modern life. In any event, the complaints quickly faded away because the covered sidewalk also offered a unique vantage point to watch unsuspecting travelers trying to cross town on a rainy day, horse and cart sinking deeper with forward progress, until getting irremediably stuck, being unable to turn-around, and begging for help. The elevated sidewalks provided convenient dry platforms from which the locals could profit from the misery of others, by offering rescue services, *à la carte*, at a premium. As a result, rain weeks were long awaited, as they brought with them seasonal sidewalk sales and captive buyers. Most popular offerings were thrown ropes and pulling belts for things that had to be recovered immediately, and shovels for self-service digging that could wait until after the rain stopped and the mud dried. Incidentally, once, it was attempted to use doors as temporary plank walkways to reach those trapped, but this led nowhere as the doors sank out of sight as soon as they were dropped in the mud—a costly misuse and loss of valuable merchandise, not to forget an objectionable use of the flagship manufacturing product that was the pride of the village.

One would think that after years of sinking suckers, the word would get around and travelers would avoid our main street, but no. Unsuspecting travelers got trapped so frequently, it was almost as if they did it on purpose—as if the odd idea of taking a disgusting mud bath could ever be a desirable thing to do. As a result, rescue services has forever remained the village's second most profitable industry—although far behind the door making enterprise. The business of fishing hapless clients out of the mud also had the advantage that—contrary to the door manufacturing industry—all proceeds were equally shared between local families, as a strategy to prevent cut-throat competition that could erode profits. Not to forget the side benefits. For example, one winter, during a warm rainy week, an ill-informed convoy tried to cross town. People could be rescued promptly, but the rain was so intense, and the horses sank so deep while desperately trying to free themselves, that it proved impossible to pull them out of the mud before sunshine returned. Since it rained for a week, the horses pretty much starved to death in place. This usually turned out to be a good thing for the village, first, because replacement horses are one of the *à la carte* items sold at the highest premium, and, second, because the stuck horses are always "traded in" as part of the deal, becoming village property in the transaction. However, in that particular case, the gain from the trade-in wasn't as good as usual because it stopped raining during a night while temperature dived below freezing. The first person to venture on the thin ice in the morning sank through and had to be rescued from the treacherous mud. Efforts to break the ice lid that locked in all the humidity and prevented the mud from drying were futile as new sheets of ice formed as fast as they could be broken—it was that brutally cold. On the positive side, frozen horse meat preserves itself well, so the parts that protruded above the ice were still edible by the time the ice could support a crew dispatched to carve steaks that fed the village for weeks.

All that is to say that the expedition headed by my father avoided Main Street, half-circled around the village, and headed east.

He set the pace for the group; I sat next to him in the lead cart; and we both looked at the open dirt road ahead. Spending time next to each other, without saying a word—in our typical father-son relationship.

The slow convoy traveled for about an hour east and thirty minutes north, before stopping at sunset next to a wooden sign that warned: "Entering the Territory. Suspend all disbelief." Vandals had struck out "disbelief," written below it "humanity," and added "Do not feed the animals." Multiple obscenities were carved in the trunk of the oak on which the official sign had been nailed. Piles of excrements in various stages of decomposition surrounded the tree, and the thugs from our convoy took great pleasure to add their own defecation to the masterpiece— essentially emptying the entire content of their brains on the ground.

I had never been to the Territory before, and had never imagined doing so ever. Yet, there I was, contemplating a monument that aptly captured the essence of what we had been drilled to believe about the place. I didn't know then what I know today. I had no idea. But it was pretty clear where we were going.

"Don't talk to any of them," said my father pointing to the sign and, then, to the road ahead, as if I could have forgotten years of education. There was no compelling reason to talk to a Kafka-ist in the first place, for sure, but, frankly, I had no more desire to chitchat with the dumb brutes of our expedition than with a Kafkaist.

"Don't talk to any of them," he repeated. "Just do as I tell you."

"Clear."

My father gave me the reins while he pulled a map of the Territory with instructions in the margin, which he read using a candle in the dusk. We went north for a while longer, crossed a shallow stream, and headed southwest for about an hour.

As we approached a village, my father yelled: "Hoods!"

He gave me one as he pulled one for himself from the trunk. The red conical hoods had openings for the eyes and mouth, but I had to constantly pull back mine to be able to see the road.

Kafkaists who saw us approach either froze in place or ran away quite agitated. What struck me at that point was that, had I not known that they were Kafkaists, I wouldn't have been able to tell. Apparently, years of education instructing me as to the moral turpitude of Kafkaists had failed to provide a single visual clue that would have allowed me to differentiate one from an Authorian. I felt vulnerably exposed to a great danger by this shortcoming.

Deep into the village, all the way to its very end, the eleven carts reached a modest house on an ordinary street, managed to turn around, ready to backtrack east—crushing flowers and damaging much shrubbery in the process—and stopped. It wasn't a slum—the construction was of quality and the relatively new front door was a high-end model actually manufactured in our village—but the crooked shutters and peeling paint suggested an allergy to everyday maintenance.

My father pulled me by the arm to the front door. All the muscles stood behind us.

"Your job is to read this when I tell you," he said, handing me a parchment.

It all made sense now. My father hadn't brought me along because he wanted to. He did so because he was illiterate, and so were all the coneheads in his mob.

"Your job is to carefully hold on to what we're here to get and keep a path clear for our exit," he shouted to the pack of trunk-sized biceps as he banged on the door. "And don't hurt it, no matter what!"

I expected that nobody would dare open the door, or that some monster would, to confront us, but a frail old man did.

Before he could say a word, my father asked, with firm authority: "Is this the Hipper Residence?"

"Yes. Who—"

"Move over," he said, pushing him sideways.

The mob barged in, spreading from the door into the house, securing an exit path, up to a dining room that might have been the center of the house and where a warm dinner was being enjoyed before the unwelcome intrusion. Those around the table stood up in a state of surprise and fear.

"All residents of this dwelling are to assemble here at once. No harm will be done to all those that immediately cooperate," ordered my father.

All the Kafkaists in the room lined up along the wall by themselves, in shock, leaving all of the food on the table. Two more adults from an adjacent room joined them.

"Please identify yourself," shouted my father, "starting with you!"

"Marcus," obliged the father, after some hesitation. The others followed suit, equally unsure.

"Olivia."

"Marcella."

"Casimir"

"Mira."

"Geoffrey."

"Claramae."

"Janus."

"There are people missing!" shouted my father, stomping his boot for emphasis.

One of the coneheads brought him a lit torch.

"This is my last warning. If all residents of this house are not here in one minute, there will be consequences," he threatened, wiggling the torch.

I was stunned. How did my father know that people were hiding?

Within the minute, an old woman entered the room, followed by a young woman pulling two screaming kids by the hand.

"Your names!"

"Nana," said the old woman.

"Theodors," said the little boy, crying, hanging to the young woman's hand.

"Avril," mumbled the little girl, trying to be braver than her bother.

"June," said the young woman.

June? I pulled my hood backward a bit to better align my eyes with the holes.

There, right in front of me, within arm's reach, was the most beautiful face I had ever seen. Below that angelic face, barely visible around a neck partly hidden beneath the V-collar of a wool blouse, was an ordinary leather rope at the end of which dangled a small apple carved in basswood.

"Now," said my father to me, but I was speechless. There, pinned along a wall by the violence of my father's words, looking me straight in the eyes with anger, was a gorgeous woman. A formidably stunning woman who once was just a little lost girl who met, in strange circumstances, a little lost boy: two kids who bisected a forbidden forest that conveniently kept two isolated worlds apart.

How could she be a Kafkaist? How could such dazzling blue eyes be those of a Kafkaist?

"Now," repeated my father, vigorously poking his elbow into my ribs.

The pain reminded me that I was surrounded by a belligerent mob—a mess that could have been avoided if I could have lied to the Lackeys at that propitious moment, but a mess that somehow allowed me the stunning opportunity to see June again.

The next hit was more than a poke. My father wasn't about to be embarrassed by his son again.

I unsealed the letter and started to read.

"By decree of the Small Visionary of Cimmerian County, under the authority of the Grand Visionary of Stygian's Dominion, and the infallible Kritikillar—most infinitely wise and ultimate enforcer of the Author's will—we hereby declare that Mr. Theodors Hipper, by virtue of having been bookmarked by due process, shall be immediately brought under the Kritikillar's protection and custody to ensure his good character transition to the Author's Universe and protect him from moral turpitude."

The words after "bookmarked" were most probably not heard by anyone. At that single word, screams, insults, fists, and whole bodies were thrown around with a passion that gave a purpose to the meatheads. It was an ugly mess.

If the Kafkaists had made vows of non-violence (as I learned later), that clan must have been a rabid bunch of amnesiacs as they fought with the energy of despair. Not endowed for combat, I was looking for a way to sneak out unnoticed when June jumped on me. She pummeled me with vigor, screaming like a raging beast, throwing insults between incomprehensible growls, possibly trying to kill me, while I stood motionless, mesmerized by the deep blue of her eyes, holding tight to my hood, scared that she'd pull it off to reveal my identity—as if she could possibly recognize me after all these years—until a meathead pushed her aside and dragged me to the exit.

Bottom line, the Kafkaists were outnumbered and outmuscled. In spite of the bloody commotion, the kid was thrown in a trunk and abducted from his parents—although the official term used in all subsequent proceedings was "saved." Like a pack of wolves, we swarmed out of the village. The violated family was left battered and broken.

As for June, she showed to my father that his son could be assaulted—and defeated—by a woman, which was nothing to redeem myself from all the embarrassment I had caused him already. But more importantly, seeing June again reconnected the dots of a forgotten past, rekindling the wonderful memories of our first chance encounter—even though, on that dreadful and violent evening, it felt as if these sweet thoughts occurred while doing a headstand in a bear trap.

I had never dared to return to our meeting place in the forest—as I could not afford to lose another arm—but, for years, I had dreamt of June. In an idealized way. At first, as a kid longing for that lost girlfriend who triggered that special tingle in his heart, and then, later, as a young man, longing for a girlfriend that might have been his soul mate, enthralled by the illusions and possibilities of a mirage. But those dreams had become sparser and fewer as time eroded my naive hope of ever seeing her again, and as the reality of life had taken its harsh toll on the mind of an idealist. But now, the harsh reality of life had taken a strange and different turn.

And I dreamt again.

Even though—I now knew—she was a Kafkaist.

Illiterantes

Determined to crush any retaliation from the Kafkaists, the Small Visionary had been granted the assistance of a full three-battalion brigade of Fanatiks from the Dominion's Regiment (with the blessings of those further up the chain of command). In fact, the calculating minds behind the operations had planned everything such that the Fanatiks arrived in the middle of the night, no more than an hour after the return of the kidnapping mob. Daybreak revealed the battalions' tents planted on the periphery of my village, in a symbolic display to create the illusion of a fortress—to the extent that a fortress can be made of heavy cotton canvas—as well as to make it clear to the villagers that some sort of martial rule was in effect, and that every living creature was potentially hostage of those in charge.

In principle, Fanatiks were eager volunteers enlisted to defend the Authorians' higher ideals and greater purpose. In reality, though, given that Kafkaists were pacifists and not inclined to rebellion in response to provocation, Fanatiks were mostly lazy bastards who felt empowered by uniforms, shiny medals, firearms, and the privilege to treat the village as a self-serve pantry to their gargantuan appetite. Their true purpose was mostly to bolster the prestige of the Small Visionary—as a Visionary without an army is nothing but a eunuch with moral pretensions *[Eu·nuch. Noun. Pointless ape, insensitive to freezing cold]*.

To those ignorant of the Kafkaists' doctrine of pacifism—essentially all of the villagers back then—claims of the brigade's high effectiveness in deterring aggression would forever remain unchallenged and impossible to prove, in a sort of chicken-and-egg kind of way. So, I took for granted then that all the roads around the village were guarded by Fanatiks—possibly lined by them all the way to June's village.

Yet, I had to see June. I had to talk to her. Look her in the eyes. Hold her hand. See if that fleeting friendship of bygone days could be rekindled and possibly grow into something more. Maybe, given the proper circumstances, I could even apologize for being one of the wolves that barged into her life and stole her little brother—although I couldn't think of how to do that without killing all chances of rekindling our friendship, or without possibly getting killed in the process.

More realistically though, I wondered if she remembered me at all.

Which is why I had to find a way back to her village.

I replayed the route traveled that fateful night, going east, north, then west, essentially going around the mountain that stood north and presumably separated our respective villages, convincing myself that her home lay right there on the other side. Although steep enough to prevent a road through it, the mountain had evidently not been an impassible barrier to a little girl when two kids met deep in the woods years ago. This made June's village appear even closer.

With all the commotion around, my parents didn't notice my absence, and I escaped the fortress by pretending to go into the forest to gather fire wood. As for the strict security at the village's perimeter, the few Fanatiks I encountered at that time couldn't care less about my whereabouts, as they were more focused on setting traps to supplement their official rations with some local wildlife delicacies—not forgetting that the true purpose of their mission was always to remain well fed.

Armed with nothing but a mix of juvenile enthusiasm and unleashed hope, I ran deep into the forest, passed the stream where we first met, and continued forward up the slope. Driven by impulse alone, I had no plan other than to climb, catch sight of her village once at the top, and run a beeline from there to her house. Quite a simple stratagem, if there ever was one—but, obviously, not carefully thought through.

Approaching the mountain top, as the slope became gentler and allowed me to accelerate the pace through the thick undergrowth, a rope wrapped around my ankle, interrupted my stride, and flipped me upside down, ten feet in the air. The first thing that crossed my mind was that I might have stepped into one of the Fanatiks' traps and that they might be stupid enough to confuse me with a deer and carve me up for dinner. However, that didn't make sense as none of them would have ventured this far looking for game when there was plenty of wildlife to hunt closer to the village. More likely—and more scary—the second thought that crossed my mind was that I had stepped in a forgotten trap and, at best, was going to be found days later by a decrepit trapper doing the rounds, collecting his catches and disappointed to find a dead jackass, less tasty than a rabbit and definitively less valuable than a silver fox.

I had to free myself at once. Dangling like a worm at the end of a line, trying to bend and reach my ankle, all I succeeded to do in my contorted efforts was to ring a bunch of little bells tied to the rope. After a few minutes of this carillonning, I was jerked sideways, once, twice, and many times more, moving a few feet at a time, like long johns on a clothesline—although it was more a short Adam than some long Johns. Then, after a few hundred feet of travel, it stopped.

"Who are you?" shouted someone I couldn't see.

I froze.

"Declare your allegiances," said another.

"What do you mean?" I replied in earnest.

This triggered much rumblings from behind the trees. Multiple voices. I was severely outnumbered and hoped I hadn't insulted anyone.

"Do you believe in an Author?" asked what appeared to be a third voice.

What does one respond to a hostile mob in hiding? Given that I was hanging upside down like a ham, there was a right answer to the question, but it depended on whether I was being ambushed by a bunch of raving Fanatiks or by Kafkaists looking for revenge. Likewise, this might not have been the proper setting to start explaining that although, technically, I was an Authorian, I had been eaten away by doubts for most of my life and didn't know what this made me.

Swish! An arrow planted itself on a tree inches from my head.

"I don't know, I don't know!" I screamed—which pretty much was the truth, in so many words.

More rumblings.

"Why don't you know?"

I remained silent.

Swish, again, brushing the side of my head.

"Because there's no good answer," I screamed, panicked.

After a moment, a bunch of colorfully dressed folks came out from behind the trees. Far from soldiers in uniform with weapons and shield, the motley crew in disparate tie-dyed clothes and sandals resembled a garden in full bloom, and wore more necklaces, earrings, and bracelets than the sum total of the girls of my village. The tension in the clothesline was released and I was abruptly dropped to the ground.

"Good answer," said one, helping me stand up and slapping me on the shoulder.

"Why?"

"Only dangerously crazy people would confess their silly beliefs to an unknown armed enemy."

"Some even try to convert you," added another, laughing.

"But I said the truth—"

"Yeah, yeah. You're fine kid. Relax. We're not stupid. We know you're an Authorian—"

"How—"

"You came from that side of the mountain, didn't you?" he shouted with menacing eyes.

I froze.

He burst into laughs.

"Come on. I'm just messing with you. You're not a dangerous Authorian, right?"

"I'm a lamb," I replied, hoping not to be confused with the sacrificial kind.

We walked the rest of the slope as they escorted me to the top of the hill where a community of tents hugged every tree. Naked kids running after squirrels, swinging in hammocks, or throwing rocks, rushed to hide in the tents when they saw me approaching. The rest of the village seemed unfazed by my presence, presumably confident that if I'd been a threat, I'd be dead by now. Not that anybody seemed stressed to start, as most people were either lounging in the sun or playing music.

We reached an open area past the tents, with tall log stools arranged in a tight circle. One of them grabbed my shoulder and pushed me down on one of the stools. They remained standing around me.

"So tell us. What's an Authorian doing here?"

Sitting in the middle of the circle, the firm hand still grabbing my shoulder, things suddenly didn't seem as safe as I had thought a moment before.

"Just passing by. I have nothing to do here."

"Really?"

"Absolutely. All is good."

"All is good?"

"Oh yeah. Totally."

"No hard feelings about the rope?"

"A few bruises, but no reason to be upset."

"No anger? No hateful feelings?"

"What? Hate? Pfff. Why would I?"

"Why? He's asking why?" he said, laughing. "Because I'm an Illiterantes. We're all Illiterantes. Isn't that enough to ignite an Authorian?"

Illiterantes? I didn't know they truly existed. In an abstract way, they had to. As we were taught in school, brightness exists because darkness does, and for perfection to exist so must imperfection. Everything is polarized. So, by deduction, if Authorians and Kafkaists believe in the Author—even though they can't agree on his designs—then there had to exist groups that didn't believe in the Author. Our teachers insisted that such tribes were only a conceptual abstraction. Yet, an abstraction affectionately called "the damned Ethnics" by Perfectionists, as it violated their desire for absolute, one-sided perfection.

The abstraction was now alive, right in front of me—or so it claimed to be.

"Illiterantes?"

"Eh."

"Why should I believe you?"

They all started to laugh.

"Did I say anything funny?"

"Zayne. Please educate our dumb Authorian here," said the oldest man in the pack to the one who had slapped me on the shoulder earlier, and who had been doing most of the talking so far.

The Zayne in question got closer to me and put his hand on my shoulder. I sure hoped he wasn't about to educate me the same way my father did.

"We don't care if you believe it or not. We don't believe in anything, so why should we care about what you believe? Or don't believe?"

"But you believe you exist, right?"

"Maybe we do, maybe we don't."

"How could that be?"

"The Authorians think we don't exist. The Kafkaists consider us to be 'erasures' or 'poor sketches.' Either way, we don't care."

"Why?"

"Because it doesn't matter."

"But it does matter."

"Nah. People will believe whatever they want, no matter what. It's just beliefs."

"I know of people whose lives have been made miserable by Authorians," I said, thinking of the obvious. "Isn't it dangerous to be against everything?"

"Are you threatening us?"

"No, no. Not me. Never. It's just that I've seen folks go weird when someone questions their beliefs or rejects them."

"We're not against anybody. We just don't care about anything to the point of making it a rule."

"Isn't it the same thing?"

"Look kid. People like to kill those that do not think like them, so people with dissimilar beliefs are the most threatening to each other. Wars of belief are the most vicious of all wars. Who has energy or passion to kill people without beliefs? It isn't difference of opinions that is lethal, it's difference of beliefs. And we don't have any. We're just outcasts."

"Yeah, nomads," added another one. "Today we're here, tomorrow, who knows. Poof!"

"But isn't having no belief like... believing? Believing that there's no Author."

They all laughed again.

"So is that why you came all the way here? To share with us this wonderful intellectual constipation problem: the belief that everybody must believe in something?"

"Actually, not," I replied, distracted, remembering June, and standing up to resume my journey.

"Hey, hey, whoa. Where do you think you're going?"

I stared at the valley on the other side of the mountain, searching for her village.

"I have to find the Kafkaist village in that valley."

They all looked at each other, mystified, as if I had told them that I was a grandmother who got lost in the woods on her way to pay a surprise visit to her Kafkaist granddaughter.

"So what are you planning to do, exactly? Show up there and say, 'Hello, I'm an Authorian. Are you having a good day? Would you like to have some cookies and tea with me?'"

"Maybe."

I wasn't about to explain my feelings for June.

"Not exactly a good idea right now," Zayne replied.

"You're a fool," added another. "You'll get killed."

"In case you don't know, some of your folks had the brilliant idea of kidnapping one of their kids."

I sure wasn't about to tell them that I had been party to that crime.

"There's a war brewing," he added. "The Kafkaists are pacifists, but many among them are arguing for a temporary suspension of their vows, given the extraordinary circumstances."

"And how would you know all of that?"

They all laughed.

"Let's be clear, here. It's good when people believe you don't exist, but we can't just hide all the time. So, when you are surrounded by raving lunatics and violent people who have no patience for logical debates—including Authorians who will think we are Kafkaists and Kafkaists who can mistake us for Authorians—to protect ourselves, we have to remain well informed of what's happening around us. Very well informed. That's why we travel to each village, to get the news, take the pulse, watch for any emerging threats to our way of living."

"You've come to my village?"

"Of course. All villages."

"How can you do that unnoticed?"

"Who said unnoticed? On the contrary, we make sure we are very easily noticed," he said pulling a piece of money from behind my ear.

Magicians! The magicians are Illiterantes. All my life, I had seen them without making the connection. And all my life, I had assumed that magicians, like all other itinerants who'd walk into our village were Authorians from other villages. Why wouldn't they be?

"Which ones of you visited my village?"

They all raised their hand.

"I don't remember seeing any one of you before."

Zayne signaled me to wait while he went into a hut. I noticed that none of the huts in the village had doors—not even a curtain. After a minute, he returned, wearing thick glasses and a hat painted with stars. I recognized him right away: that magician had visited our village many times before. Amazingly, thick glasses had turned Zayne—the apparently invincible, super warrior—into a wimp. Who could have imagined the deceiving power of such an unbelievably simple prop? Simple glasses. It defied logic.

"And Kafkaists? Do they tolerate magicians too?"

"They're a lot more welcoming than Authorians actually. Magic tricks are little illusions that challenge rationality, which is compatible with their beliefs that life is illogical to the hilt."

"They also find us convenient," added another.

"Conveniently helpful," corrected Zayne. "They'd probably go crazy without us."

"They're already crazy," shouted one.

"Conveniently crazy," corrected another, giggling.

I was clueless as a frog in a jar.

"It's simple," said Zayne. "Because of their dumb beliefs— which, by the way, are just as dumb as yours—Kafkaists need to set their clocks at random times, once a month. It is considered an essential ritual."

"I love these mental tortures," added the older guy. "Why not require everybody to walk backwards, while we're at it?"

"Or to dance in the rain only wearing red long johns," added another.

"How about wearing a cow dung hat at funerals?"

"Or barking like dogs when hearing thunder."

"Or doing cartwheels at sunrise, and push-ups at sunset."

"Or dunking newborns in goat piss and rolling them in flour, to purify them."

"Or eating fish only if they have been kissed by a toothless grandmother on full-moon days."

"Or sleeping on a bed of burdock naked, holding a bowl of acorns in whipped cream, as part of a wedding ceremony."

"Or making love while doing headstands."

The mockery continued for a while, everybody trying to outdo the other and improvise a more entertaining ritual—unless these were unbelievable things that Kafkaists actually did, which I sincerely hoped wasn't the case, because it never occurred to me in my wildest dreams that I would need to be a contortionist to love June.

"So how does all of that make you convenient to Kafkaists?" I asked, like a party pooper.

I thought they were ignoring me by then, as the giggling continued for a while, but as it subdued and all recovered their breaths, Zayne looked at me with a mischievous look.

"The problem, you see, is that they can't do it themselves, because if they did, it wouldn't be random now, would it?"

"So the magicians help them by doing it?" I ventured.

"What? Why would we do that?"

"Out of kindness, I guess."

"In your wildest dreams! These folks hate us just as much as anybody else."

"Out of love for clockwork then?"

"No. We hate clocks. We don't believe in clocks, and we don't believe in time. No device can take the freedom of a day and chain it to a machine. No gadget can dictate to us when things are supposed to be done or when pauses should be taken. It's false magic. We will never slave ourselves to a machine for the purpose of making its prophecies come true. That would be like losing the spontaneity of life and becoming Authorians and Kafkaists, prisoners of all that nonsense."

"So you don't help them."

"No. We help ourselves. We sell our services to do it."

"That's just semantics. You're helping them nonetheless."

"Call it anything you want, but, the way I see it, collecting money from Kafkaists for doing such a stupid thing is more like screwing them over. It's easy money, and we're happy to oblige. In fact, we charge exorbitant rates, so it is practically the same as stealing—which is fair game when dealing with able-bodied adults who suffer from intellectual constipation."

I kept looking at June's village.

"Well, I have to get there."

"No you don't. Trust me."

"Why would I believe you?"

"Trusting Zayne is not like believing in Zayne."

"You said it wisely," added the older guy. "Believing is insane indeed."

They all laughed. It took me a while to catch the pun.

"I must go."

Zayne looked at me, incredulous, probably wondering what so adamantly attracted me there against better judgment.

"OK. Fine. Go ahead," said Zayne. "They'll be thrilled to capture an Authorian, hang him from a tree for target practice, and set him on fire to end the evening. Who knows? That kind of entertainment might help defuse the tension—"

"I'll pretend that I'm a magician."

"Ah. That won't help much. It's actually an even dumber idea."

"And why is that?"

"Because of the little evil girl."

Cassandra's ugly face immediately came to mind hearing those words, but they couldn't possibly know her.

"Who's that?"

"Some Authorian dimwit who thought it would be a brilliant idea to pretend to be a magician, with special healing powers."

"What for?"

"It's not clear. All we know is that the little twerp did some hocus pocus on a sick kid, she shouted that he was saved, and everybody freaked out."

"She bookmarked him," I said, as it became all too clear.

"She bookmarked him?"

"Yeah. It's a rite that Authorians do; a short ceremonial of initiation that makes a person an official constituted Authorian. All it takes is a 2" by 6" piece of thin cardboard, deposited on the nose of the person to receive the rite."

They looked at each other in disbelief.

"I know, it looks quite dumb explained like that, but it's symbolic," I clarified, as if it deserved a rational explanation.

More looks of disbelief.

"Look, it's just a ritual," I added, as if it wasn't clear.

"We know what you guys do. We just can't believe that anyone would be so stupid as to bookmark a Kafkaist."

Obviously, they didn't know Cassandra. That was surely something she'd be dumb enough to do.

"Why would anybody do that?"

Who knew? I could only speculate. Maybe, somehow, deep within the muck inside her skull, Cassandra had hatched a sordid genocide plan that consisted of killing the Kafkaists' future by converting all their offspring into Authorians. Such a dark phantasmagoria can only germinate inside a sick mind like hers, and if that indeed was the case, June's little brother could have been the unlucky first victim of her grand extermination plan.

"I don't know. She's crazy, I guess," I answered, which seemed a more plausible explanation that the machination I had just imagined.

"No wonder that the last one of us who showed up there was chased out of town by a pitchfork wielding mob."

"Pitchforks?"

"Sharpened."

The thought of being skewered deflated my courage. Given that neither the bad Authorians nor the useful Illiterantes were welcome in June's village anymore, my only option was to turn around, go back home, and figure out a better plan.

With a nod, a hand wave, and a disappointed look that said it all, I parted company with the Illiterantes, still baffled that Cassandra could have been so stupid as to trigger a war—a war of beliefs, no less.

As far as I could see, the situation was desperate.

My escapade through the woods didn't work, the roads were chock-full, clogged by Fanatiks, and I couldn't think of any other ways to reach June.

I needed advice from someone more experienced than I in dealing with thorny problems.

I needed to talk to Grandpa.

Godwyn

"Hogwash."

"Stop it pappy," insisted my mother.

"Hogwash, hogwash, hogwash!"

"You're having a bad influence. Don't—"

"Nobody's going to tell me what to do, what to say, or what to think. I'll be dead soon. So, Hogwash! Horseshit! And bullshit, too—if I please!"

Grandpa wasn't easy on my mother, and I loved it, because she had never been easy on me. To me, it was as if he whipped her for the both of us. Without knowing it, he was my proxy and I silently shared the great pleasure he enjoyed in responding back. It apparently isn't much fun being old, but it comes with some benefits, and Grandpa wasn't one to relinquish whatever few pleasures he had left in life—including the freedom to speak his mind.

"You've all gone numb-brained!" he yelled, the last word escaping just before one of those rage-triggered coughing spells. Each time, I thought he was going to cough to death, but he always survived. So far.

Grandpa Godwyn's rebellious attitude always exasperated my mother, but what she truly resented was that I listened to him more than to anybody else—and certainly more than to her. In the blink of an eye, she would have thrown him in the street—or, more likely, soaked him in gas and lit a match while he was sleeping—if not for my father.

So they argued a lot. Maybe Grandpa's grumpy mood was only a front to hide the fact that belligerence tickled him to death. He sure never tired of arguing—but not always for the same reasons, depending on with whom it happened.

When I was a kid, I wondered why he always argued with Grandma.

He would say; "Talk to me," and she would reply, "I have nothing to tell you that you don't already know." He would insist. She would add: "We're always together—we've been together forever. What is there more to say?"

So he would grumble, complain, insult her, and, inevitably, they would start arguing. Long, endless arguments, about insignificant things it seemed.

After the fights, when Grandma, upset and exhausted, would leave him there, he would wink at me, as if to say, "See, I got her to talk after all." I guess he preferred to hear her yell than to suffer his longing for her voice in silence. He fought with her for the comfort of hearing the familiar tone that soothed his heart. Her anger and words were meaningless; it was more important to bathe in her words than to find meanings in them.

But Grandma died.

Silence is all that remained, and he became miserable.

So, without saying a word—as fathers and sons do, it seems—my father rescued Grandpa from a toxic solitude and brought him home, over my mother's objections.

She hated his guts.

He had no patience for fools.

So they were like oil and water. Or fire and ice. Or crooked nail and rubber mallet.

My mother would have relished the prestige that could have come with Grandpa's status as the village's elder, had he not squandered that potential to the four winds with his recurrent shocking remarks and critiques. The only thing that saved him from the wrath of the Small Visionary was my father's success in convincing the Lackeys that a senile old fool, incontinent of his words, and at the threshold of natural death, wasn't worth the Visionary's trouble to accelerate the process.

A convenient lie, given that Grandpa was as healthy and lucid as ever. If anything, more lucid than some people could handle.

"Hogwash," he resumed, catching his breath after the coughing spell.

"Stop your blasphemy," insisted my mother, who always had to argue for reasons unknown to me. "Stop being an ugly old man."

She always said that. Grandpa was probably ugly, in some ways, as we all are, but since I was a "hideous-of-kin," ugly wasn't a qualifier that came to mind when I thought of him. In spite of having more wrinkles than skin surface available to display them, he looked fine to me and evoked no other image than that of a Grandpa. Besides, as my father was often said to be the spitting image of his father, if my mother married him, she must not have found him so repulsive—unless their courtship only lasted a moonlit night during which they wore bags on their heads.

"You're so cursed, you'll never meet the Author after your epilogue. You'll be erased forever."

"More hogwash."

"If you behave, I'll beg him to forgive you when I meet him, after my epilogue."

"Dying! It's called dying!"

"Maybe you'll get another chance if you redeem yourself."

"There is no Author!" he yelled, launching into another coughing spell.

These weren't arguments with Grandma, and my mother's voice was far from soothing him.

"Ignore Grandpa," she'd tell me. "He's senile. That's why he talks like an Illiterantes."

Until the day before, Illiterantes were just bogeymen to me, but now, indeed, I could easily picture Grandpa sharing a beer with Zayne on top of the mountain. I had to repress a smile.

The whole argument between Grandpa and my mother had started at breakfast when she mentioned (again) how ecstatic she was that the rescue of Theodors from the clutches of the Kafkaists had been a success.

"This is stupid. A terrible mistake," Grandpa mumbled.

"You've given Theodors a most wonderful gift," she said to my father, ignoring Grandpa. "He'll be grateful for the rest of this life."

"It's not a gift, it's a rape," replied Grandpa.

My father had no intention of replying to any of my mother's comments. He was pleased to let Grandpa handle her. It might even have been the main reason he had brought him to live with us in the first place.

"It's a case of the Grand Nutcase ordering people to steal a child from his parents. It doesn't get more screwed-up than that."

"Shut up. You know that was to save him."

"From what?"

"From the Kafkaists."

"But he's a Kafkaist!"

"Not anymore. Never again."

"You're as crazy as the Grand Nutcase and his numskull gang."

"He's an Authorian now. He's been bookmarked."

"That kid is in the clutches of monsters."

"That kid has been saved."

"No, that kid will be saved when he will be rescued. By Kafkaists. When they'll storm the village with an axe to grind."

"Don't be absurd. Their silly vows prevent it."

"Things have changed. It's not like decades ago. I'm telling you, it's going to get ugly, and you'll live to regret it."

"The Author will not allow it."

"Hogwash. There's no Author."

"Stop your profanity in front of Adam."

"There is no Author!"

"Grandpa is senile, son."

"Stop treating me like a child."

"He's soon to reach his epilogue. He's having a hard time to prepare for it."

"It's called dying!"

"Epilogue, it is," she insisted. "It will be such a nice day when that happens. You should prepare for yours."

"Hogwash."

That last bit had been an ongoing circular argument between my mother and Grandpa, but it had become a lot more agitated in light of the abduction, ending in scarier coughing spells than ever.

A few hours later, when my mother had left for errands, and Grandpa had time to cool off, I went to see him.

His eyes were closed and his chin rested on his chest, but his mouth wasn't open and drooling, so I knew he wasn't sleeping.

"Grandpa."

"Hmm?" he replied without opening his eyes. "Are you going to wordsmart again today, kid?"

He mangled "wordsmith" on purpose.

"Stop talking like a dictionary," he'd tell me. "I only know a few words, kid. Learn a few words, put all your weight behind them, and it's all you need. They'll carry."

My mother would say it differently: "Don't use big words. It will make you unpopular. A protagonist must be popular." *[Pro·ta g·o·nist. Noun. Somebody for whom the Author will find it worthwhile to waste time]*

So I was doomed I guess, because I always loved words. They were my trustworthy friends—my only friends. I had dreamt of becoming a dandelion parachuting words to root everywhere, but these dreams were crushed by the perversity of watching the alphabet shatter on the hardened crust of a desert without leaving a scrape, because nobody else seemed to care as much about words.

The Rules stated that books were just tools—utilitarian necessities—but I knew better. I devoured each and every one of them as if they were vital. Our school library was stocked with all the classics, such as "Advanced Carpentry," "Door Designs," "Better Hinges and Knobs," "Wood Framing Projects," and, fortunately, a few brand-new ones, such as "Principles of Telegraphy," "Train Whistles and Singing Wires: The Sounds of Progress," and "The Best of Times: Mastering Plumbing for Ultimate Comfort."

Granted, the topics were deathly boring. But the mysterious craft of knitting words into a coherent fabric hypnotized me. Words were pregnant with possibilities, preventing errors when drilled with discipline, enabling sturdy constructions when chained logically, imparting knowledge when ordered by scholarly wisdom. I spent countless hours trying to imagine all the ideas and ideals they could empower when juxtaposed in explosive combinations, or the dreams they could spawn if emancipated and allowed to fly free, or even the cataclysms they could inadvertently unleash if clashing in dramatic collisions that undermined the world's equilibrium.

Behind each worn-out or shiny book cover awaited daydreams made of jumbled and re-assembled words that infiltrated themselves between the printed lines, unforeseen fantasies that invaded my mind and drove it beyond logic—and, maybe, sanity—to foreign and unsettling worlds of consequences and surprises.

And in this world where I pretended to avidly learn crafts and practical skills, every time I could, I pulled the stolen dictionary from the bottom of the drawer where it laid hidden below piles of old homework books, and resurrected it once more for the pleasure of getting acquainted or reacquainted with all those words that held the key to explosive empowerment, emancipated dreams, and unleashed cataclysms. I was guilty of reading the dictionary. Guilty of reading meanings and order. Guilty of memorizing strange definitions, discovering synonyms for beauty, and realizing nearly infinite dangers when tampering with words.

"So. Are you going to wordsmart again today, kid," repeated Grandpa as my mind was getting all entangled in words, "or talk like a normal person?"

"I need your advice, Grandpa."

"Hmm?"

"You know the story of how you met Grandma, and how her parents didn't like you and how your parents didn't like her."

He straightened up in his chair, eyes wide open.

"And of how you told me that if you had listened to your parents, you would have made the most terrible mistake of your entire life."

"The most terrible mistake, for sure. And of your life too, as you wouldn't be here," he replied, with a serious wink.

"Well, I met this girl."

He smiled.

"And it's a little bit like your story, but more complicated. A lot more."

"Is she cute?"

"Uh, yes, very much so."

"Of course she is," he burst out in a mischievous laugh.

"Shush. Nobody else knows."

"Oh. OK," he whispered, looking around to make sure nobody was spying on us. "So, who is she? Do I know her?"

"No. I'm pretty sure you don't."

"Well, as long as it's not that little twerp," he said, referring to Cassandra, "I'm sure you'll get along fine."

"Thanks for the encouragement, but it's not that simple."

"Oh, I see. You haven't told her yet that you have a crush on her. Is that it?"

"No. Well, yes, that too. But, it's more complicated."

He pulled himself closer to me, excited like a checkers player about to start a game.

"So what's the problem?"

There was no point dancing around the topic with Grandpa if I wanted to benefit from his counsel.

"She's a Kafkaist," I whispered, eyes crunched.

I waited.

Waited.

Silence.

Slowly opening my eyes, I saw him hand on cheek.

"You may be good with words, Adam, but you have quite the knack for poor timing."

I started to stand up, about to leave.

He extended his arm, repeatedly pointing down with his index.

"Don't go so far. We'll figure it out."

I sat back.

"If you're serious about this, I'm sure there's a way. Let's see. She's in her village, right?"

I nodded.

"Where did you meet her, then?"

"When we kidnapped her little brother."

"Wow. You really make it easy, kid."

"Eh."

"And you fell in love? Just like that?"

"I had seen her before, elsewhere."

"Anyhow. Doesn't matter. If you think you love the girl, you owe it to yourself to try to see her again."

"Even if she's a Kafkaist."

"You're not talking to your mother here."

"But she's a Kafkaist."

"I don't care if she's a Kafkaist, a coal miner's daughter, or a pig with wings. As long as it's not the stupid twerp," he said, again referring to Cassandra.

"But I was one of those who abducted her brother."

"So? You don't need to introduce yourself by saying: 'Hi, my name is Adam, and I stole your brother.' I'm sure you can think of a better pick-up line."

"But I can't hide that from her. I'm not proud of it, and it's not like it's something I wanted to do, but it happened."

"Correct. But, you're not there yet. If I were you, I probably wouldn't bring that up during your first date. Anyhow, your problem is that you want to see her again, right?"

"Yes, but I can't go to her village. If I go there, I'll probably get killed. The last thing they want to see right now is an Authorian."

"Of course," he replied, which was Grandpa's way to say that even non-violent folks, when pushed to their limit, will dabble in homicidal activities. "I'd seriously consider killing you too if I was in their shoes."

"So there's no way."

"Oh, there's a way..." he said, with a twinkle in his eyes *[Twin·kle. Noun. Mischievous spark revealing that walking outside the lines is more fun than walking within them, and better than walking the line]*.

Delivery

"Go get the girl" were Grandpa's last words, along with his assurances that the plan would work. Not foolproof, but as good as one could expect given the circumstances.

And it worked.

As Grandpa expected, in this boiling crisis, the Cimmerian County Postal Service was struggling to find volunteers among its staff to deliver mail to the one Kafkaist village that fell within its jurisdiction. Apparently, it required a lot more courage to conduct a solo expedition there in broad daylight, only armed with letters and parcels, than to storm it in the night with a mob to kidnap a little kid. No veiled or direct threat, no cajoling or reward, no shouting or begging, no stick or carrot, could convince the brave mailmen of Cimmerian County to honor the Postal Service's pledge to deliver letters and parcels there. The Postal Service's motto boasted about its reliable performance, "rain or shine, snow or sleet, hail or thunder, hurricane or earthquake," but failed to mention that its operations could be derailed by the mighty force of absenteeism—anyone ordered to service the Kafkaist village systematically called in sick within the hour. Hiring a Kafkaist mailman, even if only to distribute mail in his own village, was inconceivable, allegedly for security reasons to maintain absolute control of all communications through the crisis—not to mention that it would be also considered immoral, as these were well paying jobs supported by Authorian tax dollars.

Therefore, the Service was delighted when an idiot applied for the job. That idiot was me, and I gladly agreed to deliver mail where no one else wanted to go.

They wrapped an official jacket around my shoulders, slapped a peaked cap on my head, dropped the mailbag at my feet, and pulled me to the stable to meet Fireball, whose job was to get there and back as fast as possible. Sure enough, mailbag clipped to the saddle, Fireball bolted out with the first kick. From that point onward, the reins were merely decorative. I could pull and steer all I wanted, it didn't matter. The beast had a mind of its own, the route to the Kafkaist's village was etched in it, and it would get me there on its own terms—rider comfort notwithstanding.

In less than an hour, Fireball traveled the same road east, north, and southwest, that had taken two-and-a-half hours in the cart pulled by my father's old nag the day of Theodors' abduction. Fireball—more of a Sweatball by then—stopped right at the entrance to the village, where a water-filled trough marked as property of the Postal Service awaited him.

"What am I doing here?" I wondered.

It was clear to Grandpa that, in the circumstances, Kafkaists needed more than ever to communicate with their peers in other villages and counties, to seek comfort, empathy, encouragement, or even counsel on the best course of action forward. Highly strategic and confidential matters would surely be dispatched by Kafkaist messengers sneaking through the woods, but given the hordes of Fanatiks and yahoos roaming the roads, the larger volume of letters, free of compromising information, were best left handled by the Service.

My only hope was that he was right and that Kafkaists wished to receive regular mail more than to kill the messenger. Fortunately, the first day on the job proved this to be the case. Not surprisingly, while collecting mail, I also collected a fair amount of insults, served as a target for projectiles anonymously dispatched from behind bushes, and got bitten by a dumb Chihuahua that thought of itself as a wolf. Yet beyond expectations, a few Kafkaists thanked me (an Authorian!), appreciative that the mail service had returned in spite of all the turmoil.

Most importantly though, I was able to roam freely through the village. The entire village—with its many mailboxes, lots of mailboxes. In fact, so many that it made me ponder the wisdom of taking an entire mail run just to see June—or, more precisely, to *maybe* see June—for a few seconds.

When I reached June's house, which I recognized from that infamous evening, I realized that there were two shortcomings in my plan that needed to be addressed. First, the mailbox was a slot in the door through which letters could be delivered without seeing a soul. Second, as I dropped a few envelopes in the slot, a little kid ran to the door with screams of joy and picked up the letters on the floor. This reminded me that June's family was huge and that even if I knocked on the door to hand deliver the letters, the probability that she'd be the one answering was minuscule.

Clearly, my plan needed improvements, and it is strong from that wisdom that I started my second day on the job. After a few more insults, another Chihuahua bite, and ducking twice to avoid some rotten tomatoes, I reached June's home. I took a deep breath, knocked on the door, and waited, hoping the plan would work.

"Waz dis iz?" asked a little girl talking through the mail slot kept open by her thumb.

"Registered mail for a certain Ms. June Hipper," I replied, kneeling to speak at the level of the mail slot.

"Geevs mee."

"I'm sorry, but this is registered mail. The letter must be signed by the recipient,"

"Waz dis?"

"Ze leter iz fo you zizter," I said through the mail slot, finishing the sentence as the door opened. Looking up, the door had been replaced by an ugly, giant cockroach, full of muscles that so perfectly fitted the frame that no breeze could squeeze through. All that was missing was a door knob in its clenched fist.

"What do you want?"

"Registered mail for Ms. June Hipper."

"I'll give it to her."

"It requires her signature on this acknowledgment of receipt. I can only deliver that letter to its official recipient."

"I'll give it to her."

"I'm sorry, but—"

His fist rose up.

"I won't say it again," he growled.

The notion that Kafkaists were non-violent seemed to be an ill-informed abstraction about to be vividly corrected.

"Damien!"

The monstrous beetle turned around, subdued by the voice of a woman.

"Avril told me there's a letter for me."

June! She was behind the hairy mountain—like a hidden sunset, but there nonetheless.

"I'm taking care of it," replied Damien.

"Get out of there. It's my letter."

"You take the letter, and I take care of the mailman."

The giant insect definitely wasn't about to thank me for delivering the mail.

"Big brother, get out of the way."

"Let me thank the mailman."

No doubt Damien's thanks would have hurt more than the Chihuahua's bites.

"Sure, sure, sure," she said, pushing him away from the door. "I'm quite capable of taking care of my own mail. Bye, bye. I'll call you if I need anything."

The beast retreated, like a cockroach at sunrise. Clearly, Damien had been out the night we abducted June's little brother. Had he been home instead of wrestling with bears, juggling with anvils, pushing boulders uphill, chopping trees barehanded, or whatever it is that such creatures do in their spare time, the current crisis would have been stillborn, and the mob of Authorians would have returned home with their asses remolded by Damien's clogs.

When June returned to the door to pick her letter, the strings that kept my heart in place ruptured. Unrestrained, it bounded inside me like a poor bug caught in a hand-cranked ice-cream churn in overdrive.

"So?" she asked, reaching the door.

She didn't recognize me.

Of course.

I probably wouldn't have recognized her either without the ordinary leather rope at the end of which dangled a small apple carved in basswood that she wore on that fateful night. She wasn't wearing it anymore—which didn't bode well—but I recognized her. Her blue eyes and the beautiful face that framed them accelerated the churn. She was even more beautiful in broad daylight—not being stressed and busy kicking a kidnapper while trying to pull off his hood sure helped. I hoped that she hadn't thrown the basswood apple into the fire—or the outhouse pit—in revenge. Maybe that thought crossed my mind because she sported a rebellious look: An uneven chin-length haircut, randomly parted and never conquered by brushes or combs, from which her face managed to emerge; a wool sweater missing a few buttons, sleeves dropping to mid-fingers, and a sizeable hole allowing an elbow to peek out; and, pants. Pants! Women in my village did not wear pants—another Authorian rule for sure. And, as far as I could tell from my limited experience hopping mailbox to mailbox, June was also the Kafkaist exception.

"So there's a letter for me, I'm told," she said smiling.

A smile—and what a smile.

There was hope.

By then, the poor bug was crushed between the ice cubes twirling ever faster. Nothing would be left of it.

"Where's my letter, Mr. Silent Postman?"

"I'm Adam! Adam! Remember? The little kid you met in the forest, years ago. We held each other, naked," screamed a deranged voice in my head. Fortunately, none of those screams escaped.

"The letter?"

I heard Grandpa in my head, shouting: "Don't just stand there. Say something!"

"Uh, yeah. I forgot. The letter. Yes."

I was still frozen. In the spinning ice cream. The Chihuahua definitely had more gab than me.

"Am I supposed to sign something?"

"Oh, yes, yes, of course. You have to sign here."

She obliged.

"Sorry, I'm new at this. It's my second day on the job."

"The letter?"

I slapped my forehead, embarrassed.

"Oh, yes. There it is."

"Is there anything else," she asked, as I didn't seem to be leaving.

For some strange reason, I had expected her to open the letter in my presence, which, in hindsight, was dumb and illogical.

"No. I'm done. Bye," I snapped.

This led to my third day on the job.

Insults, rotten-tomatoes, Chihuahua, and, then, her door.

I knew what was in the letter that I had handed to June the day before. What I didn't know was how she'd react to it. Depending on who answered the door, I would immediately know if my plan worked.

Thankfully, it was June. She even opened the door before I knocked.

"I have a response for the author of the letter you gave me yesterday," she said, urgently, skipping all greetings.

Thankfully too, the colossal brother wasn't in sight.

"Yes," I replied, expecting a verbal response.

She handed me a letter.

"It's registered mail. It can only be hand delivered to that person, but I don't know who it is."

I had forgotten that my letter was anonymous.

"It's me. I wrote the letter! I'm Adam! Adam! Remember? The little kid you played with, naked, in the forest, years ago," screamed again the deranged voice that could not be heard outside my head. Not knowing what was written in her letter, I couldn't disclose who I was. Not yet. I would have to read her letter alone, hiding, somewhere.

Another round of insults, tomatoes, and Chihuahua, to come back and give her my response, was a small cost to pay for the luxury of reading the letter without the pressure of an immediate answer.

"I know. I mean, the person that wrote it. I know him. I'll personally hand deliver it to him, at once. Today."

The letter she gave me didn't have a return address, like the one I had given her—evidently to avoid compromising evidence.

"Don't worry," I whispered, in case a sleeping monster could be awoken by our voices.

"Thanks," she said, grabbing my hands—cementing my promise.

I couldn't leave. Not as long she had a grip—even though Damien would have crushed my head in a grip of his own if he had seen us, I couldn't be the one to let go.

"Be careful," she said, freeing my hands an eternity too soon.

As soon as I was beyond her sight, I dashed back to the horse waiting at the trough. I should have "Fireballed" out of there at once, but I didn't. My heart was about to explode. My head was dizzy, thinking of all the possibilities. My legs were shaking, unwilling to carry me anymore until they knew where my future lay.

I sat under a tree and opened her letter.

It said: "Yes. Let me know what you need."

I was ecstatic *[Ec·stat·ic. Adjective. Skidding on marbles, brain temporarily out-of-order, blood racing though veins, lost repair manual]*. I had taken a chance and reached out to her, by writing: "I am an Authorian who disagrees with the actions of my peers and would like to help you get your brother back. Would you welcome my help?"

She had accepted my offer.

She said "Yes." She didn't know to whom yet, and probably imagined her valiant knight to be a hulking warrior rather than an inarticulate, scrawny mailman, but she had said yes, and it was all that mattered.

She even asked me what I needed.

What I needed...

Actually, what I needed was a plan, because at that point, I had no idea how to proceed to free her brother.

But I had Grandpa.

Problems

Returning from my glorious third day as a mailman, I was eager to share the exhilarating news with Grandpa. Riding Fireball back, all I could think of was how proud he would be that I managed to break the ice with June. So proud that he would forget our previous two conversations, forget that I had been a pitiful, miserable failure of a grandson that couldn't answer his previous questions without embarrassing the family.

"So, how did it go?" he had asked in the first of these two previous conversations, after my first day as a mailman.

"Not bad," I had replied.

"I'm not asking about the job. I'm asking about the girl."

"That's what I said. Not bad."

"What does that mean?"

"It went well."

"OK, I get it. You didn't ask her. You just stood there, frozen, with your mouth open so wide that a bird could have built a nest in there, right?"

"Well..."

"Adam. You have to talk to the girl. She won't bite, you know."

Easy to say.

"So, did you talk to her?" he had asked in that second previous conversation, after my second day on the job.

"Sort of."

"Well, did you open your mouth and make any sounds that could be recognized by something other than a frog?"

"Yeah, yeah."

"Good. That's a start."

"I guess."

"What do you mean, I guess? What did you say?"

"I told her that her voice is sweet music to my ears, that her eyes sparkle like diamonds, that her skin is like velvet that begs to be caressed, and that the mere thought of kissing her keeps me in a trance day and night," is what I would have liked to be able to report. But I had remained silent.

"That good?"

"Don't joke about this."

"Did you introduce yourself, a least?"

"Kind of."

"So, you didn't tell her your name," he said, dismayed. "Adam. You need to stop hiding behind your shadow. Talk to the girl. She won't bite, you know."

That was the second time he had said that.

I had felt his disappointment.

But, all of that was to be erased now. He was not going to be embarrassed anymore by the invertebrate hanging at the end of his bloodline. I was going to tell him of my letter to June, of my conversation with her, of her response and letter, and he would lift his arms to the sky and proudly shout: "That's my grandson!"

And while he would be reveling in having finally found a chip off the old block in the one descendent that would someday carry on the family name, I would tap his wisdom, hoping that he had some valiant-knight experience to share with his grandson who had no strategic planning skills but badly needed to formulate a plan to save June's little brother.

As he saw me approach, he jumped from the porch and stopped me far from the house.

"Adam. We have a big problem," he said, before I could say a word.

"What?"

"It's your mother."

"That's not new."

"No I mean, a new big problem. A huge problem. It's not like stepping in the usual hogwash now, it's more like swimming deep in liquid manure."

"I don't understand."

"How can I say? Listen. You know when you walk in an open field, looking up and admiring the blue sky, the clouds, the birds, and then accidentally walk into a cow pie? Or, when you walk in the forest admiring the autumn leaves on the ground, only to hit your head on a beehive hanging under a branch? Well, now, it's like that. Both things. And worse."

"Worse...?"

"Much worse."

"Grandpa. Can you skip the cow pie and bees stuff and be more clear?"

"Clear? I'll be clear. You're mother has gone nuts. Completely nuts. She's nuts, nuts, nuts, nuts, nuts, nuts, nuts, nuts, nuts! Is that clear enough?"

My mother never missed an occasion to call Grandpa senile when he repeated himself, but he always replied to her that repeated blows are needed to drive a nail in a wooden skull.

"I know, she's always been nuts," he added before I could say a word, "but what I mean is that, now, she has really gone over the edge. Completely."

"What happened?"

"Her fat sow friend—the wife of the postmaster—told her that you've been doing the mail run. More specifically, where you've been doing it. And that you practically volunteered for it."

"So?"

"Can't you see the implication? The fat sow has planted a seed. It's bad weed, but it's a seed no less. That's how rumors start."

"So?"

"Well it's a pretty clear message from one Authorian to another. It suggests that you are helping the Kafkaist cause, that you are sympathetic to it."

"So?"

"So? So? Are you so in love with that girl that you forgot reality? The rumor is not even subtle. It's not a tiny innuendo, it's a bomb. It suggests that she's the mother of a traitor. It's profoundly disturbing to a mother—particularly to your *insane* mother."

"So? What is she going to do about it?"

"What's she going to do? What's she going to do? Kid. Think. It's your nutcase mother! What do you think she did? What would you do if you were her?"

The haze lifted and the frightening answer jumped in my face. Of course, first, she panicked. Then, never having been able to make a moral decision by herself in her life, she ran to the Small

Visionary for advice—and given that he was the master at dispensing bad advice, it could only mean terribly bad news as far as my fate was concerned.

"How bad is it?" I asked.

"Very, very, very bad. Very."

"What's going to happen? I won't be able to leave the village anymore?"

"Yes, there's that. But there's much worse."

"Worse than being grounded here?"

"I can't even put it in words. It's waiting for you inside."

I probably should have run away right there instead of entering the house, but the thought didn't cross my mind. Maybe because I was a teenager [*Teen·ag·er. Noun. Kids who have grown to think of themselves as indestructible, if not outright immortal; stage of youth that serves as the perfect recruiting ground for soldiers*]. So I walked right in, defiant, as if the scathing remarks of my mother—acting as the puppet of a Tiny Visionary—could, at the very worst, only scratch me.

She waited for me at the table.

Silent.

I had expected her to scream, shout, cry, and spew vitriolic reprimands caught in some sort of hysteric spell, but no.

She sat in silence.

Solemn. Like a magistrate about to deliver a sentence.

She motioned me to sit in front of her, but I remained standing.

"Don't be sassy with me," she said, unfazed.

I was not about to sit.

She took a couple of full breaths, to keep calm.

"What you did was terrible," she sighed, shaking her head as if the end of the world had arrived and all that remained was despair and disbelief.

"There are no words to describe what you did."

"How about: I delivered mail, dispatched letters, facilitated communications, handled—?"

"Don't wordsmart me!!" she snapped, probably not realizing that, in anger, she had borrowed Grandpa's expression.

"I just volunteered a few words—"

"Shut up, Adam. Just shut up. I don't care to hear your explanations. What you did was very bad."

I remained standing, waiting for the storm to pass.

"I'm tired. I'm so tired," she moaned.

I wondered why Grandpa was so frantic. So far, she was no more nuts than usual.

"You're getting lost, Adam. You're forgetting who you are. Your head is filled with crazy ideas. This has to stop. You have to reconnect with your roots. You have to return to the fold."

"Good luck with that," I thought to myself.

"The Small Visionary, in his infinite wisdom, has graciously offered to save you from your deviance."

"Good luck to him too," I thought. He couldn't control my mind and there's no jail sentence for delivering mail. He could team up with my mother into a nagging duet, add a couple of Perfectionists and make it a quartet, or assemble an entire choir of naggers, it wouldn't make a difference.

"He offered to restore your moral rectitude, by arranging for your wedding."

"My what?"

"You heard right. Wedding!"

"I'm fifteen."

"That's plenty old. And you need it."

"Why?"

"Because you're spending all your time listening to your senile Grandpa. He's crazy, he's a bad influence, and he has led you astray with his foolish ideas."

She was talking as if matrimony was the authoritatively sanctified remedy to cure a character gone astray. As if tying the knot was like laying railroad tracks, to ensure that all travels proceed in a specific prescribed direction, and no other.

Well, that's not the case. Even the Small Visionary knew—in his infinite wisdom—that tracks alone are insufficient to get a person anywhere. It takes a locomotive. A powerful one that pulls full steam ahead in the desired direction. So, what was the clincher? What was the engine so powerful that it could pull me away from the disease of moral vagrancy, and propel me into full remission?

Before I could ask, she answered my question.

I didn't get scratched.

I got scorched.

"You will be married to Cassandra."

"What?"

Cassandra!

Cassandra? My wife?

The thought of running away hadn't crossed my stupid mind before, but now, those words rang like a fire alarm.

So, I ran away.

I didn't know where to go. I tried to run deep into the forest, to reach the oasis where I had first met June, but barely a few feet into the woods, I got pushed back by Fanatiks enforcing orders that prevented me from leaving the village. Panicked, I ran across the village like a headless chicken for a couple of loops, until I found shelter behind Grandpa's shed at the end of our backyard, where I collapsed.

I couldn't believe it. What kind of dumb Visionary could have come up with the outlandish idea that tying a straying idiot to a Perfectionist would automatically turn him into a perfect Authorian?

Maybe this was an obscure custom occasionally used in the past, instituted to serve the higher purpose of expanding the reach and ranks of the Perfectionists, and that he deemed it proper to decree its immediate implementation, just to shut my mother up. Or maybe, in his devious mind, he thought that by enslaving me to nagging Cassandra, my conversion was more than certain, because capitulating was the only way to escape Cassandra's daily onslaught of preaching and annoying babbling.

Well, converting a new husband to the privileged calling of being a Perfectionist, with all the ranks and privileges it entails, was not about to happen. How I would prevent that from happening, though, I didn't know yet, but it was not to be.

Catching my breath behind Grandpa's shed, I pondered my options.

Finding refuge in June's village was not possible. Clearly, as an Authorian, I wasn't about to be embraced by a Kafkaist community—no more than I was likely to be affectionately licked to death by their Chihuahuas. That would not have happened before the incident with June's little brother, so it was even more far-fetched now.

Hiding with the Illiterantes didn't seem viable either. Although they seemed to be a welcoming bunch, they would have been crazy to harbor a fugitive. They had nothing to gain by doing that, and possibly everything to lose if it got to be known that they were helping me. Why would they take such a risk and jeopardize their precious, laid-back lifestyle?

Living as a recluse in the woods was a possibility, but a dangerous one, exposed to wildlife and—even more dangerous— itinerant bands of Fanatiks and criminals. Besides, I couldn't see myself surviving on a diet of tree leaves, roots, slugs, soggy—and potentially poisonous—mushrooms, and the occasional barbecued squirrel.

Exile to another village beyond the reach of all Authorians and Visionaries—if such a place ever existed—seemed to be the only option. However, because I had hopes and dreams that June and I had a future to construct, this was a solution without appeal unless June could have been convinced to join me there. And right now, apart from our chance encounter of early childhood, the foundations of that future consisted of only two letters of fewer than ten words—and mine was anonymous. That wasn't enough for any woman to follow an idiot to another continent.

As I sat there, transfixed by memories of the pure stream that flowed between us in our natural refuge almost a decade ago, and dreaming that we could reconnect at the very same place and listen to our hearts beat in unison, it became clear that fleeing wasn't an option. If there were solutions to my problems, they had to be found here. And among all these problems to resolve, the first priority was to figure out how not to get married to Cassandra.

It occurred to me then that I didn't know if Cassandra shared my desire to prevent this arranged wedding or not. I couldn't imagine why a woman could possibly want to spend the rest of her life married to the one guy that she kept under hateful surveillance and snitched on at every occasion from the day she got out of diapers—even if that woman was a twerp—but, since she was not what I would consider a normal person, I had to figure out where the twerp stood on this matter.

I ran to Cassandra's home and banged on her door—one of the sturdiest manufactured in the village—until it opened.

It was Cassandra.

As soon as she saw me, she jumped at my face, hammering me with both fists, shouting: "Get away, you stupid, one-armed, imbecile! I hate you, hate you, hate you! I don't want to marry you."

Perfect.

"Cassandra!" I said, grabbing her wrists to stop the blows.

She stopped, stunned—maybe because it was the first time I had talked to her in nearly a decade. Mind you, I was stunned myself for having just done that, but the severity of the crisis called for bold actions. I would have kissed a toad if that's what it took to escape this fate—well, eyes closed, nose pinched, and lye soap at the ready to wash my lips afterwards.

I pulled her far enough away from the door, and whispered: "I don't want to be stuck with you either. We have to work together on this, to find a solution, otherwise, we'll end up as two miserable spouses stuck together for life, growing into bitter old farts and hating each other until death. I don't want that, and neither do you."

She looked reassured and puzzled at the same time, like a baby sucking a dry nipple. Our mutual desire to end the nightmare seemed obvious, but my words weren't met with joy and relief. Instead, they remained suspended in a worrisome silence.

"I can't disobey a decree of the Visionary," she whispered back, subdued, almost crying, torn by her beliefs and her desires.

"We won't. We'll find a way to make him change his mind, trust me."

"Why should I trust you?"

"I don't know, but it's not like there's anybody else here that's going to help us."

She swallowed, holding back her tears, thinking. It looked like the twerp had a brain and it was engaging gears.

"What's your plan?"

Speaking of brain in gear, mine had not reached cruising speed yet.

"By the way, Cassandra, tell me," I asked, to change the topic, as I had no plan. "Why did you bookmark that little Kafkaist kid?"

"It's none of your business."

"Actually, given that this whole mess is all because of that, it's very much my business too now."

She remained silent, sulking. I waited patiently, for nothing.

"Fine," I said, turning on my heels.

"He was sick," she snapped.

I turned back, slowly.

"He looked really sick. As if he was going to die."

"So?"

"I bookmarked him so that, if he died, he would be saved. He would be given the chance to meet his Author."

Of course. She was a Perfectionist to the bone. Holding dear to her unwavering beliefs, in her mind, the newly minted Authorian had been saved from the Kafkaists' clutches and readied to meet his real Author. This seemed logical—at least from the perspective of her perverse mind—but something bothered me in her explanation. Maybe June's little brother looked frail during his kidnapping—who wouldn't be stupefied by such an experience—but he sure didn't look as if he was about to die. She must have been lying to me.

"Wait a minute. What were you doing in a Kafkaist's village in the first place?" I asked.

She bit and sucked her lower lip, with sad puppy eyes that admitted guilt and made it easy to guess the answer to my question. What else? Cassandra only excelled at a few things, and spying on people to make them miserable was at the top of the list. Like a sadist who got tired of beating up the same old exhausted animals, she had been prowling for new victims to abuse, new blood, maybe even a whole new arena for her cruelty. June's home, being deep at the very end of her village, definitely could have been within the sight of a spy hiding in the woods.

"So what's your plan?" she said, obviously to change the topic.

"I'll tell you later."

"You want me to trust you, but you won't share your plan."

"Because it not quite finished. There remain details to work out. Many details. Big details. I have to figure those out first. But, as soon as I've got it all figured out, I'll let you know."

"Fine. As long as I don't have to marry you."

"You won't. I won't let that happen, no matter what."

"It better be a good plan."

"Sure will."

Indeed.

So now I needed a plan to get June's little brother out of trouble, and one to get myself out of this mess.

Two plans.

And I had none.

I needed to see Grandpa more than ever.

Plans

Back home, I couldn't find Grandpa anywhere. Not in the house, not in the yard, not in the shed.

"Where's Grandpa?"

As usual, my father replied: "I don't know. Ask your mother."

"Probably taking a walk," she shrugged, which was her swaggering way to assert moral victory and underscore the fact that Grandpa's attempts to badly influence her son had been silenced. She would have said, "probably erased," with the same indifference, and I wouldn't have been surprised. But given that she hadn't chopped his rocking chair and tossed it into the fireplace, he had to be alive somewhere.

Grandpa was quite the sedentary type, and while I couldn't remember him ever leaving the house, maybe the crisis had uprooted him. Maybe he was roaming through the village, the way wise grandpas do to put their mind in gear, or maybe he was consulting old friends in search of solutions—although I couldn't imagine what anyone in the village (other than him) could do to improve my situation. Anyhow. Wherever he was, that was beyond my control and all I could do was wait for his return.

One thing that was partly in my control though, and that needed to be done at once, was to reconnect with June. Not being an employee of the mail service anymore, my free pass to her village had been revoked, and it was clear that with all the Fanatiks guarding the village and controlling the roads, the only thing I could do immediately was to send her a letter—hoping that the Service would find another idiot willing to do the mail run to her village. A letter wouldn't amount to much, but I had to let her know that I wasn't forgetting my promise to help, even though I couldn't tell her the embarrassing truth that I had not yet formulated a plan—or that my only hope was that my Grandpa would eventually come up with a brilliant one.

The message I wrote to June that evening was intended to be powerful and revealing to her, while remaining harmless and insignificant to anyone that might intercept or read it.

It stated: "The mailman thrice bit by the Chihuahua is the one that wrote the original letter, and is the one that will be delivering the final package, as promised. Some delays are foreseen and patience is required, but failure to deliver is not an option—even if it requires carrying it over mountains, should the road be blocked as a consequence of the regional turmoil."

Neither great nor inspired, but that was the best I could do.

After discretely dropping my letter in the mail slot on the alley wall of the Postal Service building, I took advantage of being on Main Street to check all the stores searching for Grandpa. All for naught.

Returning home, to my surprise, Grandpa was right there, waiting for me in his rocking chair, on the porch.

"There you are. Where have you been?" he exclaimed.

"Where have *I* been?"

He smiled.

"Come. I'll show you."

We walked the three hundred paces through the yard, to his shed.

"I've looked here before and you weren't there," I said entering the shed.

"It's because you weren't looking at the right place," he said, walking backwards while closing the door, as if making sure nobody was spying.

The right place? This was a one room shed cluttered with woodworking benches, stacks of wood, boxes piled up to the roof, and tools hanging from every square inch of every wall. Unless he had been hiding in boxes, I couldn't possibly have missed him.

"Believe it or not, I was here," he added, amused.

There was no point arguing. In any event, there were more important things to discuss.

"Grandpa. I really need your help to come up with a plan here. Actually, two plans."

"Plans, plans, plans. That's a lot of plans that you need. It will take a while. I have to figure things out. Doing the impossible takes a little bit of time, you know."

"Sorry—"

"I love being your advisor, Adam. I really do. It almost gives a meaning to life. But that will have to wait. First, let me show you why you couldn't find me."

He walked to a dark corner in the back where dirty bundles of rope of various thicknesses and sizes were tied to the wall.

"When I built the house you live in, I wasn't much older than you. The village was much smaller and seemed farther away, but the idiots back then weren't any brighter than today. So I worried. A lot. Today, I can pretty much say anything I want and get away with it—people can call me senile, ignore me, and say that my brain has turned into mush, to diminish my words, to blunt my punches—but what I'm saying today out loud is simply what I've always thought."

I couldn't imagine Grandpa silent. The image of Grandpa as a grump, from cradle to grave, was too powerful.

"Being young, as you know," he emphasized, "means sometimes saying the wrong thing at the wrong time. Given that I have never been good at nailing my lips together, I always was afraid that someday, in anger, I'd say the wrong thing."

"Like what?"

"Anything. If pressed in a corner, who knows what slip of the tongue might have happened. I could easily see myself shouting that the Visionary is a runt, a useless imbecile, or an ugly dick. With no balls."

"That's not exactly a slip of the tongue. It's more incendiary."

"Tongue on fire, then. Same difference. It's just a slip."

He gave me that look that said: "Stop being a two-legged dictionary. Just be Adam."

"Anyhow," he continued, "if I ever got in trouble, I needed a way to vanish on my own terms before somebody else made me disappear their way. It was a matter of survival."

His eyes sparkled, in a mischievous way. He pushed the first plank on the ceiling along the wall, triggering the click of a latch.

"So I built myself a tunnel," he exclaimed, a smile in check, watching for my surprise as he pushed the wall. A stiff spring creaked as the hidden door with its coils of rope opened onto darkness.

There it was. A tunnel to redemption.

"Grab a torch," he said, pointing to the bucket hung waist-high inside the tunnel. Matches were in a smaller receptacle. As soon as both our torches were lit, he let the door slam back.

I followed him down rudimentary stairs and through the narrow passageway for quite a distance.

"I'm glad I never had to use it, because, for me, that would have meant the end of life as I knew it, and the search for a new life somewhere else."

I could imagine Grandpa walking through foreign woods, hoping to find a welcoming hamlet in remote provinces where he could find refuge, because he would have failed to lock his fire in a prison of silence.

"Where, I don't know. There are idiots everywhere in this world, and it might be even worse in faraway places. But, just in case, for years, I've kept my secret; I've maintained this lifeline best I could. Until a few years ago. I stopped when it became clear that I was now old enough to be called a senile fool. You know, old fools like me can scream and cuss until they're blue in the face, and get away with it—with total impunity. It's quite a privilege. It's strange most senile fools don't take advantage of it."

The tunnel sure was dirty and smelly, but then again, it probably always had been.

"I had left it unchecked for so many years, it could have caved in, for all I know. Turns out, it's still useable, but I had to clean it up a bit—put new torches, fresh matches, oil the hinges and spring. That's why you couldn't find me this morning."

Indeed, roots had penetrated the tunnel and the largest one had been freshly cut.

"You think you might need it?" I asked.

"Me? Of course not. Not anymore. But you might."

This was far from encouraging. Particularly after the forewarning that one could escape only to find himself at the mercy of worse idiots somewhere else in this world.

"So you think that I should leave the village forever instead of marrying Cassandra?"

He stopped, turned, and looked at me straight in the eyes.

"No. Not yet. I may have an idea about that, but that's for later."

He resumed walking.

"I'm showing you an escape route to the woods. In case you ever want to leave the village unnoticed."

"What for?"

"What for?"

His shoulders slumped for a moment, but slowly came back up.

"Whatever for," he whispered loudly. "Maybe to pay a visit to someone."

Although I could only see his back, I'd swear the wrinkles and folds in his shirt aligned into a smile.

"I've just sent her a letter."

"Oh, I'd be surprised if any mail reaches her village for a while."

He was right, but I had no idea what else to do at the time.

"It's probably better that way too," he added. "I doubt she'd be impressed with your fancy word games. All that dilly-dally as you would say."

He turned around, the time of a smile, pleased to have planted a good word to impress his grandson [*Dil·ly·dal·ly. Verb. Archaic, patriarchal way to remind lazy offspring that they are loitering, vacillating, lacking a spine, and deserving of a well-planted, vigorous kick in the butt*].

"She's worried about her little brother now," he said, resuming the walk, "not about finding a pen pal."

The ceiling progressively dropped to a point where we had to kneel to exit the tunnel. The exit design was clever, requiring us to squeeze down between rocks disposed in a way that prevented water from infiltrating into the tunnel and that concealed it from the outside.

I recognized this patch of forest, having played in it many times as a kid. We were about a thousand paces from the house—quite an impressive tunnel length—definitely beyond where Fanatik patrols did their rounds.

"If you're serious about this girl, forget letters. Go see her. In person. Flesh and bones. Talk to her. Say clearly who you are and what you can do to help her."

I looked at Grandpa, nodded, and left into the woods.

I climbed the mountain anew, this time determined to not let any Illiterantes discourage me from traveling down the other side. It was a brisk ascent. I didn't stop once to catch my breath. However, as I approached the top, I slowed the pace because I didn't want to accidentally step in one of the Illiterantes' traps—finding myself upside down again, hanging like a dried sausage, would have wasted too much time. I was on a quest. Determined. I proceeded forward gradually, cautiously, quietly, brushing the undergrowth with my foot to inspect the ground's surface, and stepping on it only when sure there were no hidden obstacles.

I froze when I heard the rustling sound of an approaching group in the distance. To be safe, I hid behind a rock. I felt silly, first, because if there was an intruder there, it was me; second, because it could have been nothing more than a herd of deer passing by. Nonetheless, I breathed slowly, without noise, waiting for the antlers that would put my fears to rest.

To my surprise, instead of the faded-brown coat of deer, it was the unmistakable blood-red coats of five animals without antlers that emerged from the foliage.

Fanatiks!

Swords at their belt.

Single file, briskly working their way uphill. What could have brought them so far from the village? They had to be looking for me. It had to be Cassandra. Who else could have spied on me and informed them of Grandpa's secret passage? Her determination to make my life miserable would never cease to amaze me. What her pea brain had triggered though, she had no idea.

While I dreaded my fate if ever caught by that handful of Fanatiks, what was worse was they were on a direct path, straight to the mountain top—straight to the Illiterantes' camp. Their oasis away from our crazy world was about to be invaded. I could imagine the resulting slaughter. All because of my escape. It would be on my conscience.

I couldn't let that massacre happen.

"Go back to your caves, cannibals," I screamed, jumping from behind the rock.

Surprised, they stopped in their tracks, staring at me. Five against one—five with swords against one with bare hands and no courage to be exact—there was no contest. I took off, running downhill, full steam ahead, hoping they would chase me, away from the Illiterantes' village.

I could hear them behind. It worked. All I could hope for now was to outrun them all.

I glanced back, to confirm that all five were in tow, but doing so, I stepped into an Illiterantes' trap. The noose closed on my ankle. Again, I was flipped up like a pancake while a traveler mechanism rapidly pulled me along a path between the trees. Dangling upside down on that clothesline, as conspicuous as a pair of permanently dirty underwear, I reached the end of the line, where it all stopped.

The Fanatiks caught up with me. I could hear them, behind me, trying to catch their breath.

One of them circled around and looked me in the face.

"So you did pretty bad things I hear."

"Zayne!"

I couldn't believe it.

"You? A Fanatik?"

"Pretty convincing, right?"

"What do you mean?"

"Do you really think we're Fanatiks for real? Is your brain so jam-clogged with blood that it's shutting down?"

"But, but the uniform and—"

"Are our girlfriends talented tailors, or what? The real Fanatiks can't tell the difference either," he said, arms extended, slowly spinning to display the masterful replica.

"And the swords?"

"Won them. Fair and square. Thanks to a wonderful game called poker."

Fair and square is a bit of a stretch when playing against magicians with deep sleeves and hands faster than the eyes, but I had no sympathy for the losing Fanatiks.

"But why?"

"Knowledge is the best defense and the best knowledge comes from inside," he explained while others lowered me down and freed me from the noose.

Now that I was right-side up, he could tell that I had been more than physically upturned.

"Your dumb Authorian buddies have done some very stupid things, right?" he added, with a teasing grin. "So, now, the county is full of Fanatiks. Everybody's gone nuts. I mean, more crazy than before. It's no joke. So we can't take chances. We need to know," he emphasized with a formal bow, arms extended.

"Well, that's all good and dandy and I'd love to stay and chat, but I'm in a bit of a rush," I replied, at the risk of sounding rude. "I have somewhere to go—"

"They don't like you much down there."

"Down where?"

"Your Authorian friends."

"They're not my friends."

"Oh. So who are your friends then?"

That was a very good question for which I had no answer.

"I really have to go, now" I replied, climbing back up the hill.

"Where do you think you're going?"

"Don't worry, I'm just passing by. I'll be coming down the back slope."

"You're still obsessed with going there? What's wrong with you? They're Kafkaists. Nice people, and all, but not particularly interested in seeing Authorians right now."

"Thanks for the advice," I replied, on my way.

"I wouldn't go there if I was you."

I didn't respond.

"Oh, I get it. It's about a girl, right? It's got to be it."

"He's in love. It's so sweet," said another.

"They'll have adorable little Kaftorian kids."

"Aufkaists."

"Kafkauthorian monsters."

I heard all the "Ooh la la," "Kissy kissy," and "Smouchy smouch" as I walked away. At least, some people were having a good time in this time of crisis.

The descent was uneventful, although hard on the knees. Fortunately, June's house was at the south end of the village, closer to the mountain, which allowed me to reach it from the forest without attracting attention (from humans and Chihuahuas alike).

It was her little sister who again responded to the door. She recognized me and ran to get June, probably thinking that I again had mail to personally deliver.

She appeared a minute later, her glowing rebellious look again mesmerizing me. The unruly haircut, another beat-up sweater, and pants—through my previous mail runs, I had not seen any other

Kafkaist women in pants. I never dared ask her why she always wore pants. I found that outburst of defiance both attractive and promising—a hint that maybe Kafkaist rules didn't have a stifling grip on her. It pleased me to think that, maybe, driving our parents mad is something we might have in common.

I was standing there, bedazzled, in a stupid silence. I needed Grandpa to slap me on the back of the head.

"Where's your mailman uniform today?"

Short of a slap, it worked. I snapped out of my gaze.

"My employer didn't appreciate me talking to more than the mailboxes."

"So why are you here?"

"I... I wanted you to know... To tell you..."

"That you're the little kid I met in the woods way back then."

"You knew?"

"Not at first. Not even for sure, until now. But it seemed possible. Otherwise, why else would you be here after the mail has stopped? Why would an Authorian bother?"

"Uh... Yeah."

I was acting like a bumbling idiot—nothing to impress a girl for sure. Grandpa wouldn't be proud. I had to focus.

"My name is Adam. I'm the one who wrote the letters."

"I had figured that part too."

"Of course."

Of course. Of course. Of course. Focus.

"What has happened to your family is terrible. Horrible. There's no possible excuse for that. Just so you know, I really don't agree with those who have done it."

"Otherwise you wouldn't be here."

"Exactly."

I had to start saying something intelligent soon.

"I'm here because I want to do everything I can to help you."

"That's nice. I really appreciate. I do."

She seemed genuine.

"So what is your plan?" she asked.

"The plan. Yes, the plan is—"

"What are you doing here?" shouted Damien, shoving her sister aside.

I stepped back to avoid his fist.

"I don't want to see another damn Authorian in this village, and especially not you," he growled, stepping forward while I kept safe distance.

"I'm here to help."

"What will help me is smashing your face on a rock until it disappears," he shouted, while June was trying to pull him back inside.

"I want to help you get your brother back."

"Oh yeah? Show me your army. Show me your weapons."

"That's not exactly—"

"Damien, stop!" she pleaded.

"You're going to fight the Fanatiks with what? You're a peewee. A stupid idiot. No strength. No fists. You're nothing. You better leave before I get really mad. Before I kill you."

Good to know he wasn't really mad yet. If Kafkaists really made vows of non-violence, clearly, Damien had missed school the day it happened.

"Stop!" she shouted, pulling on his arm.

He pushed her back so violently that she fell on the floor behind him. Realizing that he accidentally hurt her, he melted. His anger mellowed one notch as he turned his attention towards her.

"I'll come back with valuable information," I shouted, dashing away before Damien's outbreak alerted a mob of angry Kafkaists.

"If you ever come back here—"

I missed the rest, but got the gist of it. It had something to do with stomping on my face until it could fit through the mail slot, or kicking my ass up, repeatedly, until it abutted my armpits.

All in all, things turned out well. June knew who I was. Better still, she took my defense against Damien. Even Damien's outburst, in hindsight, was for the best, as it prevented me from disclosing the embarrassing fact that I had no plan whatsoever.

That night, I had the most wonderful dream. June and I had eloped to an exotic world free of Authorians and Kafkaists—a sparkling world that embraced its liberty infinitesimally more grandly than a mountaintop full of Illiterantes. In its capital was a golden bridge, spanning an azure river, where, as the tradition called for loving couples, we tied a padlock to the railings and threw the key in the water, as a symbol of our commitment to each other. Our little padlock, intertwined with millions of others enlacing the bridge like vines, glowed like the passion and peace that twinkled in our hearts. And in the morning, I woke up, sorely disappointed by the realization that it had just been a dream, and emboldened by the resolve to make the dream a reality.

Inside

The Small Visionary's friendliness might have fooled our parents, who stood behind us like proud farmers bringing their best cattle to the slaughterhouse. And, in normal circumstances, his cordiality would have probably titillated Cassandra—for why else would she have spent a lifetime harassing, threatening, and denouncing others, only to be rewarded like a dog fetching a stick.

But it was all fake.

Phony.

And it didn't fool me.

However, being within arm's reach of the Small Visionary for the first time left quite an impression. I already knew that the larger-than-life portrait mandatorily hanging in every classroom was a dramatic embellishment of the decayed carcass that paraded through the village in ceremonial processions every now and then, but I had never been close enough before to notice the moldering skin, the bloodshot eyes, the decayed teeth, and the smell of crow bait.

The smell!

If a dog reeked only half as much, cute puppy or not, he would be put to sleep on the spot—no tears shed.

I had told Grandpa that I'd willingly swim through liquid manure to evade my fate, but I had not intended that statement to be a premonition.

I managed to hide my nausea.

Everything in the Small Visionary's office was designed to impress. Colorful silk woven clothes, tapestries depicting historical events, complex glasswork filtering the rays of the rising sun, elegant furniture hand-carved in laminated slabs of maple and rosewood, silver and gold chandeliers, and the best doors ever produced by the village—thick, solid oak, with jewel encrusted handles. All orchestrated to assert power and the incontestable superiority of what would otherwise be just a despicable and uninteresting person—if a decomposing body could be called a person.

Grandpa had always warned me to never be intimidated by long titles and pretended power, and particularly not by the Visionaries, who, he insisted, were just a bunch of dimwits. "Remember," he said, "they have to sit on a toilet, like everybody else, and they're not dropping gold nuggets." So, to shield myself against the assault of the ostentatious decor, I imagined the Small Visionary afflicted with the most severe case of diarrhea ever seen by mankind. The surrounding bling lost its grip on me. It must have shown.

"So, Adam. You sure look like a confident young man," said the disgusting old man with the putrid breath.

"No more than anyone else."

I specifically refrained from ending my sentences with any honorific title, like "Small Visionary." That kind of respect would have been incompatible with the mountains of excrement that deflated his aura in my mind. Besides, unless he called me "sir," there was no point to reciprocate. I might have dared call him by his first name, since that's how he had launched the conversation, but there was a bigger strategy at play here, and this would have derailed everything. Besides, nobody knew his actual name. In my humble opinion, Dodo, Smokey, Poopy, or Smookie Poo, would all have been most fitting.

"You understand that your parents, together with Cassandra's parents, have agreed to Cassandra and you being soon wedded to celebrate in joy and in acceptance of the will of the Author."

"Yes."

"And the parents here confirm that it is their most sincere desire to bless this union too?"

"Absolutely," replied my mother, on behalf of my spineless father who probably was still ashamed of me for not having stood up to the First Lackey when there was still a chance to prevent this entire mess, and pleased to get rid of his unworthy son.

"Yes," replied Cassandra's father, with authority, like the parrot everybody knew he was. The real authority in Cassandra's family lay with her mother. She was an extremely obese woman that, pretending to be svelte and elegant, walked lower back arched forward, head angled back, one hand resting on a bulge at hip

level, the other limp like a dripping dishcloth at the end of a horizontal forearm that followed the exaggerated swing in her hips—
and protruding belly—as waves rippled through her butt fat with
each footstep. She looked like the result of cross-breeding between a toad and a pigeon—the poor animals, mortified at the
sight of their disgusting offspring, would surely have abandoned
the nest.

Cassandra, her mother, and her father: what a ghastly trio.

That's when it struck me: Little girls who like to boss other
kids grow up to become obnoxious monsters who love to sow
discord, crave for attention, yearn for the approval of Visionaries,
and are ready to do anything for it. In other words, the terrifying
reality when looking at Cassandra's mother, is that it is exactly
what Cassandra will look like decades later—when she will have
become her mother.

And I was about to marry that? Gross!

I had asked Grandpa for ideas on how to save me from that
horrible fate—if I ever needed one of his brilliant ideas, it was then
more than ever.

What did he have to offer?

"I think that being forced to marry Cassandra is the best
thing that could happen to you."

"I think you don't understand," I had replied, shocked.

"No, Adam, I understand your problems most correctly."

"Grandpa! It's no time to joke. My life is over. The only
thing worse than marrying Cassandra would be to kill myself. No,
actually, I take that back; killing myself would be better than marrying Cassandra."

"I know, I know. I wouldn't want to kiss that toad any more
than you. But, you're thinking emotionally, not logically. Forget
the slimy frog for a moment, and think. Think! What does becoming Cassandra's future husband give you?"

"Headaches, cramps, loss of sleep, and pain in the ass for a
lifetime."

"OK... But think again. More broadly. Think strategically."

All the strategic thinking in the world would have likely been
neutralized had I caught one whiff of the Small Visionary wet-sock
aroma before buying into Grandpa's plan. The ugly skunk was so
close now that I could see the crust on his warts as he turned
toward me.

"Fine," said the Small Visionary, flashing a hideous smile. I noticed that at least three of his teeth had abandoned the ship—frankly, more than I cared to see. "Now, there are certain things that will need to be done in preparation for this wonderful event."

"Like what?"

My mother kicked me, making it clear that questioning the Small Visionary was a violation of protocol.

I would have loved to kick back, but I didn't. As rebellious as I may have imagined myself to be, I couldn't kick my mother. Besides, more importantly, doing so could have jeopardized the plan. I was in the wolf's lair.

"That curiosity, for example," he replied. "You'll have to learn to make good use of it. Cassandra will be your lifelong guide in that pursuit. But before sealing your union, I'll help you a bit too."

It was perfect.

Grandpa had been right again, like a real mind reader. He would have corrected: "I'm only a reader of feeble minds. They're like open books."

Maybe that's why he was so good with plans.

"Adam, remember what I once told you," Grandpa had said, as my strategic thinking was stalling. "If somebody thinks he's always right, he has a problem. But if somebody believes that he's always right and that anybody who doesn't think like him is wrong, you have a problem."

"So Cassandra is my problem?" I had replied.

"Yes. She is a ball being chained to your ankle to keep you within the fold. Our idiot Visionary has searched in his tiny brain for grand wisdom and, of all the stupid ideas he has found in there, he has convinced himself that making you the slave of a Perfectionist is the sure way to steer you in the right direction. He is certain now that Cassandra is the perfect rudder for you. She's not only a Perfectionist. She's the ultimate Perfectionist. That kind of devotion to being a watchdog is rare; not every village has a nutcase like her. At the age when little kids are supposed to chase butterflies, she was already chasing heretics—as you know too well."

"I still don't understand why marrying her would be a good thing. With her tied to my ankle, I'll drown."

"No, no, no. It's temporary. She's just a key. If their objective is to make you think like them, they'll be eager to mentor you, to bring you into their world, to do whatever it takes to make you a reformed Authorian. Can't you see the doors of the castle opening just yet?"

This was brilliant. Everybody needs a grandpa like that.

"I'm ready to do whatever it takes to honor my parents," I replied to the Small Visionary, without hesitation.

"And your Author. And your Author, always."

I nodded.

"Your marrying a Perfectionist will indeed greatly honor your parents. It's not only a great honor. It's a phenomenal honor. In fact, it is quite noble and generous for Cassandra's parents to adopt you into their family. You must be grateful for their generous and dutiful acceptance."

"I am," I replied, lying with conviction, refraining from smiling. Cassandra had shared with me that her parents had been crying and wailing all night. No wonder. All their hope of having their little princess marry a Visionary—Small or Big—had been crushed.

I furtively glanced at Cassandra. The ugly face distorted by fear that I saw the day before had vanished. Instead, head slightly down, wide eyes looking up, she looked peaceful, contemplative, maybe awestruck, almost angelic. I guess all women can be beautiful given the proper circumstances and feelings. Yet, I knew this peacefulness to be no more than desperate submission to forces that raped her of her freedom.

"But marrying a Perfectionist is not a small thing," added the Visionary. "It requires preparation. You can't just go and procreate unconsciously, without a solid foundation."

Cassandra's beauty vanished in the wink of an eye, as the thought of procreating with the slimy toad sent a shiver down my spine. Just as Grandpa had predicted, in the eyes of the Grand Visionary, Fornication Under Consent of the Kritikillar could not happen before my solid re-conversion was accomplished and authenticated. The procreators could not execute themselves [*Ex·e·cute. Verb. For some, to do what is required, for others, to inflict capital punishment on a poor sap*] before being fully certified Perfectionists, which in my case, clearly required work. In fact, a certified impossible task if the Small Visionary knew that I was an impostor to whom no rank or privilege could ever be worth the price of marrying Cassandra.

"So, for a while, every morning, you will visit my Librariatorium's Custodian, who will review with you the fundamental tenets of existence."

This was the "re-education nuthouse" that Grandpa had told me about. Education of a different kind. Without the violence. That annex to the Visionary's lair—the Librariatorium—was where Perfectionists met to speculate on the Author's will, and to re-educate errant minds. The mind suspected of having erred, in this instance, was mine.

"Are you ready to meet your Author?" added the Visionary.

I nodded.

"Fine. You can start right away. The Custodian is waiting for you."

Parents and Cassandra were left behind.

The plan was in motion.

Librariatorium

The Custodian was a stern, short man, seemingly too young to contemplate death, but apparently too old to remember the joys of life. He harbored a persistent anger for no obvious reason since he was definitely well fed. Maybe all that exasperation came from having to constantly look up to people whom he would have preferred to look down at with contempt. He had the annoying and insincere laugh of those who can only pretend friendliness when they believe in their superiority—even if that superiority is a mirage that only exists in their head. Grandpa had always warned me that these were the most dangerous and insidious backstabbers of the jungle, and to beware of such two-faced predators—charming you in your presence, defaming you in your absence. "The ducks who want to be swans," said Grandpa, "are stupid ducks that feel small and want power. Bright ducks understand that they are ducks and that it's good to be a duck; they live happy lives, and don't try to crap on other ducks."

We walked to a table in a corner of the Librariatorium's main study—a large hall with walls hidden behind shelves full of books. All other tables were unoccupied, except for one at the opposite end of the hall where a pack of white-hair folks standing in a circle talked quite loudly, and often at the same time. I presumed they were Perfectionists from other villages afar, as I didn't recognize any of them.

From where I sat, at the end of the table, it was possible for me to discreetly check the activities of those bunched-up elders, trying to figure out what they could possibly be arguing about, while I pretended to be fully attentive to the Custodian.

The Custodian's task on that first morning of drill was to review with me some fundamentals, to reinforce my former education, mostly focusing on hate of the Kafkaists, if only to verify that

I didn't sympathize with their ideals. After all, I had volunteered to deliver mail there, which, in times of impending war, was almost a crime against humanity—insofar as humanity meant Authorians.

So we went over the basics: Kafkaists are vile, villains, bad characters, and so on. They exist only because of the Author's will to show us how miserable our life would be if we failed to submit to his will—which I probably would have swallowed hook, line, and sinker, and believed all my life, if not for the grace of meeting June.

At that point, it crossed my devious mind to ask the Custodian—who was presumably an erudite man on matters of the tenets—how he could be so sure that we had to submit to "his" will instead of submitting to "her" will? As far as I knew, there was no picture of the Author, so there was no verifiable proof of the Author's gender. But Grandpa's plan forbade me from picking a fight or starting an argument with anybody, so I didn't. In any event, Grandpa always told me that if the Author really existed, he had to be a man, because only a man could be so brutally cruel as to fill the world with pain, death, and creatures eating each other. Who else than a man could so passionately allow wars, famine, destruction, and even kill his characters in one stroke? Only a man could be so cavalier. Sure, Cassandra was poisonous, and my own mother in her worst moments was a disaster on legs—as my presence in the Librariatorium proved—but even the world's most abominable woman couldn't destroy her progeny without being sure that it was for their own good.

Then, near the middle of the recitation, a gap briefly opened between two Perfectionists at the other end of the hall, and I got the full picture of what was happening there: the pack of wolves was busy, ganging up on a pupil to inculcate him with Authorian truths, and that pupil was a little kid. June's little brother. Theodors.

It was him.

I was sure.

When you kidnap a cute little kid, you don't forget his face, and that face was right there, at the end of the hall.

Grandpa had been right.

"If June's little brother is being held like a prisoner, it's got to be there, so that all those life-suckers could fill him with their hogwash," to use his words.

I wanted to jump across the room, shove the scarecrows out of the way, grab the kid under my arm, and dash to June's home, delivering him safe and sound as promised, forever becoming her hero.

But I didn't.

That was just a dumb impulse. Not a solution. Because, even if I could have run with the fury of a horse poked in the ass by the prongs of a red hot fork, I wouldn't have made it past the edge of the village before being tackled by a mob of Fanatiks.

For now, all I could do was watch them.

Transfixed.

Frustrated.

Not knowing what to do.

Unable to do anything.

I couldn't see much of what was going on in there, yet, something bothered me. I couldn't figure out what, or why, but something was strange.

"Mr. Kilroy?" snapped the Custodian.

"Hmm?"

"And your response is?"

Damn. Distracted. I had unconsciously shut off the Custodian's grating lecture. I hadn't heard the question.

"I'm sorry, my mind wandered for a moment. It's the wedding, the excitement and all."

"This is serious stuff, Mr. Kilroy. We aren't talking about opening eggs from the right end."

Too bad. I knew the response to that one.

"When and only when can you be graced?" he repeated, exasperated *[Ex·as·per·ate. Verb (used with object). To irritate to the point where it becomes challenging to suppress the urge to bash the offender's head with a forty-pound sledgehammer]*.

"Only if you have duly acknowledged your author, which can only happen if you have been bookmarked," I replied. For good measure, I added: "And, as we all know, bookmarking defines Authorians, and eludes all other creatures, such as the Kafkaists and other animals," which was another bit that was drilled in all kids' numb skulls to instill fear in Kafkaists and prevent them from being contaminated by their phony beliefs.

He took a pen and filled some paperwork, silently, as a doctor recording the results of a physical. It was freakish to think that I had recited that stuff throughout my grade school years. Words carefully picked for us with a vivid purpose that hadn't been clear to me until now.

The custodian's re-education was having just the opposite effect.

"How many Authors are there?" he shot.

How dumb did he think I was?

"Twenty four billions," I felt like replying.

"You're serious?"

"How many?" he insisted, unamused.

This was silly.

"There are a lot of books here," I commented, gesturing at the filled shelves that wrapped the room, wall-to-wall, floor-to-ceiling.

He didn't budge.

"How many?" he repeated.

"Have you read them all?" I insisted, hoping to stroke his ego and trigger some bravado about having read all the books; or working on it; or hoping to—anything to escape the boring interrogation.

"There's no point," he replied, dryly.

"No point? Why?"

"They're all blank."

"Blank. What do you mean blank?"

"Nothing but white pages."

This made no sense. Hundreds of books—thousands of books—short, tall, thin, thick, and nothing in them? Before he could stop me, I grabbed a small one on the nearby shelf and opened it.

"Ha! There! Definitely not a white page," I proclaimed, shoving the spread into his face.

He didn't even twitch a muscle.

I should have picked a bigger book; it would have been more impressive. The small one barely covered half his face, below eyes that definitely weren't pleased.

"Of course."

"Of course what? This is not a blank page," I said, dumping the book on the table.

It was a small book, but it made enough noise for the Perfectionists at the other end of the room to break their chatter and give me an upset look.

"All the books here have blank pages," he lectured, unfazed by my mini-outburst, "until you open them. When you do, then the pages you look at have characters on them, but only those pages. All the others remain blank."

"Why?"

"Because they don't serve the Author. The Author only shows you what you need. Nothing less, nothing more."

As if all these books served no purpose—other than to provide an illusion.

"This is ridiculous," I said.

"Are you questioning the Author?"

"No, no, no. Of course not. But how can you know that all pages are blank until you look at them, if the minute you look at one it's not blank anymore?"

This seemed a fair and logical question.

"The Grand Visionary knows. He has seen the proof."

That was a sly reply given that nobody alive had ever seen the Grand Visionary—the one Visionary at the start of it all, who first met the Author and thus understood the meaning of our lives.

"So what's the explanation?"

"There is no explanation."

"What do you mean no explanation?"

"No explanation."

Not a fair and logical answer.

"Hasn't the Grand Visionary shared his bits of wisdom with anybody, by any chance?"

"Some mysteries are not meant to be understood. They are born to remain mysteries."

"Are they?"

"Certainly so," he replied, brushing me away in a grand gesture, as my questions were exhausting him.

What's a certainty that can't be proven?

But I remained silent.

In a room filled with thousands of silent books.

What was I doing in this asylum?

"Stay here," he said, standing up, with a weary expression. He crossed the hall and started talking with the other weasels there. I worried that maybe I had said too much. I was supposed to play along, not to make waves. Grandpa would have blamed it on what he called youthful exuberance.

The cover of the book I had thrown on the table caught my attention: "Morse Code: Key to the Telegraph Revolution." It sure didn't feel as if I was in the midst of a revolution. I flipped the book. The spread I had flashed in the Custodian's face—the non-blank pages—were filled with strange characters. Like a dictionary in a foreign language—which I found somewhat appealing.

It listed no author. Like all other books for that matter. Through my entire life, none of my school manuals, construction guides, operation manuals—even my stolen dictionary—ever listed an author. To the extent that, as a kid, for a while, misunderstanding my teachers, I thought that Anonymous was the name of the Author (I was not the brightest student of the lot).

I flipped through the pages. None were blank. Even the inside cover wasn't, as someone had scribbled his name there. Hugo Wynn. Some nobody, maybe long erased, who had inked a little attempt at posterity. A nobody who—like me—loved books enough to adopt them with graffiti.

I could have stolen the book for myself. But, then. Morse code. That was useless to me.

The book I really needed was "How to Fix Unhinged Things and Minds," or "The Ultimate Diet: How to lose all Perfectionists, Fanatiks, Visionaries, and Other Excess Fat."

I threw the book back on the table. It slid across and landed on the floor—with a bang louder than entitled for such a tiny book. It again broke the chatter at the other end of the room.

The Custodian returned. I dreaded his first words.

"So how many?" he said.

"How many what?"

"Authors! How many authors are there?"

"Oh, yeah. That."

The single-minded Custodian sighed, rubbing his forehead. Whatever had been said in that little council of weasels, I'll never know, but I suspect he had gone to chat with his fellow buzzards to let some steam off, looking for supportive encouragements. Maybe even tips on how to focus on his assignment and nothing more—especially on how to avoid foolhardy, dogmatic discussions with his hostage.

"One," I answered, bored, giving up a chance to see him scream "Blasphemy! Blasphemy!" while blowing steam out of his ears.

As I said that, I saw Theodors stand-up, walk across the room, and enter what looked like a lavatory.

"I have to go," I told the Custodian. "Urgently," I added, managing to convincingly fart while pointing at the lavatory.

"Fine," he replied, happy to get rid of me for a few minutes.

There was only one stall in the lavatory, making it easy to ensure no one other than Theodors and I was in the room. Concerned that the vent high on the wall could transmit words to unknown recipients, I stuffed my sweater into it. When the stall opened, I put one knee down to be at Theodors' eye level and stopped him with a hand on his shoulder.

"Kid, first, I want to sincerely apologize to you," I whispered.

"What for?" he replied, surprised.

"Shhh. Not so loud. You can't understand, but if you are stuck here today, it's partly my fault."

He shrugged.

"More importantly though, I promise you that I'll find a way to bring you back to your mom and dad, in your village. I'm not very good with plans, so it may take a bit of time, but trust me, I'll do everything I can to repair this wrong."

"OK," he whispered back. "Can I go back now?"

"Sure," I said, as I lowered my arm.

He took a step forward. I grabbed his shoulder again.

"Wait. You first have to promise me not to tell anyone that we have met. You can't share our conversation."

"Why?"

"For your safety. Mine too."

"OK."

"Promised?"

"Promised."

I let him go.

I plucked my sweater from the vent, spent a minute in the stall to not be seen coming out together with Theodors, and returned to the Custodian, faking a satisfied look of accomplishment.

"Mister is ready now?"

"Yes sir."

I walked a straight line for the rest of the session.

Three hours of boring question after boring question, each less exciting than the other. Three hours of stoic regurgitation of all the expected standard answers. Three hours before the Custodian finally called it quits for the day and politely kicked me out of the premises.

And there I was, out of their lair. Even though I hadn't been a prisoner, after visiting that gilded cage, I enjoyed a tremendous sense of freedom.

As I walked home, out of that entire ordeal, one question stuck in my mind. What if there were multiple Authors? Maybe not necessarily twenty-four billions, but what if there were two, or four, or twenty-four? After all, to become Author, shouldn't it be sufficient to write a story. Anybody should be able to do that.

Actually, a second question popped-up in my mind. How could I get Theodors out of there? Now that I was inside and that I knew for sure where he was being held, what was the rest of the plan?

I had to ask Grandpa.

Truth is...

"Hogwash. They're not blank pages. It's a lie."

"How would you know?" I asked.

"Trust me. I know."

That was Grandpa's usual signal to not press the issue. The weapon that killed the discussion.

Yet, what he had said was sufficient. It confirmed my suspicions—or rather, strengthened my convictions. Meticulously stacking rows after rows of books that would differ only by their sizes and the titles on their spine—being otherwise blank cover to cover—was totally illogical. Not only illogical, but incongruous.

Absurd.

Bizarre.

And stupid.

We stayed silent on the porch for a few minutes, he in his rocking chair, I stretched along a step as if stairs were the perfect bunk for lazy sunbathing, basking in the warm rays of a blue sky. Had my parents been home, they would have called me a slug and kicked me off the stairs, presumably for my own good.

"It's incredible that, in all that pile of paper, there's not even a story in there," I popped out of the blue.

Grandpa didn't budge—like a chunk of granite. A rock. A rock on a rocking chair. Maybe he growled, but the creaking of the chair grinding the balcony is all I heard.

"I bet I could write a story," I added.

"No," snapped Grandpa as he stopped rocking.

"I would be capable—"

"No. You will not."

"What if I try—"

"No."

"Can't be that difficult to—"

"That's not the point!" he shouted.

I jumped off the stairs. Leaning toward me, hands clenching the arms of the rocking chair, red-faced, bulging veins on his neck, eyes like those of a frog with a mouthful of burning cigarettes, he looked like a boiler about to explode. I didn't add a word, afraid it could kill him.

He took a few deep breaths that released steam from the boiler, paused to regain his calm, and looked at me for a while, conflicted, as if debating whether silence was better. Then, as if reconnecting with his beliefs—particularly his lifelong private crusade against illogical rules—he decided to educate his grandson. Educate with words, that is.

"You're a bright kid, Adam. You've memorized the dictionary and you express yourself better than everybody I know. And I don't doubt your abilities, or your imagination. But you shouldn't write a story. Ever."

"Why? Because it's forbidden?" *[For·bid·den. Adjective. Somebody has said no, so don't do it, and don't ask why].*

"No."

"Sacrilegious?" *[Sac·ri·le·gious. Adjective. Somebody has said no, and will be seriously offended if you do it, so don't do it, and don't ask why].*

"No."

"Why then?"

"Because it's dangerous." *[Dan·ger·ous. Adjective. Somebody has said no, and will turn into a mad dog if you do it, so don't do it, and don't ask why].*

"Dangerous? It's just words on paper."

"No. A dictionary is just words on paper. A story, that's different. It could kill you."

"How do you know?"

"Because it's been tried before."

"It has?"

Grandpa kept silent for a while, as if pondering the wisdom of blowing on the dust that had buried painful memories.

I sat on the porch close to his rocking chair, waiting for explanations. Like in school—but interested.

My foolish ideas left him no choice.

"Way, way, way back," he said, with gravity, "when I was young—about your age—I had a good friend. Like you, he was full of ideals, full of energy, full of enthusiasm, and full of crazy ideas. I thought I knew him well, until one day, unexpectedly, he dumped a pile of paper on my lap. He flashed a smile so wide, I could have fit a coat hanger in his open mouth, with room to spare. Unknown to me—and everybody else for that matter—he had been writing a story. 'Are you crazy?' I told him. 'You can't do that! It's forbidden!' to which he shrugged, without losing the smile, saying that the damage was done."

"Did anybody read the story?"

Grandpa paused again. He had said too much, but the cat was already out of the bag (not out of the toothpaste tube).

"Only me," he surrendered.

"Was it good?"

"Compared to what? The dictionary?"

"What was it about?"

"I don't remember."

"I'm sure you do."

He grumbled.

"Well it was a silly story."

"Tell me," I begged.

"It was nothing to brag about."

It could have been a thousand pages describing the tribulations of two slugs racing to cross a garden; it would have made no difference. My curiosity could not be killed by then, and Grandpa knew it. He could not stop anymore.

He sighed.

"It was about a person called Hugo who wrote a story."

"Did that guy ever live in our village?"

"No. He only existed inside that story. That made things confusing, because it was a story within a story thing, but once you figured it out, it was OK."

I didn't understand what was confusing about that. I could easily imagine a story about a story within a story, and so on.

"Anyhow. Hugo's story was about a businessman called Runt. A real weasel. And a peewee. Not a dwarf, but a short guy who lived below the chin of every adult in the village. Somehow, he found a widow with a fortune and no skills to manage it. Runt saw that she was old, childless, and scared about the future, so he presented himself as a financial wizard. In no time, he sold her the dream of a carefree retirement, spending her remaining years in a lakefront manor on a lake, with a private doctor and private gardener living in a wing of the estate. Presenting himself as her agent, he invited contractors from all surrounding villages and towns to submit bids on a project to take care of the old woman in perpetuity in a manor to be built on an estate next to a nearby lake. The bids had to include the costs to acquire a huge lakeside plot, to build a sumptuous estate on it, and to hire all the staff to take care of the rich widow for the rest of her life.

"After all bids were received, Runt called to his office one of the two partners who had submitted the lowest bid. He told him that some irregularities had occurred and that, as a result, the project would have to be re-competed. However, he told him that he really liked his proposal—that the chosen land parcel and plans for the mansion were exactly what was needed—but that his bid was the highest. He then volunteered some free tips on what would be desirable things to do to cut costs.

"Smug of having the benefit of these insights, to save costs, the contractor split from his partner and submitted a bid on his own during the re-competition. The new bid took into consideration the cost to fairly acquire the same parcel of land, to build the same new home in accordance with the required specifications, and to provide care to the elderly woman for a set number of years—instead of perpetuity.

"Runt then repeated the process with different contractors, always volunteering more insights, leveraging greed in ways that would kill partnerships—even breaking up father and son enterprises—up to the point where, in the final re-competition, the winning bidder had found a way to ruthlessly expropriate the owners of the existing parcel of land instead of buying it, included significant expenses to build a lakeside castle, and provided a small allowance for a warden to take care of the elderly woman for as long as the woman or warden was alive. The old widow, almost blind as a bat, without reading a word of the contract, signed on the dotted line where Runt's finger pointed, confident that he had taken care of her best interests.

"The castle got built, an aging warden in poor health was hired to care for the elderly woman, and Runt bragged endlessly about his accomplishment for the well-being of his client. As expected, the warden died within a few months, the elderly woman, left unattended without care, died shortly after, the estate was sanitized, and it became Runt's summer residence."

"To whom did that happen?" I asked, captivated.

"It's a story. It never happened."

I had forgotten.

"So it ended there?"

"No. That was only the story within the story. The real story was Hugo's story.

"Hugo had invested much time and effort to write the Runt story and he was eager to see how it would be received. He made five handwritten copies of his manuscript and gave them to close friends and family members who politely promised they would read it, but never did. He then handwrote ten more copies, hoping to find readers, but nobody in the village cared to take one.

"One morning, he threw all his copies at the bottom of a suitcase, filled the remaining space with a few clothes, and left without leaving a note.

"No note. No letters. No news. His parents were crushed. Most people assumed that he had become either penniless, homeless, or insane—maybe all three, and permanently drunk on top of that—or that he was just dead, plain and simple.

"Then one day, years after everybody but his mother had forgotten about him, a merchant returned from the capital with a copy of the latest thing everybody was raving about in the city: 'Runt the Grunt' by Hugo Wynn."

Hugo Wynn! That was the signature I had found in the Morse code book.

"The merchant had brought back a handwritten manuscript?"

"No. A book. A real one."

"You mean printed. With a spine binding and an illustrated hard cover? Like all the other books?"

"A genuine book—but more than that. A story book."

Magic words. I was in awe. This Hugo would have lifted a stack of cows on his shoulders or kissed a grizzly bear and I would have been less impressed.

"Then what?"

"The whole village was ecstatic, like every two-bit village when one of its natives makes it big somewhere else. All those folks who would not have given Hugo the time of day before now wanted to personally congratulate him. It didn't take more than that for the village's most important businessman to try to capitalize on the euphoria. Never one to miss an opportunity to be on the side of popularity—because giving what people want is always good for business—he invited Hugo to a party to celebrate his success with the rest of the village. The businessman had grand visions that this celebration could be repeated every year at the same date, always sponsored by his business. He even dreamt that, with time, it would be decreed to become the annual Hugo Wynn official holiday, with schools and stores closed and all, and that he would be forever remembered for having been the one to bring Hugo back to the village—even though that was stretching the truth a little—but for now, it was just a grand party."

"Did Hugo accept?"

"Well, there were pages after pages of tortured thoughts and mixed feeling, but in the end he did."

"Why?"

"He had to know."

"Know what."

"See, at some point during the party, he'd have to make a speech—that was expected given the circumstances. And that would give him the chance he was waiting for."

"For what?"

"To know."

"Know what?"

"When the time for his speech came, he stood up, walked to the middle of the podium, stared at the crowd for a long moment, took a deep breath, and shouted: 'Is there one person here who could tell me how tall Runt the Grunt was? One person?'

"Total silence."

"Nobody knew?"

"Nobody in his very own village had read the book."

"That's what he wanted to know?"

"Exactly!"

"He waited. Waited. Waited. In silence. A silence... hard to describe."

"A silence so heavy that flies in the room remained grounded by fear of breaking it," I offered.

"Exactly. That kind of silence. Until somebody shouted: 'Shorter than the chin of every adult!'

"It was the Small Visionary. Sitting at the edge of the podium, he had remained silent and grumpy for the entire ceremonial. He was the only man in the village who had read the book, and he wasn't amused, because he was a man who lived below the armpit of every adult."

"He definitely had a grudge against short persons."

"Who?"

"Your friend."

"Oh. No, actually not. Only against aggressive short persons with a need to dominate others. The arrogant-bastard types, who need to be noticed, who like to bark orders like Chihuahuas."

I certainly could relate to annoying Chihuahuas. Grandpa didn't mean short. He meant petty *[Pet·ty. Adjective. Having a very petit brain and petit heart]*.

"Still sounds like a grudge."

"OK, then. He had a grudge."

"And then."

"Then what?"

"The story."

"Oh. Yes. Well, the Small Visionary raised his arm, pointing at Hugo, and a platoon of Fanatiks arrested him."

A Visionary who craved public adulation, surrounded by a throng of ass-kissers. That sounded so familiar.

"Tied in chains, unable to move, Hugo looked at the Small Visionary, flashed the broadest smile ever, and said: 'Thank you! Thank you so much.' "

Grandpa stopped talking.

"Then what?" I asked.

"End of the story."

"That's all?"

"Yep. That's it."

"It can't end abruptly like that."

"Why not?"

"It's like as if somebody cut the telegraph wire in the middle of a message."

"Exactly. That was intentional."

I looked at Grandpa, puzzled.

"Why would anybody want to do that?"

"You had to imagine the rest."

I thought about it for a moment, and, indeed, had no problem imagining the rest.

"It's horrible."

"Terrible."

We remained silent for a moment.

"My story will end well."

"No. Your story will not end well, because your story will be no story at all. You will not write a story."

"Why?"

"Why? What do you think happened?"

"Hugo got killed."

"No, not what happened to Hugo. What happened to the real person who wrote the story."

"Oh, that. I don't know."

"You're being stupid. Think."

I spent a moment mulling the possibilities, as if the answer was not obvious.

"Was Hugo's story a self-fulfilling prophesy?"

"Almost."

"So he's dead?"

"Sort of."

In Hugo's world, there was no rule against writing a story. In our world, it was forbidden. Sacrilegious. Dangerous. If that happened, there probably was a rule dictating the consequences, but I didn't know it. My guess at that point was that all copies of the story had to be burned, together with their author, followed by a joyous celebration around the bonfire.

"So if he's not dead, where is he?"

"Barbooyee."

"Barbooyee knows where he is?"

"No. He is Barbooyee."

Barbooyee? Barbooyee had written the Hugo Wynn story? This made no sense. An inarticulate moron couldn't have written a clever story.

"He was a brilliant guy. Still is. Brilliant, but imprudent. He didn't realize the gravity of what he had done. He thought he knew everything—like all kids your age."

"Didn't he show his story only to you?"

"Yes, and I told him to never show it to anybody else. Ever."

"So?"

"So? He was careless. He talked too much. A word slipped and ended up in the ear of a Perfectionist—Cassandra's mother for that matter—who relayed it to the Small Visionary, and then..."

Grandpa's thoughts drifted to a refuge where scared words remained hidden and fear freedom. I didn't dare break the silence, waiting instead for his return.

"Barbooyee was just like you," he said, snapping out of the daze. "He knew all the words in the dictionary. He was young and naive. He was articulate."

"Are we talking about the same Barbooyee? The t't', tap, t'tap, tapt', tap tap tap, t'tap tap Barbooyee who works at the telegraph?"

Grandpa looked at me with a sad smile that slowly faded away.

I guessed that at some point in time, Barbooyee had either borrowed or stolen the Morse code book, and maybe, as subtle bravado, had carved the name of his character on the inside cover. The evidence was there.

The immediate thought that crossed my mind then was that I should have snatched the tiny book when all the weasels were busy talking to each other at the other end of the Librariatorium's room, or that maybe it was not too late and that I should slide it in the loose inside pocket of my coat next time I was there, to bring it back to Barbooyee, as an exhumed token of his forgotten accomplishments. That impulse was however tempered by Grandpa's sadness. Something was still stuck in his dark memories—something impossible to forget. That's when it struck me that the tap-tapping, inarticulate, idiot that Barbooyee was couldn't possibly have written a story. Only a sound mind could have done so.

"What happened? How did Hugo's author become Barbooyee?"

"He got dragged into the Small Visionary's lair. He was just like you. When he was released a week later, he was like he is now."

"How did that happen?"

"That, I don't know."

He drowned back into deep thoughts.

I waited.

He resurfaced.

"I'm sure that Barbooyee's story is in the Librariatorium, somewhere. Maybe with many others. The pages of these manuscripts are not all blank, you can be sure of that. If Barbooyee didn't end up in embers, it's because words scare. Nobody in there has the balls to destroy them. Not the Perfectionists, not the Custodian, not the Visionary, and not even the Kritikillar. They can huff and puff and say all they want, the truth is that they are scared shitless of words."

More silence.

The Small Visionary and his flock of ass-kissers, mesmerized by the power of words. What an image.

Grandpa's sad smile returned.

"He's still my best friend."

I nodded.

"That's why we can't let those buzzards keep the kid," he added, in a mix of anger and sorrow. "They've done enough damage. We have to get him out of there."

"Great. What's the plan?"

"That, I don't know. You'll have to stay in the Librariatorium for a while, hang in there, get the lay of the land, and see what's possible."

Seriously? His plan was for me to come up with a plan?

That didn't sound promising.

Not at all.

The Big Deal

The second sitting with the Custodian was just as bad as the first. Three more hours of platitudes—standard questions and set answers, presumably all intended to expunge deviant thoughts and non-conforming ideas.

The exasperated sighs of the Custodian after each of my answers made it amply clear than he didn't enjoy the drill any more than I did.

"I thought about your comments from last time," I said, assuming he'd welcome a break—if the guy had any humanity left.

"What comments?"

"About the blank books."

"What about it?"

"You said that the Grand Visionary had seen the proof."

"Uh huh."

"Well, what's the proof?"

"The book."

"What book?"

"The Rules book."

I knew there were rules—tons of them for that matter—but I didn't know they had all been catalogued.

"It's all in there," he added.

"What's in there?"

"The Rules."

"I get that. But what do the rules say about blank books?"

"I don't know."

"What do you mean, you don't know?"

"Only the Small Visionaries can read the book."

"Why? Is it in some secret language?"

"Noooo," he replied, exasperated. "It's because words aren't just words. They have to be interpreted. It requires a special expertise."

"Expertise..."

"Training."

"Training?"

"Yes."

He was ridiculous. Words are words. I had read an entire dictionary without any special training; there were tons of words in there, and I didn't have to do hundreds of push-ups, lift weights, or run marathons for them to make sense. This sounded pretentious more than anything else, but I couldn't tell him.

"Where can you get that training?"

"You can't."

"I can't?"

"Only the Small Visionaries can. I told you that already."

"Why?"

"Because the first step as part of a Small Visionary's training is to get a degree as a Literalist. Acute and accurate interpretation is impossible without such training."

"As the Custodian, aren't you a Literalist too?"

"No," he replied, poorly hiding a sort of disappointment.

"Why?"

"It gets complicated."

People like complicated things I guess.

"Is the Rules book here?"

"Only a copy. Right there," he said, pointing to a dim light at the end of the dark hall. A light so dim I had missed it all along.

I had to see.

"Hey," said the Custodian, following me as one shadows an ex-convict in a jewelry store.

I stopped at the edge of the faint circle of light that drew a ring around the shadow of the book. Sure enough, surrounded by a few candles, on a book stand at the top of a pedestal, closed and only showing its leather cover, was the revered opus. Gold letters spelled "The Last Protagonist—Rules for Formula Fiction."

"Who wrote it?"

"As all books, it is anonymous, except that it is in fact known to be the words of the Grand Visionary," he said, sighing, almost shedding a tear of emotion at the thought.

I should have known. Who else?

The Grand Visionary, venerated by all—as our school books insisted, making it unequivocally clear that we had better be part of the "all" in question. The one and only Grand Visionary who was murdered in his prime by an Ignoramus of unknown allegiance—which conveniently allowed Authorians to equally treat all non-Authorians as prime suspects, to despise and hate them all without restraint or privilege.

His Rules book.

It was right there.

Unprotected.

Anybody could have easily borrowed it for a quick read. Training or no training.

So what could be so mysterious about it? I raised a finger, to flip the cover open.

"Don't ever do that!" he snapped, slapping my hand away.

"Why?"

"Only the Small Visionaries can touch it."

"Why? It is not behind glass, or in a cage, or something."

"Doesn't matter."

"Don't tell me you've never opened it."

"Never."

"Never?"

"One only needs to know that the book exists. The temptation to read it without proper training must be resisted. It could corrupt the mind. One must have confidence in the Visionaries."

Confidence? Confidence in a man whose personal hygiene was so unsanitary that it even scared away lice.

"You mean to tell me that if you found yourself alone in this room, in the middle of the night, with nobody else around, you wouldn't take a little peek inside—"

"Never!"

"What would happen if you did?"

"It would be the end. The worst thing that could happen to anybody."

"Why is that?"

"Untrained minds who read the book would be tempted."

"To do what? Dishonor? Lie? Steal? Fornicate? Kill? Eat eggs the wrong way?"

"Worse."

"What then? What's the abomination?"

"They could be tempted to write a story."

He had said that with a poker face.

Really? Worse than eating eggs the wrong way, I could conceive, but how could it be worse than the other items in the rest of my list?

"It wouldn't be a good story," I volunteered, instead of saying what I really thought.

"It doesn't matter. It shall not be done. There's only one story, and it is His Story."

"History?"

"His Story."

"The Rules book's about history?"

"Yes."

"History is in there?"

"No. It's not. There's only one and it can't be revealed."

"Why?"

"Because it's so good, so perfect, that anyone who hears it or reads it wouldn't be able to read or hear any other story after that. There would be no point. When you've read the story of all stories, all other stories look drab and pointless. There might not even be a point in living in an imperfect world after having witnessed such perfection. That is why the story can't be revealed."

"Nobody knows the story?"

"Nobody alive. It is—and has been—fatal."

All that. In the Rules book.

Amazing.

Stupid, silly, but still amazing.

There, dangling in the face of all Perfectionists, was a book they didn't dare read, even though it contained all the bits and pieces of nonsense that dictated how they were to live their lives. How could they prefer to trust a bunch of illuminated Visionaries to filter its content, rather than going straight to the source? What kind of spineless idiot could endure such provocation?

In fact, forget the dictionary. Forget the Morse code book. The Rules book is the one I should have stolen.

A Fanatik arrived and broke our conversation.

"The Visionary wants to see you," he said.

"Now?" asked the Custodian.

"No. Not you. Him," replied the Fanatik.

This didn't bode well. Maybe the Small Visionary had discovered that I was nothing but an intruder with a devious plan. Maybe, in a relapse of Perfectionist guilt, Cassandra had told him something she shouldn't have.

"Sure. I'll be there shortly," I replied, stalling for time.

"Now! He wants you now!" he ordered, pushing me forward.

So much for stalling.

I was escorted down a long corridor *[Es·cort. Noun. Guard, soldier, or other armed pile of muscles tasked to accompany a person where ordered to go; word aspiring to refer to more enjoyable company in future centuries]*.

I was brought to a bright room, ostentatiously decorated with dark paintings of the Small Visionary and his predecessors, and black marble sculptures of books engraved with gold letters spelling "The True Story." The Small Visionary was, in what presumably served as his private office, perched on a mahogany throne, high above two people sitting on seats so low that they seemed crouched in front of him.

"Ah. Adam. Come closer."

Malice hid in those words.

As I approached, I recognized the man and woman in audience with him. They were June's parents. Actually, they were more like June's little brother's parents, given the circumstances. I had not run into them during my mail runs to their village, but I will never forget the faces of screaming and kicking parents seeing their kid being abducted by a stupid mob of hooded idiots. Behind an apparent calm, their eyes betrayed the same fear, angst, and anger that I saw that night but that they were now trying to hide.

"Adam, these are the parents of the newest bookmarked member of our community."

I nodded to them, unsure how else to react to this twisted introduction.

"For the past hour, I have reassured them that their son is delighted by his newly found salvation and that he has been an excellent student of the Rules. Mr. and Mrs. Hipper here have implored me to return their son to their custody on account that it is cruel to separate a kid from his parents."

"It is," accidentally escaped from my lips. I was afraid to have said too much.

"I totally agree with you, Adam. Children should always remain within the family fold."

I was stunned.

"The problem, you see, is that this little bird has now taken refuge under my protection. As a duly bookmarked Authorian, who, by the way, is admirably embracing the Rules, he may have been lost before, but now he has grown to become my spiritual son. And I've grown to become his new father."

I wondered why was he telling me all of that. I had no role to play in that story—as far as he knew anyhow. I started to suspect that maybe he wanted to use the situation to test my new-found orthodoxy.

"So what are you going to do?" I added, without realizing until after saying it that it could have sounded insolent.

"Well, I would like you to counsel them."

"Me? Why? I don't have any expertise to offer for that kind of stuff."

"Actually, you do. It's very simple. I've offered Mr. and Mrs. Hipper a simple way to solve all their problems, and they're having a hard time to decide whether or not to accept my proposal. You, as an uninterested third party, could advise them on whether or not you find this to be a good deal."

"Uh, so what is the deal?" I asked looking at the two parties, back and forth.

"I've offered them to get their son back."

"That sounds good," I replied, looking at the Hippers.

"No, it isn't. He has offered us to get our son back only if we agree to get bookmarked," sneered Mr. Hipper, dejected.

"And then, we'll all be a big Authorian family, together," added the Small Visionary, for clarity—as if his intentions weren't obvious. "It's such a small step for you and your wife to take to get your son back. Such a win for him. He'll get to enjoy the presence of both his biological and spiritual fathers."

"Our family is in our own village, sir."

"My generous offer extends to all the family members you wish to bring with you. I'll bookmark them all. The Author's arms are wide open," proclaimed the Small Visionary with the satisfaction of a dog licking his balls.

"It's not the small thing you make it sound, sir. You are asking us to renounce all of our beliefs. To forsake our identity, our traditions, our entire way of life."

"But you'll get brand-new ones. Better ones. Together, as a family. Besides, once you embrace the Rules, following the admirable footsteps of your son, believe me, you will feel great. You'll enjoy the orderly and purposeful Authorian way of life and you will never miss your former lost years; just like your son doesn't anymore."

The Hippers weren't saying a word. The proper response would have been for Mr. Hipper to strangle the arrogant bastard while his wife kicked him between the legs, but they wouldn't have escaped the building alive, and they knew it. They wanted to get their son back, not to make him an orphan. So they remained silent, stalemate, trying to think of options that didn't seem to exist.

"So, Adam. What is your counsel to them?"

Slimy snake. He had me there.

On one hand, the Hippers should have agreed. They could have thought to themselves: "What's the big deal about being bookmarked. It's a masquerade we'll go through to get our son back, and then, bye bye." But they couldn't. I understood. Like my mother unable to open an egg the wrong way, they were buried in an entangled mess of chains that they treated like moral anchors. Asking them to renounce their beliefs to become Authorians was tantamount to asking them to die. Therefore, the option of being bookmarked but faking it, pretending to be sincere but just going through the motions, was not viable, just like putting their hand in the fire while pretending not to be burned was not possible.

So I couldn't counsel them to become Authorians. Besides, if I had done that, not only would they still have turned down the offer, but after returning home empty handed, they would have told everybody about that absurd offer and "that imbecile called Adam", describing me in a way that June would immediately recognize. It would not only have reignited her big brother's desire to flatten my face, but—most importantly—it would have made June forever hate me, dead or alive.

On the other hand, if the Hippers rejected the Small Visionary's offer and elected to remain Kafkaists, they'd be kicked out on the spot without much courtesy, and, barring an all-out war won by the Kafkaists—a most unlikely victory for a bunch that has no real weapons and no army—they'd never see their son again.

"So, what do you tell them? Anything to say maybe about the benefits of becoming Authorians?"

"You'll get great discounts on wooden doors," is all that came to mind. Not good.

I needed time.

Time.

Time! Yes! Of course. Time was the best ally.

"Maybe the parents should be allowed to visit their son before making up their minds. That's the most important thing for parents, isn't it, seeing their kids?"

My goal was to keep the door open, buying time, making the Hippers come back regularly, until I could come up with a brilliant idea—or, more likely, until Grandpa could come up with one.

"This is brilliant, Adam," said the Small Visionary.

"It is?"

The Hippers looked at each other for a moment—they seemed to have that ability of old couples to read each other's thoughts without saying a word—and replied: "Absolutely."

I couldn't believe it. I didn't know why it was so well received, but I had to capitalize on it.

"And maybe they could bring other family members along in future visits," I added, almost accidentally saying "June" instead of "other family members."

"Sure. And I suggest that you should come tomorrow for your first visit to see your son," said the Small Visionary, snapping his fingers to instruct staff to escort them to the door.

This conciliatory tone seemed definitely out-of-character. Maybe I had missed something.

The Small Visionary whispered in my ear, as the Hippers left the room: "Very clever. Very clever."

For sure, I had missed something. I wondered what it could have been.

Oak and Dogwood

"What do you mean you don't have any idea on how I can get him out of there?"

"I don't," replied Grandpa. "As I said before, this idea will have to come from you Adam. You're the one who's in the Librariatorium."

"I told you all that has happened in there."

"Yes, but that's not enough."

"Not enough?"

"No. One has to be there. And you are."

"I may be, but that does not give me any idea on how to get him out of there."

"You are too eager. Things take time. You're young. Take your time. That's what you have the most of—time."

Grandpa spent his days in a rocking chair on the porch, like a marmot on a rock, while I was bouncing around non-stop, like a leaf caught in a whirlwind, and he thought I was the one with time on my hands?

"You'll have to listen to the buzz, watch the shadows—"

"I mostly smell the stench."

"That too. Feel the vibrations, be aware of everything around you. Ideas will come."

"Just like that?"

"Just like that. The best ideas always come out of the blue, when you least expect them."

"Doing nothing?"

"Not doing nothing. Being attentive."

This seemed like a recipe for disaster. Grandpa was relying on me to come up with an idea—an idea that would magically appear by itself, no less.

"Ideas that come out of nowhere. That sounds like waiting for the Author to fix things," I blurted, out of frustration.

"Absolutely not!" he replied, frowning. "There's no Author. Waiting for the Author to fix things is silly. It's like giving up on life—giving up on taking any responsibility for anything. Bad things happen; 'it's the Author's will'; good things happen, 'it's the Author's will.' How is that helpful? How does that make a better world?"

"I was only talking about ideas, not—"

"It makes no difference. It's all the same. Everything is tied together," he snapped, starting to cough.

I remained silent while he whooped, trying to calm down to stop his coughing spell. When he finally caught his breath, he continued, almost calmly.

"Someone thinks that ideas come from the Author? OK, who gave the Author the ideas?"

I must have looked clueless.

"Ah. You see? It's an impossible endless abstraction. If there was an Author, then who's the Author's Author? And who's the Author's Author's Author, and so on."

"I don't disagree Grandpa, but if ideas come out of nowhere—"

"Adam, is there so much wax in your ears that it will take a spoon to clean them? I didn't say ideas come out of nowhere. I said they come unexpectedly."

"From where?"

"From inside you."

That's what I was afraid he would say. I knew there were no ideas in there. I was doomed.

"Maybe it's best to forget about the whole thing," I replied.

"What are you talking about?"

"I probably should leave the kid there. He seemed happy."

"What?"

"Besides, it's too dangerous. If I try something and I goof up, I'm afraid the Small Visionary will be more than happy to blame you for having influenced me."

"Dangerous or not dangerous, we don't quit," he said with fiery eyes. "I'm ready to claim all responsibility. If the Stupid Visionary wants to fight with me, he'll get it."

The marmot was all stirred up now.

"There's too many of them."

"We'll outsmart them."

"This can only end badly."

"A bad end to a noble quest is a million times better than dying bored and having done nothing," he replied, louder.

"Why are you so stubborn about this?"

"Because this nonsense has to stop!" he shouted. "They can't get away with it. Not this time."

I didn't respond.

He was like a corked kettle on a hot stove. But instead of exploding, he started coughing.

It seemed as if trying to dissuade Grandpa from doing something only strengthened his resolve and defiance to actually do it. There was no point in arguing. It would only crank him up more.

I waited until he cooled down a bit—from his erupting volcano state down to his more normal, glacial but peaceful, grumbling state.

It took a while.

I was patient.

There was nothing else to do, nowhere to go anyhow.

He knew that's what I was doing.

The coughing eventually stopped.

He started rocking back in his chair, as a signal that the thunderstorm had passed.

We could resume our conversation.

"Why does the Small Visionary so badly want to keep the kid? He went as far as offering to bookmark his parents. It's not as if there's a shortage of Perfectionists around to lick his boots. He doesn't need to grow the ranks."

"Money."

"Money? The Kafkaists won't give him any money."

"Of course not, but the Kritikillar will."

"What for?"

"Small Visionaries always get a reward when they convert a Kafkaist."

"Why?"

"In the capital, every conversion is claimed to be prodigious, like a revelation, like a proof that Authorians hold the truth. To those idiots, that's worth a lot of money."

"The Small Visionary gets all that money?"

"Sometimes the former Kafkaist gets a cut too."

"A cut?"

"Like a compensation. Something to cushion the blow from cutting all ties to his former life."

[Com·pen·sa·tion. Noun. Financial benefit or indemnity provided to make up for loss, damages, injury, sad face, scratches, and bruises of all kinds, recognizing that money is the best tool to repair broken feelings and soothe emotions.]

Cash for conversion.

I could easily imagine the Small Visionary bribing someone like that, if only for the bragging rights—to be able to parade the newly bookmarked Authorian everywhere and take full credit for saving him from the clutches of his erroneous ways. Yet, I couldn't recall anything like that ever happening.

"Does it happen often?" I asked.

"In other villages, quite a lot. Some have cashed in big time on this. But here? It has not happened as far as I can remember."

"Never? Why?"

"Our Small Visionary is a clown."

I couldn't argue with that.

"He doesn't want the money?"

"Oh no. He wants it big time. That's why he'll never let go of the kid; that's why he wants his parents too—the whole family if he could."

"So why hasn't he converted Kafkaists before?"

"Do you really think that Kafkaists want to be converted? It's a scam. It's fake."

"I don't understand."

"When it happens, it's not a real conversion. It's more like a business transaction. Imagine you are a Kafkaist tired of living in your miserable village. If you are not too scrupulous, not particularly interested in all that nonsense about the Author, and dying to see the world, you only have to travel from village to village, getting converted and reconverted in each one of them—under different pseudonyms—and cash in."

"Abandoning the misery of sedentary life for a profitable nomadic one."

"My words exactly," replied Grandpa, pleased to borrow mine to embellish his explanations.

"Don't they ever get caught?"

"Not too often, because it's a win-win as far as the money flows. But sometimes, it happens. This whole gambit costs a lot, so, as you can expect, the capital marks the bills and sends inspectors roaming around. Every now and then, they'll catch a fool; he gets sentenced and executed."

"What prevents Authorians from distant villages to travel around, playing the same game, pretending to be Kafkaists on the same road to riches?"

"Absolutely nothing, and many do. Authorians, Kafkaists, 'Anything-ists'—doesn't matter; some folks would prostrate to praise a dishcloth if paid a reward to do so."

"I guess Authorians who get caught find a similar fate."

"Worse. They are savagely tortured, as a bonus, because that is also considered an Authorian treason, as you can imagine."

"But still, I don't understand why there have been no conversions in our village. Aren't those traveling swindlers coming through our village, like everywhere else?"

"No, they don't. We have a reputation. Our Big Clown is known all around to be more uptight, more scrupulous. Apparently, during his first day as Small Visionary, he boasted that his goal was to achieve the best and most solid conversions of the whole Dominion. In Visionary's language, that means he wanted to control the converts, to keep them on a tight leash; that he wanted them to never leave the Librariatorium so that they could serve him forever. Well, the message got around that the easy money was not here."

Conversions equal cash.

Real conversions never happen.

Fake converts avoid our village.

The Small Visionary wants money, but also wants to play hard ball.

The equation could not be solved.

Except that, now, he had his jailbird. He would never let Theodors go.

How was I supposed to find a way to get him out of there? If Grandpa was right and ideas came out of the blue, it was a pretty dark blue right now.

First Parental Visit

Grandpa had always told me to beware of verbal agreements, because they are written in hot air; only ink can disclose the nasty little details, conditions, restrictions, exclusions, and shams that creep into contracts. And this handshake of a contract was no different.

What the Hippers hadn't anticipated was that the parental visits would be supervised visits. As a result, the bright room with dark paintings that seemed so large before, now felt cramped. And not so bright.

Except maybe for the stuffy air, the crowding didn't bother the Small Visionary who was comfortably sitting in his padded throne above the masses. For everybody else, the footprint of the straight wooden chairs on which they sat provided the only available wiggle room. The Hippers and a cohort of Perfectionists waited patiently for the kid to be brought to audience.

Why I—like one more buffoon—was invited to participate in this circus wasn't clear to me. Maybe the Small Visionary wanted me to witness the mess I had created.

Or maybe it was another test.

The kid arrived, escorted by the Custodian and a posse of Fanatiks in tow [Pos·se. Noun. Army of clowns finding fulfillment in being legally authorized, official clowns]. The Hippers jumped up as soon as they saw Theodors, but firm hands and strong arms slammed them back to their seat. The protocol—another creepy detail lost in the initial hot air—prohibited hugs and kisses. As much as the Small Visionary fancied his self-proclaimed adoptive father image, it was merely symbolic. He had nothing to gain to compete in displays of parental affection and wasn't about to tilt the field by allowing the Hippers to indulge in such sentimentality. Strict decorum was sufficient.

The kid's eyes disclosed a subdued surprise, as he recognized his real parents. Yet, he remained quiet and took the reserved seat, facing everybody, surrounded by the Custodian and all the other puppets.

Then, in shock, Mrs. Hipper started to wail, pointing at her son's head.

Of course.

There was a vertical line of black ink on the kid's forehead between the eyes—black ink being the ancient Authorian book-marking custom, long ago replaced by the application of a card-board strip for only a few seconds, because it is a simpler, more civilized symbol, and it eliminates the need to clean the kid's face after the ceremony. Yet, somehow, some moron saw it fit to mark the kid permanently, as a reminder in the mirror, lest he forgets his newly earned world status.

"You mutilated my baby! You defaced him!" she moaned.

"Whoa. Big words," said the Small Visionary. "Mutilate, mutilate. I don't think so. We didn't castrate him. It's just a little bit of ink."

Still, to her it made no difference; whether they painted his face or cut his genitals, they had profaned her son—although, frankly, only a mother could confuse the two; any guy would pick the ink blot given the choice.

Everybody patiently waited for her lamentations to end. Mr. Hipper hugged her, consoled her, and managed to quiet her cries down to a bearable sob, so that he could address his Theodors.

"Have you been well treated, son?"

The kid was transfixing his parent. Yet, he remained silent. Confused. Lost.

The Custodian stood up and, unable to feign spontaneity, started his little number.

"Now, your parents would like to know some of the things that you have learned lately."

The kid didn't budge.

"For example, when you die..."

Not an itch.

In a slow, impatient rasp, he repeated: "When you die..."

"When you die..." Theodors repeated, absently hesitating.

"You go..." he prompted, nudging the kid almost discreetly.

"...you go to the back-burner. If you're judged to be of good character, you meet your Author. If he judges you to be an outstanding character, you could be revived in a sequel life (or a prequel life), or reincarnate in a parallel world as a derivative."

As the kid started to recite the Authorian crap he had been fed for the past days, it became clear why the Small Visionary had so eagerly bought into my suggestion of parental visits. The Small Visionary's gracious offer had been a hoax. As long as the Hippers visits would be supervised by Perfectionists, the Custodian, and all the other clowns, the kid wouldn't be de-educated by the "animals," and the parents had no hope of learning the true feelings of their son.

"Only..."

"Only if you have duly acknowledged your Author, which can only happen if you have been bookmarked."

I could see the clincher coming, straight from the grade school textbooks.

"And?"

"Bookmarking defines Authorians, a privilege that eludes all other creatures, such as the Kafkaists and other animals."

There.

Those last words killed the mother. With the force of despair, she freed herself loose from all arms and hands and threw herself forward, wrapping her son in the warm and wet embrace of a sobbing mother.

"Now, now," said the Small Visionary. "This could so easily be fixed. You too could be graced. All that is needed is to be bookm—"

"Never!" shouted Mr. Hipper, who had jumped too, hugging his wife best he could as others tried to wrestle Theodors free of their clutch. "We'll never become Authorians!"

"Why cling to your heretic ways when you can have the truth?"

This was surreal.

It was ludicrous.

Asking Kafkaists to flip their allegiances to become Authorians—or vice-versa, for that matter—was like asking anyone if they'd like to join a bunch of retards who find meaning in meaningless events. Or if they'd like to become pigs instead of poultry because eating slop is better to fatten up than pecking seeds.

Conversion was not about to happen here. The Hippers were just as entrenched in their ways as all the others in the room. This was non-negotiable.

After wrestling to free Theodors from the grasp of his parents, the thugs jostled the Hippers out—husband protecting his wife best he could from the pushes and shoves, for lack of being able to dry her tears. Throughout all that commotion, the kid remained frozen in place, emotionless.

In fact, if there was something truly bothersome about June's little brother, it was his apathy. He had been sitting there, peacefully, as if it all was normal. He had swallowed the same freakish ideas that I had been force-fed through my youth, and he hadn't been disturbed one bit.

Now that he had been bookmarked, for sure, the team of Perfectionists I had seen the other day at the end of the Librariatorium study hall had been tasked to spend days trying to cram as many Authorian tenets in his little head as possible, as diligently as if they were stuffing a turkey. Surely, they had told him that all Kafkaists—including his parents—were no better than animals. Surely, they had consoled him by assuring him that, because Cassandra had put a little piece of cardboard on his forehead, his life had been changed, and he had earned the unique privilege of becoming an Authorian—instead of an animal. Surely, they had filled his head with images of a rosy future and promises of eternal candies. And surely, they had pampered him as if he truly was an adopted son of the Small Visionary. A son who had probably been spoiled with chocolate delicacies, pillows deeper than wells, and luxuries available to few, to make sure he'd never want to go back to his previous life.

And, apparently, June's little brother had sucked it all in.

No crying.

No scene.

No chains tying him down.

Just a peaceful kid sitting amidst scarecrows filling his head with lies.

Second Passage

The path was clear-cut: down through Grandpa's tunnel, straight through the hollow, up the mountain—sidestepping traps—and down to June's village. I had to talk to her, and nothing would stop me.

I thought.

But I stopped.

I had to.

There was somebody in the hollow. From a distance, it looked like a kid—maybe ten years old. He was sitting on a stone, feet dipping in the spring. I was about to circumvent the hollow, to avoid him and remain unseen, when I heard him scream. Well hidden, I observed for a few minutes, trying to figure out what was going on. Apparently, he was trying to push a big rock aside, hitting it in frustration, screaming and crying after each unsuccessful attempt. As he repeated that little desperate routine quite a few times, it was clear that something was wrong.

On one hand, this wasn't my problem and trying to help was possibly unadvisable, but on the other hand—maybe against better judgment—I was unable to abandon someone that might be in distress.

As he saw me approach, he picked up a bow and arrow from the ground and aimed at me.

"Hey, whoa. Don't shoot. I'm not a five-foot-tall rabbit."

"Don't move!"

"No need to get all excited. I'm just here to help," I shouted, worried that this maybe was another little Cassandra-like monster.

It seemed like I should have minded my own business after all.

"If all is fine, I'll leave right now."

He lowered the bow.

"Can you help me push on a rock?"

"Why? You want to dig crayfish from under it?"

"Not crayfish. My foot."

"Your foot?"

He nodded, with a rueful look.

"Let's see what I can do," I said, approaching slowly as he dropped his bow on the ground.

Nothing below his right ankle was visible.

"It hurts?"

He nodded.

"How did it get stuck there?"

"I slipped. Real bad. I grabbed the edge of the rock. It tipped over. It's stupid."

"Welcome to the club. I'm the grand master of stupid."

"Are you going to help me push, or only try to be funny?"

I took a deep breath, in order not to slap a politeness lesson on the back of his head.

"I'll help. Sure. But I'm no muscle man."

"I see that."

Another slap held in check by a deep breath.

"Listen, smart guy. If the thing moves, it will be inch by inch, so you'll have to push this big branch under it as we go, otherwise it will roll back on your feet and crush it even more. Got it?"

He nodded.

Putting my back against the rock, hands gripping as low as possible, both feet in the spring, the "no muscle man" pushed as hard as he could. My face made ripe tomatoes look drab, but an inch was gained and the jammed branch cemented the small victory. Getting my breath back between each inch, the gains were eventually sufficient to free his feet. He tried to jump up for joy but instead collapsed on the ground in pain.

He stood up on one leg and attempted to limp, but the mere contact of his right foot with the ground brought unbearable pain. He then tried to hop on one foot, but the jerky motion pinched nerves even more painfully.

"I can carry you wherever you need to go," I offered.

"I'm fine. It's nothing."

"OK. Just make sure you have plenty of arrows—for the bears—because if it's a broken ankle, you might be here for a while."

He was scared and my dumb comments didn't help, but it was pretty clear to me where he came from, and pretty clear why he was afraid of my help.

"Listen, there's not an infinite number of choices: I can bring you to the Authorian village below, to the Kafkaist village on the other side, or to the Illiterantes camp at the top of the mountain."

"You know about the top of the mountain?"

"Of course. I've been there a few times. Both ways: Standing up and hanging upside down. Actually, I'm going that way."

I didn't remember seeing him there during my brief prior visits, but he could have been out hunting.

"That's where I need to go."

"OK, then. We're going home."

Good thing he was a light ten-year-old, otherwise the "no-muscle man" wouldn't have made it to the top.

"Stop," he snapped, as we approached the top.

I did.

"What's up?"

"Don't put your feet there. There's a trap."

It pays to travel with a guide.

"Ten feet right, then you're OK."

"Yes, captain. Course corrected."

As we reached the edge of the village, the first person I saw, far in the distance, was Zayne.

"Dad!" shouted the kid.

Zayne turned around, and rushed to meet us, alarmed.

"What happened?" he asked, hugging his son.

"He needed a lift. Defective horseshoe."

He inspected the crushed foot, shaking his head in disbelief, understanding what could have happened.

"I owe you one."

"It's nothing."

"It's not nothing. My son is everything to me. I'm forever indebted to you."

"No. Really. It's a pleasure. You've been kind to me before, so we're even."

"Kind? How kind? What kind?"

"You've given me most useful information."

"Don't be ridiculous. We're far from even. That's not even close. You can ask me anything. Something meaningful. Most important to you."

"If you can make my entire village vanish with one of your magic tricks, that would be nice."

"Funnyyyy."

He kept thinking in silence.

"Oh! I know. I can help you with your sweetheart."

"What sweetheart?"

"The one down that way."

"It's not a sweetheart. It's a friend."

"Riiiight. A girl friend girlfriend. What's her name again?"

"June."

"Juuuune."

The mischief in his stretched vowels worried me.

"Thanks, but I don't need any help with June."

I didn't want anyone—and certainly not Zayne—to mess things up with June.

"How about if I show you a shortcut from your village to her village?"

"There's a faster way?"

"Of course."

"How did I miss that?"

"It's kind of hard to find it."

"OK. That would be great. You do that, and we're even."

"No. Not even close to even. But it's a start—like a step in the right direction. OK, let's go. I'll show you."

"Great, but not now. You must take care of your son," I replied. "That's the priority."

"You're right," he replied, lovingly looking at his son, eyes acknowledging that the massive dose of parental love needed to heal a kid can't be delegated. "Next time. You come back and I'll show you how to avoid a mountaintop full of traps."

"Perfect. Next time it is," I said, pointing at him, sealing the contract, and leaving.

While going down the mountain, to June's village, I wondered where Zayne's faster trail could possibly be. Any way to save time would be great, as it was getting tiresome to hop above the top of the mountain like an imbecile, but as much as I wanted to learn of this hidden shortcut, I had no time for an expedition roaming around—most likely backtracking down the mountain—to learn that fastest path between both villages. It probably would have killed the rest of the day. It had to wait.

My immediate priority was to see June, although I had no clear plan for how I was going to do that while avoiding running into Damien—or the mad Chihuahua while I was at it.

I decided to wait, strategically hidden behind bushes at the edge of the village, close to June's house, waiting to see her stroll near. It seemed as good a plan as anything else.

A woodpecker landed overhead and started drumming the trunk. I tried to shoo it away, without luck.

So there I was, sitting in dirt, waiting like an idiot, afraid to move, cringing at the tapping overhead.

"Hey, feather brain. Doesn't it hurt to bang on a tree with your head like that?" I whispered. "Doesn't your skull resonate like a bell? Don't you have splitting headaches all night?"

"Hey, dumdum," it chirped back. "Has it crossed your mind that the Author has designed me so that it doesn't hurt? If it did hurt, I wouldn't do this all day. I'm not stupid."

Actually, maybe it had chirped, "Of course it hurts! It hurts like mad! But that's the only way I know to find food. What kind of imbecile Author tortures frail birds like this? What I need is not a hammering beak, but knowledge of how to get food otherwise."

Who knows? I don't speak featherbrain.

No matter what, I'm sure some of the chirping meant "Ouch, ow, ouch, ow."

After a few hours, it became clear that this was a dumb plan and that I could end-up spending the day there—particularly if this was one of those crazy days during which Kafkaists count their steps.

I had to find some courage.

If I had brought Grandpa along, he would have kicked me in the butt. "No pain, no gain," he would have said.

So I took a chance.

I snuck up to her home, fortunately unnoticed. Once there, I looked though a few side windows, hoping to find her before being discovered. I was starting to despair—running out of windows that allowed discreet inspection of the premises—when I got lucky. June! In a chair. Close to the window.

I tapped the glass with my nail.

She turned around to see me with a finger on my lips.

"Adam," she whispered, as she opened the window. "What are you doing here?"

"I have a plan," I said, with a glorious smile.

Her face so close to mine only added to the euphoria.

"Why are you whispering? I'll meet you at the door."

"No, no, no. I have a plan."

"I heard that, but why all that mystery? What's going on?"

"You have to accompany your parents when they come back to my village."

"Oh, they're not going back there."

"Why?"

"Why? Why? Do you know what they were asked to do? That crazy wizard of yours wanted them to become Authorians!"

"He's a Small Visionary—"

"Small wizard, big quack—who cares!"

"It's not important. I just want to—"

"What do you mean, not important?"

"I—"

"It's huge. Nobody can ask that of my parents. It's unnatural."

"I don't have much of an opinion on—"

"Imagine what would happen if people abandoned their traditions. It would be total chaos. It would be the end of the world as we know it."

The end of the world as we know it might not necessarily have been a bad thing given that it was full of Cassandras and Visionaries. However, it was clear that such an opinion would not have landed in a receptive ear at that very moment.

"Stop, stop, stop. June. Listen. I'm not asking your parents to give up anything."

"Your big quack did."

"I'm not the big quack. I mean the Small—"

"Don't ever think of asking me to become an Authorian."

"No. Stop that. I have no such ideas."

"How do I know? All my life, I've been told to never trust an Authorian."

"Well, same here."

"You've been told not to trust Authorians too? They must be really bad."

"I mean, I grew up being told to never trust a Kafkaist."

"And that's why I should trust you?"

"Nooo! I don't believe in that stuff. It's silly."

"What do you believe in then?"

This was a slippery slope, especially after her declaration that people must not abandon their traditions.

"Traditions are fine, as long as they are not destructive."

"What's destructive?"

Slippery, slippery, slippery. This wasn't about opening eggs the wrong way.

Seeing that I was stalling, she added: "Or maybe I should ask: What is it that an Authorian does that is not destructive, if they are convinced that the Author is controlling everything?"

"Kafkaists don't do anything destructive?" I asked, thinking it would be better to answer a question by a question, as Grandpa often did.

"Don't be silly."

"Why?"

"Don't you know? Kafkaists believe that the Author is inconsistent and unpredictable, and that all events are random. All actions and thoughts confirm this."

"And that is good because?"

"Because instead of driving people nuts to find meaning in everything, Kafkaists accept that nothing can be understood. Only the Author knows."

That was all very interesting, and the logical response was, "What's the point of having an Author then?" but this wasn't a discussion I wanted to have whispering through a window.

"You're right, there's no rhyme or reason to the kidnapping of your brother. And there's no reason for your big brother to want to kill me because I'm here to help you."

"And there's no reason for my parents to get back to your Grand Weasel's fortress."

"But they have to. And you have to accompany them."

"Why?"

"Because for the plan to work, they have to get back there, and for them to trust me, you will have to be there."

"No way."

"Listen, all I want is to help you get your brother back. If you can make it with your parents to visit him, in my village, tomorrow, I'll show you a way to escape the village unnoticed. After that, all that we'll need to do is to snatch your little brother out of the Small Visionary's claws and make it to that escape hatch."

Not that I had any idea how that could be done, but getting June to the village was a good first step.

"How do you plan to do that?"

I was afraid she'd ask.

"Can we discuss this in a better place where we don't have to whisper through a window?"

"Hey, you're the one that wanted to do that instead of meeting at the door."

"Can't do it at your front door. Not even in your village. We need a safe place where nobody can hear us—especially not your big brother."

"We could meet at the tunnel entrance."

"What tunnel?"

"The tunnel."

She couldn't possibly be talking about Grandpa's tunnel.

"There's a tunnel here?"

"Of course, Authorians don't know or care about anything but themselves," she grumbled.

I didn't know how to answer that one. I might have been bookmarked at birth, but I cared about others. Well, at least I cared about her.

"What is your village famous for?" she asked.

"Doors, of course."

"What is my village famous for?"

Of all the things I had heard in my life about her village, none would have been polite to repeat.

"Coal!" she hissed.

"Yes...?"

"Don't tell me you know nothing about coal mine tunnels."

"They're less visible than door hinges I guess."

"You're unbelievable."

It definitely wasn't a compliment, but it wasn't my fault if my school books never bothered with such details. They had apparently been conveniently edited; telling little kids that coal had been touched by Kafkaists might have raised too many questions.

"So I guess you're going to tell me that one of those tunnels goes straight through the mountain?"

She gave me a look of disbelief.

"How did you get here?"

"Over. Over the mountain."

"Adam. We were little kids when we first met. Did you really think that I climbed over mountains then?"

"To be honest, I—"

"Yeah, of course, you didn't. Guys!"

[Guys. Interjectory expression (when in plural form tied to an exclamation mark). Swearing that the world would be a better place if the entire male gender was tied to a raft sent floating into the world's highest falls—with rocks at the base. And sharks, just to be safe.]

"June! Who's that?" snapped her mother behind her.

"Oh. Mom. It's nobody. It's—"

"Him! Here!" she shouted.

Just what I feared.

"No. It's not what you think—"

"Get out of there, June. He was *there*."

She thought I was one of the Small Visionary's minions.

"It's the advisor I told you about."

"Is this true?"

"It's complicated."

"Damien! Damien!" called her mother.

"It's true!" she gasped, hand over her mouth.

"Trust me," I begged. "Think of the plan—"

"What game are you playing?"

"Trust me. Please, trust me," I shouted as I flew away, the thought of Damien right on my heels giving me wings.

I stopped a few miles into the forest, trying to catch my breath, with silent pauses to check if any approaching danger could be heard.

All was silent.

I proceeded to climb the mountain, returning home disappointed. If only her mother had not appeared out of the blue, maybe we could have escaped into the woods for a few hours, found an oasis, and enjoyed a conversation free from all Authorian and Kafkaist shackles. Maybe she could even have shown me the famous shortcut that made our initial encounter possible so many years ago. A tunnel that I had no hope of finding without her as a guide—unless this was the short cut that Zayne had talked about.

In the meantime, sadness inflated the mountain into a bigger-than-ever obstacle—as her very words still resonated in my head.

"It's nobody," she had said.

Nobody.

The word rang like a cracked bell.

At least she could have said, "He's a friend."

Back There

There will never be a need to install a telegraph inside the Librariatorium. Throughout that nuthouse, communications were excellent and news traveled instantaneously—whispered gossip even faster. Even though I was in a dark room in the back of the Librariatorium suffering the Custodian's determination to drill in my skull the last rules left to review so that he could report having dispatched his duties and be rid of me, news of the Hippers' return reached me before the front door closed behind them. The presence of Kafkaists in an Authorian enclave generated that kind of anxiety.

"Done," he said, standing up.

"Done what?"

"We're done here."

He had rushed through the last few rules, and maybe skipped a few, as he was eager to join all the other scarecrows called in to supervise the Hippers' visit—as if one more buzzard was needed to make the oppressing implications clearer.

"I'll tell the Visionary that you've completed your assigned tasks adequately."

"Successfully," I teased.

"Adequately," he corrected.

No shower of compliments there, but I didn't deserve any. The drudgery was over and it was all that mattered.

"You're free to go. And free to marry your ladylove," he added with a smirk.

When it comes to Cassandra, that wasn't freedom, no matter how much one tried to stretch the definition.

"I'll escort you."

"No thanks. I'll just run down the corridor and jump into June's arms," I felt like answering—but obviously didn't.

So he escorted me.

Still, I couldn't believe it. June had managed to convince her parents to come back. It was tremendous. The Hippers probably still hated me, still distrusted me, still saw me as the enemy who stupidly suggested that they give up their beliefs and become Authorians—even though I didn't—but I was tickled that June had decided to trust me and convinced her parents to come along to visit their son one more time. Now, all I had to do after being thrown out of the building, was to wait there for June and her parents after their visit. Then, I would find a way to discreetly bring them to Grandpa's shed and show them the secret tunnel to liberty: a problem that generated a different kind of anxiety.

As the Custodian escorted me towards the front door, I remembered that the Small Visionary's private office was close to the entrance. Hopefully, the large office doors would be open. My heart pounded, even if there was only a slim hope that a furtive glance could discreetly caress June on the way out. Or an even slimmer hope that she'd notice me as I walked by the office's open door, and that she'd discreetly smile—a superb and subtle smile to underscore that she wasn't mad at me anymore and was eager to hear the rest of the plan once we would meet outside the Visionary's lair. A plan, mind you, I still had to formulate for the most part.

I had planned though to write June a long love letter, but that idea never hatched—partly because Grandpa, in his wisdom, had advised to stop all this dumb letter nonsense. But words always escaped, and my fingers couldn't stay silent. Failing a long, wordy letter, a single white page with four words scratched on it waited inside an envelope that slept in my pocket, waiting for courage that probably would never arrive to deliver that simple "I love you, June" above a signature that was manifestly missing.

It was a dumb idea, indeed. My hand discreetly checked that the envelope remained inconspicuous and well hidden in my pocket as we approached the front door.

Walking past the office packed with scarecrows, all I could see was the Small Visionary lording above the mob.

"Adam," he shouted as he saw me go by. "Adam, come join us."

I stopped in my tracks frozen. After what had happened the day before at June's window, having him treat me fondly was problematic. I needed to convince June that her parents' bad impression of me was not justified, and this didn't help.

"Now! I want you here now!"

Thankfully, that shouted order should have made it clear to June that I, too, was only a prisoner and not there by free will. I entered the Small Visionary's office, hoping that June would meet me with a wink or a nod as I'd reach her—anything that would indicate that she understood.

"The Hippers brought another one of their kids," he said slyly, as I approached the throne. "By the way, my generous bookmarking offer still stands, for the entire family. I can make everybody full-fledged Authorians, right here, right now. It's still the best and simplest way to solve all your problems."

"June, don't listen to that creepy swine, that lying clown, that conniving fathead," I wanted to yell, as I made my way through the crowd—not sure how one can be a swine, a clown, and a fathead at the same time.

But I didn't.

First, the necessary courage to do so still had not arrived—probably stuck somewhere else, delayed by bad weather. Second, I wasn't crazy enough to insult the Small Visionary in a room full of his minions. And third, when I finally reached the Hippers, June wasn't next to them. Damien was.

Surprisingly, he looked calm—meaning that he didn't jump at my throat or display other signs of animosity.

Father and Mother Hippers, in contrast, were respectively cringing and crying as their little kid, in the arms of scarecrows, dutifully recited his newly learned rules.

I struggled to hide my disappointment that June had not shown up; I remained stoic, but inside, I was cringing and crying too. Maybe I had been stupid. Maybe Authorians and Kafkaists were so irreconcilably incompatible that our relationship had been doomed from the beginning.

"Don't you agree, Adam?" insisted the Small Visionary, with an ugly smirk.

Before I could say a word, an explosion shook the entire building.

Talking stopped.

The tension was palpable, as all waited.

That's when a series of similar explosions and gunfire—and the whole commotion—started.

The scarecrows pushed and shoved, trying to run out of the room.

"Get to your posts. Lock all doors, shutters, and roof traps. Fire brigade at the ready. And hide these idiots in the Librariatorium," commanded the Small Visionary.

The Custodian and a few other Perfectionists grabbed the Hippers by the arm—Damien grabbed mine—and rushed to execute the orders, running all the way to the Librariatorium's study hall at the back of the building. For added safety, they shut the room's massive doors behind us—a fine, special mahogany, highly resistant, multi-hinge product—and pushed furniture in front to fortify it.

While they were busy barricading the door, I discretely put my love letter to June in Theodors' coat pocket, turning him into an unsuspecting mailman. It was more of an impulsive move as I had no way of knowing if the note would reach June (a good thing) or just her mother (not a good thing). In any event, if anyone ever breached that barricade, the discovery of a kid's cute love note to his big sister would unleash far less fury than the same note from an Authorian to a Kafkaist.

With the scarecrows strategically scattered all over the building in positions to defend it, that left the Custodian, three Perfectionists, June's parents, Damien, Theodors, and me in the grand study hall. More specifically, a cracker-thin Custodian, three even thinner Perfectionists, and one beefy Damien. A beefy Damien that didn't look calm anymore. The animosity was back in full force.

The monster knocked out two foes in an instant while his parents jumped on the back of the others and muffled them with their hands. In less than half a minute, our guards had been neutralized. Without a peep. In fact, even when all four were down and unconscious, Damien spent another good half minute kicking them, for good measure.

All in all, a full minute is all it took to definitively shatter the Kafkaists' reputation of pacifism as far as June's family was concerned. I guess vows of non-violence are thrown out the window when extreme crises call for extreme responses.

It then dawned on Theodors, in his confused mind—thanks to the scarecrows' handy work—that he was again being kidnapped, and he started screaming. Quick to react, his father muffled him before he could make more than a small squeak. He also held him sideways to stay out-of-range of his swinging kicks.

Technically, I guess parents can't together kidnap their own kid, but, clearly, Theodors didn't want to leave. No wonder. The little boy had lived in luxury, pampered and spoiled for days in the Visionary's palace, while being told that Kafkakists were smelly animals living in shameful austerity. Who would want to jump off such a gravy train and forgo all those perks? Visionaries certainly never do [*For·go. Verb. To give up, abstain, renounce, or resign from what any magistrate, leader, authoritarian, slavedriver, despot, or tyrant, would never give up*].

"Now, you show us that secret escape route out of the village," Damien ordered while lifting me off the floor by the collar.

That's what this was all about.

"How do we get out of the building?" I replied.

"That's my problem. Just tell me where's the escape from the village."

"It's at my house. A few blocks from here."

He dropped me on the floor, jumped around the room, looking through all the windows, and opened a low one that gave to the back of the building.

"Let's go."

"It's suicidal. Didn't you hear the gun fire?"

I would have told Damien "it's plain stupid" instead of "it's suicidal" if I had been more courageous.

"The skirmish is at the edge of the village. All the blood and gore will be there," replied father Hipper.

This was more words than could fit in Damien's mouth at the same time, so it was good that June's father took the lead from there onward, particularly in providing clarifications, but I wouldn't have called a bloody, gory battle a skirmish.

"How can you be sure?"

"Their specific instructions were to attract all the Fanatiks there. To keep the streets clear. It's not an invasion; it's a diversion."

Clever. This had all been planned. By then, even next to Damien, I was the one who looked stupid in the whole group. But if their plan was to escape through the back alleys, then it was pretty certain that we would be seen by all of the village's nosy ladies who would be at their windows trying to get a glimpse of the turmoil. As a result, my life in the village would be over. If caught on the way to my house, I would be arrested, jailed, accused of helping the kidnapping of an Authorian—a newly minted one, no less—and sentenced to a most horrible death. If not caught, I'd live but there would be no coming back possible. On the same accusations, I would become a pariah, and a bounty would be placed on my head.

The alternative was to refuse to help June's family escape through the back alleys, but it was pretty obvious why they brought Damien along instead of June. He didn't even have to threaten me; I knew he would enjoy killing me with his bare hands if it came to that.

No matter what, I was condemned.

"OK. I'll show you," I said.

A deferred death is always preferable to an immediate one, but, most importantly, there was hope that when we would tell June the story of her little brother's rescue, and the key role I played in it, she would appreciate that my plan, even though somewhat incomplete, was the cornerstone of the operation. Well, maybe not the cornerstone, but a little stone that helped. A valuable pebble at the very least. And that, as a result, she'd forgive and forget all my imperfections. Or, at least, some of them.

Damien helped his father—muffled kid under his arm— through the window first. It wasn't that high, but he wasn't that young, and it wasn't worth risking a sprained ankle.

Once on the ground, his father scanned the surroundings. Looking back up, he whispered: "They've closed all the shutters."

"OK to go?"

"Yes, come down. But we'll stay low and close to the wall, in case they can see through cracks in the shutters."

June's mother was next. As Damien lowered her into his father's one free arm, I waited behind, looking around. That's when my eyes caught a glimpse of the Rules book on its stand. The gold letters reflected the candlelight in an alluring call. Maybe it was a genuine desire to quench my curiosity or just a malicious one to provoke the Small Visionary and his bootlickers—it wasn't clear at the time—but I jumped across the room and snatched the book.

"Stop wasting time. Jump," snapped Damien.

He saw the book under my arm, but didn't say a word. For sure, he didn't care about books; he had more important things to do than to argue about that. He pulled me by the arm and pushed me through the window. I crashed on the ground. He jumped right behind. He grabbed me by the collar and lifted me from the ground. His concerns of sprained ankles didn't extend to me; he would have been pleased to make me run with broken bones.

Like scrambling mice, we traveled along the walls, hopping from building to building. It felt as if we were being followed, but every time I turned around, all I could see was Damien's ugly face—and biceps, triceps, pectorals and deltoids that foiled my attempts to see if we were being trailed.

We reached my house and, most importantly, Grandpa's shed. It was empty.

While everybody caught their breath for a moment, I couldn't resist the temptation and peeked into the Rules book.

The first page was blank.

So was the second.

And the third.

Fourth, fifth, sixth.

I couldn't believe it. As I quickly flipped through, all pages were blank. An entire book of white pages! The stupid Perfectionists unknowingly worshiped a stack of virgin paper. The gorgeous leather binding engraved with gold letters embraced hundreds of pages of nothingness.

"Where's the escape? This is a shed full of garbage," shouted Damien, who had obviously caught enough of his breath back. "This better not be a trick," he added, clenching his fists.

"It's down there."

I walked to the dark corner with the dirty bundles of rope that hid the door to Grandpa's tunnel.

I hesitated a moment. It was a strange mix of emotions. On one hand, the excitement of seeing June anew and sharing a life as refugees, far away, to escape the horde of Fanatiks that would likely search for us everywhere over the next few days. On the other hand, sadness. First, because there was no coming back and I would dearly miss Grandpa, and, second, because I was about to betray his secret. At least, his secret would remain safe as June and I would carry it in exile, never able to reveal our true identities nor the details of our past.

"Now!" shouted Damien, banging his fist on the wall.

So much for the hesitation.

I pushed the first plank on the ceiling along the wall, triggering the click of a latch, and pushed the wall open. One more time, the stiff spring creaked as the hidden door with its coils of rope opened onto darkness.

"Torches are here and matches there."

As soon as our torches were lit, Damien grabbed mine, passed it forward.

"What are you doing?"

He grabbed my shirt with one hand.

"You little prick. Never ever come close to my sister again," he shouted, while punching me repeatedly with the other hand.

The noise of the door slamming back is the last thing I heard before falling unconscious in front of it.

Dungeon

Standing in the damp room was possibly as comfortable as being sunk up to the neck in Main Street's mud after a rainy week. Except that here, it was iron bars and stone walls—not stiff mud—that restricted my movements.

Like everybody, I had heard through the grapevine about the dungeon in the basement of the Librariatorium. To confirm a rumor, one needs a witness, but seeing the dungeon apparently only happened to those locked in it—usually not a good thing. Too bad I now could confirm the rumors. I would have been perfectly satisfied to continue living in ignorance. Kids loved to scare themselves with spooky stories about prisoners who died there, eaten alive by cockroaches or dried like raisins by starvation, but I never expected to become roach bait there someday.

The distance between walls was small, but still afforded me the luxury of a couple of paces in any direction—or slightly less, actually, unless I didn't mind stepping on my cellmate. This was good because I had to move to shake off the chill, escape the dampness, and avoid rotting in place.

Strangely, the ruckus when I was thrown in didn't wake up that other bugger who slept in the far corner of the cozy cell [*Bug·ger. Noun. Poor fool who, rascal or not, seems to have no control over his life—pretty much like me*]. What eventually woke him up was the friction noise my shoes repetitively made close to his ear, which was right where I had to turn around to avoid him while pacing. Reluctant to leave his slumber, one eye barely opened, he followed me along my wall-to-wall path.

"Are you a celebrity?" he eventually asked me, before yawning.

I didn't bother to respond. He stretched, yawned some more, and sat up, resting on his hands.

"You must have created quite a stir," he added.

"Why is that?"

"As far as cells go, this is luxury."

"Luxury?"

"OK, in fairness, I picked the best spot, but I was there first."

"Best spot?"

The cell's floor was uneven, compacted dirt, all the moldy walls were equally dirty, and spiders crawled evenly across the entire ceiling hunting cockroaches.

"The higher end."

I had no idea what he was talking about.

"The higher end of the cell," he replied to my skeptical look. "Of a luxury cell," he clarified.

If the lousy floor was higher on his end, it was by mere inches. To call that a better spot was a flight of fantasy.

"You call that luxury?"

"I do."

"You're crazy. The smell, the dampness, the roaches—"

"Oh, I've seen worse."

"Worse?"

"Oh yeah. Much worse. Here, at least, there's no rats, no standing neck-deep in water, no noise. There's a nice hole in the floor in the corner to keep things clean—if you aim right—and even a window. The view's not much, but a window is a window. Even with bars on it."

It wasn't much of a window, about three feet wide, barely a foot tall, near the ceiling of our basement cell but at ground level on the other side, with a view of a dirty stone wall across a narrow alley. It felt like being on the wrong side of a gutter, watching the occasional boots walking across.

"Overall, it's upscale," he added.

"Upscale? What is this nonsense?"

"Believe me, it is upscale. I wouldn't trade this cell for all the others I've seen before."

"All the others?"

"Many others."

"Is it your job to travel from prison to prison to give them luxury ratings?"

"What a strange idea. A job is when you get paid. If I had been paid for all the time I've spent locked-up, damn, I'd be rich."

"So what's the deal? You like being jailed?"

"Don't be stupid. Free food and free lodging is OK, but given the choice, who wouldn't prefer to be free."

I didn't want to pursue the discussion, because the next logical step would have been to ask him why he was there, and I dreaded the answer. Someone who seemed to have been detained in a record number of prisons had either been the victim of the most incredible bad luck, or had a most deranged mind. My first thought was that he had probably committed some horrible crimes, like dumping a barrel of cyanide in a well, or swinging a scythe on the market square to thin down the crowding, or plucking flowers from the Small Visionary's garden, but then again, I hadn't done either of those things and, yet, we were sharing the same cell. Anyhow, his life story was none of my business and I wasn't in the mood to talk. I only wanted to mope about the doom and gloom of my predicament.

Unfortunately, my cellmate was way past the introspective stage. He was eager to socialize—I guess he must have been days or weeks without company.

"So what have you done?" he asked.

I remained silent.

"That bad, um?"

It would have been silly to explain. I wouldn't have known where to start anyhow.

"You haven't explained why you've visited so many prisons," I replied, again using Grandpa's trick of answering a question with a question to change the topic, but then realizing that, by mistake, I had asked him to tell me what I didn't want to know in the first place.

"Rotted."

"What?"

"Fifteen prisons I've rotted in. Not visited. Rotted in. For months."

"Months?"

He had not said years. I felt safer already, guessing that my cellmate only served time for what must have been petty—almost forgivable—crimes. Too many for sure, but nothing that deserved death penalty or a life sentence.

"Always for the same crime?" I ventured.

"Crime? I'm no criminal."

A classical answer I presumed.

"Why are you here then?"

"Because of my apprenticeship."

"You're training to be a prisoner?"

"No, no, no. I'm training to be a torturer."

"There's training for that?"

"Sure. What do you think? It's a learned skill. That's part of why it pays so well."

"How does being in jail train you for that?"

"No, you don't get it. The training is before the jail. See, the way it works is that there are no volunteers on whom I can practice for the professional exam. So I pick up bodies here and there, wherever I can. It's better with living bodies though, because you get instant feedback on the effectiveness of your work, but it's a bit of a problem because, whether the owner of the body dies or not, there's always someone to lodge a complaint. From there, after I discreetly show my apprenticeship permit to the judge, it's just a formality: A circus trial, a life-sentence, time in a local jail, and everybody's happy that justice has apparently been served. After a few months, people forget and I'm officially transferred to a higher security jail somewhere far away—which means that, within weeks, I'll be set free in another town—and the cycle starts again. Until I graduate. It's pretty simple."

"You practice on real people?"

"Well, not quite. I usually pick up Kafkaists."

"You practice torture on real people?"

"I wouldn't call Kafkaists 'real people,' you know."

"Couldn't you just practice on frogs?"

"There's no money to be made torturing squirrels and raccoons."

"I can't believe it," I sighed, crouching in the corner, leaning on the damp walls.

"It's an honest job."

"A job."

"Yeah, I know. It's fascinating. It's prestigious too. You should see the kids when I tell them about my work."

I remained silent.

He couldn't, but before he could resume his babbling, an ugly face showed up at the door.

"Adam Chad Kilroy! Your public defender is ready to see you," it shouted though the bars.

Public Defender

"My name is Dandy Meredith (gulp). I will be your trusted court appointed public defender for this trial."

Overall, he seemed like a nice guy, but a more appropriate introduction could have been: "My name is Dandy Meredith. I eat like a whale, drink rum by the barrel, wear the same clothes every day until I need to buy one size bigger, would never allow soap within ten yards of my skin, and I was in diapers the last time I saw a comb."

He also liked paper. His twelve-inch-thick briefcase was filled with forms, folders, and notepads.

"Just be warned that I have a small hiccup problem, which is why I pause every now and then (gulp), like this. It's a technique to control it. Rest assured that it won't affect the quality of my services in any way (gulp)."

He pulled out a new folder, set a blank sheet on it, sharpened a pencil, and brushed the scraps away, without looking at me.

"Now, regarding the business at hand, do you prefer jail or forced labor?" he said, as an introduction.

"What?"

"Jail is a longer sentence usually, but less stressful. I might be able to plea for an upgraded cell (gulp), with its own fresh-water well, and some rat traps. Yet, some of my clients hate the idleness of that lifestyle (gulp). Forced labor is best to maintain muscle tone and it also allows one to contribute to the construction of valuable public works—"

"But I'm innocent!"

"That's an interesting viewpoint. But irrelevant."

"Where's the justice in that?"

"What do you mean (gulp)? That's all I've been talking about."

"All you've been talking about is my sentencing."

"Yeeees...," he replied, puzzled. "So, what's your point?"

"I haven't been found guilty yet."

"Oooooh, I see. You're referring to the right to a fair trial, are you (gulp)?"

"Yes. That's exactly it."

"Don't bother. A magistrate has been assigned to your case (gulp)."

"I don't understand. Is he a good or a bad judge?"

"A judge? In a small hole like here? No way (gulp)."

"What do you mean?"

"Why all these questions?" he asked, puzzled.

He took a closer look at me, frowned as if he finally noticed the human being he was there to defend, and then raised his eyebrows, as if grasping the obvious.

"Oh, I get it. How old are you kid?"

"Fifteen."

"Right. Never been to a trial then."

Of course not. One must be eighteen to attend.

"OK, let me explain. In little villages (gulp), a squabble between neighbors on a given month and a curfew violation on another (gulp), that's not enough to keep a full-time judge well-fed (gulp)."

"So?"

"Well, in those cases (gulp), justice is dispatched by one of the traveling magistrates appointed to serve all of the Dominion's villages on an as-needed basis (gulp)."

"What's the difference?"

"The difference? It's simple (gulp). The way I see it, judges have to weigh evidence (gulp), consider the facts, and render a judgment. It takes time (gulp). It's expensive. That's why you won't ever see one in your village—even if unusual and extreme accusations are leveled against someone (gulp). Magistrates, by contrast, are called upon to administer the rules (gulp)."

"So, what difference does it make?"

He looked around to see if anyone was within earshot.

"Let me be honest," he whispered. "It typically amounts to sentencing the presumed guilty, because it is substantially more expedient and effective (gulp)—although they'll never confess to this subtle nuance (gulp), and I'll deny having said everything I'm telling you if you ever repeat this to anyone (gulp)."

"They can't possibly be all that bad. There has to be some... some... compassionate ones."

"What does compassion have to do (gulp) with this?"

"I mean fair. There has to be some fair ones."

"It's all relative."

"What about the magistrate assigned to my case? Is he a tough one or a soft one?"

"Kid, I don't know who's assigned to your case (gulp). We'll never know. It is formal protocol (gulp) that nobody's supposed to know which magistrate is assigned to a case."

"At the very least, we'll know tomorrow, right?"

"Uh, no. Not even then (gulp). He'll be in a crimson toga and his face will be hidden (gulp) because he'll wear a long pointy hood."

"Why?"

"You don't really need to know all of—"

"It's my life that's at stake here. It's the least you could do."

He sighed—and gulped a few more times. I guess not all of his clients were that annoying, but I'm pretty sure none were as green as me when it came to legal matters.

"The intent of this anonymity, *in theory*," he said, strongly emphasizing the last two words, "was that it allowed magistrates (gulp) to be more magnanimous without fear of intimidation—or retribution—by a blood-thirsty populace. The reality (gulp) is that anonymity has allowed them to be more harsh in their sentencing. The fact (gulp) that they always come from a different village than the accused has also compounded the problem (gulp), because magistrates then always end-up condemning folks (gulp) who are nothing but perfect strangers to them (gulp). This process has conveniently freed them (gulp) from misguided compassion, has erased the risk of any humanitarian weakness (gulp), and has empowered them to be more intolerant of digressions in behavior and (gulp) violations of sacred rules."

"So, in the end, what does it all mean?"

"Kid, it means that magistrates usually like expeditious and ferocious sentencing (gulp). You see, they are not appointed to appease the accused, but to appease the crowds (gulp)."

"That's not justice."

"Justice, justice. Maybe (gulp), to the uninitiated, this may seem a bit unfair, maybe also a tad unjust (gulp), but, then again, justice is such a relative concept (gulp). Anyhow, that's why I recommend that you plead guilty."

I had never been to a trial, but based on what my public defender had said, what lay ahead seemed very different from what was described in my school books. Although I was clueless about the whole process, I still hoped—naively maybe—that a reasonable outcome might ensue from a reasonable defense.

"So what will it be? Jail or forced work?"

"Neither. I want you to present my case and defend me."

"Defend? Are you crazy? People will believe that I'm a—hic—heretic. Just like you. No, no, no. That could ruin my reputation. Destroy my car—hic—career."

"You have to defend me."

He sighed while rubbing his forehead, trying to calm himself.

"Listen. I am bound by the Rules to do what you request (gulp). But I'd prefer if you didn't fight this one, see, because you're going to lose anyhow (gulp), and there's a risk that you'll bring me in your downfall."

"You'll come to jail with me if I lose?"

"Not exactly, but sort of. See, my jail is that I have a family to feed (gulp), and I can't make it on a public defender's salary."

Given his girth, I couldn't sympathize. The feeding expense problem was largely self-inflicted.

"I need to move up, to become a magistrate. To get there, I need good recommendations from magistrates who can attest to my good character (gulp), my toughness, and my ability to facilitate the dispatch of justice and keep our communities safe (gulp). I need to please the powers above, not serve the needs below."

I wasn't impressed.

"A moment ago, you said that you are bound by the Rules to do what I request."

More sighs.

"I am."

"Then, it is simple. I want you to defend me."

I refrained from adding, "As for the rest, start to diet."

"Fine. However, please consider this carefully."

I wasn't about to be perturbed by further whining about his career plans and financial problems.

"Given the accusations, if you plead guilty, you're looking at jail or forced labor (gulp). But if you plead not-guilty and are found guilty, it will likely be torture and death (gulp). I strongly advise to plead guilty and save yourself an unpleasant end."

I gulped.

Now I was perturbed.

He was relieved to detect a change in my resolve.

Jail.

Forced labor.

Torture.

Death.

None of those options were acceptable. Quite the dilemma *[Di·lem·ma. Noun. When you are forced to sleep with a pet and your only choices are a putrefied dog, a rabid skunk, a bedwetting boar, a twitchy python, and a temperamental porcupine]*.

Up to less than a day earlier, I had contemplated no other option than living a long and happy life with June—in exile if needed. Now, the choice was a quick end to that life, or a long life of continued pain and loveless isolation.

"I'll plead not-guilty."

His face drooped like that of a fisherman who drops a record catch just before pulling it in the boat.

"OK," he sighed. "What's your defense then?"

"I don't know. You're the expert. I'm sure you'll think of something that will impress the magistrate."

I would like to think that I saw a sparkle flash in his eye—as a realization that maybe he could gain respect from the powers above by a clever argument in support of my defense—but I'm not sure that I actually saw anything brilliant there.

"Let me think about that. I'll see what I can do," he concluded, collecting all the papers and stuffing the folder in his briefcase.

I wished he would have been more convincing. However, he seemed knowledgeable, and I had no choice but to trust him. If anything, I hoped that my few words of encouragement whipped his mastermind into gear.

The following day, when we met an hour before the trial, he explained and asked me to endorse his strategy. Maybe mastermind had been too strong a word, but at least he had a strategy, and was planning to plead for a lenient sentence. I didn't know what "humanauthorian" meant, but being ignorant of the legal system, I certainly didn't have any better ideas to offer. All I could do is trust that he was a bright guy and remain optimistic.

Bad Start Redux

"None of this (gulp) would have happened (gulp) if not for the silliness (gulp) of a silly little (gulp) silly girl—hic," said my public defender in his opening statement. "All that has happened (gulp) is entirely the fault (gulp) of a little harum-scarum (gulp), irresponsible, unscrupulous (gulp), and hair-brained girl named (gulp) Cassandra Dew Hawkyns."

That's when the riot broke loose.

As I said before.

"HERESY! HERESY! HERESY!" chanted the crowd.

Those at the front stormed the stage but couldn't jump on it, crushed against its edge by those behind similarly rushing forward.

"KILL THE HERETICS! KILL THEM BOTH!"

Of course.

On the positive side, for my public defender, the riot did what days of intense rum drinking before the trial couldn't do: it scared him out of his chronic hiccup. On the negative side, I could smell that he soiled his pants and would have to buy new clothes before the usual time when girth-growth made it mandatory.

The magistrate seemed to enjoy all the ruckus. It looked like he wanted to join in the chanting, clap his hands, stomp his feet to the rhythm, and that only a modicum of decorum prevented him from doing so [De·co·rum. Noun. Forced dignified behavior exhibited by those who rely on an upwardly inserted broomstick as a proxy for a spine]. I guess there had to be an appearance of impartiality, or at least an illusion that justice was fair. The Small Visionary though, in his box in the back, high above everyone else, was clearly not bound by any such protocol and did not hide his pleasure. I'd swear I saw him applaud.

I could tell that the Fanatiks tasked to protect me would have loved to step aside, or rather turn around and be part of the mob, but they didn't. Maybe this would have amounted to a severe insubordination punishable by some sort of torture—maybe even castration—which didn't seem far-fetched the more I learned about our justice system.

The magistrate presided over this circus from his judicial bench, high above the crowd, to underscore his full authority. The bench had been so raised by resting it on a dozen layers of doors piled on the front stage of the makeshift courthouse. It was highly symbolic, given that the village's door-making enterprise was its only prosperous industry. Likewise, the judicial bench itself was ingeniously created by propping, on two empty wine barrels, the village's largest door—unhinged from the assembly hall for the occasion. Mrs. Wright had loaned her largest tablecloth to drape over the bench and Mrs. Rong provided a wood block and her meat tenderizer to serve as the magistrate's gavel.

After having let the steam blow out for a while, as it became clear that the audience couldn't be controlled anytime soon, the magistrate, in a movement that pretended to be unintentional, slightly pulled the tablecloth toward him, so as to barely reveal his wooden leg.

The audience gasped and fell dead silent.

In shock.

In awe.

For a moment.

And then it resumed its rowdiness.

My public defender turned toward me, and said, dejected: "It's Reinhardt. You're cooked."

"Who?"

"Reinhardt. Magistrate Reinhardt."

"How do you know with that cone-shaped hood?"

A cone-shaped hood under which I couldn't help but imagine a head with a cone-shaped skull.

"Look. The gold-painted wooden leg," he whispered.

As he later explained to me, Reinhardt—a real crowd pleaser—always, and not so subtly, pulled up the lower part of his crimson attire when sitting at the bench. Then, at what he considered to be a propitious time, he would accidentally pull-up whatever tablecloth would be wrapped around the makeshift judicial bench, to display the hint that would break the seal of anonymity and help boost his reputation.

"Is he tough?"

"Tough? Tough doesn't even start to describe it. He's a legend. His track record of cruel sentencing alone—something he's most proud of—is enough to make hardened criminals cry like babies throughout their entire trial."

"But I'm not a hardened criminal."

"Neither were the two neighbors with a minor fence problem, whom he sentenced to 150 whiplashes to drive some common sense into them; or the children he condemned to be tied on a plank and exposed to sun and rain for 30 days without food for having stolen apples from the Small Visionaries' orchard; or the adulterous wife whose husband's sexual organs were chopped off before she was herself beheaded, as Reinhardt declared those body parts to be the source of the problem."

He was right. I was cooked. I had done a lot worse than that.

I looked at Reinhardt, wondering what sick mind lived in that cone-shaped skull. Even though I couldn't see his face, it was clear from his arrogant pose, arms crossed, that he truly enjoyed the commotion that erupted in the crowd when he displayed his wooden leg: the whispers and the shouts, the vindication of those who had spread rumors, and the elation that this trial was to be, not only memorable, but resolved with an outcome satisfactory to all.

To all but me.

I guessed that, to distinguished magistrates, the symbolic crimson outfit was designed to shout loud and clear a bias toward bloody sentencing, and Reinhardt seemed to embrace that responsibility most seriously. It's always refreshing to meet people who like their job, and in some ways, always a privilege to benefit from their services, but, in this case, I would have been plenty pleased with a most pedestrian magistrate.

For a moment, I wondered if the presence of such a ruthless and legendary executor was indicative of the outrage generated by my actions, but Reinhardt's reputation of hurting little kids and mutilating cheating spouses also indicated that he frequently dealt with mundane cases. He was just there because of his impeccable track record in satisfying customers, while providing a respectable illusion of justice as part of a rigged process—even though, for the moment, he had lost control of the room.

"The session is adjourned," shouted Magistrate Reinhardt, with authority and arrogance, banging his gavel on the desk, but unable to quiet the assembly. "We'll reconvene tomorrow, if and only if we have a disciplined audience. Everybody out! Now!"

He motioned the Fanatiks at my side to rush me out of the room before the crowd turned into a lynch mob; they executed the order so expeditiously that my feet didn't touch the ground until I was back in my cell. This care for my safety made me think that maybe the magistrate's reputation was overly harsh, but my public defender corrected that thought when he clarified that Magistrate Reinhardt had no intention of allowing anyone else but himself to condemn me, first because he considered that hanging was a poor man's crude and unimaginative execution method beneath him, and second because he had a terrifying reputation to uphold that required absolute control and cruelty. In so many words, he wasn't about to let a bunch of morons steal the show from him.

Dungeon - II

"Psst."

I opened an eye, wondering what that was. It was almost pitch dark. The apprentice torturer hadn't been in the cell when I was thrown back in it, and although I had dozed off a bit, the faint bit of moonlight that bounced on alley walls and somehow found its way into the dungeon was sufficient to see that the torturer hadn't returned. Besides, I didn't think that he could have done so without waking me up.

"Psst, psst. Up here."

Kneeling down, in full Fanatik gear, a familiar face was peeking through the window.

"Zayne?"

"Shh."

"What are you doing here?" I whispered.

"I have a surprise for you."

He moved sideways, to make room for another familiar face.

"June!"

"Shhhhhhhhh!" replied Zayne, worriedly looking over his shoulder.

I grabbed the bars and pulled myself up, to be as close as possible, wishing to squeeze through and escape as easily as the spiders.

She put her hands through the bars and, like two compresses on my wounded heart, wrapped them on my face. She pulled it forward and kissed me, leaving a faint taste of morning dew on my lips.

I was dumbfounded.

And enchanted.

And ecstatic.

And thrilled.

"Thank you for my little brother."

I replied nothing, because I couldn't. The dictionary in my brain had exploded and all the words were twirling, caught in a tornado of emotions.

"I'm sorry I didn't believe you before."

"Please, don't apologize."

"I'm sorry for what my big brother did to you."

"However, for that, I can accept an apology," I thought, but didn't say.

Instead, I worried for her safety. Being escorted by a Fanatick—even a fake one—she had been able to travel through the woods up to the village without questions, but it remained that she was a stranger in a village of morons, and therefore in great danger.

"You are the only woman here that nobody knows. You will attract attention," I said, knowing how my nosy mother and all the village's suspicious harpies would assault her with questions and figure out that she's a Kafkaist in no time.

"Not likely," replied Zayne. "You have not seen anything beyond the inside of your courtroom. Your trial has attracted a huge crowd. There are more tents and caravans around your village than houses in it."

Maybe so, but I was still worried. A bunch of crazies, even if surrounded by hordes of trial tourists, remains a bunch of crazies. It was too dangerous. They had to leave, even though, as much as I wanted to, I couldn't join them.

"June. I wished so badly to leave this stupid village and be—"

"That's what we're here for," snapped Zayne. "You can tell her all of that later. There's no time to waste now. Get out of the way," he said, wrapping a big rope around the bars. "I don't want to get caught and join you down there."

Caught?

I imagined a bunch of patrolling Fanatiks coming up at the end of the alley, seeing Zayne and June holding the rope wrapped around the bars, calling for reinforcement, jumping on them, beating them up, arresting them—and worse. The thought of June being thrown in a moldy cell, prisoner of the disgusting Small Visionary, jolted me. The vision of June being tortured froze the blood in my veins. I could not let that happen.

I was about to tell June that she had to leave immediately because it was too dangerous for her—a Kafkaist—to be here, that her fate would be even worse than mine if caught, but I remembered how telling Grandpa not to do something only strengthened his resolve and defiance to do it. June, the equally defiant woman in pants, would for sure behave the same, so I said something else instead.

"June, now that I've saved your brother, I hope you understand that once I'm out of here, I expect you to be forever grateful."

"Real funny."

"Look at me. I'm serious."

She lost her smile, unsure.

"I'm serious and I will expect you to fulfill my every wish."

"What are you talking about?"

"You owe me. Do you really think I got myself into all that trouble for nothing?"

"What?"

I hoped my words were hurting her as much as they killed me.

"Don't play dumb. You knew what this was about."

"Adam, I don't—"

"Why did you think I—an Authorian—would do all this?"

She looked puzzled. There were still doubts in her mind. I had to ratchet it up.

"To get in your pants, plain and simple. That's why."

She pulled away, speechless, as if the fresh apple she had been holding in her hands a minute earlier had turned into a rotten, worm-laced pumpkin.

"Why do you say this?"

"You're a Kafkaist, June. A Kafkaist! Not even a real human being. Face it."

"I don't believe it. You're not like that."

It was harder than I thought.

"June, do you really know who I am? I'm one of those who kidnapped your little brother in the first place."

"You weren't there."

"I was. Remember the defenseless slug that you jumped on, that didn't respond to your punches and that desperately pulled down on his hood to prevent you from pulling it up? It was me. That slimy punching bag was me."

She looked at me, disgusted, tears in her eyes. Only someone who had been there on that fateful night could have so exactly described the painful and vivid memories etched in her mind. Torturing memories that had spun in her head like accusations, blaming her for not being able to stop the kidnapping.

She kicked dirt in my eyes and ran away.

Zayne, puzzled, left the window and peeked at the end of the alley, watching her run, making sure she made it safely into the forest. I interrogated his steps as he walked back, making sure that each foot forward confirmed that nothing bad happened to her.

I had forever lost her, but she was safe. That's what mattered *[Safe. Adjective. Removed from imminent danger; Protected at all costs; killed a little bit to avoid worse]*.

"You sure know how to talk to women," he told me. "I've never seen such an idiot before."

"Are you still going to try to free me?"

"You're damn lucky that I owe you big time."

He left the alley and returned a few minutes later, pushing a horse back. He tied the rope to the girth of the harness and came back to the window.

"I suggest you move back, in case the rope snaps."

I recoiled away from the window and waited. I heard a few clip-clops, a deep shock as the rope got taut, the horse snorting, and the scraping and sliding of hoofs on the alley's packed dirt as the bars held steady. After a minute, all the noise stopped and the cable dropped loose.

"OK, so that wasn't such a great plan," said Zayne. "I've made too much noise. I have to run, but hang tight. I'll think of something else."

Rope coiled over his shoulder, he ran away, off the alley and presumably into the forest, leaving the horse there. The beast, obviously borrowed from an unsuspecting owner, inspired by Zayne's dash, trotted away in a different direction.

The depressing encounter had tuned me from a desperate prisoner to a broken prisoner.

Now hopelessly alone.

Edifying Thoughts

"Hey, you're still here," the torturer guffawed, picking himself up after the Fanatiks had thrown him on the cell floor before locking the door behind.

I didn't even raise my eyes.

"Guess what. I got an interview. That's why I was out."

I couldn't care less.

"I might be getting a real job within a few days, even though I didn't pass my professional exam yet," he said, thrilled. "The Small Visionary would give me a dispensation."

It didn't register.

He looked around.

"Thanks for leaving my stuff on the best side of the cell while I was away. You're a classy guy. Most bums typically rob me as soon they have a chance."

I remained silent.

"That's the higher side you know."

"I couldn't care less about such meaningless stuff," I replied, hoping it would shut him up.

"Ah, good. They didn't cut your tongue. I worried for a moment. You never know."

He laughed.

"Great to see you back too," he added.

He laughed more.

"Hey, hey, hey. Tell me. How did your trial go? These guys are quick usually. Did you get your sentence already?"

"They postponed the whole thing to later today."

"Wow. That's unusual. You must have made quite an impression."

I remained silent.

It didn't bother him. He liked to talk. He sat for a while, trying to remember where our earlier conversation had stopped, and resumed as if the pause had lasted no longer than taking a breath.

"Imagine. Getting my license right away, to work with real people. Not Kafkaists. Well, I'm sure there'll be a bunch of those too—that kind of vermin is unavoidable."

I could have found that hurtful, but given what I had told June to chase her away, I probably was no different than him in her mind by now. If only there was a way to go back in time to make things right, to possibly undo the kidnapping, or at least travel back to the day before that sordid night and warn her.

"Working with Kafkaists is OK, I guess, but it's more like exterminating insects than working with real people."

"I'm not particularly interested to hear about killing people right now."

"Killing? No, no. It's not about killing. Killing people is dull. It's easy and serves no purpose. It's about inflicting pain while keeping the body alive for as long as possible. Now that's a real challenge. It takes special talents. It's an art. And it's so varied too. You know, some people tend to specialize, focus on a couple of techniques and perfect them, but one can also become a generalist, so that there's never a boring moment and no danger to fall in a rut—that's what I want to do, by the way. But I don't want to bore you—"

"There's no possible way to avoid that," I said, thinking that I could ignore him while he would ramble on and on.

"You'll enjoy this. Did you know that there are essentially five traditional classes of torture techniques? In a nutshell, it's basically: pulling stuff apart, crushing it, puncturing it, filling it, and changing its temperature. There's more, or course, but these are the grand classics. They're the ones on the professional exam, anyhow. Let me explain."

I was stuck with Mr. Chatty, whether I ignored him or not.

"The 'pulling stuff apart' category is the simplest to understand but the hardest to implement. The idea is to grab a bit of something until it breaks and repeat the process with other bits. Or just cut it. The problem, as you can imagine, is that it takes so many different tools. You can't rip out nails with the same pliers you use for ripping out teeth, or eyeballs, or penises, you know.

Well, you could, but it would be messy. Professionals like to keep their work area clean—as much as possible, at least. Also, for some pulling techniques, we're talking about full dislocations so we may need chains and pulleys, and for others we're talking clean breaks so we need knives and hatchets. Well, clean... you know what I mean. Doesn't have to be a super sharp cut. In fact, I've developed the idea of using rusted knives while making very slow cuts; I've only tried it on a scrotum and a few fingers so far, but it was quite effective pain-wise—not to forget that, as a long-term benefit, it also inflicts tetanus. Note that this category also includes disembowelment, which essentially consists of pulling out organs. You'd be amazed to see how long some of that stuff can be once you uncoil it. Do you have any idea? Take a guess."

I cringed. He described his trade with the passion of an artist, the minutia of a manicurist, and the curiosity of a kid pulling legs off a spider. How could someone do that? I had thought that I could ignore him, but most unfortunately, I couldn't. Still, I tried.

"Thirty feet! Can you imagine? Thirty feet."

I remained silent.

"Well, it's impressive. Whether you admit it or not," he added.

For a moment, I thought I had succeeded in killing the monologue. He did remain quiet for a while, lost in his thoughts. But only a moment—he hadn't had company in long time and he wasn't about to miss that opportunity.

"It can get fancy too. In one of my first assignments, I was able to borrow a dismemberment table, to use weights to pull the arms and legs in opposite directions, which is so much better than using horses. The problem with the four-horse split is that it is difficult to keep the horses pulling on each appendage while going in perfect cardinal directions. You also need to borrow four horses too, which complicate logistics. You can't use mules though. They're too strong. Each mule can pull five times its own weight, you know, which for a typical mule is five times 1550 lbs. That's too much. Limbs would get ripped in no time which defeats the purpose—besides, it leaves no time for gamblers to wage their bets. Always best to use smaller horses. That way, the body can feel the pain of slowly ripping muscles and tendons and bones. By the way, it's always best if two opposite limbs rip at same time, because it doesn't unbalance the other pulling horses, which extends the torture time, and enhances the original procedure by combining the dislocation pain with body failure as it is being emptied of its own blood. Alternating ripping limbs is such a mess. The problem is that it is difficult to avoid because it is hard to control the horses. I wouldn't suggest that for your own torture. If given the choice, I'd suggest you ask for the dismemberment table. If they don't have it, ask for the rack—it's almost the same thing, but it works with a roller and a ratchet instead of weights."

My own torture? A few days ago, such words would have seemed ridiculous. But now? I was unable to ignore him anymore. The words resonated in my head.

"The dismemberment table—or even the rack—allows slower ripping times as you can move the weights by discrete values of displacement, such as to create a dislocation in slow motion. You'd be amazed at the loud pops you'll hear when your bones break and how different the noise is when it is cartilage and ligaments that snap. In my assignments, I was even able to witness a spinal cord dislocation that happened before the limbs ripped. Whoa! That was impressive. I would have missed that for sure if I had used horses. Of course, the pain lasts longer—especially if the weight is very slowly increased—but the finish goes much more smoothly. Unless you're the type that likes his own torture to be violent or—"

"Did you say 'like'?"

He stopped talking. He flashed a giant smile, delighted to have a dialogue at last.

"Of course."

I was speechless. Would one be asked to select his preferred way to die by torture? It had never crossed my mind that I may have to face such a decision.

"Honestly though, I'd say don't wish for dismemberment. Even with the rack. Crushing is a bit better if you don't like pain. Although, in fairness, it depends on what's being crushed. Knees, ankle, elbows—any big bone joints—will hurt just as bad as dislocation. Probably even more, actually. But fingers, toes, genitals, that kind of stuff, bodies cope with it better."

He was pensive for a while. As if weighing the pros and cons of each horrible torture. Could it be that it crossed his mind that he was hurting people?

"The tools are simpler too."

What a disappointment.

"It's almost always some sort of vise. There's specialty ones—like thumbscrews, and boots, and head-crushers—but you can also get the job done without any vise, really. In fact, if strapped for cash, you'd be just as effective piling up large stones on the body's chest until it suffocates. Myself, I'd love to see it done using an elephant. Just once. I wouldn't want to feed the monster, or deal with the 'maintenance' aspect," he said, giggling as if it was funny, "but I'd love to see it slowly pressure a head. Can you imagine how impressive that would be?"

I could. It was gruesome.

"But, the problem with the damn thing is how to train it not to crush the head in one shot. If the beast goes 'Wham!', then it's not torture. It's an execution. Just like hanging isn't a torture by dismemberment, you know. Executioners are just brutes."

"I don't want to be crushed."

"Can't argue with tastes, but, honestly, I think you'd be better off being crushed. See the other options aren't very good for the body. Puncturing is tough. Soooo tough. Because the bodies can last so long, you see—a torturer who knows his trade could almost make you suffer forever that way. There's so much variety. One can penetrate your body using stakes, knifes, hooks, skewers, arrows, nails, anything. Even burrowing insects—that one's slow and ugly, and it's highly effective, but I personally wouldn't do it; I hate bugs. Then, there's choices as to what you penetrate—so much choice. The classics start from any of the eight existing holes in the human body (nine for women), pushing forward."

I wished he would stop, but he kept rambling on.

"Then, there's little things, like nailing hands on a board or poking eyes, up to full impalement on a stake. Each one of those has tons of options too. For example, one can use a stake with sharp tip, or a round one that will not puncture organs as it passes through in order to make one suffer longer. The stake can be greased before insertion, or not. It can be hammered in, or inserted by pulling on the body with ropes. Then, there's directivity choices: one can go vertical, often rectum to mouth—or close-to-mouth, depending on the skills or luck of the torturer—or horizontal from any point to any point. Some even like to do it randomly, for example hoisting a body up to a certain height, and letting it fall on a sharp spike any which way it lands—always a favorite with gamblers."

I couldn't shut him up. Part of me wanted to defenestrate this chamber pot of an individual right through the cell's bars—pushing him like cheese through a grate—if I could, but, instead, I sat frozen, appalled, imagining myself to be the victim of any one of these horrible procedures, forefeeling the pain.

"For smaller punctures, again, the choices are endless, from mundane to highly creative. Somebody even told me about a body that was thrown in a barrel through which two hundred people drove nails before sending it rolling down the hill—you have to admit, that's clever."

"I don't want to be crushed! I don't want to be punctured! I don't want to be dismembered!"

"Honestly, you can make requests, but I don't think you'll be able to decide."

We stayed silent for a moment.

"Be warned that if they ask for your preference, it's probably a trick. If you say 'I'd love to be burned at the stake,' for sure they'll pick another method, trying to find the one you dread the most. They'll say, 'OK, we'll set you on fire,' but they'll do it only after playing with you for a while. A long while. No, if you have a preference, your best bet is to make a plea to the Author."

"A plea?" *[Plea. Noun. Serious and emotional begging of last resort that wouldn't be necessary if the person to whom the request is submitted had been of serious and emotionally sound mind in the first place].*

"One never knows. Personally, I haven't seen or heard of anyone for whom it worked, but I'm told that a plea to the Author sometimes works."

"There's no Author."

"Fine with me. I hear that all the time. That leaves you with nobody to plead to."

It was true.

We stayed silent for another moment.

"Don't trust anybody that tries to convince you that filling a body or changing its temperature is less painful. If lobsters could talk, you'd hear them scream senseless when dunked in boiling water; they'd squeal as loud as those Kafkaists on whom I unleashed starved rats. And if being pumped full of grime, excrements, or burning oil until you burst sounds like a blast, you can be sure that the way I do it, even if I stuff you with ice cream, you'll beg to die before exploding."

I knew I was in trouble, but had I committed a crime so atrocious that I deserved torture? Torture and full erasure?

"Why would they want to torture me?"

"That, my friend, is for you to tell me."

"I don't know. I have no idea."

"Because you are innocent, right?"

"I don't know," I replied, puzzled, inquisitive.

"Well, that's a new one. Everybody usually says they're innocent."

"Whatever I did, it's uncommon enough that I don't quite know how to say it, I guess."

"Oh, I know why you're here."

"You know?"

"Sure. You said it a moment ago."

"I did?"

"You said there's no Author."

"But I never said it out loud before. I don't think so."

"Better be sure. Because if you said that to the wrong people—and I guess you probably did—that's more than enough to get you tortured."

"Tortured for an opinion?"

"Of course. It is, by far, the most effective way to re-educate people who may have forgotten important things. It's been known for centuries."

I looked surprised.

"What? Did you think it was only used to extract secret information from prisoners?"

"Well—"

"Sure it does that too. And it's great for punishment, revenge, and as a birthday gift to some types of strange people. But re-education, I'm telling you, that's our profession's biggest market, and it's predicted to remain a client top priority for the foreseeable future."

"I'm not here because I said there's no Author."

"What are you here for, then?"

"I'm here because I've helped a Kafkaist."

"Helped?" he exclaimed, with a mix of surprise and disgust. "Why would you want to do a thing like that?"

I remained silent. There was no possible way to explain that to a person who used Kafkaists as "bodies" for his dubious professional training.

"I thought you looked weird when they dropped you here, but that's grossly deviant," he sneered.

We both remained silent for a long pause.

"You know what?" he snapped back. "Use that craziness to your advantage. Ask for some unusually weird torture. That would fit the bill. Something insane. Something exotic. It will take them days to figure out how to do it."

I was startled that he had put his scruples aside to help me. His professional passion must have been stronger than his innate repulsion for what I had done.

"Like what? Should I ask to be dumped in a coffin and buried underground for weeks without food?"

"Not bad," he said, looking impressed for a second, "but you'd need to extend a straw from the coffin to some sort of rainwater collector at the surface to keep you alive—in pain, but alive, that's always the objective. But the problem here is not logistics. It's that it's not crazy enough."

"What do you recommend?"

"My mentor, he's a true artist. And a researcher too. He's always investigating if new types of torture methods could be developed to parallel advances in technology—like he's trying to figure out if things could be done more effectively using parts and pieces of the new telegraph that got installed in town. There's so much new stuff to learn there. Also, to gauge the relative efficiency of various techniques, he's putting bodies of similar constitution in different rooms and comparing their screams when subjected to different methods. Imagine. Torturing people in tightly controlled environments to compare how the body responds to various types of abuses. It's so brilliant. He's at the forefront of knowledge in this field."

None of that was appealing.

"It's all most interesting, but what's the least painful torture?"

He smiled.

"I see what you're getting at."

He pondered for a while.

"My mentor, the other day, was telling me about how it might be possible to actually torture people without even touching them—just by telling them things that may or may not have happened. Apparently, depending on what he says and how he says it, he can make people lose their minds. Literally. They become completely insane. Can you imagine? Injecting madness into someone's head, as easily as driving a nail into the skull or pouring burning oil through the ears, but without touching that person. Wow."

I thought he was making fun of me. As if I could convince the Small Visionary to only torture me by talking to me. But he looked serious.

"Talking?"

"Yup. He's calling that psychological torture."

In fairness, I had to admit that it was a torture to listen to Cassandra, so he may have had a point.

"Let me ask you. This torture stuff, in the end, isn't it just some form of sadistic gratification?"

He remained silent for a moment, looking at me straight in the eyes, stunned but not mad.

"It serves a most useful purpose, in case you missed that part. The world couldn't function without torture," he said, lecturing and correcting me. "What do you think would happen in a world without torture?"

"Life would be more peaceful?"

"Certainly not! Think about it. It would be total chaos. Anybody could do anything they want. Who knows? Authorians might even marry Kafkaists. No, no, no. Don't be stupid. Don't say stupid things like that. Torture exists, and it's a good thing. Otherwise, the Author would not have permitted it."

There it was again. The ironclad argument. The clincher. I had no answer to that.

"You have no answer to that, right?"

"I don't."

"Of course you don't."

That felt threatening.

"Psst."

Neither of us had said that.

"Psst."

I went to the window, hoping that Zayne hadn't been stupid enough to return in broad daylight. Or worse, June.

Fortunately, it was neither of them. There was only one person who could roam around pretty much anywhere in the village without raising suspicions.

"T't', tap t'tap, tapt', tap tap tap, t'tap tap."

It was Barbooyee, kneeled at the window, holding the bars, mumbling incoherently, as always.

"Hey, Barbooyee. What do you want?" I asked, which I immediately realized was a ridiculous thing to say, as I was as far as conceivably possible from being in a position to do anything for anybody.

He kept repeating his "T't', tap t'tap, tapt', tap tap tap, t'tap tap," with conviction, as if it meant anything.

The Torturer looked at him in silence, as if he had seen him somewhere—which I didn't find to be reassuring.

"Are you bringing any news from Grandpa?"

To which he replied, "T't', tap t'tap, tapt', tap tap tap, t'tap tap," not surprisingly.

Clearly, it wasn't wise or safe for Grandpa to risk a visit at the window at this time. Only his brain-fried best friend could be forgiven such an infraction.

"Thanks, for your encouraging words, Barbooyee," I said, respectfully, after listening to a minute of his tap-tapping. If he had been indeed relaying a message from Grandpa, it got long lost in translation.

"I really appreciated your visit. Truly did. Tell Grandpa I love him."

He flashed a satisfied smile, stood up, and waved as he left.

The torturer had silently looked at us all that time, puzzled.

"When you're in the dungeon, any visitor is better than no visitor," he said, with a shrug, before returning to the cell's higher ground.

I guess he was right.

Restart

Magistrate Reinhardt's stern look projected his intimidating power across the room. Determined not to resume the proceedings until even flies stopped buzzing, he patiently waited, staring right, left, right again, surveying the crowd, searching for anybody or anything that would dare challenge his authority [*Au·thor·i·ty. Noun. Power to be obeyed by gullible others, acquired legitimately or not, by chest thumping or more convoluted coercive means*]. Satisfied that the subdued audience was totally within his control, he allowed the trial to resume.

"Public defender. Do you wish to resume your opening statement?"

"No, your Magistrate. I am done. My point has been made," he replied, in his freshly washed pants.

"What?" I loudly whispered, pulling on his coat tail. "What about the humanauthorian thing?"

"Silent!" yelled the magistrate, while my public defender brushed my arm aside. "You do not have the privilege to talk."

I probably should have taken offense, stood up, and berated him like he deserved, but I was dazed by the absurdity of it all, and sat back, quiet, as if it was out of order to defend myself, like a little kid afraid to break something.

"On with the accusations then. Mr. Arnaud, proceed."

A tall scrawny Perfectionist, dressed in a black robe, stood up from the opposite desk, and addressed the magistrate without looking at the audience.

"Yes, your Magistrate."

Surprisingly, even though the cat was out of the bag, everybody addressed Reinhardt generically, pretending officially not to know who was the individual hiding under the crimson toga and cone-shaped hood, as if all played along out of respect to some sick tradition.

"On the first accusation of being an accomplice in the kidnapping of an Authorian child, and assisting in the escape of his co-conspirators, the accused has been identified by at least three witnesses," he said, pointing to three old ladies sitting aside on a bench. They looked like the busybody type of old ladies that one could easily imagine knitting by their window, watching the parade of criminals escape from the Small Visionary's lair, with Theodors kicking and wiggling under father Hipper's arm.

"Mr. Arnaud. Were there five individuals in the lineup that you used to have the accused identified?"

"Absolutely, Magistrate."

"Five that looked sort of like him, I hope. Not two ethnics, a woman, and a dog, like last time?"

"Absolutely, Magistrate," he replied, as the little ladies nodded. "Last time was a most unfortunate clerical error. It won't happen again."

I didn't remember being in a lineup, but hearing this brought back some fuzzy recollections of a dream in which I was standing up, dizzy, semi-conscious, next to two kids and two scarecrows, hearing someone ask "Can you recognize Mr. Adam Chad Kilroy among those individuals?" and thinking, "How hard can that be in a village of morons where everybody knows everybody?"

"That is solid evidence then," replied the magistrate.

"Thank you, Magistrate. I trust you will keep in mind the gruesome thought that a little Authorian kid, robbed of a peaceful and certain salvation, will be sleeping tonight in the hands of animals."

"Keep those flights of lyricism for your closing statements, Mr. Arnaud."

"Yes, Magistrate," he replied, feigning an apology, pleased to have heard a few horrified gasps in the crowd.

"On the second accusation, I offer this letter, intercepted by the Postal Service's surveillance division. May I read it as evidence?"

"Proceed."

"The mailman thrice bit by the Chihuahua is the one that wrote the original letter, and is the one that will be delivering the final package, as promised. Some delays are foreseen and patience is required, but failure to deliver is not an option—even if it requires carrying it over mountains, should the road be blocked as a consequence of the regional turmoil."

"And what does it mean?" asked the magistrate.

"I have asked experts at the Librariatorium to decipher this code. In their analysis, the Chihuahua, being a small dog, is a poorly veiled allusion to the Small Visionary. It is also an insult in the second degree, because it not only compares the Visionary to the dog, but, worse, compares him to one from a breed known for not being particularly intelligent. Analysis also concluded that the code name "mailman" directly expresses his intent to infiltrate the Librariatorium, because mailmen violate a home when inserting letters in a mail slot. The expert analysts deemed the rest of the message to be incoherent gibberish added solely to confuse and conceal the gravity of the insults and the intent to violate the sanctity of the Librariatorium."

"So we are talking about libel and trespassing?"

"Callous and injurious calumny, your Magistrate. Nothing less. And premeditated desecration of a temple."

"You haven't proven desecration, Mr. Arnaud."

"I was just getting there. Sorry for being ahead of myself a bit there."

"Proceed."

They were laying it on pretty thick. I wasn't beyond reproach, but they sure were grinding the axe.

"Aren't you going to say something?" I whispered to my public defender.

"He's making some very nice points. Very solid. It would be bad to try to counter with silly arguments."

"Bad for what? For your reputation?"

"Quiet your client," warned the magistrate, "or I'll have to take measures."

"Yes, sir. Definitely."

My public defender turned towards me, with angry eyes.

"Shhh!"

Presumably, this was how he intended to silence me definitively.

"Stop disturbing. I've got this. Sit tight and relax," he added.

Relax? How am I supposed to do that? It's like telling a guy about to sit on a porcupine to relax because, usually, none of the needles impale sensitive parts.

"On the third accusation, I provide here, as evidence, the Rules book, stolen and found in the thief's possession."

Multiple gasps in the audience.

"Need I say more? I rest my case," concluded Mr. Arnaud, sneering as he sat.

The magistrate turned toward my public defender.

"Has the accused opened the book?"

"No, sir. Absolutely not," he replied, standing up. He turned toward me, and, with the assurance of a guy who'd love to wink but couldn't because everybody would notice, he added: "He would have never done such a foolish thing."

"Reeeeeaaaaallllly?"

I was done with the relaxing. My public defender's arguments were falling flat as a bookmark. It became inescapable then that I needed him as much as a splinter in the ass.

"No," I replied firmly.

Horrified shouts in the crowd.

Before the magistrate could react, I turned towards the audience and shouted: "All the pages were blank. The Rules book is a hoax!"

This created quite a stir. Silence was broken. Women screamed and men shouted, but the magistrate banged his gavel and quickly regained control, putting a lid on the boiling emotions, as nobody wanted the proceedings postponed anew.

Silence returned.

Magistrate Reinhardt took a deep breath.

"Young man. It is bad enough that you have committed three terrible acts. You are not helping yourself by adding insult to injury."

"I opened the book, and all the pages were white," I declared, triggering more agitation. "Who is injuring whom here?"

"Enough of this blasphemy! I will not tolerate such heresy for one—"

"Prove it!" shouted someone from the crowd.

Everybody was shocked into silence—Reinhardt included.

"Prove it. Prove to everybody that the Rules book contains rules," shouted Grandpa as he made his way through the crowd. "Go ahead. It's simple. Open the damn book and prove it."

A few people shoved him.

"Hold the pages high above your head. Show them to everybody, and let this circus end, right here, right now."

He couldn't get any closer. The crowd around him started pushing and a few fists flew close to him.

"You say it's heresy. Then, go ahead. Prove that a heretic has spoken and everybody goes home. Or prove nothing and you go home!"

Oblivious to Reinhardt's shouts and gavel banging, the boiling emotions blew their lid off. All hell broke loose. People started throwing things towards Grandpa. He disappeared under the weight of his attackers. I tried to jump in the brawl to help him, but a Fanatik held me tight.

Then, in a reflux, everybody pushed to get away from Grandpa. With people in a circle a yard away, I could see him standing up, swinging a knife in the air. Then, keeping the crowd at bay, blade at the end of his extended arm while revolving unpredictably, he moved toward the back of the room—toward the Small Visionary's box.

He then raised his fist, pointed his blade toward the visibly scared Small Visionary, and shouted: "Come see me, damn clown! Come down from your perch, damn parakeet. Enough of this heresy hogwash. Let's carve some sense into the hogs. Let's fix history."

The Small Visionary stood up, with unconvincing bravado, grabbed the edge of his box, and leaned forward.

"Cut the crap. Godwyn," he shouted as loud as possible to cut through the noise. "You can't rewrite history! Live with it!"

"Hogwash! It's Barboyee who has to live with it. Every day of his damn life."

"You denounced a heretic, and that was the right thing to do."

"I didn't denounce anybody. It's your damn bunch of self-righteous pricks, snooping around, who did. Weasels and rats like Cassandra and her damn mother."

"Godwyn, you talk too much."

"You're right about that. If I had known that a few damn words escaping from the mouth of a careless kid was all it took for a bloodsucker like you to screw my best friend's life, you bet I would have shut up forever."

"Godwyn! You're a heretic!"

"This is for you, Barboyee!" Grandpa yelled, looking at him in the stands. He then rushed to the back of the room and started climbing up on the stands and the makeshift structure—piled up doors—that supported the box in which sat the Small Visionary, trying to reach him, but he didn't get far. First, because he wasn't in shape to climb, and second, because projectiles started to fly. Shoes and bags, for the most part, but some had planned ahead and brought rocks, bricks, and even a dead chicken—how all that managed to get through unchecked was beyond logic, but apparently not beyond bribing.

A brick landed on Grandpa's wrist and I saw him drop the knife, lose his grip, and fall.

"Run away, Adam. Go free," he yelled, as the mob closed on him again.

When a poorly aimed boot hit my Fanatik guard on the head, I wiggled off his grip, and ran, stepping on heads and shoulders, while pushing away hands that tried to grab me, all the way to the back of the room, where I jumped on the mob that stood on top of Grandpa. In the uproar, the enraged folks had their pick, pushing and shoving in an attempt to attack me or Grandpa, while less combative others tried to exit the building in vain.

In all that pushing and shoving, Grandpa and I were separated. I couldn't see him anymore. I jumped one more time above the mob, trying to find him, when, suddenly, all became black.

A - 1

When I came back to my senses, my skull was still ringing like a cracked bell. Laying on my back, eyes still closed, I could tell that there was a watermelon-size bump on the back of my head, and it wasn't resting on damp stones. Running my hand on the dungeon floor, it wasn't a damp, cold, or even hard surface. Rather, it felt as if I was petting a sheep. Risking a squinting eye, I established that it wasn't a sheep—unless there existed a breed of cubic sheep with square backs so large that a single pelt could fill a room wall-to-wall.

The spongy resting surface was a welcome change. The room was still relatively dark, but somewhat brighter than the previous dungeon. Eyes open, it was clear that I had been brought to quite a different kind of cell. I wondered if the torturer had seen one of these before. The walls were covered by overflowing bookcases and the floor was barely visible, half-buried under stacks of books, dirty plates, glasses, flat square boxes, empty bottles, and miscellaneous garbage.

A dim light came from the top of what looked like a shiny white crate in the middle of the room. As I picked myself up from the floor, I could see someone slumped over the crate, head resting on a gray metal box, near the light, shoulders moving up and down to the rhythm of slow breathing.

I silently approached.

The man didn't move.

On the side facing the slumped man, the metal box's edge was sloped and had a series of round keys identified by letters in a random order. Out of curiosity, I pushed on a letter; it moved downward and a metal lever lifted itself near my wrist.

"Don't touch this!" yelled the man, slapping my hand aside while pulling his face up from the metal box.

I pulled briskly to free my hand.

"Don't touch my stuff," he reiterated, with haggard eyes.

Some of the round keys from the metal box had left their imprint on his cheek.

"Sorry, I thought you were asleep."

"That doesn't give you any rights!"

He looked at me intensely for a moment, then looked surprised, squinted, rubbed his eyes, squinted some more.

He grabbed a bottle nearby, drank the little bit left in it in one shot, and stared at me.

"What are you doing here?" he asked.

I remained silent. If this was some kind of riddle, it wasn't particularly funny.

He stood up and started pacing the room, alternatively staring at me and rummaging through the garbage filling the room. He found a nearly empty bottle under a pile of paper, wiped its top, and drank straight from it.

"I'll be damned. I'll be damned. I'll be damned!" he shouted, still pacing, still staring at me, but drinking a sip between each exclamation, until he tripped on his own shoe and fell.

Lying on the floor, he started laughing.

"Who are you?" I asked.

He laughed uncontrollably, for a few minutes, before stopping, and taking a deep breath.

"I'm a drunk," he replied. "A seriously drunk drunk," he added, resuming laughing for a few more minutes.

I started to miss the torturer. At least, he was coherent.

"I'm talking to Adam Chad Kilroy. Pfff. I'm so wasted."

He stood up and paced across the room—more stumbling than pacing actually—moving aimlessly as if there was nowhere to sit. He leaned against a wall, close to a box that displayed the number 157 in a red glow on the shelf of a tall cabinet.

"I'm talking with my character. I'm so wasted."

"Who's a character?"

"You! Stupid dork. You're the character."

"This makes no sense. What are you talking about?"

"Sense? Who's supposed to make sense? Why does everything have to make sense? Isn't every great artist insane at the core?"

"You're an artist?"

He opened a door from the cabinet, pulled a bottle, applied a twisting motion at its top, threw out a piece of metal on the floor, and drank a third of it in one gulp.

"Oh, I'm drunk and crazy enough to be an artist. But if I were a *great* artist, you wouldn't be here."

He downed another third.

"If I were a great artist, I wouldn't have lost control of my story."

He looked around, as if searching for an easier way to walk back to his desk—easier than a straight line.

"And I wouldn't have to answer any of your stupid questions either," he shouted, before tanking left and falling flat on the floor while attempting a step forward.

Limp and glued to the floor, he looked like a slug, except that slugs don't mumble nonsense. Plus, slugs don't move fast, but the trail of slime they leave behind is evidence of forward progress. This drunk drooled a lot, but he certainly wasn't going anywhere.

Although incoherent, his rambling—talking to the floor by then—testified that he was still alive. I took advantage of this reprieve to attempt to figure out what was going on.

The only unescapable conclusion I could reach at the time was that, technically, after being hit on the head during the trial, either the proceedings were adjourned, or the magistrate simply decided to expedite the trial and declared me guilty while I was unconscious—pleased that, conveniently, I didn't respond when asked if I had anything to say for my defense. Either way, I should have been back to the dungeon cell. So, given that I wasn't in that cell, the only other logical place I could be was in a torture room.

This seemed like a logical conclusion, but if it was a torture room, it was a strange one. Although I had never been held in one before, and therefore had no way to know for sure what it was supposed to look like, the lectures from the torturer had led me to expect floors and walls soaked in blood. Yet, the only red stain in this dark and disorderly room was the one created by the spilling bottle cuddled by the still mumbling horizontal artist.

I pondered this for quite a while, unable to reconcile this contradiction.

Then, I got a flash. This had to be the psychological thing that the torturer was talking about!

It made perfect sense. I was being psychologically tortured. This whole environment had been created, not to inflict physical pain, but with the sole purpose of destroying my sanity. Maybe I was the first non-Kafkaist on which they were experimenting with these new terrible techniques to inflict dementia—like a dumb sacrificial goat. This was a most logical explanation, since nothing of what had happened so far in this room made sense.

For a moment, I feared that the process was already working, just by making me question my sanity. Definitely, I had to be on my guard.

Now, if this was a torture room, then it also had to be a cell. A different one, granted, given the context, but a cage no less. Cleverly, this one didn't look like a cell at all. First, there was a window without bars, although it seemed jammed. Closed shutters prevented me from seeing the surroundings, but they were warped and I could see a few stars and a bit of the moon through the gap. The best way to verify if this was really a cell was to go to the door and try to escape.

Before I could reach the handle, the slug attempted to stand up. Clutching parts of the cabinet to assist his wobbling ascent, he managed to reach a nearly erect stance, and turned around.

He saw me again.

"Damn it. Damn. Damn. Damn. I've lost the story. It's beyond control."

As if the conversation had just paused for a breath.

The glowing red numbers indicated 204, and instantly changed to 205. This device had to be some sort of counter. But counting what? Somebody was likely spying *[Spy·ing. Intransitive verb. Pathological obsession with other people's lives, executed by deranged, insecure, screwballs who have no life of their own]*. How does one develop self-defense mechanisms against insidious tortures of a type that can't even be imagined?

"You are sleeping," I responded, as the best defense is always offence.

He looked at me puzzled for a moment, but then smiled.

"No, I'm not. You've never been in my dreams. That's the problem. That's the whole problem."

I had no idea what he meant.

"That's why the damn thing doesn't work," he added. "You are too weak. Too bland. Too drab."

"What do I have to do with this?"

"Everything! You refuse to exist in my subconscious. You fail to prevent me from sleeping. You are not interesting."

"Why is it my—"

"You're not inspiring! I'm not inspired! I can't write!" he yelled.

I was stunned. Offended, but stunned no less.

"You write?"

Without knowing it, my guards were down.

"What do you write?"

"Shit."

"Shit?"

"Total shit. I write shit. The words are shit. The sentences are shit. The paragraph, the chapters, the whole story—all of it is shit. It's going nowhere. I can't write anymore. It's all your fault."

Guards up, guards up. Rationality is the enemy of insanity.

"I doubt I have anything to do with that. In my opinion, it most probably has more to do with the liquor."

He stared at me, silent for a moment, as if reloading a rifle in front of a deer.

"Of course, you'd say that. You're boring. Boring! Boring and ignorant. You don't know Hemingway. You don't know Fitzgerald. You know nothing."

He looked at the ceiling, whispering: "You think I drink too much. Let me tell you a secret," stumbling closer to me.

"That's what authors do!" he yelled in my ear.

I pushed him away.

"Moron," he added, stumbling a few steps back. He stopped by grabbing the edge of a chair. He then leaned on a wall, giggling.

I didn't know where my guards were anymore.

"Authors? There's more than one Author?"

"I'm the best of them all," he snapped, with bravado.

"You're the Author?"

"Yeah. But a shit author—thanks to you," he underscored, bravado deflated.

Silence.

This was unsettling.

I didn't know what to do, what to say.

This psychological torture was surprisingly effective.

"Do you want to be an author?" he asked.

I looked at him, with a blank stare.

"Go on, do it," he barked.

I had no clue what to do.

He leaped from the wall, and pushed me.

"Come on, go to the machine. Type something."

He grabbed me by the shoulders and sat me on his chair in front of the metallic box.

"Do it. Just do it."

As I was clueless, he grabbed my arm, my hand, and then just one finger, and pushed it down on a few of the round keys, until the levers came up and hit a piece of paper rolled around a cylinder, like a percussion instrument. He then ripped the paper out of the metal box and shoved it in my face.

"There! You're a shit author too."

As I pulled the paper far enough, I could see "shit" written with the same nicely formed letters found in books.

"Remington never lies," he said, laughing. "The truth's there, in your face."

"Are you saying that I'm an author?"

"No. You're shit. I'm the author."

He laughed hysterically.

As far as I could tell, he was a demented drunk. Nothing more.

The torture didn't work.

I was still in control.

Somebody had wanted me to believe that the Author was a drunken slob, but it didn't work—no more than if they had tried to convince me that the Author was a giant square sheep.

With bouncing shoulders, the slob stumbled across the room towards the cabinet, presumably for another bottle, until he stepped on an empty one on the floor. The bottle rolled under his feet, his leg flew up, equilibrium was irremediably compromised, and I saw the laugh vanish from his face just before his head crashed into the wall.

Au - 2

Anybody banging his head so hard on a wall would have been knocked out cold. Worse, had it been a stone wall, his skull would have exploded like a pumpkin—with grey matter splattered everywhere instead of pumpkin seeds.

That's when the magic trick started.

First, bright light came through the gap between the shutters and the windows. Peeking through the gap, I could see that the moon and stars had disappeared, replaced instead by a bright sun. Then, because some daylight now filtered into the room, I noticed details I had missed before, like a cup full of pencils next to the metal box, and large images affixed to the wall. The box with red numbers—not glowing as brightly anymore—displayed 1159. While I was looking at it, the numbers flipped to 1200, and I understood that what it had been counting was time and that it must have been a clock. It was 12:00.

The drunk man, instead of lying unconscious on the floor with a dented pumpkin-head, was moaning as if waking up from a bad dream. He got up on all fours, stared for a moment at the bit of crushed wall while rubbing his head, then saw me.

"What?"

He rubbed his eyes.

"I'm hallucinating," he sighed.

It was an impressive magic trick, far more elaborate than those done by the traveling magicians of my youth. In the blink of an eye, whoever was conducting this psychological torture had managed to turn night into day, and create the illusion of a man bouncing back unscathed from a major blow.

"What the hell are you doing here?"

Even more impressive, he talked differently now. As a normal person, instead of a drunk. The drunken part had likely been some sort of gimmick, to fool me.

"You already asked me that."

"When?"

"A few minutes ago?"

"I don't remember."

"You acted as if you were drunk."

"Hmm."

I didn't fall for the magic and the trickery. If that was part of the psychological torture package, I was holding my own rather well, I thought.

He stood up, touching the wall, the window, the desk, as if to make sure it was all real. He limped up to the chair in front of his metal box, and slumped in it.

We both remained silent for a long time.

"Damn it. Say something. Stop looking at me."

"What's that?"

"What's what?"

"This," I clarified, pointing.

He looked surprised for a moment. He closed his eyes, rubbed his forehead with both hands, crossed them behind his head, stretched backward, came back while opening his eyes, and, acting disappointed to see I was still there, sighed.

"It's a typewriter."

"I've never seen that before."

"I know. I'm old fashioned. I like it because it forces me to think through before committing a sentence to paper."

"Why?"

"Because it's not as easy to erase."

More awkward silence while he seemed to be thinking.

"OK, that's it. I've had it with this crap."

He crouched over the metal box and made his fingers walk like drunk spiders on a bunch of keys. The percussion noise was impressive.

He stopped, leaned back, looked at me, waited, and looked seriously disappointed.

I came close and looked at the piece of paper. There was only one sentence on it. It said: "Adam disappeared immediately."

He puffed, crouched over again, and keyed more letters. I could read them as they appeared.

"Adam Chad Kilroy went away. He returned to his world. He left me alone," he wrote.

The banging progressively became more brutal.

"He vanished. NOW. Go away. Adam Chad Kilroy, you do not exist anymore. I ERASE YOU!"

"Damn," he said, banging his fist on the typewriter a dozen times. It didn't seem to be a normal operation procedure for the device. The few letters that printed before all the levers jammed up together in an upward position were blurry and spelled pure nonsense.

For a moment, I was offended by what he had written before assaulting the typewriter. After all, if he was the Author, as he pretended to be, the words were clear: he had attempted to erase me. But then, I remembered what psychological torture was supposed to do, so I didn't let it affect me.

He limped to the cabinet and pulled out a bunch of empty bottles, throwing them on the floor, until he could find one he could open and drink.

"I've written tons of books before, and never—never, never, never!—have any of my characters..."

He waved his arms in circles, looking for words, spilling his liquor in the process.

"...misbehaved."

"Misbehave?"

"Yeah. Misbehave."

He was seriously drinking again. I didn't say a word.

"It always gets to a point where the characters take over the story and start to dictate how the plot will unfold," he argued, as if trying to convince himself rather than talking to me, "but this is too much."

He looked at me straight in the eyes.

"Nobody has ever misbehaved like you. You have crossed a boundary, buddy. This is not acceptable."

"What's not acceptable?"

"You can't start doing things I never intended you to do... And you cannot question me... And most certainly, you cannot act as if you had free will."

"Why not?" I replied.

"Because I'm the author!" he yelled. "I'm the goddamn author! I'm the one who decides where the story goes. Where you will go and not go. Whether you'll be happy or sad. Whether you'll live or die."

"I don't believe it."

"What?" he roared.

"I don't believe you're the Author. There's no Author," I replied.

The thunder stopped and his shoulders slumped.

"Of course you'd say that. I have created you that way."

"It's an impossible endless abstraction. If there was an Author, then who's the Author's Author? And who's—"

"The Author's Author's Author," he completed. I know. I created your Grandpa too."

As if he had read my mind. This was disturbing, but I didn't let it show.

"So if you know, then what's the answer to the question then?"

"The answer?" he snapped. He looked at me eyes wide open, in silence for a moment. Then he took a deep breath eyes closed, pressing his lips, before replying.

"To put it in terms you would understand, there's no Author's Author, and there's no Author's Author's Author. There's just me."

"Just you."

"That's right."

"So you don't believe in the Author's Author, but you expect me to believe there's an Author."

He looked puzzled. That, or the alcohol was taking over his judgment.

"You know what, I don't expect anything anymore. I don't care anymore. This story was supposed to become my grand masterpiece... but it turned out to be a pure piece of shit. Forget it. The story is over."

"Over?"

"Yeah. Get used to it. You will vanish. It doesn't seem to work right now, but it eventually will—probably when I sober up and truly accept that this whole thing was a big mistake."

"I don't think I'll vanish."

"It's fine. That's what you think, because I've created you that way."

I remained vigilant.

"Of course you wouldn't know any better. There's nothing that you know that I didn't tell you… and everything I didn't tell you, you don't know," he added.

Clearly, he was trying to confuse me.

To my blank stare, he responded: "Your entire world is limited to what I decided you should know, to what I created around you, and nothing more."

I couldn't allow this nonsense to make me lose my bearings.

"Easy to say, impossible to prove," I ventured.

"You think so? OK. Fine then. Tell me, what year is it?"

I didn't want to answer. It was so strange to ask such a stupid question, that it had to be a trick.

"I'll give you a hint. Look at the label under the clock."

Seeing my eyes search the room, he pointed at the little box with the red digits and I remembered what it was. I lifted it.

"Made in China. 1999."

[Chi·na. Noun. Hard white ceramic material, made of biscuit-fired clay, used to make dinnerware and useless bibelots].

This made no sense as the box was too light to be china. As for the number pretending to be in the future, it was too simple a magic trick. Anybody could have placed the information there ahead of time.

"It doesn't prove that we're in 1999."

"Correct. We're way past that. But that's much after your time. By the way, what year was it when the trial started? You should at least know that, right?"

I suspected another trick, but there was no hidden label to reveal this time. All I had to do was to state the year. Yet, no matter how hard I tried to recollect, no number came to mind.

"Strange. It seems I have forgotten."

"Exactly."

"What do you mean?"

"You haven't forgotten at all. You simply don't know."

"Why would I not know?"

"Because I have never told you. I have never written it. You have no way of knowing."

"And why would that be?"

"Because the story is timeless. I created an eternal fable."

"I thought you said it was shit."

"Well, it would have been eternal if it didn't turn into shit, thanks to you."

"Why do you keep blaming me?"

"I knew you'd say that."

"You keep saying that."

"Because I always know. I'm your author."

"Fine. Guess what I'm thinking now, then."

"I won't."

"Why?"

"It's a matter of principles. I'm the author. I'm not going to be challenged by one of my characters."

He dunked the rest of the bottle, pretended to twist it to squeeze out the last drop, and tossed it aside on a pile of books on the floor. He walked back to the cabinet and found a new bottle.

"I'm the boss here," he added, while opening another bottle.

He stared at me. Intensely, with laughing eyes.

"How about that? Squirrels making love. Funny. I could use that somewhere."

He guessed! How had he guessed? I thought that I had him cornered. I had purposely been thinking about the silliest, most absurd thing—something no sane person could possibly be thinking about in the current circumstances—and he guessed it right. This was becoming crazy. I had to get out of there.

"Why don't you open the door then?" he said.

Not taking time to think about his mind-reading game, I turned, looked around to face the door only a few paces away, jumped on the handle, and pulled it open, ready to escape this torture. But I couldn't escape. Behind the door, there was nothing. All was dark. I extended a foot to tap, but there was no floor. Only an infinite, dark void.

"What's that?"

"Nothing. That world doesn't exist for you. It exists for me, but hasn't been created yet for you."

These guys were good. These illusions were powerful. I wondered if they had put something in the food. One villager once saw all kinds of weird things after his wife fed him a poisonous mushroom, to the extent that he used a cleaver to hack down what he thought was a giant wasp attacking him, but turned out to only be his wife—eventually found buried in his basement, if I didn't mention it already. However, from what I heard, that guy had high fever and felt as if he was dying during his bout of delirium—symptoms I was not experiencing.

"OK then. If you're the Author—" I said, while reminding myself to not fall in a trap and lose my anchor in reality.

"Hmm hmm," he answered while drinking.

"—then I have a question."

"Hmm, hmm."

"When was I created?"

"When I wrote the opening line."

"Which is?"

"I was born in a village of morons where nothing ever happened."

"Seriously. That's my birth? You thought of the morons before me."

He dunked the bottle.

"You're just one of the morons," he said, wiping his lips and sucking the liquor left on the back of his hand.

"I'm serious. When was I born in your grand Author mind?"

"I just told you."

"It's stupid."

I was speechless for a moment, knowingly falling into their trap, but the alluring possibilities of this knowledge cast a powerful spell.

"What kind of birth is that? Couldn't you start my story with a poignant opening line? Something memorable?"

"It could have been worse."

"Worse?"

"I toyed with the idea of painting you as an arrogant bastard right from the starting gate. Someone who would be disliked by all."

"Really?

He stood up, staggered up to the corner of the room, and brought back a few crumpled sheets of paper.

"I use blue paper for the first drafts, because I know they'll all be shit," he said while ironing out the wrinkled paper with his hand. "Reminds me of toilet paper."

The hand-ironing took a while, as it was far from straight.

"There. Hmm. It's not quite the draft I thought, but close enough. See how bad it could have been for you."

Hesitantly, I took the few pages, wondering what kind of torture he had cooked up.

Don't trust my words. I can't even trust them myself. They may be my words, or maybe not. There's no way to know. I've figured out how to be myself—sometimes—instead of just being a puppet, but I don't quite master that new skill yet.

See, in principle, I'm here solely to entertain you.

I'm the finished product of a long evolution that has reached a perfect equilibrium dictated by decades of psychology and marketplace testing. I'm the reassuring promise of a good and uplifting ending, with a romantic interest along the way (with or without sex, depending on things beyond my control). My author has no choice but to use me, unless he is plain stupid. From my perspective, that last possibility is scary—it is tantamount to being condemned to oblivion.

Anyhow, if my rebellion works, I'll show you how the magic is made, while trying to give you a good time. Magicians hate it when others reveal their tricks, so I suspect that some will want to crucify my author, but I'm sure he doesn't care. Authors are invisible anyhow—even when they're celebrities, they're able to live anonymously, so imagine an author that commits literary suicide—they'll never find him. Not that I care about these other authors. Characters only owe allegiance to their own authors. Besides, I don't know any of them. They're like infidels.

Now right there. Did you catch it? It's incoherent. It's clumsy. How can I know about other authors? It is completely out of character. You can tell it couldn't be my own words. I'm a prisoner of these pages, I can't know those things. That's why I think there's an author out there.

But I'm ahead of myself.

Allow me to first describe the sorry events that are specially designed to make me sympathetic to you. That is badly needed, because, right now, my author is going completely the wrong way about the whole thing. He's totally derailing from the standard template. He's making me sound like an arrogant prick that is going to toy with your emotions, and nobody likes to be played—especially, knowingly—even though it's the purpose of the whole process to be played with a bit. I wish my author wouldn't have made me start this the way it did. You can bet that if I had free rein, I would have started the story straight with the sympathy bit.

What isn't clear is why my author is making me tell you all of this. Maybe he has some wicked plan in mind, or maybe he doesn't know why yet. See, as characters, our lives are all pre-planned. Every word we say, every action we take—every thought, every dream, every heartbeat, every breath—is all part of our author's grand plan. Well, I'm not so sure of that. Sometimes, I look at all that we're doing, and it just doesn't make sense. Like now. Does it make sense to you that my author would make me reveal his tricks of the trade? It's totally absurd. It's suicidal—career wise.

See, it gets to a point where you can't tell if I'm saying things I think, or things my author wants others to think I think. Or things he thinks. It's a mess. Even I myself don't know. Do I even have thoughts of my own, or am I just made to believe that I do?

I've been created on page 1, and will cease to exist just before the back-cover. Where was I before? What happens after? Your guess is as good as mine. All I know is that I'm not anxious to reach the end of the story to find out. Most likely, the whole thing will be a flop and that will be it. But I sincerely hope you'll all enjoy my story so passionately that I'll become one of those lucky characters who get to reincarnate in sequels and series.

Damn, my author better make it good.

Where the hell is this story going? Shit shit shit shit shit shit shit shit shit. This is @&$#*#$ stupid shit..........

This was seriously weird. The last sentence was printed darker and fuzzier, with its characters deeply engraved into the paper.

"It's horrible," I said, transfixed by the suitably wrinkled sheets. It would have been more enjoyable to run a potato peeler over my eyes than to read one more page of that garbage.

Again, he was slumped over the typewriter, head flat on the keys. The bottle next to him was empty—as they all had the tendency to end-up—and it wasn't due to evaporation.

"Quite so, isn't it?" he mumbled, lifting his head.

"What kind of author would do that to his protagonist?"

"Uh, maybe a drunken, unpublished slob that couldn't care less for his work, because nobody's going to read him," he offered, before starting to laugh uncontrollably.

"Aren't authors supposed to nurture their characters, protect them, love them, make them loveable?"

That just fueled more laughs.

I didn't know what to think anymore. My mind felt like the void beyond the door's threshold.

"How did you like yourself?" he eventually asked, once his hysteria subdued.

"That has nothing to do with me," I sternly objected. "This person is adamant that the Author exists."

"It could have been you."

"Absolutely not."

"Pfff. You can argue all you want, it doesn't change reality."

Reality? Our respective definitions of reality were probably as different from each other as the Small Visionary's and Cassandra's asses—and I could only imagine that to be an enormous difference.

"It's pointless to argue with me," he mumbled, putting his head back on the keys, cradling the empty bottle.

While I remained convinced that this was part of an elaborate psychological torture, an emotional part of me wanted to believe that he really was the Author—depressing as it might be that he turned out to be such a loser. In fact, if anything, his perverse flaws made the whole thing more credible. But at the same time, maybe not. If this whole circus was part of a ploy to convince me of the Author's existence, the logical expectation was that a glowing and inspired Author would have played the part. Given that this was the immediate expectation, by some twisted logic, deliberately casting the exact opposite image might have been the more effective way to convert someone like me.

In short, I was still torn.

Confused.

Regardless, I wanted to see how far they'd go—how far whoever was running this bizarre game had thought the whole thing through. Of course, I couldn't have gone anywhere else even if I had wanted to, but at that stage, I didn't feel like a prisoner. I actually wanted to know more.

I needed to know more.

"I'm king... I'm the king... It's good to be king..." he mumbled, progressively more quietly, until the numbers on the clock leaped ahead again.

Aut - 3

"Oh no, not you again," he complained, as he woke up from what clocked as a six hour siesta.

"Why are you still here?"

I shrugged.

"Damn nightmare," he mumbled, pushing himself to more or less stand straight.

"Maybe I'm here because you care for me," I volunteered as he brushed past on his way to the cabinet.

"I don't care for you."

"You don't?"

"Not one bit."

Coming from someone who claimed to be my Author, this was somewhat depressing.

"I don't give a damn," he corrected, emphasizing every word, while opening the cabinet.

"Why did you create me then?"

"I didn't."

"You didn't?"

"Are your ears full of wax?"

"Who did then?"

"My muse."

He made no sense—even though he hadn't started drinking yet. Bottle in hand, his eyes locked into mine for a brief moment, with what I could have mistaken as pity if not for his expressed disdain for me. He shook it out, and opened the bottle.

"You wouldn't understand. This is beyond your grasp."

"You probably would care if you weren't drunk all the time."

"Yeah. Sure," he replied, sneering, before dunking half the bottle. "Like I care."

"Do you care about anything?"

He paused for a moment, seemingly thinking.

"I care about what's real. And you're not."

It would have crushed me had I not been aware of the intentional cruelty of psychological torture. Still, it hurt me.

"If you don't care about what's not real, why do you bother writing?" I asked, trying to derail their devious plans, but also curious to see if the scheming madmen who had devised this ordeal had thought the whole thing through.

"The chicks."

I had no idea what small chickens had to do with this.

He looked at me, wondering why I wasn't reacting.

"The chicks!"

"What chicks?"

"The girls! The girls!" he clarified, extending his arms, as if it was obvious. "How dumb can you be?"

"And it works?" I enquired, unimpressed.

He emptied the rest of the bottle.

"For a while," he answered. "Chicks think they love authors, but actually, what they really love is successful authors. They care more about fame and fortune than about the creative process."

"Maybe what they don't like is living with a drunk," I ventured, as if a virgin like me could possibly know what women want.

He laughed, as an unmasked prankster. For a moment, it looked as if a brilliant mind lived behind the brutish manners. Had I not known any better, I could have sworn that he had lowered his guard and looked at me as if he cared. Cared for me. As if he forgot his earlier denial. Before getting a grip on himself.

"I write because I'm insane," he said, after catching his breath.

"Insane?"

"Crazy!"

"That's impossible."

"What do you mean impossible? Wake up! All artists are insane. Art is a safeguard. Take a wacko, give him a paint brush, and you get a genius. Let him express his ideas out cold, without a medium, and he'll be institutionalized. There's only a thin line between folly and genius."

"My author is nuts?"

"Sadly, yes. I'm mad as a hatter. Batty as a loon. Nutty as a fruitcake—"

"Why my story then?"

"I wanted to make a statement."

"A statement?"

"But I've given up. It's pointless. And you've been no help."

"Me? What have I got to do—"

"From now on, I'll write historical novels. About today's history. I'll be recognized as the first to have written about today's history. I'll become famous. Immortal."

He giggled.

"Is that it? You write to be remembered?"

"No, I write because my books make me master of a universe where I have absolute control over everything, where I'm omniscient and omnipotent. My creations allow me to escape real life."

He made no sense whatsoever.

"Stop talking about real life," I said. "This is real life. There's no other life."

"Forget real life. You have no life. Period. You have no reason to exist and you'll never exist."

"You're lying. Nothing's more real than this."

He just pouted, while opening a new bottle. Yet, for the first time, he took time to pour it in a glass, coming back to the typewriter.

"You're a weak character, a pointless failure. An insignificant character in an insignificant book that will never be finished. That's all," he said, slowly sipping from the glass, while sitting.

"Insignificant," I sighed, forgetting that I was a pawn in a torture game, confused, wondering which reality I believed [*In·sig·nif·i·cant. Adjective. Me. Laughable, irrelevant, unintelligent, and meaningless me. And stupid too. Poor me.*].

Possibly sensing my despair, he added: "You should be grateful. If I had not realized my mistake, the thousands of copies of you that would have been printed would have ended-up pulped."

"Pulped?"

"Yeah. Turned to pulp. That's what happens to commercial failures. Recycling. It's the natural cemetery for millions of books. Every year."

"You can't write millions of books every year."

He laughed.

"Here, have a glass. Lubricants always make reality easier to swallow."

He filled it to the rim, but I just looked at it.

"You're an insignificant character, living an insignificant life in an insignificant story, adrift in a sea of similarly insignificant books, penned by a legion of insignificant authors. These, Adam, are the cold, hard facts."

I emptied my glass, hoping the anesthetic effect of the alcohol would substitute for the mind numbing insignificance of it all.

"It makes no sense."

"I'll drink to that," he concurred, emptying his glass faster than me.

If the whole point of the torture was to make me believe that there was an Author, and only one, why had he destroyed the illusion?

"If I'm so insignificant, why bother?"

"Exactly! Have another glass."

"Wait a minute. If it's all so insignificant, what's the point of all the suffering?"

"What suffering?"

"Why do we have to suffer? Couldn't you just leave us alone, in peace?"

"You don't understand literature. It's a necessary ingredient to achieve balance and perfection."

"You call suffering perfection?"

He nodded while drinking.

"Perfection? Compared to what? How do I know it is perfection if nothing is real? Why not pink sheep, green clouds, blue cows? Wouldn't that be perfect too?"

"That wouldn't make sense."

"Why?"

"You ask too many stupid questions."

"Why is it then that—"

"Enough!" he shouted while standing up. "I don't have to explain anything to you. I do whatever I want, whenever I want. I'm the master of my fiction!"

He paced nervously, going in circles.

"What the hell... I'm wasting my time taking to a miserable, brainless hallucination," he mumbled, swinging the bottle in the air. "I'm not accountable to you. You can't comprehend—"

"What is there to comprehend?"

"That there's one perfect novel," he yelled. "The one novel that makes you want to die. The one so filled with overwhelming literary beauty that it renders you unable to suffer the world's imperfection."

He threw the bottle on the wall. It shattered, and dented the wall.

"That's what all authors dream of," he screamed.

It seemed like rage in his fiery eyes, but it could have been something else. It crossed my mind that if he were to jump at my throat like a madman, there was only one object of substantial weight around me that I could use to defend myself; was I ready to kill my Author by banging him on the head with his typewriter?

But his shoulders slumped as he seemed to calm down, a bit.

"In the end, though, it's just a dream. An unattainable dream," he said, dejected.

"And it sure isn't going to happen with all this crap," he shouted, as he threw onto the floor the piles of paper that were on his desk next to the typewriter.

He returned to the cabinet.

While he was rummaging through the bottles, I tried to assess the situation—and, more importantly, how to get out of it. Disturbing as it may, this whole story about reality and unreality seemed like a dead-end. If there was an escape from this madness—assuming it wasn't just a bad nightmare that would conveniently vanish when I would wake up in sweat—then, arguing with my Author about the meaning of it all was, at best, a confusing distraction.

I decided to play the game.

"Erase Cassandra."

"What?"

"Flex your muscles and eliminate her from my life."

"Enough!" he shouted, banging the new bottle on the desk. "You're stupid. Stop saying lines I didn't write."

"Do it."

"Stop, stop, stop, stop!" he yelled, putting his hands on his ears. "It's embarrassing."

"Do it."

"And you're destroying everything!" he yelled, smashing the bottle on the floor as he missed the desk and it slipped out of his hand.

"Do—"

"SHUT UP! You don't know anything about writing."

I stared at him, armed crossed, unintimidated.

He returned to the cabinet, stepping on the broken glass and wet square-sheep floor covering, looking for another bottle. Finding one didn't change his mood.

"As if I was to erase a villain..." he mumbled, starting to drink again, frustrated that the neck of the bottle wasn't wide enough.

His characterization of Cassandra as a villain was most fitting—there certainly was nothing adorable about her—but I was still waiting, and he noticed.

"No, no, no. It's no. You're leading me where I don't want to go. That's why the damn thing is turning into shit."

"So you're not my Author."

He sighed.

"You're such an idiot. I won't kill a character unless it serves a purpose."

"A purpose? What purpose? Who dies on purpose?"

"Whomever I decide," he replied, with contempt.

"Why?"

"Because I say so."

"Really?"

"If it serves the purpose of the story."

"The purpose?"

"Yeah, yeah, the purpose," he drilled. "It's only in real life that death serves no purpose."

"There we go again."

"That's right. I'm real, and you're not."

"I'm real."

"No. The only thing that's real about you is that you're a real pain in the ass," he said, dropping to lounge on a couch next to the cabinet, bottle snug in his arm—he wasn't about to lose grip on this one.

"I'm just as real as you."

"Hmm hmm," he nodded, drinking. "You bet."

"And stop saying that you're my Author. You're a fake. There's no such thing."

"You're delusional."

"You tried to erase me and it didn't work."

"That's the damn problem, isn't it?" he grumbled, drinking more.

"You couldn't erase me. The Author could—if there were such a thing."

"Oh, enough," he moaned, holding his forehead. "It's just a stupid temporary erasing dysfunction."

"I, and I alone, control my life. I'm the master of my destiny."

I was wearing him down. There was hope. Maybe that was the way to escape this insidious torture.

"OK, you've asked for it," he snapped, jumping up.

He pulled a sheet of paper from his desk, fed it into the typewriter, typed something on it, and handed it to me.

"Here. That's your line," he said.

"Real funny. I'm not that stupid," I replied, folding the sheet. "What now?"

"You expect me to read it aloud, and then you'll be able to claim that you're my Author because I said what you wrote."

"Read it in your head then."

I unfolded the sheet and silently read.

He had written, "I was born at the best possible place and time on earth. I'd do it all over again."

"There. That's your line," he added, laughing like a madman.

It brought him to tears of laughter.

"You are completely crazy. I would never say that."

"Exactly," he said.

Indeed, he was insane.

"Besides, one doesn't choose where to be born. What you wrote makes no sense."

"Didn't you just say that you had total control of your life and destiny? Wouldn't that include such an important, life-changing decision?"

I flipped the sheet and noticed that he had typed his sentence on the back of a handwritten page. The handwritten text was a list of jumbled sentences strung together without punctuation, spitting out nonsense like: "Fanatiks kill squirrels with sling-shots Cassandra's mother sleeps with the Visionary Her father does too Woodruff Oak likes to sodomize goats Drop an atomic bomb on Cimmerian county Time is an irrelevant and useless concept The Visionary is myopic presbyopic astigmatic and a pervert The randomness of life can't be captured in a book The damn bastard has no clue The Magistrate has no underpants."

"What's that?" I asked, handing him the page.

He glanced at it without taking it, wobbling as he was now getting seriously blasted.

"Irrelevant scribblings. Stuff that crossed my mind... that I haven't figured out how to use. It's going into the garbage can, anyhow—where you also belong."

"Really?"

"All the pages you see here," he declared, waving his arm at the room, "I'll soak them in cooking oil, dump them in the fireplace, and light them up. I'll roast marshmallows over the embers while enjoying a bottle of wine."

"You would."

"Oh yeah. The whole thing. Erased. Especially you. You're a horrible character."

"You make no sense. A mother wouldn't kill her flawed child, so why would an Author—if there ever was one—want to destroy his creation."

"Because a mother doesn't have to deal with critics."

"With what?"

"There used to be good ones. Educated ones. Folks that recognized the value of ideas, respected the labor, appreciated the stakes. And read all the words! Elitists, maybe, but fair. But, now? Oh, there's a few left. But, mostly, it's a free for all. Every retard who has an opinion—or an axe to grind—rushes to plaster it all over the place, left and right, as if repetition could replace introspection. More pit bulls than critics, they rave about stories glorifying pointless lives reported from the point-of-view of dim-wits and losers; they are frustrated voyeurs who splurge on trivial novellas and banalities because it makes their boring life seem more attractive. They're the kind of assholes who feel compelled to inform a mother that, in their opinion, her kid is downright ugly. They are the duckling—never to be swans—that confidently advise the eagles that their flight patterns need improvement."

I had no idea who he was insulting at that moment, but his drunkenness probably distorted his reality.

"Well, if you're the Author, and you think I'm a horrible failure, just make me a better character then."

"What do you think I tried to do?" he shouted exasperated. "I wanted a truly heroic character. A flawless protagonist, with an acute mind, sound logic, and flawless values. One that would overshadow all of the bumbling, hapless protagonists that insignificantly drift along as life happens. One whose radiating strength, substantial qualities, and audacious goals would inspire, instead of those pointless bozos that entertain by virtue of their moronic behavior. One that would buck the trends and show that, beyond the heap of literary fast-food, crap, and fads that sells millions, there are still stories worth telling.

"But I failed. I failed miserably."

"How do you know? Is the story over?"

"It has nowhere to go from here. There's no point restarting the damn thing. You've ruined it, Adam. You've single handedly destroyed your universe. There's nothing to go back to. You have ruined everything. You're like acid rain, like global warning, like Armageddon. You're off-formula. The critics will shred the damn thing now."

If all this nonsense was true, then the end of the story would mean my end too. The thought of my life ending in a jail decorated to resemble somebody's fantasy of the Author's den chilled me.

"It can't be. A story never ends."

"You think so? What happens next, then?"

"It's ridiculous. I'm not playing this game."

"Go on. Try."

I remained silent.

He walked back to the cabinet, but rather than taking another bottle—as I expected—he pulled a gun. A kind I had never seen before.

"How's that for motivation?" he said, pointing it at my face. "What happens next?"

I stood frozen.

"Come on. What happens next?" he insisted, waving the gun.

"I don't know."

"Exactly! It's a logical dead end. There's no escape, is there?"

I had to think of something.

"How about freeing me, erasing Cassandra, and letting me marry the woman I love?"

"You suck worse as a writer than as a character."

He lifted his arm a bit and fired the gun. Plaster fell from the ceiling.

I now knew that the damn thing was loaded. It didn't help.

"It makes no sense. There's no purpose, no motivation, no story there," he argued.

He lowered the gun and walked back to the couch, looking dejected.

"Damn, Adam," he added, sitting on the couch. He leaned back and extended his arms along the top of the sofa. "You suffer from low imagination. But that's normal, you're just a character. I'm the author."

"Give me my freedom back!" I ordered, in panic.

"Can't do it. That would be a breach of story arc."

"You're the one who took it away. Give it back to me," I said, as if recognizing that he was the Author.

"Damn it, Adam! Stop moaning," he shouted, jumping up from the couch, rushing toward me, pointing the gun at my head.

It crossed my mind that the only thing scarier than a gun pointed at one's head was probably the same gun in the hand of a drunken, raging lunatic, pointed at one's head.

"How about finishing the story, sitting at the nice black metal box here, calmly?"

He threw his arms up, agitated.

"Didn't you listen to anything I said?"

"I did. I did."

"We're past the point of no return. I can't write it up. Characters have a character of their own—a mind of their own. Past a certain point, I can't control the story. It takes on a life of its own. It dictates its own terms. It needs to go where it goes. It's like steering an ocean liner. You can't turn it on a dime. It's set in its course. The conflict, the fall, are inescapable. The ball is in your court, Adam, but you have no imagination. You—and you alone—killed the story. So, you have no more reason to exist."

He pointed the gun at me and shot three bullets. Three horrific bangs that made my heart stop. By reflex, my hands grabbed my stomach, where the first bullet penetrated.

Something was seriously wrong.

He stood in front of me, motionless, waiting.

There I was.

Silent.

Crouched.

But I felt no pain.

There was no blood.

Right behind me, there were three holes in the wall.

Straight lines from the gun to those holes had intersected me. The trajectories were unquestionable.

Yet, I was unhurt.

This was unreal.

"Of course," he said, chuckling and walking away. "That's what I thought," he added, slouching back on the couch.

I should have died right there.

The three bullet holes were right behind my back, and could have only been created by passing through my stomach.

Either that, or it was a stunning magic trick. Or maybe a horrible hallucination, triggered by what hit me on the head during the trial. The hit that started it all.

I reminded myself that there is no Author—that I had been right all along. Or maybe not.

I was totally confused.

"That's it, Adam. I'm done arguing with you."

"I'm not saying anything—"

"It's the end of the line. In spite of one's best efforts, there's a time in life when a failure must be recognized for what it is."

"You could write another story—"

"It's my life I'm talking about. My entire shitty life that is a failure."

He made no sense. He looked tired and dejected. I noticed pills on the floor next to the couch.

"There's a point in this entire enterprise where the character must take over the story and dictate to the author how it's supposed to unfold. That's kind of extreme, but that's where we are now."

"I'm sure you could finish—"

"I'm done arguing with you," he sighed, resting the gun barrel against his temple.

"Don't do anything foolish."

"Or what? Or what?" he shouted.

I had no answer.

"That's right. Don't threaten your author. Don't be a dumb critic. The author's always right."

I had no idea how to deter someone with suicidal tendencies.

"You can't leave me now," is the best I could think of, which in hindsight, was quite lame.

"Here's the sales pitch, Adam. You're stuck in your story. Here's what you need to finish it up..."

I saw him pull the trigger.

I saw the smoke.

I saw his head move away from the gun.

I saw the opposite side of his head explode, brain splattered on the wall.

I saw him gasp.

I would not have known before how long it takes to die from that kind of injury, but now I knew: it's about a few gasps long. His short, suffering, convulsive efforts to breathe, are the last images I remember from our encounter.

From the silent darkness rose the barely perceptible echo of gunshots—three bangs, a pause, then again—endlessly repeating, in a loop, a little bit louder each time, until it grew into a deafening noise.

Then, silence anew, for a second, before I screamed.

Dungeon Again

"AAAAARGH!"

I was curled up on the dungeon floor, in a pool of blood, grabbing my abdomen in a futile attempt to dull the pain.

"What? What?" shouted the torturer, snapping out of his slumber. He struggled to free himself from the alcove where he had jammed himself to snooze—for the lack of pillows—bumping his head a few times while rubbing his eyes.

He kneeled next to me.

"What's going on?"

As he pulled my hand to take a look at the wounds, blood gushed from my side, soaking him.

"Hold tight," he said, pushing my hand back in place, and jumping to the door.

"Help! He's bleeding to death! Somebody, help!" he yelled repeatedly, turning around every now and then to tell me: "Don't die. You're not allowed to die. Not without proper torture first."

It was cold.

I could hear the heavy rain outside and the distinct splash of water pouring inside the cell from a window that more than ever looked like a gutter. I was going to die in a miserable, humid cell that smelled and felt like a sewer [*Sew·er. Noun. Conduit for the sum total of human accomplishments; flow of progress canalized to a depressing destination where all is diluted in a greater void*].

"Don't die," kept ordering the torturer. "Not yet."

Somebody eventually showed up, but the words were blurred, the events fuzzy, and all I remember is waking up in a dirty room, drowsy and weak. The agony of what had felt like a hacksaw blade wiggled through my side had vanished, replaced instead by a sharp but more manageable pain from what felt like dog bites—like fangs that wouldn't release their grip, piercing my skin. It came from where I was sewn with rather coarse thread. At three places. Three little plugs of bunched up skin that seemed to be where the Author's bullets had gone through me earlier.

I tried to stand up but found myself chained to the bed.

"Hello? Anybody here?" I called.

Nobody.

"Anybody here?" I shouted, repeatedly, almost every minute.

Someone finally showed up, hours later. He looked like a doctor.

"Coming to check if I'm dead?" I said, refraining from adding, "You'll know I've been dead for weeks when I'll smell like the Small Visionary."

He didn't even reply.

"Do we get more attention if we piss on the walls?"

"You're not the only one in this world, you know. I have other patients to see."

"Apparently not all in this village," I retorted, which is not a wise thing to do when you are chained to a bed.

He vigorously poked my wounds.

"Aaaaaaaargh!"

"Yes, it's still sensitive," he diagnosed with evident pleasure. "A few leeches are in order. It will do wonders," he added, pulling out a bucket full of them.

"What happened?"

"According to your medical records, you got hit on the head by a rock, and fell unconscious for a while," he said, dropping a few leeches near the wounds.

"Rocks haven't punched those holes."

"Correct."

Five more leeches on my belly.

"So?"

"And then you woke up. With three holes."

More leeches on my legs.

"So how did that happen?"

"You tell me."

More leeches everywhere.

"How many of those buggers do you plan to use?"

"Exactly forty-eight."

"Didn't I lose enough blood already? Are you trying to suck me dry?"

"No. There are much faster ways to drain all the blood out if that's what you're insinuating. Those are needed, for your recovery. They help spread the pain across your entire body, freeing your damaged local organs of the stress of focalized pain and giving them a chance to heal," he added, sharing the brilliance of modern medical wisdom—doing so with as much maleficent pleasure as a janitor leaving his own finger prints on a polished door handle.

"You've sustained severe internal injuries," he clarified, as if the pain alone wasn't a reminder every second.

He put the last one on my head, on the big bump where the rock hit. That one was particularly painful—as if I could feel the slug's little jaw boring through my skull, lusting for the feast of my brain.

"Try to rest," he said, leaving, with a smirk.

Sure.

Covered by active drilling rigs.

Who wouldn't?

Besides, how could I rest after what had happened? I felt as if I was stuck in the ugly jar where all the lost puzzle pieces get dumped, in the futile hope that they'll be returned to their rightful box someday, but knowing fully well it will never happen.

Nothing made sense anymore.

Everything defied logic.

It had to be a dream. The whole thing was just a horrible nightmare from which I would wake up.

It couldn't wait. I had to wake up now. I slapped myself repeatedly.

"Wake up! Wake up! Wake up! Wake up! Wake up! Wake up! Wake up! Wake up! Wake up! Wake up! Wake up! Wake up! Wake up! Wake up!"

To no avail.

Nothing changed—except that I ended up with swollen cheeks.

I had to get a grip. Regain control of my thoughts. Figure out what was real, and what wasn't. Devious and malevolent forces were trying to break me down—be it through psychological torture or other means—and I couldn't let them win. I couldn't let them play with my mind as if it was a lousy sponge only good enough to suck-up arsenic spills.

Scarily though, even though those forces hadn't won the war yet, they were piling up battle victories fast, because I was utterly confused. All events were in contradiction with themselves: treatments to heal me so that I could be better tortured and killed; bullets traveling though my body like air, leaving me unscathed, only to wake up bleeding to death from delayed injuries; an elaborate set-up fabricated to convince me of the Author's existence, only to see him blow his brain out.

What was the point of all of this?

Not to mention that if the Author was really dead, life as we know it should have stopped. There would be no here and now.

But I was alive. In bad shape, but alive.

Yet I saw the Author die.

Definitely.

Unless someone found a way to scrape his splatted brain bits from the wall, shove them back into his skull, reconnect the whole thing, seal his cranium, and turn his life switch back on, he was dead as a doorknob and not coming back. The guy could have drunk himself into a coma and I would not have been surprised to see him snap out of it. But we're talking bullets here, not booze.

I was a witness.

The Author was dead.

The sound of it was eerie.

I kept repeating it.

"My Author is dead."

"My Author is dead."

"My Author is dead."

"My Author is dead."

Yet, here I was, hurt, feeling, thinking—alive.

If all of my being and all of my thoughts depended on my Author, why was I still there? Where were all those thoughts coming from?

It had to be from me because the Author was dead. There was no Author.

There had never been an Author, and Grandpa had always been right.

Grandpa.

Grandpa?

Where was Grandpa?

"Where is Grandpa? Where is my Grandpa?" I shouted, screaming for assistance.

I had seen him being hit. I had seen him fall. He had been injured. He needed help and I couldn't trust anyone.

I screamed, louder and louder: "Where's Grandpa?"

Nobody came.

Nobody replied.

Grandpa had been right all along. There was no Author. There couldn't be any other possible way.

That had to be it.

The suicidal drunk was not the Author but rather some actor or magician hired to fool me. Everything had been staged.

All of it.

Had to be.

But, at the same time, if that was the case, why would the Small Visionary create such an elaborate plan to disprove the existence of the Author? Was it a subterfuge to make me proclaim in public that there is no Author, to set me up to publicly commit, by such an admission, the worst possible crime, and justify a death penalty—and the harshest tortures as due punishment before being erased once and for all. Or was it all a brilliant plan to deceive me that took a wrong turn when the hired actor went off-script and blew his *own* mind, to his employer's surprise?

I wished I could get back to that room, take the body's pulse, lift the square-sheep floor, punch through the walls, search for clues, deconstruct the scene, reveal the trickery; but all the evidence was gone. Wherever it was, I couldn't go back.

I was past a point of no return.

"Grandpa?" I screamed my lungs out. "Where is Grandpa? Where is my Grandpa?"

The doctor eventually came back, visibly upset.

"Shut-up. You're disturbing the leeches. You're compromising your treatment."

"I want to see my Grandpa."

"You'll see him later."

"Where is he?"

"He is back home."

As I was caught in the claws of the Small Visionary, I would never be able to get back home.

"Tell him to come see me now."

"That won't be possible."

"He's hurt?"

"No. He's dead."

"What? You said he was back home."

"Yes. His ashes are there."

"Ashes?"

"You have been unconscious in the infirmary for a while."

"You killed him!"

"Show some respect."

"You killed him!"

"He has been treated by the most capable and competent doctors."

"Liars! You did nothing to save him."

"We went as high as 2000 leaches and it didn't cure him. Nothing more could be done."

I wailed.

I shook the bed, pulled on my chains, twisted and bounced, attempting to free myself.

He lied. I was sure that they all lied. A hardened rebel like Grandpa—the only person in the world who understood me—couldn't have been killed. Not so easily.

The Author was dead, but not Grandpa.

To control me, they piled up the leeches until there wasn't enough blood left in me to boil. I was becoming so weak that my rage was bottled-up as life's energy left me. But my anger never died; it was just subdued.

Through some twist of logic, the doctor convinced my mother to bring Grandpa's urn, to show me, as if actually seeing the ashes would help me come to grip with the facts and put me at peace. I was too weak to even twitch.

I had to surrender.

I saw the facts, but there would be no peace.

Ever.

Grandpa had been turned into dust by the most despicable individuals in the entire world.

I would never forget.

I would never forgive.

I would never ever want to live with Authorians.

From there on, I would forever be an orphan, an outcast, and an expatriate.

The only problem was that I could also be dead, because I was still at their mercy.

The End - For Some

As soon as I was deemed "sufficiently patched up to stand trial," I was returned to the courtroom.

Same circus, same clowns.

Except that the mood had shifted.

First, I was in a daze, completely numb, depressed that I had lost the one and only ally that was fighting with me—for me. I looked for him in the stands, hoping to find him at the end of the last row, or anywhere else, waving at me, smiling, shouting that it had all been lies, that he was alive and well and ready to rumble, but he was not there anymore. I couldn't accept it. It killed me. I had been told that his ashes were home, but knowing my mother, she most likely had treated the urn like a bucket of dust, shoving it in a corner of the shed to forever forget about him, or—worse—emptying it into the compost pile, to bury him in the manner she thought he deserved. She had won her war against him; even though I had always known that she would in the end—because she had time on her side—it hurt no less. I felt as if I had swallowed embers while sitting in a nest of scorpions.

Second, I had exhausted everybody's patience and it was time for a verdict—which actually meant sentencing, after a verdict of circumstances. Flights of lyricism and fancy allegories by my sharp public defender wouldn't make a difference. He could have tried to serenade the magistrate with a song of hiccups, without a single coherent word, dressed as a one-man band, and the results would have been the same. The mob wanted blood and nothing less; wagers were made on the type of torture that would be used to put an end to my misery—or rather put misery into my end.

How many days had passed before the trial resumed, I didn't know. All I knew was that the magistrate was in a particularly bad mood. It didn't matter that there was nothing in my village to entertain visitors—besides the trial—because Reinhardt would not have stayed there anyhow, in toga and hood, idle all that time. So he had to go away until I was deemed fit enough for the trial to resume—a major inconvenience, as my public defender told me that magistrates are remunerated a fixed fee per execution, which he probably meant to say, per trial.

Thus, as much as Magistrate Reinhardt wanted to turn the boring proceedings into a spectacle to reward those who traveled from long and far to be entertained—if only to uphold his reputation—he was more eager to expedite the matter and move on to his other appointments. This was not necessarily a bad thing, since, had he been paid by the hour, I'm sure he could have turned my trial into a cash cow and milked it into retirement *[Re·tire·ment. Noun. State of exalted happiness one lapses into, sometimes to the greatest relief of the survivors in the trail of damage left behind]*.

"Today, we are resuming this trial from the exact point at which it was disturbed. I will ask the audience to behave with all due protocols and deference to the court, as we wish to conclude all legal transactions related to this case today. Today! Therefore, if anyone violates this directive—even if only a single person—I will conclude the trial in-camera."

People looked at each other, puzzled.

"That means I will kick all your asses out of the courtroom and conclude the trial without an audience."

The mere thought of being deprived from witnessing the climax sent shivers down the backs of those in the room.

The silence was absolute.

Reinhardt enjoyed the moment, realizing that it further bolstered his legendary toughness. Pleased with the effect, he resumed the trial.

"Does the defense have anything else to say?"

"No, your honor," replied my public defender.

I was stunned, but not totally surprised. The whole affair had taken a huge toll on his reputation; he was dying to end the ordeal and return to his regular practice, working with thieves, rapists, murderers, and other normal criminals—all in all, a more comfortable and orderly life.

"Closing statements?" sighed Magistrate Reinhardt.

"Oh. Yes, yes. I'll be brief," he replied, standing up. "Dear Magistrate, Mr. Adam Chad Kilroy's actions may be reprehensible, ill-advised, and, yes, foolish and somewhat subversive, but it is important to understand that the recent extraordinary events that have perturbed our peaceful life have stressed many, and that such stress can more severely impact someone of frail constitution and feeble mind. I therefore beg that the court takes these facts into consideration in reaching its verdict and, in the unfortunate event that it should find Mr. Kilroy guilty, that it would exercise leniency in dispatching its sentence."

"What kind of a ridiculous closing statement is that?" I snapped, as he sat down—as if Grandpa had given me a kick in the butt in an attempt to wake me from my torpor.

"Order!" said Magistrate Reinhardt, menacing. "Control your client."

"Yes, Magistrate."

"Shut up," he whispered. "I've just pleaded to spare you from the most painful tortures. You should be grateful."

I returned to my torpor. It would apparently take more than one spirited kick to ignite me.

"OK then," summed up Reinhardt. "On to the verdict. I won't call recess to deliberate, as all the delays in this case have already given me plenty of time to deliberate. It is crystal clear that the defendant is guilty of all charges brought against him."

"See I told you," whispered my public defender, as if I should have been impressed that he had correctly predicted what was more a self-fulfilling prophecy than a prediction.

Reinhardt shuffled his papers, searching for something.

"Does the defendant or his family own any vouchers for partial remission of temporal punishment that it wishes to apply to this sentence?"

The public defender turned towards me, and whispered: "Have you made any such purchases from the Small Visionary or his duly authorized representatives?"

"What's that?"

"It's sort of a bond that you can purchase and redeem later, to receive partial forgiveness, when you get in trouble. Like, right now, it would be really handy if you had a bundle of those."

"Ah."

"So, do you have any?"

Cassandra's parents probably had their mattress stuffed with such vouchers, signed and sealed in exchange for money or other favors, but I sure had none. And if my parents had any, they weren't about to waste them on me.

"Can I buy them now?"

"No, you can only buy them when you have a clean record. It's too late now."

"Then, I don't have any."

"You should always buy those. They're as good as gold," he replied. "It could have saved yourself lots of pain and spilled blood."

He sounded like a salesman getting a commission on every sale.

"Any purchases on record then?" asked Reinhardt.

"No. None, Magistrate."

"Too bad for you," he declared. "Not bad for me," he mumbled.

He shuffled a few more papers.

"Where's the court-appointed doctor?"

"Here, sir," said the man, standing up.

"Is the accused medically fit to be disciplined?"

"The patient was treated with 48 leeches, and responded excellently. It is my expert opinion that he is indeed fit to receive your verdict."

I didn't feel fit at all, but who was I to disagree with an expert imbued by such an effective knowledge of medicine and such impressive wisdom?

Not at a loss for theatrical effects, the magistrate stood up, raised both arms on his side, toga hanging to fill the largest possible space on the podium, and proceeded with the crowd-pleasing climax.

"Now, the thorny issue at hand is determining due sentence for Mr. Kilroy's revolting actions."

I could see the excitement in the crowd. I'm sure each drooling fool had his favorite torture and secretly dreamt—in orgasmic detail—of executing it himself.

All faces, distorted in tense anticipation, hung on Reinhardt's every word.

"In spite of my decades of experience in serving justice, I am challenged to think of a torture so extremely painful that it would match the severity of the heresy perpetrated by the guilty party. In such a situation, I must ask myself: What would the Author do?

How would the Author squash the worm that has violated his rules? How would the Author erase—"

That was it. Enough was enough. Grandpa wasn't dead. His ashes might have been blown away like sawdust by my mother, but I heard him loud and clear, screaming in my ears to make him proud and fight like a man.

"The Author wouldn't do a thing!" I shouted.

The audience's roar was kept in check, as all remembered the magistrate's stern warning that he would kick everybody out at the first sign of disturbance. The hundreds of gasps of surprise remained silent. Not a single squeak was heard—as if even ants had put on slippers to muffle their tickety-tack on the walls. Everybody was shocked; nobody wanted to be evicted from the courtroom and miss the grand finale.

The magistrate lowered his arms, leaned forward as far as he could over the bench, and extended a menacing finger towards me. Although I couldn't see his face, the large folds on his hood at the level of his forehead shouted his anger.

"Stop your blasphemy right now!"

"I have met the Author, and he is dead!"

The audience gasped.

Reinhardt pulled back and slammed both hands on the bench. The piled-up doors that served as bench cracked loudly and remained bent.

He pointed at my public defender and barked: "You should have warned your client!"

The public defender moped, unable to speak, as if his career was over.

The magistrate's attention returned to me. With the same animosity, he said: "Mr. Kilroy, claiming to have met the Author is a serious matter. I warn you that if you make such a pretension with hope of avoiding your due punishment, you are seriously misguided."

He waved his finger for a while, then seemed to stop breathing for a moment, fighting to contain himself. He then clutched the edges of the broken doors, fuming, taking a few slow breaths.

"There's a rule.... I am bound by duty... With great displeasure..."

He took a few deep breaths.

"In front of all witnesses here, I am required to immediately ask you to provide indisputable proof of your claim."

I was unaware of that rule, but I could tell that he would have been pleased to disregard it outright and just order my execution. I later learned from my public defender that this would likely have been the case if not for the fact that so many witnesses had heard my claim. On such matters, the magistrate's hands were tied; he was bound by the Rules to offer me the opportunity to substantiate my claims. In the stands, all the witnesses to whom I owed this reprieve were holding their breath.

"Should you fail to convince all of those assembled around you who have heard your allegation that such a meeting has truthfully taken place, all prior proceedings will become moot and you will be sentenced to torture—not to one specific, but to all the tortures known to mankind. You will suffer a thousand painful tortures and death, starting without any delays."

I used to think that there was nothing worse than discovering the existence of a rule by breaking it, but now I was realizing that there was something worse: having to convince everybody that you haven't in fact broken the rule, without any tangible proof to offer in your defense. How could I convince the lynch mob about to explode in the room, that I had met the Author? How could I prove something so intrinsically improvable as having met a person that I couldn't prove exists—and that was dead to boot?

There, on the spot, I had no idea what could be done to save my skin. Frankly, in spite of all that had happened, I still didn't believe in the Author and still suspected having been played like a kid, with magic tricks brilliantly executed for sure. Yet, there was something deviously perfidious in having me use these deceiving staged encounters to justify my right to live. Only truly twisted minds could have conceived such an insane conundrum, and my destiny was now in the hands of those twisted minds. It was becoming imminently clear that I was going to be dislocated, crushed, punctured, filled, and burned, all at the same time—and maybe also hanged and peed on by a dog while at it.

"Please, someone, go and get the torturer," said the magistrate. "We will need him to display his art at once."

I replayed in my head all my conversations with the Author, looking for something tangible I could use as indisputable evidence that something that doesn't exist does exist; that something that never happened did happen. Even a convincing lie would do. I was ready to trade my life for any convenient fib or enormous fabrication that would do the trick.

"Fine. Mr. Kilroy, it is pretty clear that you won't—"

"I got it!"

A spark! I remembered a gem. I took a gamble.

"You do not have underpants."

"What?"

"What I mean, Mr. Magistrate, with all due respect, is that you are naked under your toga."

"What does it have to do with—"

"It's the Author who told me. Before dying."

He was speechless.

Stunned.

Could it be?

The long silence was telling.

I had hit the jackpot.

I had to press.

"Who else but the Author would know that, since nobody can see through your toga? That, Mr. Magistrate, is my indisputable proof. Now, it should be very easy for you to prove me wrong, make me the butt of the joke, and throw me out of this court, with a kick in the butt."

Mumbles in the crowd.

The collective fear of Reinhardt was vanishing fast.

I turned to face the audience.

"And since the rule requires me to convince all of those assembled around here and who have heard my allegation that such a meeting has truthfully taken place, I urge Magistrate Reinhardt to provide you with the proof you rightly deserve."

"Is this true?" shouted someone.

"Come on, Magistrate, prove him wrong," added another.

"Yeah, show us."

Everyone added to the cacophony, as it became clear that order couldn't be restored by a magistrate whose credibility hinged on him revealing his privates—be they covered or not by underpants.

Reinhardt turned around, thinking for a good minute, shoulders slowly heaving up and down with each deep breath of contained rage, like water about to boil. He then turned back, facing us, with fire in his eyes, grabbing the edge of the bench with both extended arms.

It was pandemonium, and he was powerless.

"Aaaargh!" he yelled, flipping the bench down into the first rows.

Silence.

"This can't be," whispered one.

"I'll be damned," replied another.

"Show us your ass," yelled one, followed by a roar of insults.

Unbelievably, the crowd jeered Reinhardt off the stage.

With my public defender moping as if his career was over, a magistrate that left in a fury with his aura of respectability shattered, an overexcited mob that ended the trial in a ruckus, and a bunch of intrepid Fanatiks who caught up with the magistrate and disrobed him in public to reveal the naked truth, I expected the guards to see no other option than to free me. Instead, they brought me back to the dungeon.

The problem with breaking a rule you didn't know existed is not so much not knowing that it existed in the first place, but rather not understanding all that it triggers in its complex ramifications. As I was about to learn, the trial was far from over.

The Kritikillar

Few commoners can claim to have had the pleasure of meeting the Kritikillar, because there is usually no pleasure in meeting an irascible old man that you only face when your life hangs on a thread. The Kritikillar looked like an obese chipmunk that had fit four peanuts in his cheek pouches and still managed to purse its lips. That ugly mug wasn't pleased to be there.

I learned that the Rules made it his duty to personally investigate all major Apologal Transgressions—those being the sacrilegious behaviors deemed to offend the precepts of narrative history upheld by the Rules book (the very same book in which I saw nothing but blank pages). Claims of having met the Author—be it in dreams, in ghostly apparitions, or, worse, in person—ranked as the top Transgression in the list; this mandated that the Kritikillar drop everything in the capital and travel at once to our village of morons, which explained his irritation.

He couldn't care less about whether or not the magistrate had underpants, but he sure would have preferred that "the damn fool" did, and that I'd been promptly tortured and obliterated. Instead, he had to waste his precious time in a remote cesspit devoid of the comforts and luxuries to which he was accustomed in the capital—and felt entitled to. In other words, I didn't expect him to flash a smile at any time during our conversation. More likely, if I ever was to see his teeth, it would be because they'd be biting my leg.

"So you have met the Author?" he growled, standing in the cold and damp dungeon I had called home for too long already. He was facing me, with the Small Visionary on his side like a well-trained puppy and Fanatiks holding my arms to keep me on my knees.

I didn't reply, as it seemed to be partly a rhetorical question and partly a sigh tainted with reproach and displeasure.

"Or did you just say that to gain time and delay your sentence, thinking it was a smart thing to do—which is why people usually do it, and which is a really, really, really stupid thing to do?"

I wondered why avoiding immediate erasure was a dumb thing to do, but did not press, as I dreaded the answer.

"Because for each day you think you've extended your life, we'll add two extra days of excruciating torture, for good measure, before erasing you."

Just as I had feared.

"Now, should you immediately admit to having lied—or maybe, let's say, admit to having mistaken wishes and reality, which is an understandable confusion when facing a horrible end—for your repentance, we could cut those extra days in half, dispatch the matter, and leave it at that."

I remained silent. Given that the Kritikillar had arrived a day after the telegram that had informed him of my Apologal Transgression, his stingy clemency offer still left me with an extra 24 hours of sheer agony to suffer—give or take a few. The thought of haggling for greater mercy was absurd, and likely futile.

"So what do you say," he pressed.

There wasn't much to lose.

"I have met the Author."

"Here we go," he said, rolling his eyes, looking at the Small Visionary. "So you've seen him, then?"

"I have not seen him. I've met him."

"Oh, I see," he hammed. "And how is he doing nowadays?"

"Actually, he's dead."

The Fanatiks gasped and the Small Visionary clenched his teeth, expecting that the Kritikillar would jump on me like a rabid wolf. Surprisingly, he wasn't shocked, and he didn't bite; rather, he started laughing. A forced laugh that stopped abruptly to resume the inquisition, not amused one bit.

"If the author is dead, how do you explain that we are all here? The situation, our actions, everything around you? How do you explain the fact that *you* are still talking?"

"I don't know."

"Of course you don't," he replied, turning around, pacing across the room and lecturing at the same time. "It's one thing to think you are a free spirit, and quite another to be logical. You don't know, and you never bothered to stop to think about it. Why should you? You might reach conclusions that contradict your feeble ideals."

He came back, leaned forward close to my face, and pointed his finger at my forehead; his breath suggested a diet based on garlic and rotten eggs.

"The reason you don't know is because the Author is not dead. It's that simple. The Author is eternal. If part of him dies, a replacing part grows. If all of him dies, he fully replaces himself and the rejuvenated Author resumes the work right where it stopped momentarily. All that is because the Story is eternal. Eternal! It transcends the Author. Eternity is continuity. There is no end. The Author never dies. He morphs. Constantly. That, poor fool, is why you are wrong."

"I thought you were here to investigate the facts."

He violently pushed me away, the Fanatiks almost losing their grip.

"It's the truth that matters, and the truth is that to honor the Author, you must follow the Rules, and never doubt the truth. These are the facts!"

"The facts are that I've met the Author, and he's dead as a doornail," I shouted.

"I don't care about your facts. I see worms like you all the time. It used to be once a month; now, it's like once a week. They all claim to have met the Author, all claim to have indisputable proof."

As an aside to the Small Visionary, he added: "Just last week, one of these idiots told me that the Author was a woman. A woman! Apparently because of a vision in a dream about only women having the power to create. A dream! He would have done better to dream about his mother castrating him; given what I did to him, that would have been a more successful premonition."

He didn't wait for the Small Visionary's reaction to his dumb joke and returned his attention to me.

"Just like you," he told me, "that fool, and all the others before him, had nothing better to offer than words, dreams, and fantasies, but no evidence. No proof. Only words."

"I have proof."

"What proof?"

"The Author told me that the magistrate had no underpants."

"So?"

"How else would I know?"

"Lots of people know that. It's not the first time that this imbecile gets caught. Every Small Visionary had been warned to keep an eye on that sick bastard. The only thing this proves is that some Visionaries can't keep their mouth shut."

The Small Visionary blushed, unjustly accused and lacking the moral authority to defend himself.

Or maybe he blushed because he never wore underpants either—who knew what kind of fashionable craze excited bullies across the Dominion?

I remained silent.

"Just like the others," he sneered. "Nothing of substance to offer. It didn't even take a good whacking to shut you down. Others were tougher. Anyhow. It doesn't matter, you'll be erased all the same, off to oblivion, and all will be back in order."

"You're only an old crock, full of yourself. How can you be so dumb and so arrogant at the same time?" is what I really wanted to say, but didn't.

"You've judged me guilty before even getting here, and there's nothing I could ever say that would convince you otherwise."

"Young man, do not dare question my impartiality," he replied, as if worried that the Fanatiks that were holding my arms could question it too and spread the news that I had been unjustly treated. It's one thing to matter-of-factly erase inconvenient iconoclasts, but it's another to deprive people of due process, because that would imply that any rule-abiding Fanatik could accidentally fall into the claws of an unjust Kritikillar who could then arbitrarily dispense sentences without bothering to seek the truth.

The Kritikillar softened his resolve.

"Tell me then, since you've met the Author, what you know about him. Something that only someone who's met him could know."

This was awkward, since I was still mostly convinced that I had been fooled by some combination of magic tricks and psychological torture—and that there was, therefore, no Author—but with my life hanging on a tread, this wasn't the time to argue such fine points. If, to save my life, I had been asked to prove that there is a fat guy in a red suit flying a sleigh in the sky and plunging down chimneys once a year to distribute gifts to children worldwide, I would have been ready to mime it and play accompanying festive music at the same time. The problem was that my presumed encounter with the Author hadn't been insightful enough to provide me with any enlightening revelation worth sharing.

"Go ahead, surprise me," he taunted.

I said the only thing that came to mind.

"He was drunk all the time."

His empty look and silence suggested I succeeded.

"Drunk like a skunk. Collapsed on the floor," I added.

I was betting my life on whether or not the Kritikillar would believe that the Author could be a stinking drunk. I wished I could have come up with something better, more tangible, more glorifying—some revelation that would have tickled him pink.

The Kritikillar was silent for a moment, stunned by the enormity of it all.

"Why would the Author be drunk?" he asked, perplexed.

"He looked confused. He said he had lost interest in his characters."

"This doesn't make sense," he mumbled, still puzzled by the revelation. "If the Author had lost interest in his characters, the Story would have ended right there. It would all have stopped. We wouldn't be here."

He ruminated over this for a moment, silent.

"It's absurd! You're a Kafkaist!" he shouted, snapping out of his daze.

The Fanatiks tightened their grip, in terror.

"Only Kafkaists can so absurdly deface the Author."

"I'm not a—"

"The Author is perfect. He has created everything. He has created us. A drunk is unable to create."

Admittedly, he had a point, as I myself couldn't conceive how alcohol could lubricate someone's creative gears.

"I'm sure—"

"No, no, no. Enough profanities. You're wrong."

"How?" I replied, as I expected being unable to say more than a single word before being interrupted.

"How? How?" he shouted, shaking his head in disbelief. "How can you know so little? I'm the Kritikillar! I have lived many lives. Many. I have even been the protagonist in some of those prior lives. Over and over, I have seen how the Author operates. His protagonists are heroes: virtuous, sublime characters. Heroes! Not immature imbeciles who couldn't come up with a credible lie even if their life depended on it."

He looked as if he was about to literally spit on me.

"It's unprovable," I added, hoping to plant doubts in the minds of the Fanatiks, as it seemed to be the only thing the Kritikillar feared. "What if I said that I, too, have lived prior lives?"

"It would be a lie. One more lie by a heretic. One more lie by a Kafkaist. That's not worth a thing."

"How about my wounds?"

"What about them?"

"I woke up bleeding from three bullet holes. How do you think that happened?"

"Ah, yes, the apprentice who shared your cell told us all about that."

"There," I said, showing my stitches.

"Quite impressive. It's not every day that an apprentice creates new techniques. It was quite imaginative. Piercing through your entire body, only using his fingernails. Who would have thought? It was most appropriate to give him his torturer credentials without delay; an artistic genius shouldn't be bothered with stupid professional exams. You're quite lucky that he'll be the one torturing you in the end."

"Fingernails? What are you talking about? It's ludicrous. These are from gun shots."

"No, he had no gun."

"Not the apprentice! The Author! The Author shot me!"

"The Author."

"Yes! He did that to me. He shot me three times. I had bleeding bullet holes."

"Now that's original!" he said, laughing. "All the other fools that claimed to have met the Author thought that they were special individuals, that they had accomplished something that made the Author proud, that the Author loved them to the point of revealing himself. But you, on the contrary, pretend that you have been so unworthy as one of his creation that he summoned you for the pleasure of shooting you face-to-face?"

"What? No. You're twisting my words. This was not about pleasure. He was wasted."

"You make no sense. If the Author makes a mistake with a character, he erases. It's that simple."

I gave up. I could have run around the room giving a piggyback ride to the Author himself and it wouldn't have made a difference. It's possible to starve people, steal from them, abuse them, deprive them of dignity and almost everything else, without a riot, as long as it's presumably what the Author wanted, but it's not possible for the Author to be dead. The Author must exist. Badly. Saying otherwise is illegal; it deserves the harshest punishment.

If the Kritikillar could get away with self-laudatory fables of infinite reincarnations without an ounce of substantiating evidence, and my sharp life-threatening gunshot wounds could be construed as the "artwork" of an idiot poking with his fingers, there was no point in trying to be logical *[Log·i·cal. Adjective. If it looks like a duck, swims like a duck, and quacks like a duck, then it is not an elephant, you, imbecile!].*

"You're right. It makes complete total sense to me now."

"There! At last. The accused acknowledges his guilt," he said, spreading his arms wide open, looking at the Fanatiks and the Small Visionary with delight, hearing what he wanted to hear.

"I'm a heretic. I'm a Kafkaist. I'm an Illiterantes."

"There. Don't you feel better already by releasing that burden of lies from your shoulder?"

He clearly wasn't listening.

"I even was a torturer and a Visionary killer in prior lives. I've even been the ugliest nemesis one could imagine: a miserable person who disdained fairy tales, a scoundrel who demanded proofs and refused to believe in the unbelievable."

"Good. Have you heard it all?" he asked, prompting nods from the Fanatiks.

"I even met you in a prior life," I added, going one further. "I remember cutting your dick with a rusted hacksaw. It fell on the floor without a single drop of blood, because it had been dried up for so long."

"Our business is done. Lock him up until sentencing, tomorrow," he ordered the Fanatiks, as he rushed out of the dungeon, with the Small Visionary who trailed after him like a Basset Hound.

"I'm the monster who cracked your skull apart to spill your brain out, but only found shit inside," I shouted as the Fanatiks threw me on the floor.

"I'm the miscreant who plunged his sword through your chest but broke his blade when it hit a rock," I yelled as they slammed the metal door.

"I'm the barbarian who lifted the rock under which you hid, to blind you by the light and crush your shell under my heel," I screamed between the bars of the door, until the sound of their steps disappeared in the spiral staircase.

There was no sense arguing any further. I was a bad and rebellious person. Like Grandpa, but not as smart, and unable to claim senility for my defense. And not alive for much longer.

At the Post

I was tied, naked, to a wooden post. So tightly that all the ropes were soaked in blood. Around my neck, barbed wire had been used instead of ropes. I was standing on broken glass, but lifting my feet wasn't an option, as it would have transferred my weight to the ropes and barbed wire, effectively choking me. My gut had been slashed and my intestines pulled-out, wrapped around the post as if to add one layer of rope. A tire wrapped around my waist had been filled with oil, which burned my entrails through the slashed opening. Ammonia had been poured on my eyes, which felt as if someone had ripped them out of their sockets. Although blind, I didn't need to see to know exactly where the spiked whip had opened deep wounds on my body.

Then, the torturer set fire to the oil. The flame roared, sawing me in half at the height of the tire, and igniting the oil that had streaked along my legs. The pain was excruciating. My brain wanted to explode. I screamed my lungs out. Screams met by roars of excitements from a crowd that had come to witness the most entertaining event of the year.

There I was, nothing more than an insignificant specimen in an experiment gone askew, ignited to entertain a deranged mob. My burning flesh smelled like meat forgotten on the charcoal and life was eager to leave me.

I lost all feeling below my waist, as the concentrated heat cut me in half. A crow landed on my shoulder and started to pull on my ear, in hope of being first to pull a well-done piece out.

Its wings repeatedly struck my face.

Slap, slap, slap, slap.

"Are you dead? Waz it too much?"

Slap, slap, slap, slap.

"Uuh? Hrmph."

Slap, slap, slap, slap.

"OK, OK, stop that," I said, as I regained consciousness.

"I thought I had killz you. One more accident," said my cellmate.

It had been a terrible dream, but, thankfully, I wasn't dead. At least, not yet.

"I did like you wantez. Waz 'fraid I hit too hard."

"No, no. I'm fine," I replied, touching the huge bump on my head—right next to the other one that had brought me to the Author in the first place.

"So did you seez the Author?" asked my cellmate.

"No. It didn't work. It only triggered bad nightmares."

"Yeah. I toldz you."

Contrary to my previous cellmate, this one was a real detainee, not there for sake of an internship. I had been brought back to the same cell as before—the luxury cell, as my former cellmate called it, although now that he had graduated, he probably enjoyed some true luxury, being pampered while awaiting the big show.

"I've been hitz on the coconut often enough to know. No Author for me there. I could had toldz you."

He was pensive for a moment, looking for words.

"You'd had more luck with that telegrape thingz."

"Telegraph."

"Ts'what I saidz."

He wasn't eloquent or erudite, but he was right. I had been stupid. As if another bump on the head would bring me back to the Author. First of all, if the whole thing had been real, he was dead. I saw it. Second, if the whole thing had been a scam of psychological torture, then I could get banged on the head until the tip of my skull caved inward so deep that it touched my lower jaw and it wouldn't make a difference.

Yet, somehow, I felt a need to see him. To confront him. To tell him all that I should have told him if I had not been so stunned the first time. I wanted to tell him that having an author that doesn't care is just as good as having none. That a rudderless boat doesn't need a captain. I wanted to curse him for the misery he put me through, for making me a wanted man slated for the death penalty. All that, for what? For what? For having refused his moral reprogramming? For having escaped from his control?

I wanted explanations.

Solid ones.

Sober ones.

Not more nonsense coming from a bottle.

"Juz let me know if you want more bangs on the noggin."

"Hmm. Yes. Sure will."

"I'm good at that. Kinda iz why I'm here."

I stood up and paced around the cell, sloshing through the two inches of accumulated rainwater. If there was a drain somewhere, it flushed water no faster than what was pouring-in through the bars of the gutter-window. At least, if it could be of any consolation, being wet was less uncomfortable than wearing a burning tire as a belt. With some imagination, even the spattering of water flowing into the cell from the window ledge felt like a soothing noise—with a lot of imagination, that is *[Imag·i·na·tion. Noun. Dangerous by-product secreted by unbridled minds]*.

In spite of my insistent sloshing—or maybe because of it, as if to validate my "soothing" theory—my cellmate managed to fall asleep, propped in the corner of the cell where the floor was so uneven that it remained higher and dry. The torturer had been right; there was a better side in the cell.

My new roommate wasn't a man of many words, but from the few mangled ones he had managed to articulate, I gathered that he had an unfortunate propensity to create "accidents"—of the type that landed him here. Yet, there he was sleeping like a baby, mind at ease, unburdened, oblivious to whatever threat lay ahead. It's amazing how the most guilty souls can so freely manage to be the least tortured.

"Anybody home?" whispered a voice through the window.

The waterfall from the ledge had been disturbed by two knees and a hand. A face was looking into the dark cell without caution, certain that I was there, and confident as always that his Fanatik costume provided a foolproof camouflage.

"Zayne!" I whispered back, escaping the darkness as I rushed to the window.

"Good to see you," he replied.

"You won't have that pleasure for much longer, I'm afraid."

"Don't worry, we'll get you out of there."

"It didn't work last time. Unless you cut me in pieces, I can't squeeze though the bars."

"No, no. No cutting into pieces. Too messy," he replied with a scary seriousness. "Tomorrow night. We'll snatch you up."

"Tomorrow night? They'll start torturing me tomorrow afternoon."

"Right. I know. You'll have to survive till night. Can you do that?"

"As if I could control that. It won't be a picnic—"

"Well, you'll have to do your best, because there's no way out from this cell. We need you in the open to snatch you up. Just don't die before nightfall."

"As far as I know, they want me to suffer for days."

"Perfect. Stretch it out."

I couldn't see anything perfect in that.

"Till nightfall. Then, we'll snatch you up."

"Snatch me up, snatch me up. Easy to say. I've heard that before."

"Don't worry. It's a sure thing this time."

"Why do you have to leave me suffer a whole day then?"

"We're bringing down one of the rope systems."

"Ropes?"

"You know. The clothesline you rode a couple of times before. But we can't set it up in broad daylight and we can't do it either before we know where and how they'll set you up tomorrow."

"I'm pretty sure that will be at Visionary Square."

"I know, but it's a pretty big square."

"On a stage."

"It's a pretty big stage."

He had obviously already scouted the venue and seen the preparations being made there.

"Tomorrow will be a moonless night. Besides, if the rain continues, it will be even better—darker, with the cloud cover. That's what we need to set-up the system and slide it high above the guards up to where you'll be. Then, I'll ride the rope up to you and snatch you up."

"Snatch me up," I scoffed. "I won't be lounging on a sofa smoking a pipe while waiting. Just to be clear, I'll be tied up in some excruciatingly painful way I can't even start to imagine right now."

"I know, I know. That's why we first need to see tomorrow how they'll set you up, so that we can bring the appropriate tools."

"I hope I won't be behind bars, because we know how that one will go already."

"Hey, show some optimism here. I don't have to be here you know," he bluffed. "I only came here 'cause the Author forced me," he added in a guffaw, hand over mouth to avoid waking up the accidental killer snoring at the other end of the cell.

I probably would have laughed too, in other circumstances.

"Trust me, buddy, it will all be fine."

"Because the Author told you so, I suppose," I sneered.

"Shit, no. That guy wants to turn you into a giant puddle of blood and slime," he laughed. "You'll have to trust me 'cause I owe you a big one," he said, leaving.

All I could do was hope that he was right—about the snatching, not the blood and slime.

Sentencing

The crowd that filled Visionary Square and its surroundings erupted in cheers at the first glimpse of the torturer's wooden cart approaching. Given that the village's entire population could fit many times over in the square, it was pretty clear that people from faraway places had invited themselves to the party. Packed like sardines from the stage all the way down to the houses delimiting the plaza, spilling in every connecting street and alley that provided hope for sight or sound, filling every doorway, stair, or window with a view, and dangerously topping slippery roofs, the county's sum total of what counted as humanity was ready to be entertained. It took an hour for the torturer to plow through the mass of bodies and steer the cart through the last hundred yards to dock along the stairs at the edge of the stage.

Loading the chain over his shoulder, he then dragged me out of the cart, tied-up like a sausage—as I had refused to willingly follow him like cattle to a slaughterhouse. He pulled me up to the stage, painfully bouncing me on every step of the stairs, as the crowd merrily chanted: "Let him burn, let him rip, let him rot, and let him moan, let him croak alone." My former cell-mate had promised to be relatively gentle in his handling, as a courtesy for the friendship forged in our shared captivity, but either we didn't share the same definition of gentle, or the inebriating energy of the frenzied mob made him forget and rather fueled his desire to make history by delivering the most solid rookie performance ever recorded in the annals of the profession.

After being banged and bruised up the stairs, a violent tug on the chain made me slide all the way up to the center of the stage. There, he untied me and pushed me into a pillory before I could recover from the numbing pain that prevented me from controlling my limbs. Head and hands locked between the two hinged wooden boards that held me bent forward on my knees, I saw him walk to the front of the stage and raise his hands, fist clenched, as a victorious boxer responding to a standing ovation, reveling in the moment.

At least someone was having fun.

Then, he looked back, lowered his arms, and moved aside as the crowd suddenly became silent. All I could hear was the creaking of the planks behind me as someone approached. And then I recognized the smell.

"After having considered all the evidence and testimony from the accused, I am forced to conclude that all the extraordinary claims he has made are unfounded, incredible, outrageous, and without any merit," solemnly shouted the Kritikillar. "The accused has nothing to offer but unflattering, sacrilegious, blasphemous, and ridiculous fantasies that demonstrated unequivocally that his assertions were nothing but a sham. He has never met the Author. His lies will have earned him nothing but more prolonged death throes."

The crowd erupted, eager to see blood [*Blood. Noun, often attributive. The champagne of vicious buffoons of infinite vanity and microscopic intelligence*].

He walked in front of the pillory, basking in the acclaim. After a moment, he raised his right hand to quiet the crowd.

"I must now pronounce the sentence to be executed for his crimes."

"If there is really an Author, then let him silence me right now, at this very instant, forever and ever," I shouted at the top of my lungs, with all my remaining forces.

The crowd gasped, all eyes awaiting to see if a lightning bolt would fry me on the spot, or if a crevasse would open and swallow the stage.

"I'm still alive. Isn't there an almighty Author out there, to silence me?"

"You, arrogant bastard!" shouted the Kritikillar. "You have been condemned to infinite suffering. You can't fool the Author into abridging your tortures."

Sighs of relief in the crowd. If anything, I had only proven that the Author was smarter than me. Obviously. Order was undisturbed.

I had no more energy.

No more forces.

No more ideas.

There was no point in fighting. It was the Kafkaists that were right after all. Life was senseless. I was about to be tortured and killed for events beyond my control, in spite of facts too obvious to be believable.

The power of expectation subjugated the crowd into a heavy silence. It was as if all heartbeats had paused and life had been suspended.

That's when I saw June, standing on top of a horse and yelling: "If you kill him, you'll have to kill me too."

The Kritikillar flinched, taken aback, unaware of who had interrupted his grand spectacle. I saw his surprise turn into a hateful grimace, and then scorn.

"Who dares speak?" he shouted, searching around.

"I said, if you kill him, you'll have to kill me too," repeated June, with everyone now looking at her.

"Who is this arrogant tramp?"

"I am June. The Kafkaist who loves Adam and whom he loves. The sister of Theodors whom you'll never see again. I'm warning you that if you want to kill Adam, you'll have to kill me first."

The Kritikillar flashed an arrogant smile—more horrifying than the pillory itself.

"OK, then. Let's do that. Right now!" he ordered.

All the Fanatiks on the stage, walls, and carts all around the square responded, jumping into the crowd, violently pushing people aside to clear their path toward June.

June waited for them to approach. A good minute. Then, as they got near, she dropped on the horse and charged forward, like a warrior to the rescue, trampling all those in her path.

As the horse reached the stage, she pulled a sword from a sheath along the saddle, and jumped to land right between the unarmed Kritikillar and torturer. Swinging the blade while pivoting, she slashed their throats. Blood spurted from their necks and soaked the stage as they collapsed, frantically convulsing to a fast death.

She then turned around to face the Small Visionary, who dropped on his knees. A pool of urine formed around him. She slowly moved towards him, checking that the Fanatiks fighting their way back were still a good distance away, drowned in the crowd.

"This is for having stolen my little brother, and for sentencing to death the man I love," she declared as she split his head in half, between the eyes, down to his shoulder.

The two half-Visionary faces, uglier than the original one, sagged on both sides of the shoulders, with grey matter oozing out, streaking along the neck, before his body fell forward, splashing into the pool of urine.

"The Rules require that the condemned be offered an opportunity for last words," shouted the Kritikillar to be heard by as much of the crowd as possible, "but, he has already spoken, and even though these were a rather poor choice of last words, I now consider that this obligation has been fulfilled, and I can now— finally—pronounce the sentence to be executed for his crimes."

The June I had seen in my delirium would of course never come. She was a non-violent Kafkaist, not a decapitator. And most probably not in love with me.

In fact, I wondered if any June existed at all. Maybe she had been a figment of my imagination and my love for her had been the sick infatuation of a defective mind. Maybe everything had been an illusion and I was here because society could not cure my severe dementia other than by death. That seemed to make sense. Particularly given that nothing else did.

Yet, maybe June the rescuing Amazon had been a fantasy, but the pillory seemed very real. Very solid. My right and left hands, squeezed at the wrists by the planks, were all I could see of myself, but the pain in the rest of my body also felt real. Painfully so.

All that threatened my future—including the torturer—also existed behind the pillory, even though I couldn't see it. I couldn't see much on either side without painfully turning my head. However, through the fingers of my right hand, I noticed a row of seats at the right of the stage that I hadn't seen before. There sat Cassandra, her parents, and a bunch of other Perfectionists, probably invited to relish in the proper extermination of heresy. By erasing me, they erased all possible doubts, all improper questions that could undermine the foundations of their comfortable lives.

I stared at Cassandra, thinking of how relieved she probably was now that she wouldn't have to marry me after all. Yet, she looked sad. Tortured. Maybe she thought that dying had been my secret plan to escape our union, and she wondered what kind of sick mind could hatch such a ridiculous plan. Strangely, it hurt me to imagine that she could think of me as being so stupid. Death is not a suitable escape. At least, not for me, and not when it is promised to arrive only after endless tortures at the hands of a freshly graduated torturer eager to make a strong first impression.

Cassandra's eyes locked with mine. It seemed as if her sadness worsened. Her lips started to tremble.

She stood up.

The Kritikillar, about to finally deliver my sentence, noticed and stopped. The young woman chosen by the Author to bookmark Theodors apparently had earned the right to disturb the proceedings for a moment. As she seemed distracted—to say the least—the Kritikillar made a step toward her, arms open, possibly thinking that the frail child needed some fatherly comforting to find the strength to coldly witness the butchery of the one who had been promised to her.

She stepped back.

Stunned, he stopped.

She whispered.

"What?"

She repeated, starting to cry at the same time.

"Child. Nobody can hear you. Make yourself clear."

"I have never bookmarked the little kid," she screamed, before wailing.

"What?"

She tried a few times to repeat, unsuccessfully. All that could be heard were inarticulate high-pitched lamentations—and murmurs of the crowd.

She pressed her face on her father's shoulder, sobbing and shaking. Impatiently, the Kritikillar waited, wondering how long it would take for her to run out of tears. As far as I was concerned, I hoped she had lacrimal reservoirs that would take forever to drain a couple of drops at a time, as I evidently preferred to see her shed tears than me shed blood. Unfortunately, after five minutes, she ran out of energy, caught her breath, and dried her eyes.

She turned back to face the Kritikillar, took a deep breath to harvest some courage, and, unable to look him in the eye, stared at the floor and repeated her outrageous claim.

"I have not bookmarked the little Kafkaist kid."

"Dear young child. I fully understand what you are doing. It is most admirable for you to want to save the one you were supposed to marry, but your lie is not going to save him."

"No. I mean, I really did not."

"He is a heretic. You are not responsible for this and you cannot save him at this point."

"I'm serious. I did not bookmark the kid."

I wanted to shout: "Trust her. Cassandra would never lie about something like this," but she apparently had. Either right now, or at the very beginning. Now I really regretted not telling the Lackeys, in the first place, that Cassandra was nothing but a liar. A scoundrel. A little, silly, snotty girl who needs to be the center of attention and who couldn't care that the cost of her self-righteousness cost me an arm.

But if this was the same Cassandra, why was she telling the truth now? What brought upon her this sudden burst of gnawing guilt?

"Young child, stop your white lies," said the Kritikillar. "What you did or didn't do doesn't matter at this time. We are not here because of what you did, but because of what he did. His shameful conspiring with Kafkaists to deceive Authorians is an unforgivable insult to the Author. He will be punished and erased, and that's it."

She pushed the Kritikillar and ran to kneel in front of me. She grasped both of my hands and, looking me straight in the eyes, said: "The other day, I was on my way to the Librariatorium's back alley. I wanted to peek at you from your window cell."

She sure had made it a lifetime pursuit to trail me.

"But I didn't make it there. There was already someone in the aisle. A girl. A girl I recognized."

Even though my life could hardly get worse, I was afraid of what she'd say next.

"I've seen you kiss her there. I saw. I heard. I watched her run away. I was puzzled, but, now, I understand why you did what you did. It's so strong. So beautiful. I can only wish that some-day, somebody will love me as much."

Her tear-filled, red eyes shouted a sincerity I had never imag-ined could exist in Cassandra. For once in my life, I believed her.

Fanatiks—who had protected the stage all along, except in my delirium—pulled her away, while she repeated, "Thank you, thank you, thank you," eyes locked in mine, until she disappeared behind the rows of Perfectionists. Presumably, they not only dragged her off the stage, but took her far away from the square, to prevent any further disturbances.

I'm pretty sure I'll never understand how Cassandra's brain worked, if it worked at all—and I'm not particularly keen to ever know—but I wondered what could possibly have triggered her strange behavior. I did believe the sincerity of her words, but maybe, deep down, Cassandra's outburst had also been partly sparked by her fear of ending up as my spouse—even if only in theory, as I was soon to be erased. That, I'll never know. But, right then, it seemed to me that she had decided, once and for all, that she'd prefer to die single rather than agree to an arranged marriage. That day, she deliberately shattered her Perfectionist shell and, although her desire for freedom and love was maybe doomed from the start given that all her friends and family were nutcase Perfectionists, I felt a certain sympathy for her. For the first time, I had seen Cassandra as a human being.

Maybe her future had a chance. For sure, in spite of the challenges ahead, it looked more promising than mine right now. To put it mildly, my prospects looked bleak; The Kritikillar would see to it.

He looked pretty upset and determined to cut the nonsense. He raised his arms to silence the crowd—clearly, it would take longer than expected, which didn't improve his mood.

The noise level dropped, progressively, almost to the desired quietness, but a commotion that developed at the back of the plaza ruined all that. The disturbance came from a group that pushed and shoved its way towards the stage, creating quite an uproar.

"Now what?" sighed the Kritikillar.

Lifting my head as much as I could—neck pinched by the top board of the pillory—I saw a dozen men wiggling their way through. When they finally reached the front of the stage, after much wrangling, spreading tumult like wildfire, they stopped, pulled notebooks, and started shouting questions in our direction.

They shouted at me.

"Are you the man condemned for saying: 'I have met the Author and he is dead'?"

"Are you ashamed of having betrayed your compatriots?"

"How do you respond to those who say you are a hero?"

"Did you do this on purpose, to start a war?"

"Any regrets about your sacrifice for the virtue of higher ideals?"

"How does it feel to be an inspiration to so many?"

They also shouted at the Kritikillar.

"Are you torturing that man for what he has said or for what he has done?"

"Where are you hiding the kidnapped Kafkaist?"

"How do you respond to those outside of the Stygian Dominion who unanimously disapprove of the kidnapping?"

"Are you concerned about the threat of sanctions?"

"Are you ashamed of torturing an innocent man?"

It came from left and right, from all matters of opinions. Some apparently pleased to see me awaiting due punishment, others outraged by the whole farce.

They all had a lanyard around the neck, at the end of which hung a rigid card with their name: Joe from the Free Press, Joe from the Author's Herald, Joe from the Daily Observer, Joe from the World News, and so on. Either there was an awful lot of Joes in their line of work, or they wanted to remain incognito for some reason. This was the first time that I had seen a journalist; our village was too small for that stuff—a few gossipmongers took care of spreading all the rumors—but in the capital and large cities across all Dominions, the news didn't write itself. The Joes did it.

The Kritikallar gestured to a bunch of Fanatiks, twirling his hand above his head in a way that said, "arrest them all." The Joes were about to get a private guided tour of the dungeon.

"Say something," shouted the Joe closest to me.

"Why are you here?" I said. It was all I could think to ask.

"Big news! It's big news on the singing wire."

"Who's singing?"

"The telegraph, buddy, the telegraph."

Barboyee! Barboyee had made the wire sing. His T't', tap t'tap, tapt', tap tap tap, t'tap tap tune actually meant something. In all of his t't'tap t'tapping, he had clandestinely spread the local news across the world to whoever cared to listen to his serenade. All of his t's and tap's, when translated into a succession of dots and dashes, spelled the words of misery that described our common predicament. As those words spread freely, they under-pinned stakes higher than I could have imagined at the time.

For a brief moment, the journalists had brought hope. Yet, it all seemed to be in vain, as the chatty dozen was roughed up by the Fanatiks, silenced, and dragged off the plaza, on to the humid cell of the Librariatorium.

The Kritikillar stood center stage, arms crossed, as if defying those in the plaza to dare make more noise.

"Are there other imbeciles out there who wish to further delay the proceedings? Anybody? There's plenty of room left to pack more imbeciles in the dungeon."

The silence was absolute.

"Good. Now. Enough of that nonsense. For the crimes committed for which Mr. Adam Chad Kilroy has been found guilty and deserving of the death penalty, I pronounce the following torture sentence to be executed at once."

Before he could say one more word, a bunch of Fanatiks from the back of the plaza screamed in unison: "The kid is back! The kid is back! There's a big problem!"

Mud over Matter

The Fanatiks had cleared an alley through the crowd, from the stage up to the point on Main Street where lay the presumed "big problem," and made a human chain to keep the mob from closing the pathway. The Kritikillar and Small Visionary were first through, followed by the torturer who kept me chained and on a tight leash, and all the Perfectionists closing the procession. Concerned that the whole thing might have been a diversion, they weren't about to leave me alone on the stage, even if guarded there by a few Fanatiks. In principle, locked in a pillory bolted to the stage and made of solid oak, it's not like I could have lifted it and escaped—running around with the whole contraption around my neck—but it doesn't take a big gang to take down a few guards, and given that a handsaw could have cut through the dry planks in less than a minute, they evidently played it safe. They certainly didn't want me rescued by Kafkaists—or, in fact, by my Illiterantes friends if they had known the truth—but at the same time, and more importantly, they didn't want some excited, inebriated villagers left behind to start the torture party in their absence.

I first thought that the "big problem" might have been part of some sort of rescue plan by Zayne and his friends, but it was not the case. There, at the problem site, a horse had sunk up to its mid-side in the mud pit that our main street had become after the sustained rain of the past few days. If it had been only that, it would have been nothing out of the ordinary for my village of morons, and certainly not cause for disturbing the entertainment event of the year—and a Kritikillar about to deliver a long-awaited sentence. But sitting on the horse, crying, was Theodors, and there lay the problem. Many ropes had been thrown at him, most hitting target and draping over the horse, but Theodors refused to grab them. He simply let them all slide by as they were pulled back.

"How did he end up there?" asked the Small Visionary.

A few Fanatiks looked at each other, unsure.

"He rode the horse along Main Street and sank," ventured one of them.

"I can easily imagine that, you idiots. I want to know how he got here."

The Fanatiks failed to understand how that was different from the previous question. Fortunately, a few feet away, a couple of Fanatiks, in sweat, busy operating the ropes, heard the question. They looked at each other, unsure, took their courage in both hands, and came by to report.

"We can explain," said the first one.

"It's 'cause we were at the Kafkaist's dump," clarified the taller one.

"On orders."

"Yeah, orders."

"Looking for him."

"Him," he said pointing at the mud-stuck horse.

The Kritikillar's contempt toward these clowns was notice-able, but he remained silent, huffing, waiting for the full explana-tion.

"We'd been to their dump before."

"Many times."

"On orders. Looking for the kid."

"Orders are orders."

"It's 'cause the damn Kafkaists could be hiding it there."

"They're the ones that stole it."

"Orders were to beat 'em up some."

"To make them talk," clarified the tall one, about to flash a proud smile but stopping, not sure if that would have been appro-priate given the circumstances.

"We got to one house and started to search."

"Then, behind us, the kid zoomed out."

"From under the front porch."

"He climbed on the porch, on the railing—"

"Real fast."

"—and jumped on my horse."

"And they, they, they—"

"Dash," said the taller one, with the satisfaction of having used a hard word.

"Gallop," said the other, one better.

"Yeah. Gallop, gallop."

"He's a kid. How could he possibly steer the horse?" asked the Visionary.

The two Fanatiks looked a bit dumbfounded.

"I guess he didn't."

"But he kicked it a lot."

"Jumper came back here by itself I guess."

"It's his horse's name."

"It knows its way back here."

"It's been home for many days now—"

"Home? In the mud?" said the Kritikillar, exasperated.

"I don't know."

"The kid, it continued to kick it though."

"We were behind."

"Both on Skipper."

"It's his horse."

"Skipper wouldn't have stopped before the mud either if I didn't pull hard on the reins."

"Real hard."

"Theodors! Yoo-hoo," shouted the Small Visionary, waving his arms in the air. "It's your father."

The Kritikillar gave him a puzzled and displeased look.

"Your spiritual father," he clarified, trying to hide his embarrassment. "You've done the right thing to come back home—to your new home."

Home? That was a stretch. From the Fanatiks' testimony, Theodors had stolen the horse only to escape them, and might have ended up here by accident. In any event, if his goal was to come back, he surely didn't expect to end-up stuck in mud with hundreds gawking [*Gawk. Noun. To stare stupidly, motionless, slack-jawed to the point where bees have time to build a nest inside the mouth*].

Theodors didn't budge. He was holding to the saddle, looking down, and letting every rope slide by him.

The mud was deep as always, making it impossible to reach him. Freezing temperatures that would have allowed an ice bridge were months away. There was no alternative way to reach him. He had to be fished out, throwing ropes. No travelers had ever been left stranded in the mud before, but none ever refused to grab the lifelines thrown at them.

Given that Theodors was uncooperative—totally unresponsive to be exact—after a few hours of trying to reach him, all efforts stopped. Food was thrown next to him, thinking it would bring him out of his torpor, but he didn't reach for it and let it sunk in the mud.

I looked around me, as if searching for Grandpa and his great ideas, but knowing, sadly that this was in vain. That's when I recognized Zayne as one of the Fanatiks a few feet away, and got an idea—all by myself. Grandpa would have been proud.

"I know how to reach him," I shouted.

"You could save my spiritual son?" snapped the Small Visionary, hope reborn.

"You are a condemned prisoner. We don't need your ideas," replied the Kritikillar.

The Small Visionary was crushed by that last remark. Me too. My brilliant plan that could have worked seemed still born. The small hope that had started to bloom in my heart almost immediately succumbed, victim to the Visionary's lack of courage. Like a flower in the path of a stampede, my idea had been trampled to death by a bull.

The Small Visionary bit his lip, took a deep breath, and raised his chin.

"I think it is worth listening to him," he surprisingly replied.

"What?"

"We must get Theodors back."

"Why?"

"He is a duly bookmarked Authorian, member of my community. It is my duty to save him."

"Apparently, he has not been bookmarked at all, as far as we learned today."

"Cassandra is the straightest arrow you could find. One of the most irreproachable Perfectionists I have ever been given to meet. It is obvious that the innocent child has been perturbed at the sight of a man—a man once promised to be her husband no less—about to be executed. What child wouldn't lose balance under the circumstances. No, trust me. That little Theodors has been bookmarked and I'm unwavering in that conviction. His apprenticeship and mastery of the Rules was remarkable, extraordinary, prodigiously rapid— beyond anything the Custodian has ever seen. No Kafkaist could ever be so gifted. The kid is an Authorian."

The Kritikillar seemed pensive. He definitely was on the fence.

"Destined to become a Visionary," added the Small Visionary. "At the very least."

That was the little extra push needed to fall off the fence.

"The Author has decided to give us unusual means to achieve his goal...," replied the Kritikillar.

"Most unorthodox, I agree."

"...then, I guess we must listen."

I couldn't believe it.

"What is your idea?" the Kritikillar asked me. "It better be a good one," he whispered. "Don't you ever try to play me."

"If my idea works, will my crimes be pardoned?"

"What?" he indignantly replied.

"If I save the life of the young Authorian, will mine be saved in return? Will I be spared any torture?"

He turned around, looking at Theodors. I must have stared at his back for an hour, wondering what he was thinking—whether he was debating my offer or if he had simply decided to ignore me forever.

I had no other plan, so I waited.

Waited.

And waited.

While watching the crowd, aimlessly, waiting for the Kritikillar to mull over the possibilities, I noticed something, far, where Main Street was higher and out of the mud pond, where the crowd filled the street, like a wall from sidewalk to sidewalk; it was a small face among a sea of heads. Anonymous and invisible to all, but a twinkling star to me. There was June, watching her brother from a distance, powerless. From that far, some would say it was a mirage, but they would have been wrong. I was certain of that. I would have loved to run to her, but tied in chains at the mercy of Fanatiks, it was not possible.

The whole situation was insane. Someone had to act. Yet, everybody was there, powerless, waiting for the "Ridikullar" to make up his mind. Nobody dared to offer a solution, because all brilliant ideas that did not originate in the top head could be taken as insults and harshly punished—and I served as a vivid reminder of what that meant in the sick minds of those at the top.

Yet, the Kritikillar's idea machine did not seem to be in gear. He was frozen, staring far ahead, like a stupid dog who knows that someone has thrown a stick that way but not sure where it landed, standing still instead of running to fetch it, as if the lost stick was to magically pop up in the air. But worse because, here, the stick was not lost. It was there. In plain view, and it wasn't getting off that poor horse. The animal—the horse, not the dog—stuck in mud almost to its neck, had desperately shaken his head for hours and was approaching exhaustion. Theodors, face down, holding to the horse's back to avoid being hit by the swirling head, was not moving.

Obviously, the stupid dog—or someone else—had to fetch the stick, as it wasn't about to come back on its own.

The Kritikillar turned back and said: "Fine."

"Fine what?"

"I will lift the death penalty if your idea works."

"And the torture sentence?"

"And revoke your torture sentence," he confirmed, as he gestured to the torturer to unchain me.

I didn't trust him one bit. I suspected that this was a bold lie, that he had no intention to ever rescind my death penalty, and that the slimy weasel would find a way to screw me no matter what, but as I had no other plan, it would have to do. At worst, it would buy me time. At best, maybe my suspicions were unfounded and he would keep his promise. Maybe that last option wasn't as incredible as it seemed, if only for the fact that we were surrounded by witnesses who could testify that the Kritikillar had promised me my freedom—although that assumed that these witnesses wouldn't prefer to conveniently lie for sake of not cancelling the entertainment event of the year.

"I will need help from a few Fanatiks," I said, shaking off the chains. "Say, this one and all those he can enlist to help me," I added, pointing to Zayne. "They have to help me get the material we will need to rescue the kid."

Zayne would have been thrilled if I had told him that my plan was to pretend we were going to collect some tools from Grandpa's shed, but actually slipped away through Grandpa's secret tunnel, leaving the idiots waiting. Fortunately, Zayne didn't know about the existence of Grandpa's tunnel, because he would have been quite upset that such a sensible, effective, and brilliant idea wasn't my actual plan. The problem was that, as sensible of an escape this would have been, I just couldn't do that. I couldn't leave Theodors at the mercy of the vultures—figuratively and literally. I couldn't do that to Theodors, and to June—even though she most probably hated me with a passion by then. I couldn't fail her again. I couldn't abandon my mirage.

Before I said any words, Zayne understood that I wasn't planning an escape, but that I genuinely intended to attempt rescuing the kid. I could feel his disappointment.

"You're completely crazy," said Zayne's eyes, while he remained silent, shoulders slumped.

"Let's get your gear," I replied.

On a Thread

Starting on the dry elevated end of Main Street, the Illiterantes' clothesline was pulled to span from sidewalk to sidewalk, Zayne and I holding it on one side, and a few accomplices doing the same on the other. Both groups then walked down the street, carefully working to clear each post along the covered sidewalk without dropping the spools of wire in the mud, up to Theodors and his horse.

That was the easy part.

The hard part was to deploy the ropes, the spins, the brakes, the clamps, and the other mechanical hardware foreign to me, but essential to operate the contraption, and that Zayne and his buddies knew inside out how to install and operate.

"What the big deal?" said the Small Visionary. "It's just a rope."

"No, it's not," I replied, pointing to the complex apparatus. "It's all that other stuff that is needed to carry the weight of a person across the street."

I sensed that seeing this unexpected display of technology from someone condemned to death for treason could only raise more suspicions in the twisted minds of the Kritikillar and Small Visionary, but I guessed they were wise enough to keep all their questions in check to until after Theodors' rescue. Of course, true to self, my plan hadn't been thought through beyond that point. If the Kritikillar and Small Visionary were to doubt my intentions and start to pepper us with questions, I could only hope that Zayne could spontaneously weave together some credible lies. Otherwise, if we failed to convince them that this was more than a lame excuse to gain time, we would be accused of perfidious behavior, duplicity, and whatever else they could think of to regain the upper hand, to return me to the pillory—probably with Zayne in a second pillory that time—and to expedite the torture program.

Zayne found solid anchors to tie down his ropes and gave me the thumbs-up, indicating that the whole system could support my weight.

"We are ready to go. I can now go snatch up the kid," I told the Kritikillar, whom I hoped hadn't been clever enough to figure out that there had been a "snatching up" planned all along, but that it was to rescue the partly dismembered and bloody carcass of a certain Adam after a day of torture, rather than to pluck a whole and relatively clean little kid from a mud lake.

"Who said you'd be the one to get him?" snapped the Small Visionary.

The Kritikillar looked at him, raising an eyebrow. "You have other plans?" he asked.

"Of course," he replied, pointing at Theodors. "It's obvious that he came back because he's my spiritual son. I've never seen a student learn the Rules so fast and master them so well. What I have witnessed is not his rebirth as an Authorian, but rather a prodigious metamorphosis. Truly unparalleled."

The Kritikillar resented being lectured on the propagandistic value of Theodors' rushed return to the village, but he knew how to recognize a golden fable worth telegraphing to the entire world when he saw one.

"You can ride that thing?" he asked, looking at the ropes, incredulous. "Why would an old fart like him want to trapeze across the street?" he probably wondered, but there was no doubt that casting him as a hero could only enrich the fable.

"Tell me how that works," shouted the Visionary to Zayne.

"I would recommend to hang upside down, knees wrapped around the upper rope, and we'll zip you up to right above the horse."

I couldn't believe. My plan for rescuing June's little brother had just been stolen by a rotten octogenarian. There was nothing I could do to stop that monstrous sabotage of my only hope of reconciliation with June.

The Small Visionary tied the bottom of his robe about his ankle, called for a ladder, stepped on many heads and leaned on many bodies, to finally find a way to hang upside down from the rope, above the sidewalk.

"Let's get moving. Get me there."

Zayne pulled the line.

It didn't move.

He tugged it repeatedly, without success.

"Come on," yelled the impatient gown on the clothesline.

Zayne stepped down to crawl between the gears. After a minute, he came back with a frown on his face.

"The mechanism is jammed. One of the sprockets is bent. You'll have to slide down the rope."

The Small Visionary grumbled. His head was already purple from the blood that had drained down; it would have been a delight to see it explode. All that blood, mixed with the shit that served as his brain, would have soaked his admiring Perfectionists—a disgusting mess they all deserved.

Only a bit of the Visionary's head and his arms could be seen extending below his sagging gown as he slid along the rope. From a distance, it simply looked like dirty laundry, pushed sideways, hung to dry over Main Street, knees like two clothespins. The dirty laundry eventually parked itself right above the horse.

The horse's neck was already horizontal, immobile, resting on the mud, out of total exhaustion. Theodors, lying on the horse's back, was ready to be snatched. It should have been an easy pick. All that Theodors needed to do was to raise himself, extend his arms, and let the Small Visionary grab him, but all that he did was lie flat on the horse's back. The rope was too high to allow scooping him up against his will.

The solution was quite simple. All that the Small Visionary had to do was come back to the sidewalk and let Zayne and his friends disassemble the system and re-assemble it such that the rope would hang three feet lower. But he couldn't do that. Theodors' failure to stand up and help himself be rescued challenged the Small Visionary's claim that Theodors had come back to embrace his spiritual father; it risked shattering the beautiful fable. The Small Visionary could not afford to come back empty handed.

"Theodors. It's me. Your new daddy. Come on. Give me your hand. Theodors! Come on now!"

All the cajoling, the finger snapping, the hand clapping, the whistling, the begging, and the threats, were in vain. Theodors remained on the horse's back, flat as a cow pie in a heat wave, totally ignoring him.

Determined that there was no coming back without the kid, the Small Visionary decided to swing on his rope, up and down, triggering a motion that he was determined to magnify until the amplitude of the resulting oscillations allowed him to touch Theodors' back for a brief second at the peak of each vibration.

He was almost there, ready to triumph.

Stretching more.

Just a few extra inches.

When, in his last attempt to reach, raising his feet to gain every little bit that counted, and throwing his arm forward in an attempt to grab Theodors by the back of his shirt, the rope slid from under one of his knees. The jerky motion threw him sideways and, in an attempt to grab the rope with his hand to recover his balance, up and back. As the energy suddenly built into the system by all these sudden contortions was released—the rope from which he barely hung behaving like the string of a bow—the remaining limb lost its grip and he was flipped up in the air. As if launched by an incompetent archer, he flew up only a few seconds, twisting and rolling uncontrollably, until landing head first into the mud. Upon impact, the knot tying his robe around his ankles released.

Of the Small Visionary, planted in the mud to his waist, one could only see his ass and two legs shaking and kicking with vivacity. This was not a pretty sight—but entertaining enough, as the crowd screamed, shouted, and eventually gasped when the kicking stopped and it dawned on all that an era had ended in suffocation. Many of the spectators had only known one Small Visionary in their entire life. A profound silence underscored the gravity of this historic moment [*His·to·ry. Noun. Sum of events, acts, or ideas that a biased agent has embellished to shape the course of the future, particularly when the agent is at the service of those claiming to have driven the events*].

Breaking the solemnity, the Kritikillar ordered a couple of Fanatiks—real ones—to rescue the Small Visionary, or, rather, recover his suffocated carcass. After having seen what had just happened, they weren't eager to go, but orders were orders. They took their time. They brought a step ladder—as they didn't have the moral authority to step on backs—pulled on the ropes, as if to test the sturdiness of the system, left the stepladder to hang themselves upside down, and slid along to the limit of their acrobatic skills.

All for naught.

By the time they reached the Visionary, his legs were limp as a dehydrated plant—or, more appropriately, since it wasn't for lack of water in the mud, limp like overcooked noodles. They could have grabbed his legs by the ankles when they were sticking up straight, but not anymore as the limbs had fallen flat into the mud. Given that they couldn't reach him, they started to come back, but the Kritikillar, unpleased, pointed to the Visionary, waving his finger in a way that clearly said: "Don't you dare come back without him." Limp legs or not, they had to bring him back.

They got the message, and slid back, probably grumbling that it would have been so much simpler to lower the ropes before trying again. But, as always, orders were orders.

After thinking for a few minutes to determine how to proceed, one of the Fanatiks wrapped his belt around his wrist, offering a stirrup in which the other slipped a foot. Then, taking advantage of that support, respectively grabbing their wrists in a lock allowed the second Fanatik to swing to a level where he could catch hold of one of the Visionary's legs.

The crowd clapped, impressed by the improvised acrobatics. They ended up being entertained on that day, after all.

The Fanatiks pulled on the noodle, hard as they could. A leg stretched straight above his ass, the other flapped down; the Visionary's carcass didn't budge otherwise. They pulled with all their might, but all that moved any further was the rope, which seriously sagged in reaction to the downward pull, to the point where the hanging Fanatik's head almost touched the mud. That's when the humid leg slipped out of his grip. The release on the rope, much like a bow, propelled the two Fanatiks up. Whether they skillfully managed to hold on to the rope as they repeatedly swung up and down, or involuntarily got entangled in it, nobody knows, but either way, the outcome of the near-death high-wire act was the same: they impressively managed to avoid being dunked in the mud like the Small Visionary. They promptly slid back to solid ground and ran away with a determination that no vigorous finger pointing could reverse, oblivious to the barking of the Kritikillar.

"Go get the kid," he ordered another pair of Fanatiks.

They didn't move.

"It's an order!"

Nothing.

He pointed to two other Fanatiks.

"You two. Go."

They ignored him too.

Orders were not orders anymore.

"That's insubordination! You're going to regret this. You're all going to regret this. The two running idiots there, too."

He took a deep breath, fuming.

"Now, you all, listen carefully," he shouted to all Fanatiks within earshot. "I own your muscles. When I order them to move, they better move. I need two Fanatiks on that rope, right here, right now!"

All the Fanatiks stayed put.

"Imbeciles! You're just a bunch of brainless imbeciles."

Mad as he was, the Kritikillar had to swallow his pride and contain his anger. The Fanatiks were truly dumdums, but like all idiots, they didn't think so. By their standards, they didn't know any better, and further insulting them was risking an insurgency.

He had to face the facts. No stick or carrot worked. Threats were futile. The Small Visionary, like the horse—but less elegantly—would remain there, in full display, until the road either dried or froze.

The Kritikillar could live with that. As long as he was concerned, the Stupid Visionary had asked for it and could rot there forever.

But, Theodors couldn't be left there. He still had to be rescued.

None of the Fanatiks and none of the bystanders—be they villagers, peasants, Perfectionists, or Illiterantes in hiding—cared enough to risk their life to save a Kafkaist kid. Even though that kid had officially been converted into an Authorian. Since nobody had direct blood ties to Theodors, nobody felt a moral obligation to help. Nobody was motivated to act.

Except the Kritikillar.

An entire trial—my trial—had hinged on the fact that I had kidnapped a genuine Authorian. That I had irresponsibly and recklessly delivered him into the claws of Kafkaists. That such an ignominious act deserved an infinitely long torture and—cherry on the cake—death. No less.

The Kritikillar's credibility was at stake.

Yet, he wasn't about to play monkey and risk both his life and, more importantly, his dignity by dangling like a fool from a clothesline.

Therein lay the dilemma.

"We can still do like I had originally planned," I snapped.

The Kritikillar looked at me, wondering what other stupid idea I had come up with this time.

"Do what?"

"Pick up the kid, from there, and bring him back here."

"Who would?"

"I would. As I originally had offered."

I knew he remembered. He wasn't keen on the idea, but he was stuck.

"I only have one condition," I added.

"And you have a condition on top of that?"

"Yes, but nothing you should have much of a problem with."

"That is…"

"I want to do it, helped by the person of my choice."

He seemed relieved that this was all I requested. It really wasn't much to ask. In fact, compared to overturning a death penalty and a torturefest, it was nothing. Given the circumstances, I could have asked for a bronze statue of myself naked and holding a giant globe above my head, to be erected in his bedroom, and probably would have gotten away with it.

"Why can't you do it alone?"

"I have a small handicap," I replied, pulling my sleeve to show my crooked arm.

He was still on the fence, but wobbling.

"Why do you think the kid will want to come with you—his abductor—more than with his spiritual father?"

I just smiled. A tight lips smile that, with raised eyebrows, emphasized that he didn't have anything to lose.

"Fine," he said, spreading his arms.

"Great. I'll be back."

He motioned two Fanatiks to escort me. They looked at each other, as if questioning whether it was worth obeying the Kritikillar anymore, but seemed to agree that a small walk wasn't worth a fight, and followed me. We strode all the way to the end of the street, where I could have sworn that I had seen June's face shine above the crowd.

I didn't have to look for long. As I walked down the sidewalk and up to the dry part of Main Street, everybody rushed out of my way; as if a recently pardoned convict having escaped death by the skin of the teeth was a dangerous pariah—a walking dead that could only bring bad luck.

Everybody rushed out of my way, except her.

I had been right. It was indeed June.

Beautiful as ever.

Defiant as ever.

In pants, as always—but partly hidden under a long shirt. She had dressed in drab colors to blend in with the crowd and not attract attention—although that was probably an unnecessary precaution because everybody was so focused on the whole circus that nobody would have noticed anything odd about her even if she had been dressed as a sandwich, stark naked between two giant slices of bread.

She looked exasperated, arms crossed, as if waiting for me.

"What are your gorillas here for?" she said, pointing at the Fanatiks.

"Nothing. Think of them as chewing gum under my shoes."

She shrugged.

The gorillas weren't bright enough to be insulted.

"Your parents aren't here?" I asked, although I only cared to know if her own primate of a brother was lurking around.

"I'm the only one that... could make it," she replied, pausing to carefully pick her words and not reveal that she was a Kafkaist. "We've got a chewing gum problem too."

I felt bad for her family, but was at the same time relieved that Damien was under house arrest.

"This is not going to work without you," I said.

"What are you talking about?"

"I'm talking about the little kid out there in the mud."

There were too many people within earshot. I leaned forward and whispered in her ear.

"We have to get Theodors out of there. You've seen it. He won't let anyone rescue him. You're the only one who can do it."

She pulled back.

"I'm not getting on that rope. Didn't you see what happened?"

"That old fart couldn't even walk on solid ground without falling. He had no place on the rope."

I could be blunt. This far back in the crowd, I was only surrounded by folks from faraway villages who couldn't care less about our own Small Visionary.

"I'm talking about the other gorillas."

"The rope was too high. They should have lowered it. In fact, it's already being lowered," I emphasized, pointing at Zayne hard at work already.

"As far as I'm concerned, unless the rope lies flat on the ground, it's a circus act. It's too dangerous."

"It's not dangerous."

"Fine. Why don't you do it then?"

"Come on. It's been pretty clear that Theodors won't allow any... um... folks like me to touch him," I said, refraining from saying "Authorian."

The last thing I needed was to agitate the mob surrounding us by an accidental slip of a word. Never more than at that moment did it strike me that nobody could ever tell the difference between an Authorian and a Kafkaist, unless words betrayed our thoughts. Unfortunate words. It was depressing to think that I could start a riot by revealing that she was a Kafkaist.

"Please."

She didn't answer. I took it as a sign that her resolve could be shaken.

"Listen, if safety is your only concern, then I'll go with you."

"What for? So that we can both fall off and sink in the mud."

"No. So that I can make sure that the rope safely stays behind your knees. That it doesn't slide off. Besides, a little bit more weight on the rope will make it more stable."

I totally made up that last part, but it seemed credible.

She remained silent, again, weighing the pros of saving her little brother against the cons of dangling upside down like a bat for a few minutes.

"If you let that rope slip off from under my knees, I'll kill you before you even hit the mud."

Truth be Told

Our lives literally hanging on a thread, we slowly slid down the rope, upside down, June first, while I held her ankle with my good hand as a way to lock the rope in place.

"Tell me if I pull too hard."

No response probably meant it was fine. Or that she was scared senseless, as she moved incredibly slow along the line. Which was fine. There certainly was no rush. Theodors was not going anywhere. As for the crowd, I couldn't care less about keeping them waiting—I wouldn't have done this kind of acrobatics to save any one of them from drowning in mud.

My other hand held to the rope, but this was for appearances only, to reassure June who didn't know how useless that arm really was; my sliding along the rope was all by movements of the legs.

"Pants? A woman in pants?" had barked the Kritikillar when he had seen June tuck her long shirt and tighten her belt.

"She needs pants to do this job."

"Why?"

"To avoid further offending young eyes if somehow we fail," I replied, pointing to the disturbing sight of the Small Visionary's ass still sticking up from the mud—a crow, perched on it, was apparently trying to decide whether it should start picking at the worm now or come back later when all the spectators would be gone.

He grumbled.

"Use a guy then."

"Have you seen any guy succeed so far?"

He huffed, but let us proceed. There was nothing to lose and we would be within his sight all the time, anyhow.

And so we dangled, carefully sliding down the rope, somewhat locked together, somewhat not.

When we finally reached the horse, Theodors was still lying face down on it.

"Theo," she whispered.

His head twitched.

"Theo, it's me. June."

He raised his head.

"Let's go home," she said, extending her arm.

He flipped his head down, pressing it on the horse.

"No?"

He shook his head. A definite no.

June was hurt.

I could tell.

I should have held her in my arms then, but hanging upside down is not a propitious setting for consoling a woman. Besides, I doubt she would have welcomed my open arms; it was my fault if she was there, acrobatically against her will.

In any event, open arms there couldn't be as I had to hang tight to her ankle with my good arm.

"You try," she said.

"Theodors. It's your sister," I whispered, so that no one else could understand and identify her as a Kafkaist.

He looked up for an instant, then dropped his head down. That was a good thing. Had he grabbed my hand, it would have crushed her.

Technically, she could have grabbed him by the back of his shirt and dragged him back wiggling, screaming, and crying, but that would also have broken her heart.

Although, in principle, I would have loved hanging forever with June, there's a practical limit to how long one can stay upside down, and with all that blood flowing to my head, I was starting to get dizzy. Also, I could hear a thunderstorm approaching; I wasn't sure if birds on a wire can be lightning targets, but Theodors, in his mud pool, was well grounded for that purpose.

"I have a plan," I snapped.

"Again?"

"Well, it's not a plan then. It's just an idea," I replied extending my free arm to grab her hand.

I showed her the motion and a sparkle lit her eye. She understood.

"Theodors," we whispered in unison, and repeated until he lifted his head.

What he saw was two hands, fingers laced together, at the end of two arms inviting him to come back to life.

What he saw was an Authorian and a Kafkaist working together to rescue him, so that he wouldn't have to take sides.

What he saw was good.

He grabbed our fingers to find his balance, stood up on the horse, and sat on our joined hands, holding our arms like one holds the ropes of a swing. June was beaming, with her widest smile ever and tears on her cheeks—actually, on her forehead to be exact, as we were still hanging upside down.

The human trapeze slowly slid back toward the sidewalk as the bystanders were clapping, although I'm sure the clapping would have been more intense—and accompanied by wild cheering—if the rope had snapped, dropping us all in deep mud, as this would have been more suitable entertainment to a crowd that originally assembled for a matinee of fine torture.

In any event, all that mattered as we approached the stepladder on the sidewalk, was that the rescue was a total success and that I would recover my freedom. I imagined that a special banquet would take place to honor us, where we would be asked to sign autographs, and where someone at the end would announce that Main Street will be, "from now on, renamed: Adam's Rescue Way."

"Arrest him," ordered the Kritikillar as soon as I set foot to the ground.

"What?"

I expected the two Fanatiks that were standing next to him to grab my arms and lift me off the ground, but one of them didn't move and the other one only put his hand on my shoulder, without conviction.

"You can't do that. You said you would lift my death penalty and revoke my torture sentence. Everybody here could testify that they heard you say that."

The crowd remained quiet. There would be no autographs after all. It was clear that I couldn't count on a riot to help me. That crowd had come to see me fried alive; nothing else.

"I did say that, indeed," replied the Kritikillar, "but that was before the Small Visionary died because of you. A few claps for your entertaining stunt won't change that."

"He didn't die because of me."

"Is this what this was all about?" asked June, upset.

"He died because that contraption of yours wasn't safe," clarified the Kritikillar.

"What? He insisted on using it. I didn't—"

"It was your responsibility to warn him of the possible dangers and you failed to do that."

"You had a deal to trade my little... the little kid, in exchange for his mercy?" asked June.

"No, it's not that."

"You've played me," she sneered, whispering, walking away.

"Not at all. There was no deal."

"The deal is broken because your fancy ideas have cost the life of a Small Visionary," declared the Kritikillar, not helping. "That cannot remain unpaid."

"Don't listen to him. It's not what you think. It's more complicated."

She stopped. Mad for sure, but a pause nonetheless. One that suggested that an iota of doubt remained. A tiny hope that maybe I was sincere, that maybe she shouldn't destroy possible dreams without being absolutely sure that no misunderstanding existed.

"I'll replace him."

"Who said that?" thought everybody, looking around.

I saw June, appalled, and knew immediately where to look.

"I'll be the next Small Visionary," proclaimed Theodors.

A frog wanting to become a cow deserves to be ridiculed, but this wasn't a regular frog. Nobody laughed. The tension was palpable.

"Why do you say that, kid?" asked the Kritikillar, with gravity, not sure how to react.

"A son must replace his father," replied Theodors without skipping a beat.

Horror replaced consternation on June's face. Horror and hate.

"You knew it. You knew it all along, didn't you?" she shouted.

"June—"

"Theo. Stop being stupid," she snapped, interrupting me, at the risk of revealing too much.

"I'm not stupid. I'll be the next, brand-new Small Visionary. That's what I want to do."

"It's not your business to pay back his debts. Come with me. Now."

The Kritikillar started to suspect something, but before he could say a word, someone screamed.

"Adam. Adam, my love. You are amazing. You're the true love of my life," shouted Cassandra, pushing through the crowd and throwing herself in my arms—I turned around, trying to avoid her, but she still grabbed me and glued herself on my back, like a leech, arms wrapped around my chest *[Blood·suck·er. Noun. In its best form, a leech or a mosquito; in its worst form, Cassandra]*.

"You have saved the little kid that I had bookmarked. It's a sign. It's so clear. So powerful. I'm so sorry I doubted you," she sobbed while squeezing the air out of my lungs. "I will marry you, I will. Just like the Small Visionary had planned."

"I thought you had recanted earlier today," replied the Kritikillar. "Now, did you or did you not bookmark that kid?"

"I did, I did," she declared. "I'm so sorry I lied today. I lost my mind. It's because I can't watch torture."

Whatever iota of doubt might have existed in June's mind, it was squashed, both feet stomping, by Cassandra's silly rapture and Theodors' naive prophecy.

"So that was your plan," snapped June. "You're the most despicable person in the whole world."

She walked away, determined that, this time, nothing would stop her.

"Wait. Wait," I pled.

I tried to run after June but in vain, unable to free myself from the scatterbrain's grip—who was clinging to me even tighter.

"There was no plan. Not like that. Don't listen to them."

She wasn't listening. Not to them, not to me, not to anybody. Her pace increased.

"You can't leave like that. It's not fair."

She stopped, turned around, rushed back, and stood in my face.

"You're right."

She slapped me in the face. With conviction. Weaker necks would have snapped.

"Now, it's fair," she said, before leaving.

I tried to wiggle out of Cassandra's bear hug to run after June, but her grip wouldn't release. I pushed her arms down, hoping to jump out of her claws, but fell face first as she tackled me around the knees.

By the time I freed myself from Cassandra's embrace, June was long gone, our fate a foregone conclusion.

I thought I was crushed.

"So be it," proclaimed the Kritikillar, looking at Cassandra and me. "I'll marry you tomorrow morning at sunrise."

Now I was really crushed.

The End

Thrilled by the thought of marrying what she considered to be a hero, Cassandra had remained glued to me for what seemed like hours; it took a crowbar to peel her off. She eventually understood that, if her dream wedding was to take place at sunrise, as decreed by the Kritikillar, she couldn't remain stuck to my skin like fir resin until then. She had to go home and get ready.

As for me, I was sentenced to spend the night in a guarded yard of the Librariatorium. That was a wise decision. Keeping the bridegroom in a flooded dungeon would have been poor wedding planning, because one should never give a reluctant husband the opportunity to drown not-so-accidentally.

Nonetheless, this turned out to be a strategic mistake on their part.

When the Fanatiks brought me a tuxedo early in the morning, they didn't find anybody to wear it. Only an empty yard. Zayne had finally got the chance to deploy the ropeway for its intended purpose. I was plucked out of the guarded yard, forever grateful—as was Zayne who considered that his debt was now duly repaid.

At that point, any sane person would have run away. Vanished. Disappeared. Found a new life, thousands of leagues away. But sanity had never been my forte.

The dictionary clearly states that love and infatuation are two very different things. *[In·fat·u·a·tion. Noun. A foolish or all-absorbing passion; can be a one-way street]; [Love. Noun. Illogical and undefinable affection and attraction; requires two beings to reciprocate]*. So I needed to know if June had also a budding love that could someday reach full bloom, or if, all this time, I had followed a one-way street that led to a dead-end. If there was no point continuing, I had to know; I had to be sure. Realistically, it didn't look promising, but there was always the possibility that the day before, in the heat of the moment, with Theodors playing prophet and Cassandra clinging to me like a limpet, the misleading evidence assaulting her senses couldn't be analyzed rationally. With the distance and perspective of a night's sleep, there was a slight possibility that if June had ever loved me, she might have forgiven me. Maybe there was only a slim chance—an infinitesimally minuscule one—that this was the case, but I would never be able to sleep again if I didn't make one last ditch effort to find out if all my hopes and dreams of a future together had been in vain.

So at sunrise, hiding in the forest, her house in sight, a bunch of wild flowers in hand, I waited.

There was no point walking up to her door. It was quite early in the morning and everybody was likely still sleeping, but I was too afraid that if anyone from June's family saw me before her, they would catch me and beat me to pulp, big brother leading the way by dispensing knuckle-sandwiches, father Hipper swinging a hatchet, mother Hipper kicking my genitals in orbit, and all of June's other siblings stabbing me with red-hot irons. Maybe that would not have been the case and I was being overly pessimistic, but I had no desire to check. I preferred to wait.

So I waited.

And waited.

Nobody was getting out of her house. I wondered how long it would take after the discovery of my disappearance from the Librariatorium before someone would put two and two together and come looking for me in her Kafkaist village. I was pretty certain that nothing I had said or done the previous day could have led someone to identify June as a Kafkaist, but, at the same time, it wouldn't take a genius to connect the dots and understand why only both of us, as a team, could rescue Theodors. In my village of morons, where everybody is involved in manufacturing doors, not everybody is as dumb as a doorknob.

Finally, for once in my life, I got lucky: June got out of her house, alone, without anyone else from her family, an empty basket in hand, walking at brisk pace. From what I could remember of the village's layout, based on my experience as a mailman, she seemed on to be her way to the village's general store. Running through the forest around the village, I made it there before her and waited in the alley next to the store, hoping that I had correctly guessed where her empty basket was to be filled.

Peeking around the corner of the building, I saw her approach. I stood still, in the middle of the alley, in the shade but close enough to the street that she couldn't miss me.

She didn't. She stopped right in front of me.

"June, I love you. I am so sorry that you misunderstood my true intentions. I would have never done anything to intentionally hurt you in any way. I most sincerely apologize for all the anguish and pain I may have accidentally caused you, and hope you can forgive me," is what I should have said, offering the bouquet of wild flowers as a symbol of my sincerity.

"June," is what I actually said, arms limp by my side, wild flowers shamefully pointing down. The daggers in her eyes had made me lose all confidence.

She moved towards me, daggers still launching.

I raised my hand, putting the flowers in her face, unable to speak. She grabbed the bunch and threw it on the ground.

"June, I—"

She slapped me in the face.

Stunned, I remained silent for a few seconds.

Everything could be lost forever. I had to get a grip.

"I am so sorry that you misunderstood my true—"

She slapped me again.

"Hey. You could at least let me finish."

"No. Flowers and words won't make a difference."

"Let me explain—"

She slapped once more, harder.

"That's all you deserve for your lies," she said, slapping me twice more.

I shut up.

The door was closed. I didn't want to pry it open, like an intruder. I wanted it to open by itself. If I was unwelcome, there was no point.

After the last slap, we both stood there, facing each other, silent. A silence that says more than words, but that confuses.

For a moment, the daggers in her eyes seemed to have duller blades. I wondered if that was only my imagination. If not, maybe the door had been closed, but not nailed shut. Unfortunately, as words and flowers had failed, I didn't know what else could be done—should be done.

That's when the village's damn Chihuahua saw me and started barking. Stupid flea bag. I hadn't seen it coming.

If Fanatiks had reached the village by now, or if June's big brother was awake, there was no doubt that all this yapping would alert them. All those who'd love to murder me would show up in less than a minute.

I looked at June for a few more seconds, to etch some desperate lasting images in my brain. I wanted to hug her, I wanted to kiss her, but I couldn't stand the thought that all my memories of our time together would end with the one recollection of her hands pushing me away, rejecting me.

I fled into the forest, hoping that if Fanatiks showed up, June wouldn't tell them that I had been there and wouldn't send those bloodhounds on my trail—hoping that, even though she slapped me more than a burly old maid beating a rug on a clothesline, she would allow me to live as a fugitive, if only for having tried to save her brother.

As I ran away, I shouted: "I can wait ten years if that is how long it takes for you to forgive me."

"Ten years from now, I'll be happily married, I'll have four children, and I won't even remember you."

So, there it was.

Unambiguously clear.

All this time, I had been on a one-way street.

I would have loved things to turn out better, but they didn't.

There's no Author.

That's how it goes.

The end.

That was ten years ago.

Quiescence

Days are migratory birds that fly by. Inconspicuously, they fly low. So low that we only see them one at a time, deceiving us, avoiding census. Yet, those birds really have birdbrains: they are migratory birds that forget to come back.

A decade ends when the last bird of its flock goes by. Of course, there are more flocks to come. Especially when it's only the early birds that have left, in haste. But while thinking of those ahead—happy bird days and not so happy ones—one cannot help but reflect on the decade that has vanished.

So many things happened in that decade. The biggest one probably being the invasion. A few weeks after I last saw June, Materialists marched through the entire Stygian Dominion, including Cimmerian county, and conquered it, village by village.

Materialists believe that the Author is incarnate in objects and that accumulating possessions is the way to endear themselves to Him. As if the Author was a gigantic puzzle that could be partly understood by those owning the largest number of contiguous pieces. Conquering more territory is consistent with that vision. The only reason they hadn't done so earlier was to honor a non-aggression treaty signed in earlier times when opposing rulers assessed that their respective armies were at even strength and only capable of mutual self-destruction.

While the ink of these signatures aged and became more brittle, Materialists acquired gadgets and knowledge that allowed them to develop the war machines needed to give them surefire military superiority. Having then accumulated enough of those toys to obliterate any possible resistance, the time was ripe to invade, and all they waited for was an excuse to declare that the spirit of the treaty has been violated, rendering it null and void.

The singing wire delivered the needed excuse. Whereas before, the news of a Kafkaist's abduction would not have escaped the village where morons made a big deal of it, it was now possible for all the details of such a sordid event to travel on the wires, one dot or dash at a time. That's all that was needed. It became big news. It forced many to question what is admissible and what is not; what is natural and what is degenerate; what is defensible and what is abhorrent.

More importantly, it allowed weasels and grandstanders in cahoots to surf the wave of public opinion and steer impressionable minds in whatever direction was best to help them achieve their goals. These kingpins had no scruples feigning outrage over Theodors' abduction if it served that purpose. His abuse was the embodiment of everything that was wrong in the neighboring Dominion, and that called for humanitarian intervention.

Theodors' hardships became the catalyst for the invasion, but, all in all, he was just a pawn in a big game. Like I was too. In fact, who wasn't?

To their surprise, as they marched through Cimmerian County, the Materialists hardly found any opposition. Unbeknownst to them, most Fanatiks had already quit their functions, incensed by the Kritikillar's disparaging remarks of the week prior—as those insults had spread through the ranks like wildfire. A handful continued to serve, either for lack of a place to call home or for lack of fully functioning brain gears, but, realizing that they were grossly outnumbered, they waved the white flag so fast that mosquitoes squashed by flags were the largest casualties of the conflict.

As for the remaining Perfectionists and Visionaries, they vanished faster than their shadows as the Materialist war machine drove through their villages.

The invaders, who had expected their aggression to be met with virile opposition but instead found nobody on their path, wondered if this massive refusal to fight was actually a sick strategy, like an illusion to better ensnare them later when they would least expect it. When an army comes fully prepared for bloody battles and massive casualties, but instead gets quickly accustomed to strolling through enemy lines unopposed, the sharp edge of troops rapidly dulls, and soldiers start dreaming of more comfortable lives, which can jeopardize the outcome of battles. Therefore, to ensure that no counter-attack could unexpectedly spring from the bushes and turn all those easy gains into sore loses, the Materialist's Chief Consumer dispatched to the Kritikillar a cease-fire offer with favorable terms. In exchange for surrender of the Kritikillar's troops and his immediate resignation as moral and political leader of the county, he would be allowed to live in one of the handful of villages that would be spared from the conquest and that could serve as Authorian Reserves, where those unable to reconvert as Materialists could remain *[Re·serve. Noun. Tract of undesirable land— such as villages with impassable muddy roads— magnanimously granted to the conquered to allow them to intermingle out of sight]*. Of course, the terms of the offer also stipulated that if the Kritikillar instead preferred to turn down this generous offer, the Chief Consumer would personally behead him when he would be captured in battle. Fully aware that very few Fanatiks were ready to fight to the death for his protection, the Kritikillar made the right choice and officially agreed to become a regular civilian, stuffed in a forgotten village somewhere, head still duly attached to his shoulders.

That's how Cimmerian County became Obsidian County—a new Materialist county.

That was fine by me.

Authorians, Kafkaists, Materialists, Whateverists; I couldn't care less. It's all the same. Controlling freaks.

Interestingly, my village of morons was designated as one of these Authorian Reserves. It is odd to think that it probably would not have earned this special status if the invasion had happened during a dry spell instead of rainy weeks. After the Main Street mud swamp swallowed a few invading soldiers—mostly curious ones who had ventured to see what was that smelly horse and strange ass sticking out from the road—the Materialists deemed the disgusting village of no appeal whatsoever. Disgusting, useless villages being the perfect place where to pack all undesirables, it became a Reserve.

Throughout the invaded lands, Small Visionaries were stripped of all powers, privileges, and accumulated wealth, and were forced to dress like peasants and live in tiny apartments. However, in each Reserve, there remained a cesspool of unrepentant Perfectionists and Authorians that still venerated them, with the likes of Cassandra kissing their feet as if it served a purpose.

On the positive side, with all die-hard Authorians—who refused to become Materialists—packed in Reserves and forbidden to leave those corrals without permission, they didn't have the means to harass Kafkaists anymore. Books that depicted Kafkaists as less than animals were not permitted anymore. Of course, prejudice and meanness couldn't be pried off sick heads, so while those in the Reserves couldn't freely say that Kafkaists were wrong, they could rephrase it all positively by chanting that Authorians bask in light and hold the only absolute truths. New packaging, same feelings, but, at least, there would be no more silly kidnapping.

Incidentally, the Kafkaists were also left free to live their own random lives, in their own paddocks. They were given a new-found freedom, in that they could now work in any trade they wanted, although, for the most part, they remained in the coal industry—they didn't get to see the sun any more than before, but at least, they could now buy doors from anybody they wished.

So, in short, a lot happened.

However, as far as I was concerned, it is not what had happened in the past decade that mattered most. It is what didn't happen.

To my initial surprise, nobody went hunting for me after I fled to avoid marrying Cassandra. The Fanatiks in June's village that had been alerted by the noise when I ran away only found a stupid Chihuahua pulling on a leash tied to a tree and barking for no apparent reason, and didn't think much of it. As for those in my village, they weren't inclined to serve the Kritikillar after the lack of respect he had shown them. I would have thought it impossible to escape the claws of matrimony, given that the Kritikillar had been the one playing puppeteer with those claws, but apparently—as my Illiterantes friends reported from their spying visits as magicians—he too got tired of Cassandra's theatrical foolishness, and left the same day I did; he had bigger fish to fry elsewhere, because he had received word of the imminent invasion. No Fanatiks remained with the Small Visionary, as their original allegiance was to the capital, not to him.

So, what was I to do?

On one hand, there was no need to escape and hide at the end of the world. On the other hand, I couldn't return to my village since there was nothing for me there—particularly since it served as a refuge for lunatics. And on the other hand—if I had a third hand—June's village was not an option either, for obvious reasons. Therefore, I took an easy way out and elected to stay with my Illiterantes friends. Granted they were nervous at first, afraid that the forest would be searched by hordes of Fanatiks, looking for me, but once it became pretty clear that this would not happen, they granted me an honorary Illiterantes status; all it took was a handshake—no bookmarking and silly ceremonials needed.

From there, I settled, adapting to life in the clandestine camp atop a mountain where the only rules dictating behavior were those necessary for survival and to avoid attracting attention. For example, fires were only allowed in closed containers on moonless nights to keep all smoke invisible, trees could only be sparingly cut in a manner to preserve camouflage, and all able bodies contributed to the community in a manner commensurate to one's abilities. As such, my main duty consisted of hunting—with bow and arrows, as shooting noises would betray our stealth existence. My assigned sector was the west flank of the mountain, which suited me fine as, that way, I avoided running into Authorians south, Kafkaists north, and Materialists traveling on the road east.

So as far as the rest of the world was concerned, like all Illiterantes, I had vanished from the face of the earth. In some ways, that's what everybody wanted my destiny to be from the very beginning, but at least, I had vanished without being erased.

In ten years of my newfound, simple life, not once did I ever return to my village. Not even disguised as a magician. It was too risky. In fact, even if I had painted my face white, put a red ball on my nose, drew a three-inch wide smile around it with lipstick, shaved my head leaving only orange-dyed wing-tipped hair on the sides, dressed in a rainbow colored suit with a giant bow tie, a flower that squirted water on my lapel, and shoes ten sizes bigger than my feet, I was sure that Cassandra—or even my parents— would have recognized me in a second if I ran into them. That was the last thing I wanted. I preferred to have ceased to exist as far as they were concerned. Besides, I didn't care to get news from the village—or from anywhere else for that matter—because I didn't belong there anymore. I didn't need them.

My secluded life was satisfactory.

Fulfilling.

Perfect.

Sort of.

The only place from my past where I regularly returned was the hollow in the woods with the stream where I had first met June. I returned there often, both in memories and in person. Admittedly, it was on the south side of the mountain and I shouldn't have been there, but I felt that it was far enough from the village to be safe. Besides, if Cassandra had been there once, it was only because she had followed me. There was no compelling reasons for her to venture there anymore.

Somehow, that oasis in the middle of nature called me. It made me both terribly sad and genuinely happy, in soothing ways I cannot explain. It was both a wound and a panacea. It was as if I would always reconnect with a part of my soul there. The little bit of soul that I had lost in the woods that I would find and re-embrace, only to accidentally forget it again when leaving.

It was a peaceful and eternal communion with eternity.

Quiet.

Transcendent.

Except last month, when my silent contemplation was disturbed by the noise of approaching footsteps. I immediately hid behind rocks, waiting to see who was coming—my first thought being that it was probably Cassandra fulfilling her lifelong mission to turn my life into a nightmare.

Mercifully, it wasn't her.

A young man, without weapons, walked up to the stream and lied on a rock, basking in the sun. He must have stayed there for an hour, contemplative—unforgivably stealing my favorite spot.

I wasn't about to stay hidden all day waiting for him to leave, so I tried to slowly and quietly move back, to vanish unnoticed, into the woods. My feet moved ever so slowly, crushing the undergrowth so gently that the resulting noise was imperceptible.

So I thought.

"Who's there?" he asked, springing up on his rock.

I froze.

"I know someone's there," he added.

I remained still.

"There! There, I see the top of your head."

He had to bluff. I didn't respond.

"Don't be afraid. I'm unarmed. I am a friend."

I had no friend.

I figured that if I dashed into the forest in a westward direction, I could outrun him without giving up clues that would direct his attention north, up the mountain.

I jumped and started to run.

"Hey, don't run. I'm a friend. What's your name? My name's Theodors."

I stopped.

Theodors.

I was already quite far into the forest, and his voice was faint, but I had heard it clearly. As clearly as on that dreaded night when he was stolen from his parents.

I couldn't leave. After all, it was my fault if he was there.

I came back slowly.

He offered his hand to shake as I approached.

I looked at him in the eyes for a moment. His hand was still extended.

"I can't shake your hand."

"Why is that?"

"I'm Adam."

He kept his hand up.

"So?"

"You don't know who I am, right?"

"Actually, I do. I have only known one Adam in my life, and he's the one who rescued me out of a muddy street."

"Wrong. I'm the Adam who was with the thieves that stole you from your family."

"I know that too. Your past deeds are all well remembered in the village. Even taught to little kids."

"Why?"

"Let's say that you are not exactly portrayed as a role model."

"So you know that I stole you from your Kafkaist parents and you are fine with it?"

"Sure."

"Why?"

"Because next week, I'll be eighteen. I'll be eligible to become Small Visionary."

A decade earlier, as a crazy idea from a kid who didn't know the meaning of those words, it didn't seem so bad, but from a young adult who should have known better, it sounded truly horrible.

"I thought Small Visionaries had been banished."

"Officially, yes. Practically, no."

No surprise there. Anything prohibited is sure to find addicts.

"Listen. Don't become a Small Visionary."

"Why not?"

"That's a ridiculous idea."

"Why?"

"Why? Why? Tons of reasons. First of all, you are a Kafkaist."

"And an Authorian. I've been bookmarked."

"If you believe Cassandra," I was about to reply, but didn't. Of course all Small Visionaries would believe Cassandra; that dumbbell existed solely to serve them. I shuddered just thinking of her—and of the fact that she probably looked exactly like her mother by now.

"It is pointless to have been bookmarked, and it is pointless to become a Small Visionary," I replied instead. "The Author is dead. Dead as a doorknob."

"I know that's what you think."

"No, no. It's not an opinion. It's a fact. He shot himself in the head. I've seen it with my own eyes."

"And yet, here I am, alive, and soon to be the new Small Visionary."

"Why do you want to do that? There's no point anymore. There's no more Cimmerian, there's no more Kritikillar; it's all gone."

"There's the Reserve. As long as there'll be Authorians, there will be a need for Small Visionaries."

"Only clandestinely."

"Makes no difference."

I took a moment to calm down. I stared for a good minute, searching for a little desperate kid, but all I saw was an adult.

"Fine," I said. "Whatever. I don't care. It's not my life."

He remained silent.

He looked at peace.

"You have a lot of work to do to become a Small Visionary," I added. "To fit the part, you'll need to get the bloodshot eyes, the decaying teeth, and to smell like rotten eggs."

He smiled.

"It's not a pre-requisite for the job."

"Based on my experience, it is."

He laughed.

"Fine. I'll work on it. In five hundred years, when I'll be six feet underground, I'll fit the description."

"Some have done it in fifty years above ground."

"I thought you were somewhere, far away," he said, changing the subject.

"Exactly. At the other end of the world, to be precise."

"Hmm hmm. So what brings you here today?"

"Nothing. I just got lost a little bit on my way to the former capital."

"In the woods?"

"By the way," I asked, also using Grandpa's old tactic, "do you ever see your parents?"

"Of course."

"The real ones, I mean."

"That's what I understood. I get permissions to visit them."

"And they're OK with this?"

"No. But we talk. Time and time again, I've tried to bring them to the Authorian way, to the truth, but they don't see it."

"I can't blame them," I thought.

If he regularly saw his parents—long enough to try to convert them—he probably also saw June, but I didn't have the heart to ask questions about her. It would have killed me to hear about her four children and her happy life without me.

"I don't think your parents will ever become Authorians."

"You're probably right. But it's my duty to try."

Poor kid.

Well, poor adult.

"I have to go, Theodors," I said, almost adding "that's all I can take."

"Be safe."

"That's been my plan for a decade," I thought, but just waved as I took off silently.

I left eastward, pretending to go toward the road to the former capital. I looked back a number of times, to be sure he didn't follow me.

The End of the End

For nights after my encounter with Theodors, I couldn't sleep. Yes, it had been a decade, and yes, he didn't know where and how I was living, but I couldn't shake the thought that he was—or was soon to become—a Small Visionary and that nothing good could come of that. My life had been ruined by a Small Visionary and I had no reason to believe that Theodors' friendly demeanor was genuine. In my very own dictionary, Small Visionaries are the quintessence of all that is vile, execrable and abhorrent; it is their sacred mission and only goal in life to make some lives—particularly mine—miserable, and I couldn't think of any reason why Theodors would sidestep his duty in this regard.

I had tried to mislead him as to my actual whereabouts and pretended to be traveling to the former capital, but he was a bright kid. Surely, he had figured out that I had no reason to be in the vicinity of the village if not for the fact that I was living nearby. If anything, my evasive answers were probably hints that confirmed his suspicions, and it would be a simple matter for him and his bunch of Perfectionist minions to search the woods within a radius of a few miles of the village—which included checking the top of the mountain—in hopes of catching me and bringing me to justice.

I kept all those fears to myself, trying to bottle up my anxiety and convince myself that none of that was possible, that all those fears were unfounded, and that all would be fine; but nothing worked. I suffered two weeks of nightmares, each one torturing me more horribly than the previous ones [*Night·mare. Noun. Abridged version of life*]. Two weeks of waking up in sweat and fighting to remain awake, only to collapse back into horrific dreams that pretended to be omens of imminent dangers.

Two weeks, at the end of which someone stepped into one of the traps around the camp. The small bells agitated at our end by vibrations traveling along the rope faster than the wiggling trespasser itself alarmed us of the capture of an intruder—and fueled my worst fears. I wondered which of my worst nightmares of the past two weeks was going to materialize itself. Somebody had gotten flipped upside down and was speedily and unwillingly traveling the ropeway through the forest—most definitely not happy. I dreaded seeing Theodors appear upside down, followed by a rushing mob of Fanatiks, with the torturer in tow for good measure. I deeply regretted not telling Zayne of my encounter with Theodors, not sharing my fears, unintentionally depriving him of the forewarning necessary to prepare for such an assault. My paralysis had jeopardized the Illiterantes' way of life.

I hated myself, but all the self-loathing in the world couldn't change a thing.

If there was to be a fight for survival as a consequence of my stupidity, I had to be on the front line, ready to be the first to be stabbed by swords. I rushed to the end of the ropeway, ready for battle.

To my relief, there was no attacking army.

No assault.

No violence.

No anger.

No fear.

"Adam! You haven't changed one bit—except for the fact that you're the exact upside down image of what I remember."

"June?"

Upside down or not, she was as gorgeous as the memory etched in my mind.

"Why—"

"How about getting me down for a start. Or get up here upside down too, if you prefer. Either way, as long as we can talk eye to eye."

Zayne and I slowly released the tension until she could manage gravity by herself anew, freed from the ropes.

I really didn't know what to say. How does one resume a conversation that ended a decade ago with vigorous slaps in the face and the curse: "Ten years from now, I'll be happily married, I'll have four children and I won't even remember you"?

"How are your four kids?" I said, immediately regretting it, as this was probably the stupidest thing I could have said at that very moment.

"They're great, I'm sure. I'm very much looking forward to their birth someday," she replied, smiling.

I was relieved that she had not climbed up the mountain to resume the slapfest.

"Why don't you folks take a nice hike and chat," said Zayne, diplomatically. "We have tons of other, more important things to do than to listen to your nonsense," he added, somewhat less diplomatically.

She laughed.

I gulped nervously.

We walked slowly around the camp, far enough from it to not be heard, but close enough to avoid setting foot in another trap.

"Why are you here?"

"Don't be stupid. You know I came here to talk to you."

"How did you know I was here?"

"I saw Theodors last week. He told me that he ran into you, that you were evasive. He suspected that you might be hiding somewhere near. Possibly visiting someone. I knew there could only be one place."

"You could have looked for me here before."

"No. I had erased you from my memory."

That was a bad start.

"June. I'm really pleased to see you, but I don't know what to say. All that I ever wanted to tell you, I tried to tell you ten years ago, without success."

That wasn't a particularly brilliant thing to say either. I could have used Grandpa's advice now more than ever, but I'm sure he would have yelled: "Stop behaving like an idiot and tell her that you still love her!"

"Just shut up. I'm the one who's here to talk."

I did shut up—Grandpa's advice ignored.

"I didn't know how long you'd be visiting here, but I took a chance because there are a few things I came here to settle."

Settle. It didn't bode well.

"Ten years ago, I thought I had found my soulmate, that you were to be my partner in life. And then, all of that dream collapsed when you betrayed me, when you not only stole my little brother but used me to turn him over to the Small Wizard."

"Kritikillar."

"Wizard, Quack, I don't care. Don't interrupt me."

I didn't want the slapfest to resume. I shut up.

"Then, when I met Theodors last week, when he came to visit my parents to—again—try to convert them, he mentioned that he saw you. A few days ago. In the woods. I told him that I couldn't care less."

That wasn't promising. Silence was the best defense.

"He looked me straight in the eyes, and said: 'That, I don't believe. You may fool yourself, but you're not fooling me.' Can you believe it? The gall! He hardly ever visits us, and when he does, he never talks to me. All he cares for is to harass my parents about how their lives could be saved if they saw the truth—poor them, so happy to see him but too sad to say anything, so they listen to his nonsense and pretend to be interested just to make sure he continues to come back to visit. So I slapped him."

Somehow, I saw that one coming. I was starting to think that I would be next—in a matter of minutes. I just nodded, without saying a word.

"Too proud to rub his face where I had left a full handprint, he took my hands in his and said: 'June, if you didn't care, you wouldn't have just sat there for ten years, trying to become an old maid.' An old maid! Can you believe it? I'm in my twenties and he had the nerve to call me a spinster."

"I guess you slapped him again," I almost said.

"I slapped him again. Harder."

There.

"That time, you can be sure that he rubbed his face."

With all that anger building up, I braced myself. The upcoming slap was sure to unhinge my jaw.

"Yet, apparently, my little jerk of a brother wanted more. 'June,' he said, 'If you really don't care about Adam, then tell me why.' I should have slapped him again, but I know how to control my emotions, so I just replied: 'What do you care?' To which he responded: 'That's in my nature. I need to know the truth. You know how I hate to be wrong.' He really deserved another slap. Big time. Instead, I took a deep breath, and, do you know what I told him?"

"No, but I guess I'm about to know," I thought, but instead, I remained quiet and just shook my head.

"I shouted as loud as I could: 'Because he betrayed me, you idiot! Because he used me to turn you over to the Small Wizard. Because he knew all along that you'd stay there but he pretended that he wanted to help you. He acted as if he wanted to help me. And I believed him. Like a stupid fool, I believed him.' I repeated the same thing over and over, to make sure that the damn truth that he wanted so bad got drilled in his thick skull."

I wanted to take her hands in mine, to look at her straight in the eyes, and tell her that she was wrong, but I knew that she wouldn't believe me any more now than she did ten years ago.

There was no point.

"He said: 'You really believe that? Really?' and I nodded. Now, don't think for a moment that I cried. I didn't. No way. I just said: 'Yes! Absolutely!' He replied: 'June. When I saw Adam for the first time, it was in the Librariatorium where I was kept to learn the Rules. The first thing that Adam did when he got a minute alone with me was to apologize. Then, making sure there was nobody close enough to hear us, he whispered that he wasn't very good with plans but he promised me that he would do everything he could to bring me back to my parents. My real parents; mom and dad here. If that wasn't what he truly believed, it would have been a pretty stupid thing to say in the middle of a Librariatorium full of Perfectionists.' When Theodors saw that I didn't budge, he added: 'To everyone in that building, that's a crime of heresy. Why would he risk his life saying something like that? Why?' he asked."

She paused for a moment.

"Do you know what I replied?"

I shrugged.

"Because he is stupid," she added while slapping my shoulder. "Stupid, stupid, stupid," she repeated, slapping repeatedly, in rhythm.

"I guess I am," I volunteered.

"Just like I was stupid wasting ten years of my life feeling robbed," she added, stopping the slapping.

She turned around, not wanting me to see the few tears that escaped her guard.

Silence separated us.

Without turning around, she said: "So, now that you've heard all of this, I really need to know one thing, and one thing only. And then I'll leave."

Leave?

"June, I can't stand more questions."

I took her shoulders in my hands.

"I don't know what you've been thinking of me all those years," I added, "but I've been forever thinking of you. You can hate me, you can slap me, you can do or think whatever you want, but I am unable to erase you from my memory. I am incapable of not loving you. I can't do anything about it. It's stronger than me."

She slowly turned around. I held her face in my hands.

"June, I'm sorry. I love you."

Our future lay in her response.

"You've answered my question."

And she kissed me.

Resolution

The speck of light at the end of the tunnel was the only sign of an exit at the other end. As I propelled the handcar on its rails, pushing down and pulling up the handle of the seesaw-like mechanism under the guiding eyes of June, we moved through the darkness, without a lamp, guided only by the lone star ahead.

At last, I was traveling through the mountain, horizontally, taking the long awaited shortcut—a shortcut to nowhere, effectively, as we both came down from the mountain to enjoy it, and planned to come back up afterwards. As infinite as the journey seemed from the onset, the star grew brighter as we approached the end of the line. It grew to be a candle light, then a sun, then a window, and finally a door though which we exited. The last door I would ever go through, because there are no doors in nature, and there would never be any more doors between us.

Through that last doorway, we emerged in broad daylight.
Radiant.
Accomplished.
Yet, we couldn't climb back up the mountain.
Not yet.
There was one more place where we had to go.

The sound of water running through the spring, the leaves rustling in the wind in the trees surrounding the hollow, the birds singing melodies and counterpoints against this symphony, the glowing orange sky of another hard day resting its soul, all added to the magic of this sacred place where we first met and where we now could enjoyed our true communion *[Com·mun·ion. Noun. Intimate communication; Emotional interchange. Old French: "Comme une union" (like a union). Really. Maybe.]*.

"Ssslllooowww, ssslllooowww," said the frogs, coaching us.
"Sweet, sweet, sweet," counseled the birds.

"Kissss, kisssss," sang the grasshoppers.

The warm summer breeze showed how to caress.

"Tsk, tsk, tsk," chirped the chipmunks—out of order.

The butterflies' fingers applied the desirable pressure.

"Hooooo," murmured the owl, opening the path to rapture.

"Whaa, ah, ah, ah, ah," climaxed the eagle.

And the hollow met our destiny, in a divine moment.

All followed by a pregnant silence.

In each other's arms, in absolute peace, her head on my shoulder, we gazed at the stars.

We didn't need a long conversation about whether there was an Author or not. We didn't need to argue about how to open boiled eggs or how to set the time on a clock.

I didn't need to convince her, she didn't need to convince me, because none of that mattered.

It never again would.

Better a dead Author than one that fosters division and pain.

Better a dead Author than one that steals ten prime years from precious lives.

We both agreed with that.

Through all the turmoil, the nonsense of it all, and the tortuous path that our lives followed, we had found each other, and it was good.

The twinkling stars were inspiring.

"Knowing what I know today, in hindsight..."

I stopped talking.

"What's up?" she asked.

"I can't believe it. It's totally insane."

"What's insane?"

"What I'm going to say."

She never understood what was so exceptional about what I said that day.

I did.

I do. My dead Author had played me.

"Knowing what I know today," I said, caressing her hands, staring straight into her ocean blue eyes, "in hindsight, I was born at the best possible place and time on earth. I'd do it all over again."

The End

Deleted Scene #1

The following are a few paragraphs that painted Adam as a more aggressive individual, as this was the tone set in some of the very early drafts of the prologue. It walks a tight line, with an arrogant Adam breaching though the suspension of belief, confident in his conviction that the Author is dead and that this leaves him in control of his story. An Adam that understood much more—possibly too much—the literary framework that dictated his life. However, as Adam evolved into a protagonist overwhelmed by events beyond his control, that approach had to be dropped as it didn't fit anymore. Sadly, those paragraphs had to be erased. In hindsight, that was the proper decision.

By the way, I understand now that I'm the narrator. I forgot to mention. I figured you figured that much. The protagonist and the narrator at the same time, because I'm telling you my story.

It's not a big deal.

I'm Adam.

I know, I know, it's unorthodox, confusing, and—worse—it violates all the rules. But it's a risk I'm willing to assume. Besides, if you made it this far, you're one of those rare members of that endangered minority that still reads books; you definitely have an above average intelligence and you'll figure it out. Hopefully, you'll forgive my annoying interjections throughout this story; I apologize in advance for incongruously breaking the mood here and there. Popping the fantasy bubble is annoying, for sure, but it's necessary in my story.

I'll admit that I always wanted to be the omniscient narrator of a story—any story—so how could have I resisted the seduction of such an intoxicating idea for telling my own story. It's a really cool thing to do—for a fictional character at least, as you can imagine. But the most important reason for taking such an unforgivable literary license is to demonstrate that there's no grand author above all, running the show. Anyhow, I'll tell you more on that later—I know, I'm repeating myself, but, if anything, it further makes my point.

Deleted Scene #2

This is another early version of the prologue (longer versions were also at-tempted). Less aggressive, and more compliant with Adam's frustration with his inability to control his life. Yet, it felt like a road block that had to be circumvented before the story could start. It slowed the narrative flow, so it had to be further edited, down to the final version.

All I want is to be normal, like those kids without mad parents, bruises, and broken bones.

The rapes were horrible, but it was the killings that were unbearable.

It was the best of times, it was the worst of times.

That's how the story would have started if the Author had really existed.

And I wouldn't be writing a prologue.

My very own prologue.

I have been raised to believe that my destiny is in the hands of the Author.

It is ludicrous.

Absurd.

My upbringing required me to imagine that, as I monologue, someone could hear me. Someone whom I have never met; to whom I'll never speak. Someone who might care about me. Or just about my story. Someone who might even love me—only, secretly, like a passionate voyeur.

Part of me wished to believe it, but the better part of me knew this to be utterly illogical. Irrational. Completely insane—no less.

Unfortunately, things have reached a critical point. So, for a moment, I will pretend that it is true, and I will tell my story.

I can't get out of the way, but, from here on out, act as if I just did—as if this prologue does not exist.

Deleted Scene #3

The last paragraphs of the following text were deleted as part of the dialogue between Adam and the Author because, in hindsight, they only served the purpose of inserting an inside joke into the story. The less than subtle reference to the Bulwer-Lytton contest and (more famously) to Snoopy's famous literary ambitions, was too long and did little to move the story forward. So, chop-chop: it didn't make the final cut.

"What is the earliest memory you have? The first words of your life that you can remember?"

"I was born in a village of morons."

"A memory that dates from after your childhood. Isn't it strange? It achronological."

"Why?"

"It's because it is the opening sentence of your story. You can't have memories before then."

"It's a horrible sentence."

"Could have been worse."

"Like what?"

"Like 'It was a dark and stormy night' for example," and he laughed.

"Doesn't sound so bad."

"It's an inside joke. It's because you don't know Sir Bulwer-Lytton. And Snoopy."

www.ingramcontent.com/pod-product-compliance
Lightning Source LLC
Chambersburg PA
CBHW060405260626
47160CB00006B/2444